NORTH

Light and Shadow
Book One

KATRINA J. DAROFF

Coffee Kat Books

A Note from the Author

Dear Reader

First of all, thank you for choosing my book. I know how many books are out there and how difficult it can be to choose which book you are going to read and love next. So, thank you for picking mine. I hope you love it as much as I do.

The Light and Shadow series is intended for new adults, emphasis on the word *adult*. This story deals with themes of choice and the choices made for you. As such, there are depictions of sex and a scene that deals with sexual assault, though it does not depict it. There will be an Asterix at the beginning of that scene. I did not add this scene lightly, but I believe it is important to the theme of choice as well as Princess Catiya's future as the hero of the story.

I hope you enjoy North and the rest of the Light and Shadow series as much as I have enjoyed writing it.

Katrina J. Daroff

For my best friend, Erin.
Thank you for being the first to take this journey with me.

The Three Kingdoms
Fire Temple
The Northern Isles
Capitol
Reinsaffira
The Border Lands
The Peach Tree
Cordawnia
The Block
The Villa
Royal City
Volentia
Rook
Salene
Highcliffs
Deslacs
Lifespring
Stone Temple

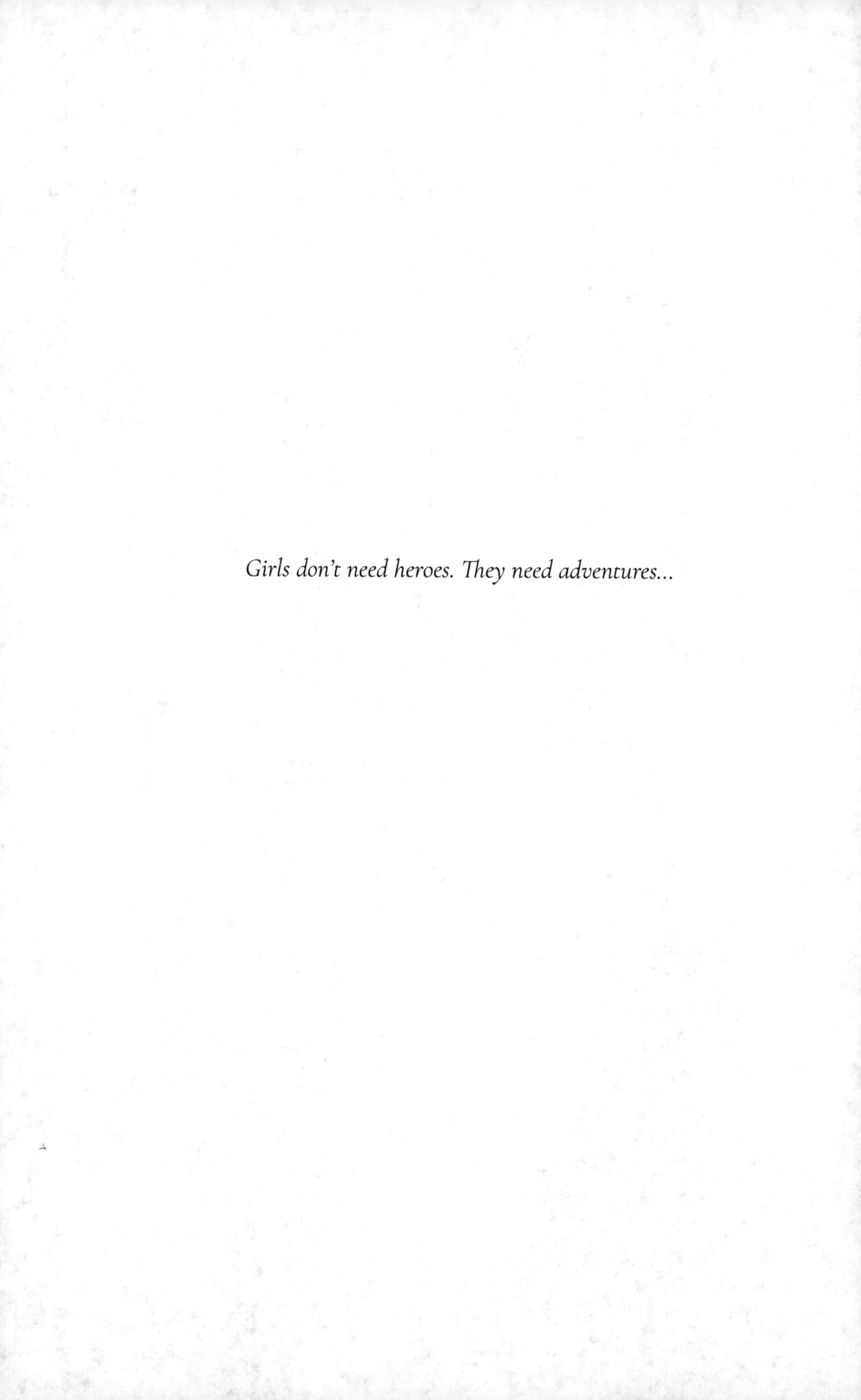

Girls don't need heroes. They need adventures...

SHADOW

# Shadow

Olivia's shadow soaked up what little moonlight there was, pouring into the ornate bedroom. It moved like a breath, flowing through the room, pausing in the moonlight beside the bed.

Through the haze of shadow magic, Olivia could see the sleeping princess. She was fully grown now, just past twenty-two. The pieces of Bastian's plan had taken years to fall into place, but everything was ready now. She was still small, so easy to crush beneath Olivia's fingers. Not so different from the child Olivia had tried to drown years ago.

Olivia's fingers tensed.

The princess did not deserve to die, but the daughter of the prophecy could not be allowed to live. Not that Olivia had the power of will to actually kill her now. She could only do what Bastian demanded.

Her wispy shadow fingers wrapped around the girl's throat. Ice cold against her skin.

"Princess Catiya." The shadow's voice was a rasping hiss that grated against Olivia's ears. This was what she had become. "I wish I could say that none of this will hurt, but I doubt you will remember it."

Her fingers tensed again, crushing the princess's throat.

The princess's eyes fluttered open, emerald green and wide with panic. Searching for her attacker, she was unable to find Olivia in the blanket of darkness. A shadow that was nearly impossible to see in the dark. Princess Catiya struggled, but Olivia pressed down, ethereal and solid. Fingers tightening around her throat, killing the scream that threatened to burst out of the princess.

One of two things would happen; either were fine with Olivia. The girl could die, taking her magic into the abyss with her. If only Olivia could be so fortunate. Otherwise, the *light* would protect her, and she would prove once and for all that she was the daughter of the prophecy, forcing King Kristoff to take action. That was what Bastian hoped for and as the crone, an instrument of her master's will, that was all Olivia could desire.

Princess Catiya gasped for breath. It would not come. She fumbled at the nightstand for a weapon but found nothing with her numbing fingers. By now every part of her would feel numb and heavy. Spots would be dancing over the princess' vision, her fear giving way to un-consciousness.

"I am sorry, little princess."

The girl made one last attempt to free herself. Fingers fumbling against a glass oil lamp. She sent it tumbling to the marble floor. It shattered with a piercing crash.

The shadow's grip loosened just enough for the princess to gasp for breath. "Help," she cried out for one of the guards that should be stationed just outside her door. Her voice wavered like the shattered glass littering the floor.

"Cat?" A man's voice sounded on the other side of the door. Muffled and far away. There was a pounding on the heavy oak door, but Olivia knew it was locked and sealed, it would take time to break through. Time that the princess did not have.

A blinding white light burst forth. Too bright, too warm, to be any candle or lamp. The shadow was forced back across the night sky. Back to the space where Olivia cast it; a barren attic room in a flea ridden inn less than a mile from the palace. Olivia's skin burned, prickling with heat. The smell of smoke filled her nose. It was done. The last pieces fell into place. Every seed had been planted, now all there was to do was hope for a plentiful harvest.

Olivia swept back her hair, releasing a wisping trail of smoke. The girl had the light and the light protected her. That was the power Bastian and The Darkness wanted to exploit.

Light poured into the room.

Through the darkness edging her vision, Cat could see Roderick, the captain of the royal guard, push open the door. He was an imposing man with shoulder length brown hair tied into a low ponytail. His eyes widened, hiding the wrinkles that had recently started to form in the corners of his eyes. He rushed over to Cat.

The velvet darkness deepened, pulling Cat away.

Then, there was something else. A warmth growing at the center of her chest. Light filled her, burning hot, until Cat thought she might burst. A wave of hot tingles washed through her body, and there was a blinding light.

The princess woke with a start. She lay under the gaze of Captain Roderick's warm brown eyes brimming with worry. Light fingers brushed a loose strand of hair from Cat's face.

"R-Roderick? I... I've just had the most horrible nightmare." Her throat ached with every word.

"It is all right," he whispered. "You're safe, Princess." The captain turned back toward the open door. A second knight blocked the light, casting a long, still shadow. A shiver ran across Cat's skin. There had been a shadow in her dream. She had not dreamed about shadows for a very long time. "Why weren't you at your post?"

"I went to investigate a sound."

Roderick stormed across the room. Exhaustion pulled Cat back against her pillows. She barely heard the captain bellowing at the guard. "You never leave the princess unprotected. Is that clear, Sir Guy?"

"Yes sir."

Cat's eyes fluttered; her energy spent. Waves of tingles still danced across her skin. It was only a dream. It had to be.

"Good. Now, go wake the king and tell him I have to speak with him, and fetch lady Emma; I need her here."

"Catiya believes this attack was a nightmare?"

A low fire burned in the king's study. Green and gold fabrics turning nearly black in the dim light. King Kristoff stood in his dressing gown, his eyes fixed on the dancing flames. His expression did not change once while Roderick told the tale of the strange shadow in Princess Catiya's room.

"Yes sire."

"Good. Keep it that way." The king sighed. "Why would Bastian come for her now? It's been three years since the war ended."

Many years ago, Roderick and Kristoff had been friends. Boys who played and fought together, young men who shared glorious adventures. Of course, that was before Kristoff became a king and Roderick became Captain of the Royal Guard. Now there were rules and protocols forcing a gap between their stations. On occasion, the old friendship seeped through, forming a bridge over the chasm.

"Perhaps, sire, the shadow is not Bastian's work but some other servant of *The Darkness*. Don't you think it would be best to tell Catiya who and what she is? So she might be prepared if... something comes for her again?"

"No." The king's auburn hair appeared almost red in the firelight, just like Cat's. It was the only thing Cat inherited from her father. The rest was all her mother. "Telling her would be far too dangerous. Fortunately, I believe I have a solution."

Roderick's mind was moving slowly. The late hour stealing his wit. What kind of solution could the king have found?

"Bastian offered me a treaty once... a chance to prove we had no intention of pursuing Catiya's birthright. If I sent Catiya someplace safe... like Reinsaffira. It is far north, out of Bastian's reach. And if Catiya marries into their royal line, she would never be able to ascend the Salenian throne."

"Kristoff... Sire..." Roderick was afraid to ask. "What are you suggesting?"

Before the king deigned to answer, the doors to the study swung open. The Reinsaffiran Ambassador, Lord Arik, stepped into the room. His clothing was wrinkled. His mousy brown hair was mussed and un-styled.

"Ah, Arik, just in time. I do hope we are not stealing you away from anything important."

"Only my bed, Your Majesty." Arik added a curt bow. "How can I, and Reinsaffira, serve you?"

Roderick raised an eyebrow, still unwilling to accept what he suspected may be the king's solution. Why else would Arik be called in on any matter regarding Princess Catiya? The young ambassador was a notorious flirt and had been found in several courtiers' beds. It was generally understood by the royal guard that Arik's antics were to be ignored, so long as he also stayed far away from Cat.

"The Captain and I are discussing a change to the terms of our alliance with Reinsaffira. We would like to see it become a more permanent arrangement. How would your crown prince respond to an offer of marriage? A Volentian princess to serve as his queen and cement the peace between our lands?"

Arik smiled.

A wave of annoyance and nausea passed through Roderick.

"I believe he could be persuaded to see the wisdom in such an arrangement."

PART
ONE

Part One

Dirt slid beneath Cat's fingers as she pulled herself up the tallest rock formation in the arbor, The Dragon's Tooth. Ages ago, before Volentia split from Reinsaffira, the northern kingdom, men would travel south to climb the rock formation. It was a test of courage. A waterfall rolled off the cliff near the top of the spire. Cat had read all about it. Men would climb the spire and fill a wine skin with water from the falls to show their courage.

Of course, Cat did not need to prove her courage, nor did anyone care if she could reach the top of the towering rock formation. They would have probably preferred it if she did not attempt to reach the great heights. But Cat loved to climb. She loved the freedom it offered. On top of the Dragon's Tooth, none of the responsibilities of being a princess could reach her. Maids, knights, royal advisers, the constant line of suitors futilely seeking her attention, even her brother could call to her, but their calls did not reach her there. Cat could simply stretch out on the burning rocks and ignore the rules and expectations that constantly pulled at her.

Cat never fell. She had started climbing the rocks three years earlier and she was good at it. Cat was strong and quick. She kicked at a boulder, making certain it was stable. Orange dirt slid down the stone.

The foothold was secure. She pushed herself up, another foot closer to the top.

From this height Cat could see the main thoroughfare of Royal City, leading all the way from the city gates to the palace. Everything seemed so small. Even the ornate carriage rolling down the main road could be crushed beneath Cat's thumb.

A single trumpet blared.

"Not today," Cat muttered, testing a new hand hold.

Three trumpets answered. Noise exploding in the palace courtyards and gardens below her feet. Cat glanced over her shoulder, pulling herself onto the topmost ledge of the Dragon's Tooth and perching on the warm rock.

The ornate carriage continued its journey down the main thoroughfare, scratching at a memory Cat could not quite reach.

She studied the palace grounds beneath her feet. It was still early. The morning sun barely reached the cliff top where Cat sat, but the gardens and training yard bustled with activity and the kitchen had been packed with kitchen maids and cooks preparing delicate morsels, too distracted to even look up as Cat snuck through. The scent of warm cinnamon bread drifted over the trees.

It all nagged at Cat's mind.

Movement on the southeastern wall caught her attention. She dug her palms into the rust-colored dirt, leaning over the edge, craning to see. A page or a squire raised a deep blue flag, just below Volentia's green and gold sigil.

Cat squinted at the flag. Blue and silver were the colors of the Reinsaffiran royal family, Volentia's northern neighbor and ally. The alliance formed during the war with Salene, more out of necessity than actual friendship. Reinsaffira's king was a kind enough man, though he always wore a calculating look, his mind always working things out to his advantage. Cat had never met his wife, Queen Cassandra, but she was supposed to be tall and willowy. Rumor had it that she embroidered all of her finest gowns herself. They had two sons and a five-year-old daughter. The oldest son, Cat thought, was somewhere around her brother's age, maybe 24 or 25, and the younger was supposed to be close to her own age. They were all supposed to be people of great intelligence.

The information leapt readily to Cat's mind.

Cat's eyes widened. "No. No. No! It can't be today!" She was so stupid! How could she forget? This was the day the Reinsaffiran royal family was expected to arrive in Volentia to renegotiate the alliance. The palace had been in full scale preparation for days and Cat had been quizzed on Reinsaffiran customs and the royal family for weeks so she could greet the king and the two princes, and on the actual day she had forgotten and wandered off. Her father was going to kill her, if the hurried climb back down did not.

Rubbing the soreness from her arms, Cat prepared to climb down. She knew she ought to wait until the tremble of fatigue was gone, but there was no time. Cat had to beat the carriage back to the palace. She swung her legs over the ledge and let them dangle hundreds of feet above the ground. She felt the rush of butterflies in her stomach. Climbing down was always just a little frightening.

"Cat? Cat, are you out here?" A sugar sweet voice echoed off the stones around her. Cat risked a glance down. A girl with wild raven hair stared up at her. Lady Emma of Highcliffs. There was no mistaking her. Emma had been Cat's companion for years, that is, until a few months earlier when Emma became engaged to Ryder and was given a new position at court. She was still Cat's best friend. "What are you doing up there?"

"Being an idiot." She dropped onto a narrow ledge. "I completely forgot what today was." Her fingers ached as they dug into the rock, making a steady trek down the cliff face. "I don't suppose you can stall them?"

"How long do you need?"

"At least 10 minutes."

"I'll do my best." Emma pushed her long dark curls out of her face and disappeared into the trees.

Cat nodded to herself; if anyone could stall a royal family, it was

Emma. There was no woman in the world who looked more natural in fine gowns and jewels. She had a classic beauty with an oval face and expressive caramel eyes. In fact, Emma was widely regarded as the most beautiful woman in Volentia. Her home, Highcliffs, was a dukedom in the mountains bordering Salene and even though she had lived at the palace for several years, she somehow still smelled of pine trees and crisp mountain air. But her looks were deceiving. Emma was a warrior and the finest archer at the palace, though very few knew that secret.

Men were always following Emma, trying to impress her. They told her stories of their valor, and she would toss her curls or flutter her eyelashes, though she saved her smiles only for Ryder. Even after her engagement to Ryder was announced, everyone who met Emma seemed to fall in love with her. It was useful at times like this, when Cat needed a diversion. A dozen drooling knights always made a good diversion. It would also be useful when Ryder and Emma finally married and became the king and queen of Volentia. A queen should be able to capture the hearts of her kingdom. How else could she inspire her people?

No matter what Cat did, she never seemed to master that same allure, despite her status as a princess. Not that it mattered. Cat would never be queen of anything and had no need to capture anyone's heart.

As she got older, it was becoming clear that Cat would never be the lady of any great house. She had been deemed unruly by most of the respectable families and rejected the attentions of those who still considered her a worthy prize. Cat refused to be a prize. If she ever married, she wanted to be in love and she doubted she would ever fall in love. She would be Princess Catiya of Volentia forever. That suited her just fine. Ryder could be king, with Emma at his side and she would fall into obscurity, left alone to climb rocks and hide in the arbor.

The sound of branches and leaves cracking underfoot rousted Cat from her thoughts. She pulled herself closer to the cliff, arms trembling with fatigue. She twisted around to see who was after her now. Leaves and branches blocked her view. It was probably just Ryder, double-checking that Cat was on her way.

Cat dropped onto a ledge that was just wide enough for her to stand, then slipped into the branches of a nearby tree. She began climbing down as fast as she could.

The ground was about twenty feet below her when Cat reached for a branch that wobbled and bowed under her grip. It seemed sturdy enough for her purposes, just thin. She swung onto it, reaching with her toes for the larger branch just below.

The branch broke.

Cat was falling.

Cat had the vague thought that she never fell and that this was going to make her late before becoming aware of a figure sitting on a low branch. A pair of hands reached out, wrapping around her waist and pulling her toward his chest. Cat's fall slowed but only for a moment. There was a snap of branches and she and the figure slammed into the ground.

A man in a leather riding jacket lay on top of her. Everything was out of focus. Though Cat could see he had russet curls and was smiling at her. She felt a twinge of familiarity, as if she had known him once, a long time ago. She slowly became aware of her aching body and of the large hand planted on her chest.

"Are you hurt?"

Cat's vision started to clear. Her breath caught. She did know him. The knight was older now. His hair had been neatly trimmed and his clothing was much finer than it had been when they danced in the gardens. It was still him. He was still handsome. And, somehow, he still smelled like crisp fresh lavender.

"You!"

He started to push himself away from her.

Pain filled her already aching chest.

Cat gasped.

Panic flashed through the knight's widening blue eyes. His hand flew away from her. "I'm so sorry. Are you hurt?"

She slapped him. The sound echoed off the cliff side. "Get off of me." She pressed her palms into the knight's chest, struggling to get out from beneath him.

"Cat?" Ryder's low voice had a tone Cat rarely heard. Was it fear? Leaves crackled under his feet. "You!" The steel point of a sword flashed between Cat and the knight, coming to rest at the man's throat.

"Ryder." Cat was still out of breath. "Th-This is not how it looks."

The man's eyes flitted between Cat and Ryder, putting the pieces together of who Cat was. Cat watched the knight brush hair out of his face and struggle to his feet, careful not to lay a hand on her. Ryder ignored the red mark forming on the man's cheek, left by Cat's slap.

"Tell me what you are doing to my sister, before I run you through."

"Prince Ryder, a pleasure, as always." He bowed with an exaggerated flourish that annoyed Cat. "Let me assure you, I meant no disrespect to your sister's honor." He reached down, offering Cat a hand. She accepted it and he lifted her lightly to her feet.

Ryder grabbed Cat by the shoulder, dragging her behind him. He was still glaring at the man who had broken her fall, and the veins in his neck were tense and throbbing.

"To be fair, I did not know she was the princess when I saw her falling. I was sitting on a low branch, and I tried to catch her, but... I seemed to only manage to break her fall instead."

Cat took a moment to study her rescuer. His name was Thomas, she remembered that from the night in the garden, when Reinsaffira last visited. He was tall and thin, though strong enough to lift her with ease. He stood several inches taller than Ryder, who Cat had always believed was too tall for his own good. He had sharp cheekbones and a healthy tan from days of travel, to match his brown curls.

"Ryder, that's true. I was..."

"Cat," Ryder pushed her away. "Go back to the palace and get dressed." Anger was definitely the tone filling Ryder's voice now. It had been years since Cat had seen him so angry; that had also been her fault.

Sore from her fall and worried about what Ryder would do to her rescuer, Cat turned back toward the palace. She hoped Ryder would understand that Thomas had tried to save her.

"Before you run me through, I think there are one or two things that you should know..."

Cat could not hear what else the man had to say or how Ryder responded; she was running through the arbor, remembering the responsibilities waiting for her at the palace.

Sweat slicked down Emma's neck. She barreled around the side of the palace to the front park where the royal blue carriage waited. The door swung open just as Emma swiped a handkerchief over the back of her neck. Cat was not going to make it.

Heart sinking in her chest, Emma dipped into a low curtsy before the visiting king and queen at the bottom of the steps. "Your majesties. Welcome to Volentia."

King James' hair had gone silver since Emma saw him several years earlier. Queen Cassandra's hair was a gleaming gold. Tall and thin as a willow tree, the queen swayed as she stepped closer to Emma. "Thank you, my dear." The queen glanced around, hesitation in her stone blue eyes. Emma had a vague recollection that everyone in the Reinsaffiran royal family had blue eyes. It felt like an unimportant detail. "Forgive me but... I don't believe you are the princess."

Emma's grip on her silk skirts tightened. "No ma'am. I am sorry to disappoint you. Princess Catiya is... indisposed at the moment and will be here shortly. She sent me to see that you were taken care of."

"And what is your name?" King James spoke in hard flinty tones that bubbled with an undercurrent of laughter. Was he laughing at Emma's discomfort? Was it so obvious that her legs were shaking beneath the miles of silk and petticoats?

"I... My name is Lady Emma of Highcliffs, I am betrothed to Prince Ryder." Emma was not certain why she added that last part. Maybe she wanted to show the king and queen that she had sufficient rank to be the one sent to greet them. Not just some lady-in-waiting sent on errands that were deemed beneath the royal family.

"I see. So, Princess Catiya does not think we are worthy of her personal attention. Or was she simply too nervous to face her own betrothed for the first time?"

Time stopped. Emma felt the blood rush to her feet. "Her... what?"

"James, stop teasing the poor girl." Queen Cassandra slapped her husband's arm. Lightly. Almost playfully. "She's so pale she looks as if she might faint. Don't worry, Lady Emma, James can be a bit like a cat with a mouse at times. You may take us to our accommodations now, or would you prefer to have us wait in the hot sun for Princess Catiya to become available?"

"I would be happy to show you your accommodations." She extended a hand toward the hall. "Right this way."

Kings and queens never actually follow anyone, so King James and Queen Cassandra stepped into the hall ahead of Emma. A young man with golden blond hair appeared at the base of the steps. Emma had not even noticed him standing behind the king and queen. One of the Reinsaffiran princes. She fell into step beside him, gesturing directions to the king and queen.

"Don't worry," the prince leaned close to whisper in her ear after a few steps. "My father enjoys making people nervous."

"I noticed." There was still a quiver in Emma's voice. She hated it. She hated the way it betrayed the tremble of nerves residing in her chest. "What did he mean, about Cat... Princess Catiya being nervous about facing her betrothed?"

"I suspect he was referring to the marriage clause in the new treaty King Kristoff sent. I believe most young women are nervous when meeting their future husband for the first time."

"A marriage clause?" Emma fought to keep her words a low hiss. Her throat tightened with the strain.

"Between Princess Catiya and the crown prince of Reinsaffira. Surely this news is not a surprise to you."

The doors to the guest tower were in sight. Emma pushed past the royal guests, throwing open the gilded doors. "These are your rooms; everything should be in order. Please feel free to ring for a servant if there is anything you require!" The words came rushing out of her.

Emma spun in a flurry of skirts and silk, her long black hair clinging to her face and shoulders. "I do apologize, but I must leave you here, Your Majesty. I have to assist Princess Catiya." She hurried to bob in a sloppy curtsy before hurrying down the corridor.

"What were you even thinking? You know you're not supposed to be climbing the cliffs, on any day, let alone when you are supposed to be greeting royal visitors!"

Cat rolled her eyes at the gilded mirror, twisting her long hair into an elaborate braid. Ryder had been lecturing her for nearly twenty minutes now. Long enough for Cat to brush the tangles from her hair and try on three different pairs of shoes. She twisted a golden ribbon around the end of the braid, securing the braid. Cat had eschewed the elaborate green and gold ball gown for a simple white and gold dress that would stain if anyone sneezed within ten feet of her. It was much too fine, but infinitely more comfortable than the mess of corsets and petticoats that had been chosen for her. Pink and green roses, like the ones covering the palace walls, were embroidered across the bodice.

"I'm sorry. I just wasn't thinking." Cat flipped open the jade jewelry box on her vanity, the lid clanking against the polished wood. A set of diamond hair pins waited at the bottom beneath a tattered blue handkerchief. Cat plucked them out one by one.

"You never think."

In the glass, Cat could see that her brother's normally pale face had turned red.

She twisted the hair pins between her fingers.

"And then the fact that you were found with that... that man on top of you."

"I already explained that to you. You didn't hurt him, did you? He was just...."

"Whatever you are about to say, I guarantee, it is not *all* he was trying to do. Trust me." Ryder folded his arms over his chest, his voice turning to a low growl.

Cat knew better than to argue with him when he got like this. So she said nothing, simmering with annoyance that he really thought she was so dumb and that she did not understand that some men might try to hurt her. As if she were still a naïve girl.

"I don't even know how to explain to Father why you weren't there to greet King James and his family. Not to mention your bruises."

"Then don't. I don't need you to protect me from everything."

"Fine. How do you plan to explain to Father?"

Cat shrugged, a purple and blue bruise was already visible just beneath her white capped sleeve. She made no move to cover it. It hurt to move too much in the tight dress. Her ribs... her everything was sore and aching. "You know me. I'll think of something."

"We're back to the fact that you *never* think," Ryder grumbled.

Cat pretended she did not hear him.

As it happened, she did not have to respond. The doors flew open. Emma stood just on the other side, a flurry of dark curls and purple silk. She pushed her way inside. "Cat! Why didn't you tell me?" Emma flung her arms around Cat, crushing her bruised shoulders in a hug. "If I had known... we could have... I could have..."

Cat stepped back, looking her oldest friend in the eye. Emma's dark eyes darted over Cat's face, wide with panic. She must have heard about her fall and the knight. The skin on the back of Cat's neck prickled with the heat of embarrassment.

"I... I haven't seen you since it happened."

"You haven't seen me?"

"It only just happened, less than an hour ago."

Emma's face hardened. "Less than... what are you talking about?"

"My fall, in the arbor and..." Cat lowered her voice, eyes dropping to the floor. "And the knight who..." She glanced back to Ryder, shaking her head. "It doesn't matter. Why? What are you talking about?"

A look passed between Emma and Ryder. A silent conversation that Cat was not privy to. Although Cat thought there was a heavy question in Emma's eyes, and she thought she saw Ryder shake his head. Almost imperceptible in the span of a breath.

"Nothing," Emma sighed. "It doesn't matter. Are you hurt?"

"Only my pride." Cat shrugged again. A jolt of pain flashed through her shoulder and arm. Cat spun back to the mirror, shoving a hair pin into her braid to cover the wince of pain.

"Thank heavens. Here, let me help you with that. You always were the worst at fixing your own hair." With a few deft movements, Emma removed the diamond hair pins and laced them through Cat's braid until it sparkled in the mid-morning light. Next came the rose gold tiara that rested just above Cat's forehead, nearly blending into her copper hair. "I... um... I met the Reinsaffiran prince today. He's quite handsome. Do you think you and he will have the chance to spend any time together on this visit?"

In the mirror, Cat watched her brother. True to form, his fingers tightened into fists the instant Emma mentioned the Reinsaffiran prince. Ryder had spent more time in Reinsaffira than anyone at court, besides Ambassador Arik, who Cat was not encouraged to spend any time with. The only thing he ever told her about Reinsaffira was how much he disliked the crown prince. She believed the exact words he used to describe him were *philandering* and *fool*.

"I highly doubt it. I'm only required to go to the negotiations to look pretty and offer the queen tea."

"Good." Ryder glared at the mirror. "Neither of you should spend any time with the crown prince of Reinsaffira. No matter how handsome or charming you *think* he is. He's dangerous."

"Oh Ryder," Emma let out a sparkling laugh. "It's adorable when you're jealous and overprotective."

Cat could hear the blush rising in her brother's cheeks.

"I will have to remember that."

"Could the two of you please try not to be adorable while I'm here. It's disgusting."

Emma's skilled hands picked up a brush and carefully painted a thin black line over Cat's eyelashes. Then she selected a second brush to paint Cat's lips a pale pink that would complete her transformation into a princess. "You know I cannot make that promise."

"All I ask is that you not actively try to seduce my brother until I'm gone."

"Very well."

The roses stitched into Cat's bodice scratched against her palms as she ran them down the gown, smoothing away any wrinkles. Everything was in place. The skirt was too long. All of her dresses were too long for her, but then, Cat was short. She would be forced to take delicate, ladylike steps everywhere she went. Emma straightened the rose gold tiara in Cat's hair.

"As usual, that is as good as it will get," Cat muttered, kicking the silk skirt out of her way before standing up and spinning around. "What do you think?"

Emma opened her mouth to speak, but Ryder beat her to the answer. "Adequate. Just try not to..."

"Be myself?"

"Unfortunately, yes."

Emma swiped a hand at Ryder, smacking his chest. "She looks lovely! Tell her she looks lovely." She gave Ryder a sharp look until he agreed.

"Just... try not to start a war. Volentia needs this alliance." He offered an arm to Emma, inclining his head. She placed a slender hand on his silk sleeve, letting him guide her toward the door. But Cat thought, after a moment, that Emma was the one tugging him toward the door.

"Start a war?" Cat called after her brother. "Not before dinner."

"Cat."

"It's the only promise I am willing to make."

Ryder spun around, his blue green eyes sharpening into a glare. "Cat!"

"You used to be fun. I'll grant, it was a long time ago." They had already made their way through the heavy oak doors into the hall. Cat folded her arms over her chest. She was alone with her thoughts and bruises until an escort came to guide her to the great hall.

The second Cat's door clicked shut, Emma turned sharp on her heel to face Ryder. A white-hot anger burned through her core, blazing against her dark skin. "She doesn't know your father arranged a marriage for her!"

Ryder's beautiful sea green eyes widened in surprise. Every muscle in his body stilled until he looked as if he may have been made of stone. "How do you know about that?"

Emma buried her fists in her long loose curls, suppressing the scream growing in her chest. "King James told me. He seems to think that Cat did not greet him today because she was nervous about meeting her *betrothed*. How could you not tell me? How could you not tell Cat?"

"Because I did not know until this morning." Ryder scrubbed his hand down his face in an act of frustration and defeat. His fingers slipped around Emma's, pulling her away from the heavy oak door. Emma let him pull her out of the royal wing into a shadowed corner before demanding he explain. "The engagement has not been finalized yet; I still have time to change it, but we can't tell Cat yet. You know how she gets. This has to be handled delicately."

"And when do you think we should tell her? Right before she walks down the aisle? When she finds out she's going to..."

"Do something rash and impulsive. And she's going to panic. There's no reason to put her through any of that when I can still fix it. Trust me, there is nothing to worry about. Prince Thomas is... an idiot and a scoundrel. As soon as my father sees that, he'll call off this mad idea. I know he will."

"What if he doesn't?"

"He will!"

Another thought scratched at the back of Emma's mind. A memory from Reinsaffira's visit several years earlier. The image of Cat standing in the arbor with a tall young man who spoke in soft sweet tones.

Emma's lips and throat felt too dry to speak. "And what if," her voice came out a rasping half whisper, "the prince is the person she is supposed to be with?"

Lightning crackled in Ryder's stormy eyes, his jaw tensed. "He's not." Ryder ground out the words. Not in a menacing or cruel tone. At least, not one that was directed at Emma. There was an anger there. "Trust me, I know Prince Thomas. He does not deserve Cat."

Cat sprawled on the large armchair beside the cold fireplace. Swinging her legs back and forth as she mentally listed the things she needed to remember; *delicate steps, a demure greeting,* she could not forget to curtsy to both kings. Still waiting for her escort.

Her hand dropped to her side. Where was her escort? It had been almost an hour. Someone should have sent for her by now.

Just as she thought it, with a small amount of irritation, someone banged on the double doors.

"Finally!" Cat jumped to her feet, balling the long silk skirt up in her fists and lifting it to her knees. *No.* Cat paused, letting the hem drop to the floor. She pressed her hands into the white silk. *Delicate and ladylike.* "I'll be right with you."

The soreness spider-webbing over Cat's muscles made the door heavy. Across the threshold stood a woman with shimmering black hair. A silver streak ran through the woman's hair. Something familiar sparked in Cat's memory.

Perhaps the woman just reminded her of a crone in a fairy story. Cat had read enough fairy tales to be wary of such a stranger; they were usually enchantresses. Cat shook the thought away. The old legends and fairy tales were *not* real.

Still, something familiar vibrated off the old woman. A shadow of a memory, like a dream she could not quite remember. Cat shook her head this time, hoping that would remove the thought.

The woman lifted her hand. Something glittered in her palm like diamond dust. Cat narrowed her eyes, studying it. Then the woman blew the dust into Cat's eyes. Cat blinked; the glittering dust sparkled on the edge of her vision. Warmth spread through her chest, chasing away the uneasiness that had, just moments before, been tightening in her chest. Why had she been uneasy in the first place?

"Good morning, Princess Catiya." The woman bowed low.

Cat nodded. Who was this woman? With all the visitors swarming the palace, it would be impractical to expect to recognize every servant and guest, but Cat thought she should recognize anyone allowed in the royal wing.

"Good... good morning." She took in a deep breath to tame her stutter. "I'm afraid I do not have time to meet with you now, but the king is receiving all of his guests in the..."

"I'm not one of the king's guests." The woman's voice sounded like it was full of gravel. "I'm here for you. That is...I am here to bring you a gift." The crone produced a bag from her flowing sleeve.

Cat definitely knew better than to accept anything that had not been inspected by a guard and she had the vague thought that there should be a guard at her door to inspect it. Her hand stretched toward the gleaming bag. It looked like it was made of starlight.

Realizing what she was doing, Cat pulled her hand back to her chest. "You must be mistaken. There is no cause to bring me gifts."

"But there is. Your mother entrusted these items to me just before her death. They were meant for just such an occasion.

Her mother? The question prickled Cats skin. There was no occasion, not as far as Cat was concerned, and her mother's death had been unexpected; had she really had time to put such plans in place? The statement drew Cat in anyway.

The woman opened the pouch, drawing out a silver necklace with a blue sapphire pendant. The necklace flashed into Cat's mind. A memory of her mother. Queen Anya had never worn any jewels besides this necklace. Cat stared at it in wonder.

"Your mother believed you might have need of it someday."

All of Cat's wariness melted away as she clutched the pendant close to her chest. No words formed, at least nothing that could express the weight of her gratitude. Besides the crown nestled in her hair, Cat had nothing of her mother's. It had all been destroyed in a fire. The gem thrummed between Cat's fingers, pulsing with memory.

"There is also this." A brass sea compass appeared in the enchantress' gnarled hand. "It will show you the way to what you need most."

The princess smirked. Cat may have read too many fairy stories, but she was not an idiot. Compasses pointed north. If she followed the compass from where she stood, she would walk directly off a cliff, into the sea. "Thank you." Cat turned to place the items on the table by the door. "I will treasure them..." When she turned back, the crone was gone. The corridor was empty. Silent. Where had the old woman gone? More important, where was Cat's escort? It was getting late.

She let the doors close with a thud, ignoring the compass, and scooping up the necklace. Cat draped it around her neck, so the stone rested just below her collar bone. Perhaps the Reinsaffiran king would be impressed by the gesture of wearing a sapphire when they were introduced, even if it did not match her gown.

She followed her feet and thoughts onto the balcony.

Cat let her arms rest on the railing. The afternoon heat soaked into her skin. Her mind twisting over the day ahead of her.

If Cat was lucky, she would only need to be charming for a few moments. Her father would introduce her to the Reinsaffiran royals. She had met the king once before, and he was not terrible, just intimidating. Cat would curtsy to him. She straightened her spine, spreading her skirts in a mock bow and lowered until she wobbled, practicing. Next, she would be introduced to the queen and the two princes; curtsies were not required for them. Instead, the princes would bow to her and kiss her hand in turn. Cat closed her eyes, stretching her hand out in front of her the way she imagined a proper lady would receive such a greeting. But her hands were rough and scratched from climbing. Would the princes tease her for her calloused palms and fingers?

She left her hand stretched out before her, practicing a friendly smile, trying to picture herself flirting with the princes. Emma and the other girls always made it look so easy. A lump formed in Cat's throat every time she tried to greet someone new. She was always afraid she would stumble over her words at the worst moment.

"It's such a ple- pleasure... to meet you." She opened her eyes again, grunting with frustration. Cat hated her stutter, and hated that it came back whenever she got nervous.

Maybe if she pictured what the princes would look like. They would be tall and broad shouldered. Both the king and queen were tall, and the king had all the markings of a man who had been strong in his youth. If they were anything like Arik, they would have easy smiles and gentle laughs.

The image of the slender knight from the arbor popped into her mind. He smiled, taking her hand in his and pressing a kiss into her knuckles. Shuttering, Cat pushed the memory threatening to surface far from her mind. Even if he did save her today, it did not change what he did the last time the Reinsaffiran court visited. She had not thought of him in years; she refused to think of him now.

Her fingers twitched, reaching for the jewelry box on her vanity, where the handkerchief he once gave her was hidden. Cat curled her fingers into a fist. No. She was not going to open that box. She was not going to think about him.

She forced her mind back to the Reinsaffiran royal family. Once introductions were made, Cat would be obliged to spend several minutes talking with the queen about frivolous things. Cat racked her brain for the queen's interests. Painting sounded right. They would discuss painting and embroidery for several minutes. Then Cat would be shuffled to a back wall, not important enough to take part in a treaty negotiation. There would be nothing left for her until the feast and ball that evening.

Cat's stomach gurgled at the thought of the feast. It must be lunch time. She was starting to wish she had snagged a crisp apple from the arbor before she left, or maybe a plum. Her mouth watered at the thought.

Where was her escort?

There was a light rapping on the door.

"It's about time!" Cat kicked the hem of her skirt out of her way and pulled the door open in a swift motion.

Two men stood in front of her. Sir Guy, a square shaped knight with long brown hair, and Evander, a slender blond guard. Evander held a tray with something that smelled savory hidden under a coverlet. It would be just like her father to send the only two guards in Volentia who had no sentimental feelings for her to exploit. Both had made it clear, in their own way, that they expected her to behave like a princess.

"You're delivering food?" Cat leaned on the door frame. "I would have thought my father would provide a meal at the negotiations."

"He did." Evander's jaw tensed as he spoke.

"Then why..."

"The king thought it would be best if you got some rest; you'll need to be your best this evening."

Cat's spirits fell, plummeting like stones to the bottom of a river. He was afraid she would embarrass Volentia, more than she already had. What else did she expect after failing to greet King James? At least he did not know about her fall.

"Oh." Cat nudged the door with her foot. "I see."

Evander stepped inside, lowering the tray to the table beside the door, hesitating when he saw the compass and starlight bag in his way. Evander locked eyes with Cat, quirking a questioning eyebrow.

Cat snatched up the compass, shoving it into the bag.

Evander set the tray on the side table. "Um... The king also asked me to be certain you were presentable for the feast. You are to wear the emerald gown and..."

"Thank you, but I know how to be a princess." Cat wrenched the tiara from her hair. Pulling the wispy fly aways free of her braid, they fell into her face.

A snicker drew her attention away from Evander. Sir Guy watched them from the doorway, dark eyes boring into her. He adjusted his surcoat; it was red with a golden rooster sewn over the heart. The symbol suited him.

"And what are you here for?"

He raised his chin, avoiding Cat's hard gaze. "As one of your personal guards, I have been asked to keep you safe. There are so many strange visitors about."

There were a great many strange visitors. She wondered where he had been when the crone appeared at her door. "Well," her eyes narrowed, and throat tightened. "I think you can manage that from the other side of the door."

She pushed the door closed blocking Evander and Guy on the far side of it.

"You should have seen her this morning!" Thomas spoke with the giddiness of a child. Almost floating around the luxurious guest room. "She was just as beautiful as ever. She was climbing the Dragon's Tooth, like in the legends."

"Didn't she fall from the Dragon's Tooth?"

"Of course, Prince Ryder is a problem." Thomas barreled past Arik's question. "She trusts him and he... well he doesn't trust me. I need to talk to her, to show her..."

There was nothing Arik could do but shake his head. He doubted even gravity could bring his friend back down to earth, let alone Arik's tenuous grasp of the Volentian royal family dynamic. And why shouldn't Thomas be excited? He was the luckiest man in the world; just days, hours maybe, from getting everything he had ever wanted. There was no other word for it. Thomas was lucky. Not only had he found the mysterious girl from his dreams, but it had been arranged that he could actually marry her. It was also the best thing for his kingdom. Even Arik could not spoil that.

"But I have a plan. I've bought some roses that I will give her when we are introduced at the ball," Thomas rambled on, adjusting his silk collar. "I know they are trite, but no one could tell me what she prefers."

"Thomas...."

"After we are introduced, I was thinking I would ask her to show me the labyrinth. We're already engaged. I doubt anyone will object to us taking a walk through the gardens. At the center of the labyrinth. That's where I will explain everything to her. About the marriage contract, how I want to marry her and will wait until she *wants* to marry me. I think..."

"Princess Catiya doesn't go to the labyrinth anymore," Arik cut in, ruining his friend's romantic notions before the princess could. "She has not set foot in it in years. Not since..." Arik shook his head, turning his eyes away from his friend and future sovereign. Why had he never told Thomas what had happened with the young lord? Probably because he was afraid Thomas would fly into a jealous rage. So, why not tell him now? The damage was long since done. "There was an incident. The princess has not gone into the labyrinth since then. Not alone, and certainly never escorted by a man she does not know or believes has already lied to her."

"Oh." Thomas picked up the small pouch that Arik knew contained a sapphire ring, chosen for the princess a long time ago, fiddling with it before dropping it into his pocket. "Well, there are other private spaces in the garden. I'll..."

"There are a few more things you should know about Cat... Princess Catiya. I... I have known her for several years now, only from a distance, but still... she's quite stubborn."

"I think for princesses the preferred term is *headstrong*."

"No." Arik nodded with more force than he intended. "Princess Catiya is stubborn. Like a mule. And she will feel betrayed when she learns the terms of the alliance. I doubt flowers and romantic gestures are going to win her forgiveness. You need to speak to her as soon as possible and tell her who you are and what has happened before she hears it from someone else."

Ryder's pale green eyes flit over the group of men in the great hall. The two kings sat at a table, leaning over a large map spread out across the surface. A parchment waited on the edge of the map, waiting for four signatures. The whole scene soured his stomach. His throat tightened around a lump that threatened to strangle him.

It was all too much. The secrecy and the lie of it.

His mind flashed back to the arbor, when he came rushing through the trees and saw his sister sprawled on the ground with Prince Thomas of all people lying on top of her. Then Thomas told him about the new conditions of the alliance. At first, Ryder honestly believed it was a lie. A clever way to keep Ryder from sheathing his sword in the erstwhile prince's heart. Why would his father even arrange a marriage for Cat, especially with the crown prince of Reinsaffira?

But it was true.

The king... his father... had changed the terms of the alliance with Reinsaffira and, worse, he kept it from Cat. Every second that passed would deepen that betrayal. Ryder had to do something.

Emma's hand slid into his. A wash of tingles spread from his finger tips to their tightly pressed palms. The dainty diamond ring on her finger pressing against his, anchoring him to the place and moment. "Ryder," she whispered against his ear before jerk her head toward the side door. "Is that him?"

Ryder followed her gaze to the tall prince who had just deigned to arrive at the negotiations. The collar of his silk shirt was open, giving him an unkempt and disheveled look, as if he could not be bothered to show up to his own engagement. He had probably been too busy trying to charm some courtier, just like Arik, who was also notably absent.

"He looks kind. Are you so certain it would be so bad? I mean... if Cat likes him..."

"It would be. Trust me." Ryder watched the prince fidget for a moment, smiling at the sight of a red mark on his cheek, the one Cat gave him.

Emma sighed. "Then, I think, he is the one you need to convince." Ryder met her gaze. Emma's caramel eyes sparked with the warmth of mischief. "If he refuses to marry Cat, this whole thing goes away and you don't have to convince your father."

It was a terrible thing, learning that Emma was usually right. Most people congratulated Ryder for winning the heart of the most beautiful girl in Volentia. They did not realize that she was also the most cunning person in the palace, which was what he liked most about her. If she was not so unfalteringly good, Ryder might have questioned if she had tricked them all into welcoming her so completely into the royal family.

Ryder nodded.

He lifted Emma's hand, kissing it lightly, before quietly sliding away. He strode over to the tall man with russet hair and rumpled clothing.

Thomas offered him an unwitting smile. "Prince Ryder. To what do I owe the pleasure of..."

"I need to talk to you now!" Ryder grabbed him by the arm, dragging Thomas out the door, half throwing him against the wall.

Thomas righted himself quickly, leaning against the wall with casual ease. "Are you concerned that I am going to try to rescue your sister again? Or is something new upsetting you?"

Ryder shoved him up against the wall, gripping his collar. His teeth grinding.

"What is it with you Volentians and assaulting your guests? What is this, the third time you've attacked me? And then there's your sister..."

"Is everything a joke to you?" Ryder's grip on Thomas' collar loosened. His trembling hands dropped to his side. His fingers were still flexing, aching to wrap around the man's throat. "Call it off!"

"What?"

"Call off this farce of an engagement. Tell your father you don't want to marry my sister. That you won't marry my sister!" Ryder kept his voice low, with some difficulty. Every muscle in his body strained against his better judgment and the voice in Ryder's head screaming that he could not kill the crown prince of Reinsaffira. At least, he could not kill him in the middle of the corridor. "Call it off!"

Thomas straightened. "No." Thomas raised his hands in a placating gesture. "Before you hit me, please understand. I have no intention of harming your sister or forcing her to do anything. From what I hear, I doubt anyone could force her to do anything she did not want to. But I won't call off the engagement, because I *want* to marry her. I've only ever wanted to marry her, but I will leave the choice of *if* and *when* entirely to her. Believe it or not... obviously not, I find the idea of forcing someone to marry a person they do not love..." he searched for a word that could encompass his feelings, "offensive. Is that good enough for you?"

"It might be... if I trusted you."

"Then trust me."

Ryder's jaw was starting to ache from grinding his teeth. The words rang true. He forced the thought away. Ryder did not and would not trust Thomas; he'd known him for too long. "If you are lying to me, if you hurt her in any way, I swear to you, I will personally crush every bone in your body."

Fixing Ryder with a serious look, Thomas spoke in low even tones. "I give you the truest oath I can, on everything I hold dear. Princess Catiya will be protected and cared for. I will hold her life more dear than my own. I also swear that if she does not wish to leave Volentia that I will never be among those who try to force her to." He smiled. A small part of Ryder wanted to slap it off his face.

The sun rested on the horizon. The sky had changed from blue to orange to purple in sweeping brush strokes over Cat's balcony.

She had been changed into the emerald gown embroidered with golden roses, each one studded with a diamond, as her father had commanded of her. It was entirely too much. Perhaps the finest gown she had ever owned; painstakingly stitched together with the finest of materials. It was also the heaviest and most uncomfortable gown she ever had the displeasure of wearing. How could silk and velvet weigh so much?

Cat waited on her balcony, watching the sun dance on the distant waves. Her fingers ached to fiddle with the intricate braid the maids who dressed her had twisted her hair into. Or to tug on the delicate curls framing her face. With all the pins and gels they put into her waist length hair, it probably weighed another ten pounds. Her neck would be aching by the end of the evening. And it would all be for nothing. No matter how much work was put into her appearance, she was still her. A girl with calloused hands who could not fall in love and would never measure up to the expectations placed on her.

She had to admit though, the effect was breathtaking. When the maid had finally let Cat see her reflection, she did not recognize it. The only feature that was truly hers was the fiery hair that had been so painstakingly styled. Her freckles were covered with a soft white powder and black ocher was painted around her eyes, which appeared much greener with the gown. Every detail was arranged so she could be the most beautiful, most princessly, version of herself. Someone she did not know. All so a foreign king and his sons could look at her for a few minutes before deeming her unimportant. Just a sparkling bauble to be displayed when it was convenient and set aside when it was not. Much like the diamond hair pins and rose gold tiara that dazzled in the evening light, casting refracted rainbows across the terrace.

"Sir!" A shout came from behind the heavy doors. "While I appreciate your dedication to your duties, you will let me through!" Emma was resorting to something other than her charm to get past Sir Guy. He was the only knight she refused to flirt with. She never said why. Cat did not mind.

The door banged open.

"I HATE THAT MAN!" Emma threw herself onto Cat's bed. Her own wild hair was intricately styled and draped with pearls. Her dress was golden with green trim, almost a mirror of Cat's. The golden cloth warmed her tan skin.

"Good evening, Emma." Cat walked in from the balcony, dropping onto the bed beside her.

Emma flapped a dismissive hand in the air above her. "I'm here to fetch you for the ball."

"A daunting task. I'm surprised they did not send an armed guard." Cat absently rubbed at the purple bruise on her arm, just barely visible under the milky powder. It was the size of an apple at the very least. "Have I missed anything exciting?"

A worried expression clouded Emma's features. Her lips formed a tight line. Then it was gone. Emma lifted an ebony lock of hair off the pillow, examining it between her fingers. Cat chewed her lip to keep from laughing. Cat seemed to be the only person in the palace amused by the fact that Ryder had fallen in love with a girl whose hair was remarkably similar to his own. They both had ebony curls that framed their faces perfectly.

"Well... the treaty is all but iron clad, once one or two final details are seen to."

"Still moving little flags around on a map?" Cat laughed shaking her head. "Deciding how much Reinsaffira's friendship is worth?"

Emma chewed her lip. Letting the lock of hair fall against the pillow. "Something like that. Do you want me to fix your hair before we go down?"

Cat's hands flew to the extravagant coif. "Does it need it?"

"Not really. But... the princes of Reinsaffira are both... adequate looking. You may want to impress one."

"Why? So, I can beguile one and run off to Reinsaffira? That sounds awful. Besides, you know I have no intention of ever marrying"

Emma sucked in a sharp breath. "Then your hair is fine." She sat up. "We should go down. The banquet will be set soon, and your father wants you to mingle with our guests before it is." Emma fidgeted with her hands. There was more she wanted to say, Cat knew there was.

"All right, what is it?" Cat stood, first taking a step toward Emma then spinning around, stalking across the room. She turned back. "Is it because of what happened in the arbor today? I'm fine! There's nothing for anyone to worry about."

"No... It's nothing. Just... jitters about the ball." Emma twisted her hands in the skirts of her rumpled ball gown. "Do you think it would really be so bad... to marry one of the princes? It's a powerful kingdom. Think of everything you could do."

"Right, and never see you or Ryder or anyone else I care about again. Besides," Cat made a show of gesturing to her whole self, her wrinkled silk gown, untenable hair, and freckled skin. "I doubt we need to worry about it. I am hardly enough of a lady to beguile a knight, let alone a prince."

"Right. What was I thinking? We had better get moving. We don't want to be late." Emma grabbed Cat by the elbow dragging her out of the room. The pair of girls pushed past Sir Guy. He trailed after them, quietly muttering that he was required to escort Cat. Cat flipped the impressive braid over her shoulder, ignoring him.

Sir Guy followed them all the way to the ballroom where Ryder waited, fidgeting with the sleeve of his shirt. Emma wrapped her arm around his waist. He promptly dismissed Guy with a wave of his hand, turning to Cat. "How are you feeling?"

"Ravenous." Cat marched past her brother to the door. She thought she heard Ryder and Emma whispering something Cat could not understand. She had gotten used to ignoring Ryder and Emma's quiet romance. "It's been ages since we had any sort of celebration." She tried to sound bright and cheery as she peered around the curtain at the top of the stairs. The ballroom looked exactly like she expected a ball to look. Groups of richly dressed nobles milling about, waiting for something exciting to gossip about. "I hope it is less exciting than the last time the king of Reinsaffira visited."

Ryder peered at the crowd over her head. "I do too."

A booming voice reverberated from the top of the steps. "Presenting Crown Prince Ryder, escorting Lady Emma of Highcliffs." Cat watched Ryder breathe a sigh of relief before he stepped into the ballroom, almost dragging Emma behind him. The seconds ticked by, and the voice boomed again. "Princess Catiya of Volentia." Her own sigh of relief lowered Cat's shoulders; carrying the weight of waiting was exhausting.

Eyes of every color fell on Cat, her skin prickled under the pressure. Her legs shook as she made her way down the steps.

There was no place to hide, so Cat turned toward a table in the corner, covered with small delicacies. At least there, Cat knew exactly how to behave.

"Ah, Catiya!" A calloused hand scratched Cat's shoulder. The gruff voice belonged to her father. He held an untouched glass of rose-colored wine in his free hand. Cat covered a wince of pain as her father's finger pressed into the bruise, smearing away the powder. "What is this?" His gaze caught on the purple bruise on her shoulder.

Cat tugged at the shoulder of her gown, hoping to hide any other bruises that might appear. "Tokens of this morning's misadventure." Surely, he already knew about the fall. Everyone else did.

King Kristoff nodded, eyes narrow. "Of course. Well, why don't you come meet our guests? It's high time you were introduced to the queen and the princes." The light pressure between her shoulders turned Cat away from the food.

"I would have thought that *high time* passed several hours ago," she muttered, trying to force a smile for the king she was being steered toward.

She had met King James of Reinsaffira before, though it felt like a very long time ago. He was still tall with strong broad shoulders, only now he had graying blond hair and lines across his brow. He stood at the center of attention. A tall, slender woman with white-gold hair stood beside him. Cat sucked in a breath. The woman was massive, taller than the king. Taller than Ryder. The third in the group was a young man Cat did not recognize. He wore a crimson cloak that contrasted with his own golden hair. Surprise, surprise, he also had blond hair and blue eyes, just like his parents. Emma had not lied about the prince's... adequacy.

Wrinkles formed in the emerald silk of Cat's gown as she balled the lengths of fabric in her fists, her knees buckling as she tried to curtsy. Cat tumbled forward, grabbing the prince's arm to keep from hitting the marble floor.

"I am so sorry!" Her skin burned with embarrassment. "My curtsy seems to be out of practice."

The gleaming king's voice boomed with laughter.

The prince helped her to stabilize before assuring her it was perfectly fine. "It is wonderful to finally meet you, Princess Catiya. I am Prince Phillip." He raised her scratched knuckles to his lips. "May I just say, word of your beauty has not been exaggerated."

Word of her beauty? Was he teasing her? The idea was so laughable it hurt to hold back the giggles that bubbled in her throat. "And here I was led to believe that only rumors of my unruliness had left Volentia." The giggle threatened to escape. Cat bit her lip, cutting it off. She glanced around at the small group. "I thought Reinsaffira had two princes. Was I wrong?"

"No, my dear girl, though I am not certain where my eldest son is." The hall seemed to boom with King James' laughter a second time. "It seems you and he are kindred spirits. He will charge headlong into reckless danger, but when faced with meeting his bride, he skulks off like a craven."

The sparkling laughter inside Cat shriveled. She nearly fell again. "H-h-his..." She swallowed hard. "His what?"

"I had hoped to find a more private moment to inform you. King James and I have agreed, the best way to cement our alliance is with a royal marriage between you and Crown Prince..."

Cat pulled away from her father. "A more private moment? I have been locked up in my room all day and..." her voice trailed off. He knew she would object. The realization hit hard, knocking the wind from her lungs. "And tell me, just wh-when exactly is this happy occasion meant to take place?"

"We were hoping, by the end of the week. Just before our guests depart for Reinsaffira," King Kristoff spoke in soft, placating tones, as if she were a child throwing a tantrum.

"I'll be sure to mark the date in my diary." She felt her gaze hardening. "I'm sure that I can fall in love with a complete stranger in that time!"

Fire blazed in her father's hazel eyes. "You are forgetting yourself, Catiya. This is not about love; it is about your responsibility to your family and your country."

She took a step back. Dancing just beyond his reach. "I am not the one who has forgotten themselves."

"Catiya!"

"You *swore* I would always have a *choice*! You swore you would never force me to marry anyone I did not choose! What changed? What did the prince promise you that was worth so much more than your word?" Anger welled inside of Cat, turning to a storm of rage, then hurt. "Please, don't say it was the convenience of it all." Her voice somehow remained even despite the tears that were starting to burn in her eyes. "You rid yourself of a useless princess and gain the guaranteed support of Reinsaffira at the same time."

"My dear." The golden queen brushed a hand against Cat's shoulder. "It is not so horrible as you imagine."

Cat spun, knocking her hand away.

Queen Cassandra's eyebrows rose in surprise.

With a twinge of regret, Cat turned back to her father. "I will not go through with this!" Her voice echoed around her. The hall had fallen into a stunned silence. "I don't care who it is! Or what they are offering."

King James, who was obviously growing tired of Cat's tantrum, groaned. "I don't understand the problem. Your father is the one who approached us with the new terms and the agreement is signed."

Cat's jaw tightened. Everything else in her softened to the ache of betrayal. Her gaze turned back to her father, one last time. A tremble started in her knees, begging her to run. She was being sold for the alliance by her own father, as if she was nothing more than a cow or a sheep to be bargained away. "Pl-please... Please tell me that isn't true."

"Catiya, there are a great many things you do not understand. If you would just come with me, everything will..."

"I'm not going anywhere with you or anyone else. I..." The words she wanted to say stuck in her throat. Choking her. "I..." There were a million eyes on her. Courtiers and ambassadors listening to her every word, and she had none left. "I..." She could not stand there any longer. The fire blazing in her core burned too hot. If she stayed, Cat would burn away. She bundled her skirts in her fists. Then her feet were skittering against the marble dance floor, pulling her away from the two kings. Hands grabbed at her arms and gown, but she fled, knocking herself free of their grip. Cat pushed herself out of the ballroom. Out of the crushing silence and stumbling into the dark hall.

She stumbled right into the knight from the arbor, falling into his deep blues eyes. He wore a blue silk shirt that deepened the ocean deep color. His hands wrapped around Cat's shoulders, keeping her from knocking him to the ground a second time. The bundle of pink roses he held fell, littering the ground at their feet.

"Princess? Is everything all right?"

"I'm sorry!" Cat pushed away from him. There was no time to answer. And this was not the time to get lost in his blue eyes. She would drown if she stood beneath them too long. Voices were booming behind her. There was no time for any of it. Cat had to get away. She had to think.

He moved without fuss, allowing Cat to sweep up her skirts and sprint down the corridor.

Thomas watched as *she* sprinted through the lamplight before turning back to the ball and being knocked to the ground by a flustered Prince Ryder. He landed in the bouquet of roses intended for the princess.

"This must be a family trait," Thomas laughed, rolling out of the way.

"I don't have time for this! Cat! Stop!" Ryder chased down the hall after the princess.

A shadow passed over his vision, Thomas realized there was still a second form standing over him. He glanced up to see Lady Emma extending a delicate hand to him with a smile. He accepted it, rising to his feet.

"I seem to have missed a great deal of excitement."

"Not too much. Only Princess Catiya's refusal to accept the marriage contract. And she may have threatened your kingdom with war. That part was unclear."

Thomas' head swiveled back to the empty corridor the prince had chased the princess down. His heart sank. Arik was right. He should have gone to her and explained things hours ago instead of insisting on some romantic gesture. "Shouldn't you be chasing after her?"

"Shouldn't you?" Lady Emma glared.

"You..."

"Know who you are? Of course. And I know that you are also the 'knight' who broke her heart five years ago."

"Great. Do you plan on knocking me down as well?"

A trill of laughter flowed from Emma's perfect pink lips. "Actually, I was planning on helping you. Come with me. I know where she is going."

Cat slipped out the first door she found, onto a brick veranda set with tables, near the kitchens from the savory scents surrounding her, set for an elegant tea the next morning.

She took in a deep breath of cool night air before turning to the lattice covered in pale pink roses.

In the moonlight, the palace looked as if it had been pulled out of a fairy story, pure white stones covered in pink roses that always bloomed, even in the dead of winter. It was the reason the royal family's sigil was a golden rose. Some stories claimed they were a blessing of protection given to the royal family by a powerful magix when Volentia first separated from the northern kingdom. At that moment, Cat did not care where the roses came from; she was just glad they were there. The lattice they grew on was sturdy, bolted into the walls, strong enough to hold the weight of one small woman.

She rested a hand on the lattice, careful to avoid any thorns, and started to climb. It was slow tedious work in her heavy ball gown, the extra weight dragging her down. Cat worked her way around several balconies and corners before reaching her own balcony. She knew the spot from the feel of the bricks and the curve of the stone wall, having used it as an escape route whenever the palace walls started to close in.

Cat pulled herself onto the balcony, tumbling onto the marble tiles in a pile of green silk. It would be quite some time before the palace guards, or even her brother, thought to search for her in her rooms.

"Cat!" Of course, Emma had beaten her there. It was the last place anyone else would think to look. Emma rushed onto the balcony pulling Cat up. "I'm so sorry! I should have told you! I found out this morning and I tried... I mean I should have... I just didn't know what to say."

Cat leaned back against the balcony railing, fixing her friend with a confused stare. With all the thoughts swirling through her mind, it had never once occurred to her to be angry at Emma. She was hurt, and angry with her father for bargaining her away, but she had never once considered how many people in the palace might have known about it and did not tell her; Ryder, her guards, Emma. How many people had she talked to that day? Did they all think she was an idiot? After this evening, Cat was not certain they were wrong. She certainly felt like an idiot.

Cat pushed her fingers into her ruined hair, pulling it free of its pins and plaits.

"I wanted to tell you. Please, can you forgive me?"

Silence pressed in around them. "There's nothing to forgive." The floodgates behind Cat's eyes threatened to break. "I... I've ruined everything, haven't I?"

"Ruined everything or created your only chance at freedom?" The voice that answered was familiar, but the aging scratch to it did not belong to Emma.

Emma spun around.

Around her twirling silk skirts Cat could see the old woman from that morning standing in the golden light of her room. She had not been there a moment before. Cat blinked. The woman cast no shadow. There was a translucent quality to her, the golden lamplight shifting through her.

Emma went stiff, backing into the balcony rail. "Where did you come from?"

"Maybe I've always been here." The old woman preened, stepping onto the balcony with her hand outstretched. "I offered you a gift earlier, but you have given yourself a greater one. The gift of opportunity." She lifted the brass compass, holding it out to Cat.

Cat's hand reached for it, driven by instinct. The cool metal pressing into her palm. Heavy.

"The compass will show you where you need to go."

"Don't be ridiculous! Compasses point north. There's only ocean north of here." Emma's dark eyes fixed on Cat, peeling away layers of fear. "Cat, you know there's no magic like that. Think about my dagger; it's supposed to only be wielded by someone worthy of it but..."

Cat traced the engravings on the metal, runes that were strange to her. They hummed, tickling her skin. As if by magic. Emma was right. She knew Emma was right. *There is no magic left in the world.* Everyone knew that all of the wonders of fairy stories had died centuries ago. Only the practical remained. Practical and responsible. Compasses only pointed north.

The cover clicked open under her fingers. The arrow spinning, capturing Cat's gaze.

It stopped. The arrow wavered, pointing east to the mountains.

"This is dangerous." Emma's voice broke through the dream state.

She no longer sounded certain. "We need a plan, not enchanted trinkets. We'll find a place for you to hide for a few days and Ryder will fix it. He's so good at politics. He could fix anything. You'll see." Fear clung to Emma's voice. She gripped Cat's shivering shoulders with trembling hands. "We can fix everything."

Cat looked down at the compass. It was so small; it did not even fill her palm. "What is in the east? What is this thing I need most?" She dared to look back to the old witch.

The crone had to be a witch.

"You will know when you find it." As the woman spoke, she stepped back onto the balcony, fading into the shadows.

Emma jumped up, peering around the curtains. The room was empty. There was no one in the room besides the two of them. "Where did she go?"

The air was still.

"Gone. Faded away... I almost doubt she was really here." For years Cat had been taught there was no magic left in the world. Magic had gone extinct along with the guardians who protected it. It should have been difficult to change that mindset. It was not. Believing magic could be real was like taking that first deep breath after swimming beneath the waves. As simple as opening a book, revealing a world she did not yet understand, though she desperately wanted to.

A sigh of relief escaped Emma. "Good. Throw that thing away and be rid of both of them."

"No." Cat's fingers tightened around the compass. Cat needed Emma to believe too. She was the only one who could understand. "There's somewhere I need to go. I... I have to... Emma, I'm not like you. I did not meet my true love at 16 and I... I don't get to choose, but there has to be something out there for me. I have to go. I have to find what is for me."

"Then," she dropped her hands to her sides, shaking her head. "You had better change. You cannot go on an adventure in your ball gown."

The kitchens bustled with even more commotion than usual. Emma flattened herself against the wall. She did not know what she expected. It was not as if the feast would be canceled just because Cat threw a fit, not with a hundred people in the palace waiting for it. Even if it had been, the kitchens would not have simply emptied.

She ducked behind a passing footman, moving to a new hiding spot, this one a behind a line of tall cakes. Just a few feet from the enormous pantry where dozens of crates full of fresh picked fruit and loaves of bread waited for breakfast. She adjusted her skirts, preparing to scurry the last few feet when a voice behind her gave her pause. Three kitchen maids were on the other side of the counter, gossiping as they arranged the trays for the feast that was already underway. Emma crouched down so as not to be seen.

"If you ask me, she gave him just what he deserved, arranging a marriage without bothering to tell her. I know I wouldn't stand for it."

"*You* are not a princess. And what else was the king to do? She's rejected every noble in Volentia and she does have to marry eventually. You think Prince Ryder wants her traipsing about the royal palace when he has his own little ones to raise" Emma's fingers curled into fists against her knees. As far as she was concerned Cat could stay in her home as long as she liked. And she did not have to marry... unless she chose to. "Besides, the princess could do much worse than a prince for a husband."

"A prince who did not even show up to the feast celebrating their engagement."

"Probably too busy at some brothel if the rumors are true. They say he's seduced half of his own court."

"Those are just rumors."

"Rumors come from somewhere. If even half of what I've heard about Prince Thomas is true, I don't blame the princess for not wanting to marry him."

"I don't think that was the reason." The third girl spoke in a low tone that was full of innuendo and subtle meaning. "I think she's still in love with that knight and that's why she rejects every suitor." Emma could picture the maid waggling an eyebrow.

"What knight?"

"I forgot, that was before you worked at the palace. They say the last time Reinsaffira visited, Princess Catiya fell in love with one of the knights who came with them and she's been waiting for him ever since."

"No," the younger girl gasped.

"Yes." There was a clank and the voices receded, heading toward the line of servers. "I heard it from Ambassador Arik himself."

"And what would he know about the princess's romances?"

The voices faded away.

Emma did not wait to see if they might return. She jumped to her feet, rushing into the pantry, closing the door behind her. Then, she forced her mind back to the task of gathering food for Cat's journey. The sack she carried rustled as she shoved apples and hard cheeses into it.

There was a creak and light suddenly flooded the small room. Emma paused, hand hovering over a loaf of bread.

She turned slowly, finding a familiar plump woman with flour and chocolate smeared across her apron. Her blonde hair was tied up under a handkerchief. A few tendrils had slipped free, framing her too wide eyes.

"Lydia! What are you doing here?" Lydia was a baker, but she did not work at the palace. Emma only knew her because her brother was a royal guard, someone who had once been Cat's friend but had not been for a very long time.

Lydia swept her hands down her apron before bobbing in a facsimile of a curtsy. "That was just the question I had planned to ask you, my lady." Her eyes swept over the bag in Emma's hands.

"Yes, but as I asked you first, and significantly outrank you, I expect you to be the one to offer an answer."

A smile played on Lydia's lips. "I prepared the desserts for the feast. I even made a chocolate one special for Cat, though I don't suppose she'll get the chance to try it now."

Emma found herself tensing the way she always did when Lydia or any of the rest of them spoke of Cat like they still had the right to call her a friend.

"Is she all right?"

"The princess is fine. I'm just taking her some food." Emma shoved the loaf of bread into her bag, pushing her way out of the pantry.

Lydia stepped aside. "And she sent you instead of a servant because she's hiding and doesn't want anyone knowing where she is?"

"I offered," Emma glared, "because I am her friend. Friends look after each other."

It was almost midnight by the time Cat was changed into her traveling clothes, a dark green vest with an over-sized tunic, breeches, and her best walking boots. Somewhere in the palace the celebration should still be going on, as if she had not stormed out and disappeared. Cat shuddered at the gossip that would have traveled around the glittering ballroom by now. It would be nothing compared to what they would say in the morning, after they discovered she was gone.

Cat wrapped the food Emma smuggled from the kitchens in a cloth, stuffing it into her small leather pack. When that ran out, Cat would have to find an inn and purchase more with the little pocket money she had saved, and the diamond hairpins also hidden at the bottom of the pack. Then she started fastening her emerald green cloak over her shoulders. The velvet was much too fine to wear on the road, but it would be warm, and she had nothing else. Hiding her mother's sapphire necklace under the velvet, the bright blue stone throbbed against her chest.

Her plan was all worked out. She would climb down the lattice work again and leave the palace through the small gate on the eastern edge of the garden. Cat was forbidden from going anywhere near the gate and had only opened it once. Cat did not know what was beyond it, other than freedom and adventure. Getting across the garden, just beyond the ballroom, without being seen was going to be tricky. If she could just get to the gate, no one would think to search beyond the palace walls for hours.

The magic compass gave Cat an unbidden sense of confidence as she stepped out onto the balcony.

"Wait!" Emma held out a small box to her. "Take this as well." She opened the box revealing a silver and gold dagger with a large opal embedded in the pommel.

"You can't give me that; it was your mother's!"

Emma shrugged. "It is a loan. You have to return it." An almost toothy grin spread across her face before growing solemn again. "My father used to tell me it was magic, that it could only be wielded by someone of great power. I want you to take it with you, just in case."

Cat lifted the dagger from the velvet lined box. The filigreed hilt hummed against her palm. "Thank you." She quickly strapped it to her hip, then finished clasping the cloak tight around her shoulders. She climbed on the balcony railing. "I'll see you again soon."

Emma watched her best friend climb, slow and careful, down the palace wall until she vanished into the night.

"Is she away?"

Emma leapt, a shiver dancing over her skin at the sound of a man's voice. She turned just in time to see Thomas pulling himself out from under Cat's monstrous bed.

"I forgot you were there." She held a hand to her chest.

"That had become obvious to me... a while ago." Thomas' legs were so long, he was at the door in only a few strides.

"Where are you going? You can't tell the king; she would never forgive you!"

"I'm going after her," he grunted. "Not to drag her back. The wilderness is dangerous for anyone traveling alone, and it will be worse if anyone finds out who she is." Thomas pulled open the door, hurrying down the hall before Emma could protest.

Somehow it was comforting, knowing he would be there to protect Cat. It was not the way she planned it, but somehow Emma knew that if Cat and the prince just spent a little time together... they could fall in love. They had been so close once.

Cat spun around, hair raising at the sound of a branch snapping behind her. In the distance, just beyond the shadows, she could see the twinkling golden light of the ballroom. Maybe it was just a couple wandering the dark paths in search of a romantic secluded spot.

She leaned into the shadow of a tree, breathing deeply until her heart stopped pounding.

There was no one. No one would see her.

The secret gate was only a few feet away. Just a few more feet and Cat would be free. Every decision would be hers to make.

Cat stepped up close to the gate. Her fingers wrapping around the cold iron handle.

It groaned, the lock sliding open.

"I had hoped I was wrong."

A shiver danced up Cat's spine. She glanced over her shoulder. Not that she needed to; she knew Evander's voice. She should have known the moment she sensed another person in the darkness that it would be her one-time friend. Her muscles tensed, hackles rising.

"What are you doing?"

"Don't you know? You are the one who knew to wait for me here."

The gate swung open.

"Cat, wait."

Her fingers tensed, wrapping tighter around the ancient gate until the handle dug into her palm. It had been a lifetime since Evander called her anything besides *Princess*. A lifetime since he had spoken to her as if she was a friend. It was hard to remember that they had once been friends.

She turned back to face him.

Evander stood a short distance away. His arms folded over his chest. "You're not really going to run away, are you? It's dangerous out there."

"I would rather face the danger of freedom than spend my life as a pawn for *them* to trade and sacrifice." Cat's thoughts strayed back to that morning. When everything had been so simple. Evander had been at her father's council meeting. Evander was one of Ambassador Arik's escorts. "Did you know?"

"I..."

"For how long?"

"Cat... I know you feel betrayed and..."

"You don't have the right to call me that!" She kept her voice low. Cat had to fold her arms tight over her chest to keep from trembling with rage. "You're not my friend. Do not act as if you care about me. All you care about is the fact that I'm a princess." The words hurt to say. Like ice shards buried deep in her heart. "What makes you think you know anything about me or what I feel?" As far as Cat was concerned, it did not matter that he was right. She did feel hurt and betrayed. Nor did it matter that Evander had known she would run away and exactly where to find her. All that mattered was he had lied to her as much as any of them. He had known for weeks. A friend, someone who cared about her at all, would have told her.

"Because I know you! Cat, I've known you for years."

"I wish I could say the same about you." Cat spared one last look at the palace. Then back at Evander. He had his hand on his sword. "I'm leaving. If you want to stop me, you will have to drag me back to the palace screaming." Cat felt her fingers inching toward the dagger at her belt. "And if you want to do that, you'll have to beat me. And we both know you've never been able to."

Across the shadowy garden, Cat could see the Evander's muscles tense. His fingers tightening around his sword.

The dagger rang clear and metallic as she pulled it from its sheath. Every muscle in her body thrummed with anticipation.

"Please, Cat. Don't make me drag you back." He stepped forward, wrapping his free hand around Cat's elbow and pulling her toward the palace.

Cat's heels dug into the dirt. She pulled free of his grip, pointing her dagger at him, dropping into a fighting stance. "Then don't."

Evander reached out a second time, but Cat slashed at his hand with her blade. Forcing him to block with the flat of his blade. The clang of steel rang across the dark garden. Cat cringed; certain the sudden sound would attract the attention of any number of guests and palace guards. She dodged, slamming her foot into Evander's. Anger and rage overtaking her. Her limbs started to shake with adrenaline.

"Cat! Stop!" His arm snaked around her waist, pinning her to his chest. "Please be reasonable."

Cat pushed his arm away, slamming her elbow into his ribs. She spun out of reach. Wrenching the sword from his hand as she moved. In a quick flurry of movement, she knocked him onto his back. Struggling to pull himself back to his feet. Cat seized her opportunity, spinning back toward the gate. She was out the gate and sprinting up the trail before she thought to look back.

PART

TWO

Part Two

Cat pulled her cloak tight around her. The wind cut through her like a knife. Her pack felt heavy and awkward on her back and her legs were aching from the long walk up the steep trail, but the path was starting to level out. She must be coming to a high mountain valley. Her stomach growled out an empty yowl and her lips were getting dry with thirst. She needed to find a safe place to sit down and rest. Cat tromped onward, farther away from the palace. She had to get farther away before she could stop.

The mountain trail curved around a moss-covered boulder. The spot was totally unfamiliar. Mist clung to the ground around Cat. Only a few miles, but it may as well have been an entirely different world. On the far side of the boulder, Cat could make out a stream with a willow tree alongside it. There was a rock almost shaped like a table hidden under the swaying branches. The perfect spot to refill her water skin and enjoy an apple for breakfast. This adventure was turning out lovely, just like a fairy story.

The sounds of Royal City had long since faded away, unable to reach Cat's ears. It had taken longer than she expected for the alarms to start after she slipped through the gate. At least a half hour, and by then she could barely hear the bells. Still, Cat had been listening for the clamor of knights from the moment she left Evander in the garden. No one had come this way yet. A few times, Cat's ears had perked, thinking she heard hoof beats or the soft nicker of a horse. Nothing followed behind her. It was just her panicked imagination.

Cat double checked her compass, clicking it open and closed. The arrow still pointed east, directly ahead.

She pocketed it.

Footsteps echoed behind Cat, catching her attention. She glanced back down the path. Nothing. Only the rustle of leaves in the wind. Why wouldn't her heart stop pounding?

She spun back toward the path.

Two large men with matted beards and stained cloaks stood before her. Their drawn knives gleamed against the swirling fog.

"Well, well, well. What have we here?" The larger of the two spoke with a thick gravely drawl.

"She's a pretty little thing." The second man had a weaselly face beneath his unkempt beard.

Bandits? Cat remembered hearing reports that the roads near the city had been growing dangerous. She never expected anyone on this remote path. Cat took a breath, deciding she was not afraid of them. They were Volentian, after all. Once they saw who Cat was and that she was unafraid, they would let her pass.

"I don't want any trouble." The long dagger Emma loaned her was in Cat's hand. She was regretting leaving Evander's sword behind. "Please, l-let me pass."

"You hear that," the weasel hissed. "The little lady don't want no trouble. Looks like you found trouble anyway."

The men were close enough that the filth of their clothes filled her nose, making her gag.

"I warn you." The steel point flashed in the torchlight. "Let me pass."

The larger man's meat hook fingers wrapped around the blade. He wrenched the dagger free without blinking. Smiling. His free hand gripped her wrist.

Now Cat was afraid. "Let me go! My name is Catiya, and I am on an important mission for the king of Volentia."

Never let your enemy see fear behind your eyes. Roderick's voice echoed in Cat's mind. He spent weeks teaching her how to disarm an attacker before they could hurt her. *If they see your fear, they have already won.* Cat's heart was pounding. She fixed the men with a sharp glare.

"I know exactly who you are and why you're here." The man flipped the dagger around, so the hilt was in his blood-stained fingers. Pointing it at her throat. "But don't worry, your highness, we're not going to hurt you, just keep you here until our *friend* arrives." He grimaced, then dropped the dagger with a grunt of pain. It was hard to see beneath the blood, but it looked like blisters were appearing on his burned palm.

Taking advantage of the distraction, Cat raised a booted foot and kicked him in the stomach. Metal clanged, hurting her foot. The man wore a breastplate under his tunic. Mountain bandits would not have proper armor. Cat did not know who their *friend* was, but she knew she did not want to wait for him to arrive.

The pounding of her heart filled her ears.

No. The sound was at Cat's back. It was familiar but far too irregular to be a heartbeat. The ruffians looked back, eyes widening. They let go and pushed Cat off the path just as a flash of brown and red barreled down on them. A lanky man leapt from his horse onto the larger of the two brutes. Cat snatched up her dagger and rolled away from the grappling pair.

"Where do you think you're going?" The weasel gripped her cloak, pulling her toward him. Cat clenched her eyes shut and pushed the blade toward him, biting through wool and soft tissue. The weasel clutched his stomach, disappearing into the bushes. The larger man disappeared behind him, engulfed by the mist.

Cat pushed herself to her feet, pointing the tip of her blood covered dagger at the rider who now sat in the dirt. His horse waited nearby, saddled and riderless. Slowly, the man slid the hood of his cloak down to hang off his shoulders, revealing a familiar set of dirty russet curls. The knight... Thomas.

He arched an eyebrow. "In my experience, a lady usually says thank you when a gentleman saves her. I have saved your life twice now and on both occasions I have had a blade at my throat for my trouble. Is this a Volentian custom?"

"Perhaps you should stop trying to save me." Cat stomped to the stream, kneeling down to scrub the blood from her hands and the blade in the cold water.

"And miss out on all this praise and your sparkling manners?"

The man followed her, carefully positioning himself between her and the bushes the men had disappeared into. "My name is Thomas." He smiled, watching the blood thin in the water. A long smudge of dirt ran from his temple to his chin.

"I know your name." She knew who this man was beyond any doubt, the knight who had hurt her heart so badly when she was young. He seemed to have a bad habit of appearing and causing trouble whenever she was supposed to be getting engaged. "And even if I didn't, why would I care?"

"I thought you might like to use it, the next time I save you."

Cat ignored the obvious bait, continuing to scrub her clean hands.

"And you are Catiya, Princess of Volentia. A bit far from the palace and your royal guards though. You wouldn't happen to be running away from something, would you?"

Cat spun to face him.

She reeled back, still grimacing. Thomas was more handsome than she remembered. "What do you want? Are you here to drag me back?"

"Right now, I want to make sure you were all right, Princess. That was quite the scene a moment ago." He brushed a stray lock of copper hair away from her face. His blue eyes fixed on her. "Are you hurt?"

Cat flinched back. She had no time for him or his false chivalry. Cat had to cover more ground if she was going to get away. "You talk like a knight." She turned away, her legs wobbling with shaking nerves. She had no reason to trust Thomas, whether he saved her life... twice... or not. Besides, she knew he was only here to strap her on the back of his horse and take her back to the palace.

He chuckled, shaking his head. "I have not met many princesses, but I should have known you were one the instant I saw you. You're so used to giving men orders that you tried it on a pair of bandits. And so used to men only being interested in you for your title that you don't recognize real concern when it is in front of you."

"I don't need your concern!" Cat pounded her feet on the moss, stomping away, fists clenched. It made her feel like a child throwing a tantrum. "I can take care of myself."

Laughter racked Thomas' entire body. A wave that started in his shoulders and moved to his knees. He hunched forward, tugging at the fastener of his cloak. "You're doing a marvelous job so far."

Normally, Cat's cheeks were pale. Not now. Anger flushed crimson, burning hot, from her chin to her forehead. Her jaw was growing tight. "Who's to say I would not have handled it if you had not come along?"

"Only me, seeing as I was the only one who witnessed it."

"Then once you leave, no one will."

Thomas folded his arms over his chest, stepping into her path. "See, that's where we have a bit of a problem. I have no intention of going anywhere without you. Chivalry will not allow me to leave you, a princess and a fair maiden, unaccompanied. The woods are dangerous, you know."

A frown etched into Cat's features. Suspecting it did not make knowing her adventure was over hurt any less.

"The way I see it, there is only one option. I would like to offer my services as your bodyguard for your travels."

"What?"

"I'll go with you. I'm traveling that direction anyway. I would be happy to see you safely to your destination."

"My destination?" Hope had the nerve to bubble in her chest. "How do... You don't know where I'm going." The brass compass was back in Cat's hand, the arrow spinning.

"It appears that you don't either." He shook his head, gesturing toward the lightening sky. "Only a princess would need a compass to find north at dawn. It doesn't matter. I am going whatever direction you are going."

Cat's frown hardened. Thomas was that perfect combination of handsome and irritating and she had no desire to waste even one more second in his company.

"Or would you prefer me to tie you to the back of my horse and carry you back to the betrothed you are running away from? Honestly, I prefer the first option. From what I know about you, you would only be gone again by sunset."

Chewing her lip, Cat weighed her options. She turned hard eyes on Thomas, searching his face for the lie. Cat could not find it. Only more blue hung behind his eyes. His clear glittering eyes. Could she trust him? She seemed to have little choice. If she tried to turn him away, he would overpower her and carry her back to the palace. If she let him go with her...

"Well, Princess?"

Cat stepped forward.

He bent his head toward hers.

"Fine, but under one condition. Do not call me *Princess*. And I'm leading."

"That is two conditions, my lady."

"Ugh."

Thomas frowned at Cat's immediate look of disgust.

"That's worse. Cat. Just call me Cat."

The horse sauntered toward them, nudging Cat in the shoulder with its velvety muzzle. Thomas put out a hand, catching Cat as she stumbled forward. She stiffened, springing away from him.

"Right, now that we have that settled, why don't you mount up while I gather some supplies." He walked away from her, leaving her alone in the icy mist. Cat's eyes rounded when they met the mare's large brown eyes.

She had ridden a horse before, side saddle, at a slow walk, for parades through city streets. Never through the woods, straddling the poor creature the way this saddle was designed. She was not even entirely certain she knew how to mount up.

"Eventually, your father's guards will realize you are not in the palace or city and start searching the mountains. I cannot say for certain how long it will take them to reach that conclusion, you would be more familiar with their stupidity than I am, but I assure you they will." Thomas smiled as he slung her pack over the saddle bags. Cat's hands flew to her shoulders; she had not even realized she dropped it. "Which means time is of the essence. Which makes me wonder why your feet are still on the ground." A quizzical look combined with concern clouded the irritating knight's features. "Do not tell me that the princess who climbs rocks cannot ride a horse."

Cat rolled her eyes; circling the beast in search of a way to mount it. Nothing was worse than someone assuming she could not do something... even if she couldn't. It was part of a stubborn streak that many courtiers, and a handful of servants, enjoyed gossiping about. She gripped the reins in her fingers. No matter what, Cat planned to get onto that horse on her own.

"Of course, I know how to ride," Cat grunted, placing one hand on each side of the saddle. Her muscles tightened as she tried to push her feet off the ground. When rock climbing, she used footholds. The horse had no footholds. And there were no steps. The stable master always brought out a set of steps for Cat to use. There were no steps here and it seemed unlikely that Thomas would run back to the palace to fetch some.

Warmth touched Cat's hips. She felt Thomas' fingers stretch across her stomach. Then, before Cat could push his hands away, Thomas swept her up into the air.

"Unhand me! I don't need your help!" Had she really been so intent on what she was doing that she had not noticed his approach? Cat would have to be less careless in the future. He was already too familiar with her. It sparked memories of Carswell. What if his motives for staying with her were not his sense of duty?

He let her back to the ground, holding his hands up in placating gesture. "I just assumed you would want to be on your way soon. Do you really know how to ride?"

"Only side saddle," she admitted. The words soured in her stomach.

Something about this man's smile was impossible to lie to. "I'm not even very good at that."

"I'll have to teach you then."

A snapping sound on the path, back toward the palace, made them both jump, searching the darkness behind them.

"But perhaps... it would be best if we wait until we are a bit farther away."

Voices echoed behind Cat, growing louder with every second.

The blood drained from her face. She knew she did not trust the man in front of her and could not shake the suspicion that he would drag her back to Volentia or on to Reinsaffira at the first chance he got. Then again, she knew the people coming up the path definitely would.

His warm hands wrapped around her waist a second time. Lifting her with what seemed like no effort, onto the horse. Leaping onto the horse behind her, he held her against his chest. Cat did not see how he mounted so fast. She intended to watch closer the next time.

Thomas balled the reins in his hand. "Well, which way?"

Cat pried open the compass. The arrow wavered for a moment before spinning off to the east. "Due east."

The horse took off across the brook.

Blankets tangled around Emma's legs. She kicked them away, rolling onto her side. The blankets only twisted tighter around her feet. The pink and orange light drifting in from her window told Emma it was just after sunrise. Sleep had been elusive for the few hours Emma spent curled in her bed. Her stomach clenched, twisting into aching knots.

Had it been a mistake to let Cat leave? The image of the crone floated in Emma's vision, startling her out of the peaceful silence of sleep.

It will be okay. Emma pressed a hand to her ribs, flopping onto her back and taking in a deep breath. It had to be okay. The prince would have caught up to her by now. He would keep Cat safe. The anxiety tightened around her ribs. She took in a second deep breath, going over what would happen in her head. It was not exactly a plan, just an idea, a hope. Prince Thomas would catch up with Cat, then he would protect her and gain her trust. A smile started to form on Emma's lips. It would be slow at first, but eventually they would fall in love. A perfect love story. Cat would choose him for herself, and the alliance would be saved.

The image of the crone shattered the magic of the perfect fantasy.

No, it was not the thought of the crone that shattered the thought.

Someone was pounding on her door.

"Lady Emma! Wake up!" Captain Roderick's voice boomed on the far side of the heavy door. "You've been summoned before the king."

Emma sat upright in bed. Her pulse thrummed in every inch of her skin. She was on her feet in an instant, wrapping a thin robe around he shoulders. Her fingers shook against the door handle, trembling with nerves.

The anxiety tightened around her stomach.

She pulled the door open.

Roderick filled the doorway, a storm cloud crackling in front of her. He looked perfect, despite the early hour, dressed in a crisp white shirt, his sword resting on his hip. The only sign of the early hour were the lines and dark circles etched around his eyes.

"Captain Roderick? Whatever is the matter?"

"Let's not play games, Lady Emma." He let out a heavy sigh. "It is quite early."

Emma's demeanor hardened. She leaned against the door in as casual a manner as she could muster. "Have you found Cat yet?"

"I believe you already know the answer to that." Roderick's shoulders were stiff, solid and strong and unmovable; every inch the captain of the guard Emma knew and feared. It was not that Roderick was ever hurtful or mean. He never tried to make Emma feel less than anyone else. It was the gossip that played in her mind kept her away from him.

Once, when Emma had been walking the halls she heard two guards whispering about Roderick and the woman he had once been in love with. The woman who raised Emma. Her adopted mother. A sense of unease raised up the back of Emma's neck every time she was near Roderick. He knew Emma was illegitimate; an insult to the woman he once loved. If anyone believed Emma did not belong in the palace, at Ryder's side, she knew it would be him.

Captain Roderick crossed his arms over his chest.

Emma mirrored him. "You know I can't tell you where she is."

"I know." Roderick's frown remained fixed, but something sparkled in his eyes, almost like a smile. "But you'll have to tell the king that. I would suggest you change, unless you want to address two kings in your nightgown."

Emma stifled a yawn. She stood on the sidelines of the great hall while a young man with messy blond hair spoke. His rumpled uniform told Emma he was one of the Volentian guards. Emma's brow scrunched; she knew him. Her fingers tapped a quiet rhythm against her legs, the velvet scratching her fingertips. He was one of the guards for the Reinsaffiran ambassador.

EVANDER!

The second his name formed in her mind, Emma knew why she knew this guard, he was Lydia's brother, the one who had been Cat's friend. Why was he here?

Emma blinked, forcing herself to focus on Evander's words.

"Princess Catiya was at the eastern gate. I tried to stop her from leaving, but..." Evander stumbled to a stop. His words tripping over his tongue. "I'm not sure what happened. I... The next thing I knew I was on the ground and Ca- Princess Catiya was gone."

"Lady Emma." King Kristoff gripped the arms of his cushioned throne as he spoke. The force of his voice made Emma flinch. "You have been Princess Catiya's lady companion for many years. I know you would do little to endanger that position. I also know..."

"That I am close friends with Cat and am probably the only person who knows why she was at the eastern gate. Forgive my interruption, Your Majesty," Emma added a hasty curtsy. "It is only that it's a bit early for long speeches meant to ask simple questions."

"It is early for insolence as well." A chill passed through the room as Kristoff spoke. "Well then? What was Princess Catiya doing at the eastern gate?"

Emma forced a smile. The expression was achingly difficult to hold in place. "I would think her reasons would be obvious. I believe she intended on leaving the palace, rather than be forced to marry someone she did not choose and has never met."

A ripple of tension swept through the room, shoulders straightening and jaws tensing. Emma swore she could hear the king's teeth grinding from the far side of the great hall. Her gaze darted to Evander. He stood still as stone, but his gaze was fixed on marble floor, his fingers curled into tight fists. She noted the slight shift in his demeanor, though she did not know yet what to do with it.

"And where..."

Emma's gaze snapped back to King Kristoff. His rumbling voice was like thunder.

"...has she run away to? She must be found so we may rectify this situation."

"Forgive me, Your Majesty. What do you mean by *rectify*?"

This time it was the Reinsaffiran king who spoke. He was seated beside King Kristoff in a plush chair, the only one allowed to be seated in the king's presence. "We mean, she is to be returned to the palace so she and my son can sign the marriage contract. They will have to be married at once. Now, where is she?"

Emma's shoulders tensed. The edge to the words cut her somewhere deep inside. Cat ran away and they still planned to use her to solidify the alliance? Cat would be still expected to marry the prince the moment she was returned to the palace, without a ceremony or a proper gown, or the comfort of a choice. Then she would be dragged away to Reinsaffira. More a prisoner than a future queen. The mere thought of it hurt. The searing pain dulled knowing none of that could happen, because Cat would not be found.

"I cannot tell you." That much was not a lie, she did not know where Cat had gone. All she knew was that Cat went east, following a compass that was meant to lead her to the thing she needed most, whatever that might be. Emma twisted her engagement ring around her finger, letting her gaze trail over to Ryder. He always knew what to do. If she could just take a few minutes to talk to him, maybe he would have a plan. That was... *if* he ever forgave her for letting Cat run away in the first place.

"You cannot tell us or won't tell us?"

"Cannot. In truth." The words sounded surprisingly weak, almost breathless, even to her own ears. "I do not know where Princess Catiya is. I wish I did."

Her every muscle was tuned to the way Ryder reacted to the statement. The smallest movement of his shoulders, the shuffle of his feet. It was not a lie, but Emma knew he suspected it was not a full truth. She could feel his jaw tensing, preparing a statement.

Before Ryder could speak, the door behind Emma banged open.

"Your majesties!" The Reinsaffiran ambassador rushed into the room. His clothing was rumpled, the same clothing he had been wearing the evening before. "I apologize for the interruption but... It's Prince Thomas. He's missing."

"What?"

"His bed is unslept in, and his horse is missing."

"Then find him!"

"I..."

Emma's eyes lit with delight. A giddiness bubbled inside of her. "Forgive me, your majesties, I do know the prince's whereabouts."

Time ground to a startled halt.

The eyes of both kings, as well as Prince Phillip and Lord Arik, turned toward her with a strange mix of surprise and confusion.

King James studied Emma's form, doing quick calculations of her beauty. Deciding if a girl engaged to her own dashing prince might succumb to the charms of his rakish heir. Unsurprising, considering the rumors of the Crown Prince of Reinsaffira's *behavior*.

King Kristoff's eyebrows arched. The quick and certain surprise of a man who knew Emma and Cat well enough to know she was telling the truth and wonder what new and horrible mischief she had gotten into.

Ryder's look of panic hurt the most. He knew the prince first hand, and very much disapproved of him.

The only eyes that did not contain surprise were Evander's. He did not move at the announcement that the prince was gone or that Emma might know where he was. He knew more than he said.

"Well," King Kristoff finally sputtered, waving a hand at her, waiting for Emma to continue.

"Well, I do not know his precise location, but I have an idea of where he is."

"Spit it out then, girl!"

"Crown Prince Thomas is with Princess Catiya."

King Kristoff let out the same derisive snort his daughter always did when confronted with an idea she thought was absurd. "I believe you have had enough attention for one morning." A wave of his jeweled hand dismissed Emma. "You are confined to quarters until such time as you choose to tell us anything resembling the truth."

Ryder stepped forward to escort Emma back to her room, as he always did.

"Not you, Prince Ryder. I still require your presence."

"I will escort the lady back to her chambers. If my king has no further need of me." Philip, the golden second prince of Reinsaffira volunteered his arm. Emma grasped it and let him guide her out of the cold room.

The doors had barely clicked shut behind them when he rounded on her. "Are you playing some sort of joke, or do you truly not know the whereabouts of my brother and the princess?"

"I already told them. I do not know where Cat is, but you can trust me when I say that they are together. He should have caught up to her by now."

"Caught up?"

Emma felt a laugh forming in her throat. "Cat ran away, and Prince Thomas went after her. Neither of them are on the palace grounds anymore. He was not far behind and if he had a horse," Emma shrugged, "he should have caught her by now."

"To bring her back? I'm sure a guard could have done that."

"Are you all really such massive idiots?" Emma dropped Phillip's arm, spinning to glare at the golden prince. "No! I sent him after her to protect her... to win her." She wanted to run her hands down her face and scream. "Don't you get it? Cat does not love Prince Thomas!"

"But he loves her. That's why he agreed to marry her."

"I know that! But if he wants to claim any part of her heart, he will have to earn it." The fire in her voice dwindled to a dim ember. "That's why, when Cat wanted to run away, I let her... I helped her. And that is why I sent him after her. So he could protect her out in the world. So they could actually have a chance."

"Oh, creator save me!" Phillip rolled his brilliant blue eyes. "You can't be serious?"

Shouts echoed in the hall as the door swung open.

"I am very serious." She glanced over her shoulder to see Ryder stepping through the large oak doors. "Listen, I know Cat. She is brave and stubborn and often rushes into things without considering the consequences. She is also true to her heart, and she will never love someone she was forced to marry. I know she will get tired of running and she'll come back. Until then, she'll be protected by the man she is betrothed to. During that time, he will earn her trust and, *if* he deserves it, he'll earn her love." The sound of Ryder's boots filled the hall. Emma smiled back at the prince. "I would appreciate it if you would allow me to divulge this information as I see fit."

"I do not believe I could explain it if I wanted." Phillip glanced between Emma and Ryder. He bowed and turned back toward the guest wing. "I shall leave you to it then."

"What was that?"

Emma turned back to Ryder, resting a hand on his arm. "An exercise in trust."

"Do you really believe the Reinsaffirans are worthy of your trust?"

Whether they were or not, there was not turning back now. Thomas and Cat were out in the wilderness and there was nothing Emma could do to help them. "Ryder." She placed a hand on his shoulder, the warmth of his skin soaked into her fingers. "There is something I need to tell you."

The sun was fully up now, illuminating the red and orange leaves that littered the path. Leaves that almost matched the princess' fiery red hair. She was made for autumn leaves.

Thomas steered the horse to the side of the path.

"What are you doing?" Cat twisted around to look at Thomas as she spoke. Jostling him out of balance.

"Woah!" He dropped one hand to her waist, wrapping an arm around her to keep the princess from falling, or knocking him from his own seat. Warmth pressed through the tunic and vest she wore. Thomas could almost imagine the press of her skin against his own. "Be careful or you'll fall. The last thing I need is a bruised and trampled princess when your guards catch up with us."

The horse slowed, drifting into the open mountain meadow. The last vestiges of wildflowers danced in the grass. Dragonberry bushes ringed the edge of the meadow.

"If you're so worried about the guards catching us, why are you stopping?"

Thomas was already climbing down from the saddle, raising his arms to Cat to help her slide down into the grass. "Because we've been up all night and need to rest. Even if we didn't, the horse is tired. It won't hurt us to take a short break." His fingers found her waist again.

"I suppose a short rest won't hurt much." Cat pushed his hand away.

Sliding down from the saddle, she landed with a hard thud that made Thomas wince.

He let his arms drop to his side. Useless. Chivalry clearly was not the way to win the princess' affection. Maybe it was not affection he was fighting for... yet. Thomas spun around, watching Cat wander the lovely green space. With her back to him he could stare at her as much as he pleased, still disbelieving that she was actually there in front of him. Thomas had spent years searching for the girl with red hair. Then, once he found her, he spent five years trying to forget he loved her. Cat was exactly the way he remembered her. Her emerald eyes were hard as stone. She tossed sharp looks that Thomas swore could cut his skin. Underneath was a deep sadness, a need or longing that he was desperate to fulfill. Her hair was a glowing copper that gleamed like the autumn leaves. She kept it tied back in a neat braid that hung down her back.

The only difference, he realized as a frown formed on his lips, was that this time she hated him. In his dreams, she did not hate him.

Cat reached for one of the deep purple flowers blossoming around her, brushing her finger over the delicate petal.

"You don't trust me. Do you?"

The princess stiffened. The motion was almost imperceptible, but he saw it. He saw the tightening of her shoulders, the flinch that crinkled in the corners of her eyes. Then she stood, sweeping her hands down her shirt, smoothing the wrinkles in her nonexistent skirt out of habit.

"Trust is earned." Cat crossed her arms over her chest. "And it's fragile. *Easily* broken."

The sharp words, though spoken softly, needled at Thomas. "You're talking about the night we met, aren't you? The ball, five years ago? I did not think you remembered me."

"Don't flatter yourself. It is not a fond memory."

"You remember dancing in the garden and..." Thomas paused. Surely she remembered their kiss. The moment was seared into his memory. Permanent, yet fragile. Somehow, he felt that talking about it would shatter the perfection of their single moment together.

"I remember you asking me to meet you at sunset! I remember you leaving me sitting there alone in the garden! Without any word! With-out..." The princess seemed to choke on the words. She swallowed hard. "Without anyone knowing where I was."

Cat hated how hard the words were to form, but the memory of being left alone where Carswell could find and threaten her was burned into her memory. It was a painful, jagged piece of glass that rattled inside of herself. Was it all a trick he intended to play on her? Was this? Would the knight wake up while they were resting and drag her home again?

He studied the ground, unwilling to meet Cat's hard stare. Now that the question had formed in her mind, Cat had to know the answer. She stared him down, daring the man to offer some feeble excuse.

"That is something I wish you did not remember."

"Why? So, it would be easier to trick me again? So, you could curry favor with..."

"Because I wanted to meet you!" The knight's eyes widened as if the sudden confession surprised even him. "I... I wanted to meet you, but I had to leave suddenly, an urgent task for the crown prince. There was no time to find you and explain."

Something in his tone tasted like a lie. But there was something else that rang true. Maybe it was the passion and surprise with which he spoke. It was difficult to fake such a reaction. Cat pushed the thoughts aside. She no longer cared what his excuses were, only whether or not he was someone she could trust. The fact that he had once been close enough to the crown prince, her new fiancé, to be asked to personally carry out a task on his behalf caught Cat's attention.

"You know the crown prince?"

Thomas shrugged. "In a manner of speaking."

She opened her mouth to speak then shut it again. The question she wanted to ask felt stupid. Suddenly tired and stiff, Cat spun around, searching for a soft place to sit down.

The light breeze drew the scent of the fresh berries dangling on the bushes surrounding the meadow to Cat. Her mouth watered at the tangy scent. She had been up all night and was hungry.

Cat took a step toward the bushes.

Without having to look at Thomas, she felt a little bolder. It was easier to ask a question when the person holding the answer could not see the curiosity on her face. "What is the prince like?" She studied the bush of deep blue berries, as if she did not care one way or the other about the answer.

"Why would you want to know what the man you are running away from is like?"

"I'm not running away from him," Cat snapped. As if this man could ever understand. He was a knight and Cat had known enough knights in her life to know they were always free. No one told them who they had to be. "I'm running away from a life that was picked out for me. A life without any choices or adventures or freedom. I can't live like that anymore. I can't sit by and let others make my choices for me."

Cat turned back to the bushes, brushing her fingers over a pale white blossom.

A heavy pause stretched out between them.

"Fine, forget I asked," Cat muttered. "I just... I wanted to know."

Thomas took a deep breath. "You could not live a life in which people expected you to be someone you are not. Yes, I know a little of what that is like." Cat spun around to look at him. Thomas was no longer looking at her. He stood beside the horse, working at removing the saddle from the beast's back. "What do you want to know about the prince?"

"Um... just... what is he like?'

"I'm sure you've heard the gossip. They say he is a great fool, endlessly chasing after the next shiny bit of nonsense that catches his eye."

Strictly speaking, that was not what the gossips said about him. They called him a rake always chasing after the next girl to fill his bed. But Cat never paid much attention to gossip. She had no patience for the people at court who prattled and bandied lies back and forth about her and her brother. Even the half-truths among them were wild exaggerations and misunderstandings. Whatever they had to say about the Reinsaffiran Prince had to hold the same level of truth.

"I did not ask what the gossips said about him. What do you think of him? You said you knew him."

"Well," he paused, thinking deeply. The silence stretched out like a forest of dark trees. "He *is* a great fool, but not for the reasons you might think." Thomas absently ran his hand down the horse's long neck as he spoke, smiling to himself. "He is a fool for not coming to you and asking for your hand himself, or even offering you a proper courtship years ago. But..." There was a lilt of joy in his voice. "He is a good man, or he tries to be. He wants what is best for his people and his family, and I think he would understand better than anyone why you ran away." A low throaty laugh burst from Thomas as he spoke. "He probably would have gone with you if given the opportunity."

"That would have defeated the purpose."

"I thought you weren't running away from him."

Cat ignored the barbed bait.

The tangy scent of the berries was too tempting. Cat reached out, plucking a particularly juicy looking berry from the bush. The juice stained her fingers. She lifted the fruit to her mouth.

"Princess!" The knight's hand was suddenly around Cat's wrist, pulling the berry away from her mouth. "What are you doing? Dragonberries are poisonous!"

"What? I... I didn't know these were dragonberries."

"How could you not know these were the most poisonous berries in the three kingdoms?"

Cat glanced at the bushes circling the meadow. The berries hanging from the vines were a deep blue, bunched together like blackberries. Now that Cat looked again, she supposed they were lighter than they ought to be.

Always unwilling to admit to being wrong, Cat wrenched her hand out of Thomas'. "I've never seen them before." As if she owed any more of an explanation, Cat kept speaking. "I've only ever left the palace once, and that was escorted by a battalion of knights."

"Didn't your tutors teach you anything?"

"Trust me, if it was not related to serving an elegant tea, they did not." That was not entirely true. Until her mother's death, Cat had learned a great deal about history and politics. Still, she had been taught nothing regarding poison; she was being taught to be a queen, not a spy or assassin.

"Oh..."

Something like pity flashed in the knight's eyes, only annoying Cat more. A bitter taste, like fire, rose in her throat. Her skin flushed with heat. "And where did you learn what plants were safe?"

"My... friend, Jason, is a physician. He could probably identify every plant in this meadow and find a use for each one." Thomas forced a tired smile, tossing the berry aside. "I'll just add showing you what is safe to eat to the list of things I have to teach you while we travel. First, the apples in my pack are safe."

They slept most of the day. Cat was surprised when she startled awake in the meadow, leaning against a tree. Then she was surprised she had not slept longer. Exhaustion hung off her skin. Every muscle in her body was tight and sore.

She held the reins loosely in her hands as she rode away from the meadow, letting the horse make most of the decisions. Thomas pressed a hand to her side, keeping Cat from sliding from the saddle as she leaned too far to one side, guiding the horse around a boulder in their path. Helping her through the movements. Just like dancing. The thought crawled against her skin. It was too familiar. Too much like the night they danced so long ago. Drawing the same feelings back to the surface.

"You're making fast progress."

Cat's face burned with a surge of annoyance. Good, annoyance was better than any other feeling. "Do not patronize me."

"I wasn't trying to patronize you. But if you would like to be patronized, I'd like to point out that it has been at least fifteen minutes since you last fell, and that fall was wonderfully graceful."

She could feel her teeth grinding as her jaw tensed. Cat worked at her jaw, trying to relax it. When that was no good, she twisted in the saddle to properly snap at him.

His hands shot to her shoulders, fingers digging into skin. "Eyes forward Princess!" Thomas physically turned her forward again. "Honestly, it's no wonder no one ever taught you to ride. You have to pay attention to what you're doing."

"I told you not to call me that."

"Oh, but it suits you so well, *Princess.*"

"You clearly don't know me." Not that it mattered whether or not Thomas knew or understood her. Cat was engaged to a prince. Even if she wasn't, she was not on this adventure to fall in love. She had no intention of ever falling in love. The fact that Thomas was irritating, insufferable, and knew nothing about her, would just make it easier to keep her mind on her quest for... whatever the compass was pointing towards.

A forest loomed ahead of them. Something moved in the shadow of the trees, routing Cat's thoughts away from Thomas. The two bandits she ran into that morning flashed into her mind. A pang of fear hit Cat's stomach. It seemed like particularly bad luck to run into the only two bandits anywhere near Royal City the first time she was ever alone. Then again, bad luck seemed to follow Cat, it always had.

"Do you think we'll run across anymore bandits up here?" The movement was probably nothing, a trick of the light.

"Probably."

Was he trying to scare her? Her father's men, even Ryder, would have lied to her to hid any danger. Ladies had weak constitutions and could not handle the stress impending danger. Maybe it was a trick to make her give up her adventure and go back to the prince? The way he spoke that morning, he seemed to want her to return to his prince, but he had not dragged her back... yet.

"Of course, we would be less obvious targets if you weren't wearing that diamond around your neck."

Cat gripped the necklace. She had forgotten she was even wearing it. The sapphire pendant thrummed against her chest. It was so much lighter than most of the jewelry she wore for court functions. She barely noticed it. Like it had always been a part of her.

The pine trees were approaching, their long shadows stretched toward them. Cat could feel Thomas' grip on her waist loosening. Her balance must be improving. The muscles in her back tensed, holding herself straight in the saddle, guiding the horse to the left.

"It's not a diamond. It's a sapphire and it belonged to my mother."

He laughed. "Trust me, that is not a sapphire. The Reinsaffiran palace was built overlooking a beach made of sapphires. I know a sapphire when I see one."

She gripped the pendant, pulling it free with the intent of proving him wrong. The vibrant blue stone that had gleamed so brightly the night before, and in her memories, was drained of color. Only the lightest hint of blue remained. It was odd. Cat had not removed the gem since putting it on. And then it had been blue. Impossibly blue. Like the ocean on a clear day.

Admitting she was wrong was not something Cat did. She closed her fist around the thrumming pendant. "I swear to you, the gem was blue when..." Cat stopped herself. The crone, like the magic of the compass, were secrets best left kept.

"When what? When a sorceress gave it to you as a protective talisman, like in a fairy story?" He said it with a sarcastic tone, but there was a certainty to it, like he had been there.

"When I put it on last night." Cat fumbled to hook it around her neck again. A difficult task with only one hand. She did not want to drop the reins.

The chain pulled from her hand, scraping across the time hardened callouses from years of climbing. Thomas plucked it from her hand.

"What are you doing?"

"You should not be wearing it, but if you insist, at least allow me to help you. You have to control the horse." He brushed aside her long braid, draping it over her shoulder. Cat's long copper hair hung down to her waist. Perfectly straight and unmanageable. She always wore it in a thick braid to keep it from tangling. Everyone told her it was her prettiest feature; wild red flames framing her emerald eyes. Thomas' knuckles brushed the nape of her neck as he moved her braid. A shiver lingered where his fingers met bare skin. His fumbling movements distracted her. Cat nearly steered the horse off the path. "Careful Princess. I do not have a free hand to catch you."

"Stop calling me that!" Cat grit her teeth, using the most commanding tone she could muster. "Especially if you are so interested in remaining inconspicuous."

"Princess."

"Honestly?"

His hand went to cover Cat's mouth, stifling her words. "Listen." A pounding sound was coming from over the hill behind them. Horses. At least six horses were speeding toward them.

"That took less time than I expected." Thomas shifted, pulling the reins from her hands. "Hold on. We're going to lose them in the woods." Cat leaned forward, gripping the horse's neck as they rushed toward the shadows.

Trees enveloped them.

It was a long time before the horse slowed to a walk again. Golden sunlight filtered through pine needles. Cat pushed herself into a relaxed position, glancing back at Thomas. "Why... Why are we stopping?"

"That's why." He nodded ahead of them.

A man sat on a tree in their path. A sword rested on his knees.

"Sir," Thomas raised a hand in greeting, smiling at the man. "Will you let us pass?"

"Not without paying the tax," the man's voice ached. It pulled at Cat's heart. Like he was sad, diminished by some great weight.

"Tax? Sir, we are humble travelers with nothing to offer you."

"I'm no knight. Addressing me as one will not make me behave like one. I know you are not humble travelers."

Thomas grip on Cat's waist tightened. She gasped at the pressure, pushing his hand away.

"What you believe is unimportant. We are what we say we are, and you will let us pass." Her commanding tone wavered.

"Sweetheart," the man stood, turning the cheap steal sword in his hand. "You don't really expect me to believe that, do you? I'll start by relieving you of that necklace."

"Sweetheart?" Cat's eyes hardened.

"Take it off."

She was not sure who she was angry with, but the bandit would receive the brunt of it. Cat pushed Thomas' hand away a second time, squirming her way off the horse.

"Cat! What are you doing?" Thomas reached out, snagging her wrist out of the air, pulling her back toward him.

"Retrieving your sword. I need it." Cat slid out of his grip. Finding the hilt of the sword. The weight of it felt right in her hand. The leather was soft against her fingers.

"No. No no no!" Thomas' bright blue eyes met Cat's. "No! That is a bad idea. You cannot do what you are thinking of doing."

"I am tired of people telling me what I can and cannot do."

She was going to die. If it was not from eating poisonous berries it would be from picking fights with every bandit that popped up within a hundred miles of her. Thomas watched Cat spin the sword in her hand, approaching the bandit. He would have laughed if he was not about to watch the girl he was trying to protect, not to mention his fiancé, die.

Volentia boasted the greatest swordsmen in the world. And Cat knew she had once been among them, when she had been allowed to train. She had always worked hard to be the best, but, even with practicing with Emma in secret, Cat was out of practice. She could feel how sloppy her movements were after years of being banned from the training yards. Still, something echoed inside of her. Her muscles tuning to the memory of holding a sword, just like they did when she fought Evander.

The bandit swung first, slashing at her, thinking the fight would end quickly.

Cat side-stepped, pushing her elbow into his stomach. Steel clanged together twice before Cat knocked the bandit onto his back, the soft leather sole of her boot pressing into the man's chest.

She was a skilled fighter.

Thomas' eyebrows rose with surprise. Princess Catiya knew how to fight.

The bandit's hood slipped back. He appeared to be his father's age. Not old, though no longer in the prime of his life. The wrinkles forming around his eyes gave him the look of someone who spent his youth smiling. How had he come to be in the woods? Waiting right in their path?

Steel flashed, and the man knocked Cat off balance. She stumbled, hitting the ground, rattling her teeth.

Everything went still.

Cat was definitely going to die… if he did not intervene. Of course, if he did intervene, she would kill him.

Another flash of steel and Cat had been disarmed.

A blinding light suddenly filled the forest.

Too bright.

Thomas had to look away. When he dared to look again, the bandit was gone. Vanished. Everything within a perfect ten foot circle of Cat felt pale. Bleached by the flash of light.

"What the…" Thomas stared at the girl, laying in the dirt. A sense of disbelief washing over him.

For a moment the gem resting on Cat's collarbone throbbed as blindingly bright as the light had been. As hard to look at as the sun.

The light faded away.

Ryder rubbed his forehead, as if that could wipe away the words that echoed in his mind. This was a joke. One of Emma and Cat's tricks that he never quite understood. "You were being serious in the throne room. Cat is gone? How could you let that happen?"

"You're mad. I knew you would be." Emma dropped into the armchair beside him. The only sign of her discomfort was her frizzing hair, which she kept twisting around her fingers.

"Mad is not so much the word for it." Ryder let his arms fall against the crushed velvet arm of his chair. Eyes flicking from Emma to the door, and then back to Emma. She had bolted the door to her room before letting the whole story pour out of her. "Just stunned. I mean… you saw them, and you still let her leave the palace."

"Them? Who?"

"The shadows. Those assassins that tried to kill Cat, and you… and you still let Cat leave. And you sent Prince Thomas, that spoiled, rakish idiot, after her as protection." The bitter taste of dislike for Prince

Thomas of Reinsaffira burned in Ryder's throat. He swallowed hard; this was not the time for his feelings to become muddled.

"That was years ago. She hasn't been attacked since..."

"A week ago." A darkness crept into the room, surrounding them, icy cold. Just speaking of the attack sent shivers through his body. Ryder could barely believe the truth himself.

Unbidden, his eyes flit back to the door. Still bolted. No one was eavesdropping. "An assassin broke into Cat's room and tried to strangle her." He shook his head, correcting himself. "A shadow broke in and tried to kill Cat. It was like magic." There was no other way to explain it. "Someone wants Cat dead. That's... that's why my father was suddenly so insistent on the marriage. He thinks she'll be safe in Reinsaffira."

"The crone." Emma gasped, her fingers pressed to her mouth. Her shoulders shook, shivering against the chilling darkness that swirled around them. "She appeared out of nowhere and vanished again. She... she gave Cat a magic compass. She was trying to lure Cat away from the palace. Why?"

"The same reason my mother was killed. She's the rightful queen of Salene."

Cat's eyes felt heavy. Her muscles ached. It was the burning pain in her chest that disturbed her. If it were not for the pain, Cat might have thought she was waking in her feather bed, wrapped in a soft blanket, listening to a crackling fire. Any minute now, Emma or Ryder would burst through the door and drag her from her dreams.

Any moment.

She only heard the quiet whistle of wind through the trees and the crackle of the fire. And where was that pain coming from?

Cat furrowed her brow in thought. She remembered leaving the palace. No one was coming to pull her out of this dream.

Suddenly unable to ignore the pain burning in her skin, Cat forced her eyes open, finding herself in an unfamiliar cavern. Water glistened on the rough stone walls. The orange firelight glimmered, dancing against the trickling water. The heavy cloak wrapped around her was also familiar. It was soft and smelled like pine and lavender.

She threw it off.

The source of the burning was a strange mixture of herbs, plastered across her collar, where her mother's necklace had rested. She had to be rid of it. Cat set her nails to peeling away the hard cracked paste.

"Leave it on." Thomas' voice struck her. Cat's hand dropped to the dirt floor. Her eyes searched for the knight. Thomas sat near the entrance of the small cavern, looking at the night sky. "It will help the burn."

What burn? Cat had been nowhere near a fire, except for the small pile of sticks burning between them.

"Should we really have a fire? If the guards..."

"I doubt your guards will notice, if they're still looking for you at this hour. Even if they are, there's dozens of caves in these woods. They won't search every single one." Thomas brushed his fingers through his hair. His gaze fixed on her again. Something about Thomas' gaze prickled against Cat's skin, like the sweet fluttering of butterfly wings. She looked away, studying the flickering fire. "I think that you owe me an explanation."

Cat shivered. The cloak hid how cold the cave really was. She pulled it onto her lap, hunching her shoulders. The material smelled like him. The soft fur lining danced beneath her fingers. She drew a quiet pattern in the lining. "Explanation? For what?" Nothing made sense. Her head was heavy with fog.

"You're a magix, aren't you?"

Cat blinked, looking up at the knight. His hair gleamed in the orange firelight. He watched her with a serious expression, as if the question was not absurd, as if accusing her of being born of a long extinct magical line was not an impossibility. "Magix are extinct... and even if I was, do you really think I would tell a *Reinsaffiran* I just met?" It was common knowledge that Reinsaffirans were suspicious of anything to do with magic. The last person in the northern court who had even been suspected of being a magix, over a century ago, had been beheaded. It was the reason for the hatred between Reinsaffira and Salene and the centuries of war that kept repeating.

"That does not change what I saw today. That light was..."

"Don't you think I would know if I was a magix?" Cat's fingers itched to curl into fists. Of all the things Cat knew and did not know about who she was, being a magix felt like it should be one of them.

"I'm not entirely certain," Thomas grumbled under his breath. "It would make sense. Explain why you ran away. Fine, a different question then? I think you owe me at least one explanation after saving your life multiple times... today."

Cat studied Thomas, calculating how wise it was to show him any of her secrets. Would he even know if she lied to him?

Cat waited another moment, his summer sky eyes locked on hers.

"Fine."

"Where does a princess learn how to handle a sword the way you did?"

"My mother was a warrior. She met my father...well she saved him in the Border Lands." Thomas studied Cat's face. Not quite enough truth to feed his curiosity. "She insisted that I be trained as well. The captain of the guard trained me. After..." The words caught in her throat. "After her death... well, that was no longer allowed.

Cat held back the fact that she and Emma still trained with swords and arrows as often as they could. That secret did not belong to her alone. She chewed her lip, hoping that would be enough to sate his curiosity.

"And your mother, she was Salenian?"

"How do you know that?" Her voice held a sharp edge. It was not that her mother's heritage was a secret, but no one dared to speak about it anymore. Cat had been lectured time and again that her and Ryder's Salenian blood died with their mother. It was not allowed to survive. Cat was not Salenian, she was Volentian. It was why she was not allowed to fight.

"It is not uncommon knowledge." Thomas shrugged, feeding a handful of twigs into the fire. "I used to love history. The people of Reinsaffira came from Brotid, across the sea. If I recall correctly, Volentia is the product of a rebellion. Bad blood or not, Reinsaffira and Volentia are the same. But the people of Salene... they have always been in these lands, and they are the ones with a history of magic."

Cat's head hurt.

"I don't know much about magic, except what is in the old stories. It is always passed from mother to daughter and was always present in the ancient royal bloodlines of Salene. And your mother was a Salenian princess? I was told King Bastian was her brother." Thomas raised an eyebrow. In the dancing firelight, his cropped curls shifted from brown to almost red. His eyes were the same color as the sky in summer and they held a smolder, like a lighthouse on an island, all but hidden behind crashing waves.

She realized she had been staring at him without responding. Cat hated that she even noticed how handsome he was. It was too distracting. He was too tall. She dropped her gaze back to the flickering fire.

"Yes, my mother was the princess of Salene, and she was banished for marrying my father. King Bastian was her twin. And I would know if she were a magix." Wouldn't she?

It was Thomas' turn to stare in a stunned silence. He was unsure of how to continue.

Cat's thumb rubbed at the burning below her throat. Green flakes of the balm stuck beneath her nail.

"It won't do any good if you pick it off. It needs water or it will make it worse. Just wait a moment." He patted his vest then his bag, searching for something that might resemble a cloth.

While he searched, Cat's hand dipped into her pocket retrieving the blue silk handkerchief he gave her ages ago. Feeling stupid for even having it with her, especially considering who she was about to hand it to. What kind of fool brings a silk handkerchief on a quest? Cleaning the salve would ruin the liquid fabric.

She held it out to Thomas. "Here."

A gentle hand reached across the fire, pulling the about-to-be-ruined square of fabric from Cat's. He did not say a word, but turned the sapphire silk over in his hands. She watched it darken as Thomas poured water over it.

Thomas extended his hand, trying to return the handkerchief.

Cat did not even notice. There were too many thoughts swirling around in her head. How was she supposed to do this? Cat did not know anything about treating burns and wounds; she could not guide a horse on her own, Cat did not even know what plants and berries were safe to eat. This adventure was a stupid idea.

Warmth spread over Cat's fingers, shattering her thoughts. Thomas gripped Cat's hand, placing the cold handkerchief in her upturned palm. Absently, Cat pressed the cloth to the salve, the burning subsiding as she washed it away.

"Thank you... for helping me." It was not something Cat had much practice in, admitting she was wrong or accepting help of any kind. The words came out in stuttered halts. "Where... where did you learn all this, about b-urns and what's good to eat... and..." She shook her head. Words were too hard to form.

"My friend Jason is one of the court physicians. The Reinsaffiran palace tends to get quiet when Arik is away. So, I spend most of my time with him. I suppose I picked a few things up."

"Arik? Lord Arik? The ambassador to Volentia? You... He..." The more Cat learned about Thomas, the more confused she became. Who was this man that he would know the crown prince and Ambassador Arik? And why hadn't he forced her home the moment he found her? "You're friends with Lord Arik?"

"Technically he is a cousin of mine. We grew up together on the Northern Isles."

Thomas grew up in the Northern Isles. That was something, Cat supposed. She crossed her arms. "Why are you traveling with me and helping me?"

"Maybe I believe running into you was fate. That you were meant to go on this journey and I was meant to help you. That it is my destiny to save you from some unknowable evil." He lifted an eyebrow at her. "Or maybe your friend, the dark haired one, sent me to find you and made me promise to keep you safe on your journey."

That did not seem likely.

"Or maybe I just like being with you. Where else will I find such obvious disdain? Now, I get to ask another question, about the light."

"I don't know what the light was." Cat found herself glaring at him again.

"See, obvious disdain. Most girls are so subtle about it, a man might almost think they like him."

"Well, I'm glad you appreciate it."

"The light though. It seemed like magic. Has anything like that ever happened before?"

The brass compass was still hidden in Cat's pocket. She could feel it tugging at her like a distant memory. Heavy and cool. The magic inside of it thrummed at her touch. It sent silver shivers dancing across her skin as she remembered the familiar icy touch of magic. It had happened before. The memory was hazy, and Cat had forced it from her mind for so long it was hard to bring it to the surface again. Almost like a dream. Or a nightmare hanging on the edges of her vision after waking. But then... the memory of the shadow that held her head beneath the water, cutting off her supply of air had been visiting her nightmares recently.

"Yes."

Morning light streamed into the freezing cave, waking Thomas from a stiff, uncomfortable sleep. He stretched out his arms, rolling onto his side. "Good morning, Princess."

The space across the fire was empty.

Princess Catiya was gone!

"Princess?" Thomas leapt to his feet, cracking his head against the low ceiling.

"Are you all right?" Cat leaned over the cave entrance, her copper hair gleamed like fire in the golden morning light. Thomas felt his breath catch when he met her gaze. Princess Catiya was beautiful, just not in the way a princess was expected to be. It was an untamed kind of beauty that drew his gaze to her. Her loose braid was tossed over one shoulder, a few tendrils falling free to frame her pale face. The powder and makeup that had been painstakingly plastered across her skin for the ball was finally gone, scrubbed away, revealing the line of freckles across her cheeks. Thomas felt like a fool, believing the girl he had met draped in jewels and silks years ago had been the real her. A girl who needed to be rescued from ruffians and thugs. Now he knew better; she was brave and stubborn and completely untamed.

Thomas rubbed the aching spot with his fingers. "Fine. What are you doing out there?"

She turned back toward the morning light, smiling a closed lipped smile to herself. She held a small brass compass in her hand. "Trying to figure out which direction to go."

He followed her out into the grassy forest. Glancing around. It was early enough in the morning that the sun was still low on the horizon. Thomas shook his head, glancing at the compass resting against her palm. "Only a princess can't figure out what direction she is facing at sunrise. If you're looking for north, it's that way. You can tell by the moss on the base of the tree." He gestured to a large pine with a thick layer of moss covering the northern facing roots. "And the sun, of course."

"I'm not looking for north." Cat focused her dark eyes on the pink and orange horizon before snapping the compass shut. "We need to go that way."

"What are you looking for?" Thomas leaned as casually as his stiff muscles would allow against the cave entrance.

"I don't know, but this will take me to it."

A laugh formed so unexpectedly in Thomas' chest that he could not stop it from bursting out of him. It shattered the quiet morning and silenced the lilting songs the birds sang. "No, that will take you north. If north is really where you need to go, then you should have married your prince. His palace is that direction."

Cat narrowed her eyes, glaring at him. An icy, hard look.

Thomas smiled back.

"Not this compass. This one is magic." She opened the cover, holding it out to him. The arrow was spinning, pointing toward him, due east.

"This one points toward something I need." Her voice burned with flinty conviction.

Princess Catiya came fully into focus in Thomas' eyes. She believed what she was saying. She believed the compass was magic. She believed there was still magic in the world, just not in her. It was hard to believe that anyone could see the princess and miss the magic flowing through her veins. Every inch of the princess was light and fire. Even if he had not seen the light burst out of her, or heard her tale of the shadow that tried to drown her, he would have known it just from looking at her. Thomas could see her in his dreams because she was light and she shined, piercing the darkness even hundreds of miles away. The red in her hair flickered with the fire burning inside of her.

"You really didn't run away from marrying the prince. Did you?"

"Running away from something is useless unless you are also running toward something." She let the compass snap close, hiding it in the pocket of her vest. "Believe whatever you want, but I'm going to follow this compass and I'm going to find whatever I need at the end of it. You don't have to come."

"Then you're in luck. The main road goes east from here. It will be easier and safer than trying to wade through a dense forest. And the Volentian guards will have a harder time tracking you on a more heavily traveled road."

The look on the princess' face told Thomas that was not the sort of response she expected from him. Her thin pink lips pursed before the ghost of a rogue smile crossed her face, the first smile she had seen fit to offer him. It was a nice smile. He liked the sight of it better than anything he had ever dreamed.

They packed up the few items each had brought in their haste to get away from the palace. Cat took the time to strap her dagger to her waist, and hide the throbbing gem beneath the collar of her shirt. Then they guided the horse back to the path. They would have to ride for most of the day before they reached the main road. That gave Thomas time to try to see her smile again, maybe even hear what a real laugh bubbling from deep within her core sounded like.

Evander paced in front of the large arching doorway of the guard's wing. It was the only place in the palace he felt he could pace, with the training yard and everywhere else crowded with royal guests. He was wringing his hands over his shirt as he paced; he had started to change for his shift but stopped halfway through. It had been two days; Cat should be back by now. If the prince had not caught her, Sir Guy must have. But Sir Guy had returned earlier that day, empty handed.

Where was she?

The rumors about the shadows and the memory... the secret... that Cat's rightful place was on the Salenian throne kept flashing through Evander's mind. What had gone wrong that she had not come back yet?

"What are you doing back here?" A flinty, familiar, voice on the far side of the slightly cracked door made Evander pause. He ducked against the doorway, straining to hear distant voices.

"The men I had waiting in the mountain are dead," Sir Guy hissed back. "And the princess is not traveling alone. I can't attack the crown prince of Reinsaffira."

"Your mission," the man growled back, "was to obtain the princess by *any means* and take her to King Bastian. I will handle any complications with Reinsaffira."

Evander felt his blood grow hot. He had suspected for years that Sir

Guy was a traitor, perhaps even a Salenian spy, though he could never prove it.

The voices dimmed. Then passed into silence. Evander leaned around the corner, just enough to peer through the crack in the door. The corridor was empty. Evander could not bring himself to breathe a sigh of relief. There was a Salenian plot to kidnap Cat. She was in danger; he had to get her and return her to the palace. Now!

He spun on his heel, heading toward the stables. Then paused again, shaking his head. He needed to find Simon and Marcus first. Someone needed to know there was a traitor in the palace. Spinning around a second time, back toward the corridor, he slammed into Lord Carswell, who stood in the now open doorway. Carswell's jaw was set in a tight grimace, arms crossed. He was cold and immovable as stone. It took Evander half a minute to catch his breath. Another half a minute to register that Carswell did not belong in the palace, that he was no longer allowed at court.

"Listening at doorways, Evander? Didn't your mother ever teach you that was considered rude?" The same flinty voice he heard conspiring in the hallway was now directed at Evander.

Every muscle in Evander's body tensed. His hand was on the dagger at his hip, squeezing the hilt, ready to attack. "I would have thought yours would have taught you not to plot treason in a public space. It seems both of our educations are lacking. What did Bastian promise you to betray Volentia? What does he want with Cat?"

"Cat?" Carswell lifted an eyebrow. He was smiling, as if the whole situation was a delightful joke. "Oh dear, that is a bit more familiar than I believe you are meant to be. You've been doing a great many things lately you ought not; listening in doorways, letting princesses run away in the dead of night, and lying to the king."

"How..."

"Do I know that you let her go? Are you sure that is the question you want to be asking right now? If I were you, I would be much more interested in what the king will do to you after I tell him. You'll lose your commission, of course, and your sister will lose her bakery, but what will happen to you specifically?" Carswell scratched at the patch of blond on his jaw that he called a beard. "King Kristoff is too squeamish for beheadings, but I think banishment is too lenient."

Evander could feel his teeth grinding together. Fists and jaw clenched. His fingers ached to drive his dagger into Carswell's heart. It probably would do no good. The man's heart was clearly stone.

"You're right, banishment is far too lenient. I doubt King Kristoff will make that mistake with you a second time."

Another smile, cruel and pointed, drew Evander's attention to Carswell's pointed features. "The king is not going to find out. You are going to resign your post and return home to your family's little bakery."

"Why would I do that?"

"Because you know it will give you the time to gather proof. Proof that you desperately need before you can accuse a duke, even a disgraced duke, of treason. Or you can charge off into the mountains in search of your princess, so you can rescue her and be the hero of this story, but you and I both know you're not, and you never will be. All that opportunity goes away the instant you tell the king what you *think* you know."

Carswell turned away from Evander, sweeping down the hall.

Bile burned Evander's throat. Everything Carswell said was true. If he went to the king, without proof, he would not be believed; he was only a guard, one who had overstepped his bounds too many times before. He could go after Cat and try to rescue her, but he was not a tracker, and she had a two day head start. There was only one thing he could do, and that was prove Guy and Carswell were traitors.

The fire flickered, keeping Cat warm and the darkness at bay. Two things she was desperately grateful for. She perched on the ledge of the steep hillside, absent-mindedly running her fingers through her knotted hair, wondering if it was safe to have a fire in such a wide open space. What if Sir Guy or the other guards searching for her saw it? She pulled her knees to her chest, resting her chin on them as she peered into the deepening darkness. It was some comfort that she could see farther from her vantage point, even if it was still hindered by the trees.

The fact that *Sir* Thomas would not climb the ledge was also comforting. It offered a moment of quiet. She had decided she could trust him. He seemed like the sort of knight she read about in stories, the heroic ones who kept the defenseless safe. But he talked too much. Thomas only seemed to stay silent long enough to think up a new joke or recall the lyrics to a folk song. The day had been filled with his voice. Cat hated to admit that she enjoyed most of it, biting her lip to hold back a fit of childish giggles. She needed quiet though, and time to think. She needed a few minutes to allow the day to wash over her. Time to decide what to do next.

Stars illuminated the deep purple sky, tiny pinpricks of light shining down on her through the tree branches. In Royal City only the brightest stars could be seen. They reminded Cat of Emma. Emma loved to watch the stars; she knew every constellation and the stories behind them. The last time Cat had seen so many was when she was sent to Rook. Cat shook the memory from her mind. This was different. This adventure was her choice.

Worry knotted Cat's stomach. What would happen to Emma, if Cat's father found out she helped her run away? Which he must suspect. Her fingers worked through the tangles in her hair. What if something happened to Emma because of Cat? She was the only friend she had left; Ryder hardly counted as he was her brother and was stuck with her.

"Cat." Thomas' voice interrupted Cat's worries. He kicked dirt over the fire, smothering it. "We may have a problem." Cat looked back the way they had come, the trail was empty. Then she followed his gaze to the unknown parts of the forest. A group of six were coming toward them.

Cat gasped.

It could not be Sir Guy; they had come down the only trail.

Faster than she ever expected, the six men surrounded their small camp. Cat stood, balancing on her perch.

The men were clean and well groomed, each wearing brightly colored tunics and cloaks that clashed. Clearly, they were not concerned with being seen. They were armed and sneering.

Seeing Thomas draw his sword, Cat gripped the dagger at her hip. It would have been nice to rebraid her hair, but adventures were not convenient things.

"Stay where you are, Cat."

"There are six of them. You cannot fight them by yourself," Cat shouted in protest. If these men were dangerous, Thomas would be killed. The thought made her heart drop, blood racing. Just because she did not want to be alone. Not because she liked him, of course.

"Smart girl," one of the men grunted. "I would listen to her if I were you. You cannot fight all six of us."

"Cat! If you ever, in your life, do as your told, please make it now."

The note of concern held Cat on the ledge. No, not concern. He was using her name. Not Princess. He had been calling her *Princess*, in a light teasing tone, for the past two days. *Now* there was a deliberate note in the way he said her name. It left butterflies fluttering in her chest. She gripped the dagger tighter, the golden filigree leaving marks across her palm. Poised to leap to his aid.

"You seem a bit far from your usual stomping grounds," Thomas addressed the leader. The man had dark hair that was cropped short and a meticulously sculpted beard. "Are there not enough unsuspecting travelers on the rivers anymore?"

"Our business is just that, *ours*," he grumbled back. "I had planned on robbing you, but since you only have one thing of real value, I am prepared to offer you a deal. There are powerful people who are willing to pay a hefty sum for any red-haired girl we find wandering the wilds. Let us take her and you can keep your life, as well as your possessions."

Cat watched Thomas stiffen. These men were slavers. Taking part in the slave trade was punishable by death in Volentia. The very existence of men who would do such a thing ignited a burning anger inside of

Cat. If she was a magix, she would have attacked without thought or question. Something kept her from leaping down.

"I'm afraid she is as stubborn as a mule. Hardly worth taking. So really, I have nothing of any value to you."

The smooth leather and golden filigree of the dagger dug into her palm. Cat felt her hands shaking with rage.

"I'll be the judge of value." The leader of the slavers drew his thin sword. It rang with a cold metallic sound.

Before the man could attack, an arrow whizzed through the night, striking him in the thigh. Cat did not see where it came from. For a moment her heart leapt, thinking it must be Emma. She was the best archer Cat knew. Then the brawl broke out, forcing Cat's attention back to the men around her. Thomas slashed his sword at the five men still surrounding him. Cat leapt, landing on the back of one of the men, knocking the him to the ground. A hooded figure, carrying a bow, rushed from the shadows, loosening an arrow as they ran.

The fight did not last long. Both Cat and Thomas were skilled fighters. When Cat got hold of her own sword, only the leader remained, the arrow still in his thigh, broken off. He spat, then fled for his horse, vanishing into the darkness.

Their mysterious helper hovered on the edge of the shadows. Cat turned toward them, once again hoping to find Emma standing there. A frown tugged at her mouth when she saw the shape of the stranger. Whoever it was had shoulders too broad and movements that were too stiff.

Thomas wheeled on Cat, grabbing her by the arm. "I told you to stay on the ledge! You were safe there! How am I supposed to protect you when run headlong into danger?"

Cat pulled free of his grip. Blood from a cut on his arm stained Cat's sleeve. "I did not ask for your protection or your company." She wished she could take the venomous words back the instant they left her mouth. Thinking before speaking had never been Cat's greatest skill. "You're hurt," she added, her voice softened.

"It's nothing."

"You need to wash that," a gruff, pinched voice, spoke behind them. Cat whirled around, knocking the stranger off his feet, the point of her sword hovering above the man's throat. She did not know who he was, but Cat had quite enough of people trying to kill her.

"Sweetheart, I would not help you just to turn around and attack you myself."

Sweetheart? Cat suddenly recognized him. The bandit from the day before. No one else in the world would have the lack of instinct to mistake Cat for having a sweet heart. Had he tracked them all this way?

"I would have an easier time believing that if you had not tried to rob us once before."

"That was before I knew you were a light magix. Only an idiot would attack a light magix... twice."

Cat could feel Thomas' eyes on her and sense the smug smirk he wore. He laid his blood stained hand on Cat's, gently lowering the blade she held. The point coming to rest in the dirt.

"If you're not here to attack us," Thomas spoke in a calm, even tone, "then what do you want?"

"I will tell you, but first you should wash that cut. River pirates dip their swords in poison, to subdue their victims."

Cat's eyes widened, turning to look at Thomas. A deep red patch of blood soaked through his shirt on his right shoulder, dripping down his arm. She did not want to turn her back on the stranger, but she also did not want anything to happen to Thomas. The pull between the two instincts was painful. After a long moment, she lowered the blade to her side, stalking to the place where the horse was tied on a picket, choosing to help Thomas.

In the saddlebags, stacked against the steep hillside, Cat found a canteen of water and the stained silk handkerchief.

"I've been following you," the stranger sighed, "and I am sorry about trying to rob you. I... well I suppose you could say I owe a debt. When I saw your magic... I knew... I couldn't let the river pirates take you."

Thomas and the man both sat before the dying fire. Cat dropped into the space between them, helping Thomas roll his sleeve up to expose the wound.

She was surprised to realize the stranger was talking to her. "Why couldn't you let them take me?"

"There are people in Salene who would use a light magix to do terrible things. No honorable Salenian would allow that."

Cold water rushed through Cat's veins. The man was a Salenian? She felt her muscles tensing, inching her closer to Thomas.

"That is not the only reason. I... I need your help. My name is Aiden."

"Why would you need my help?"

"Your magic can save my wife." The bandit, Aiden, had heavy, sad eyes. Short mousy brown hair covered most of his head, except a few patchy bald spots. He looked almost helpless. "I know it can. It's too powerful not to save her."

Thomas fed a stick into the embers of the dying fire. Cat placed a hand on his shoulder. He was the one who remembered the light, not her. All she knew was that it came from somewhere deep inside of her. She did not know where or how to summon it. She could not possibly save this man's wife.

Thomas ignored her touch.

"I... I can't."

Anger flashed across Aiden's face. "You can!" He lunged toward Cat, trying to grab her.

Thomas' hand flashed between them. Muscles tense, he gripped Aiden's wrist. His eyes were cold as steel.

"If you ever try to touch her again, I will kill you." Thomas' voice had a hard edge to it. His voice, one that Cat had only heard as kind and filled with joy, was now harsh and grave.

Aiden's face fell. Sadness etched across his features. "She's in there. I need your magic to save her from the Darkness." He pulled free of Thomas' grip.

"I can't. I... I'm sorry. I d-don't... I don't know how."

"If you plan on killing me, you need to clean that wound. Or else you'll be far too weak to kill a fly."

The forgotten silk rag pulled out of Cat's fingers. Thomas twisted to reach his wounded shoulder, starting to clean the narrow cut.

"Honestly," Cat tisked. "Let me help." She may have been clueless when it came to dressing wounds, but Cat had suffered enough gashes and scrapes that she at least knew how to clean one. Thomas rolled his eyes, huffed, and handed the handkerchief back to her. He rolled his sleeve up to his bicep. Drying red blood traced long paths down his arm.

"Your shirt will have to come off." Cat soaked the rag while the knight removed his shirt, pulling it over his floppy curls. "I'm sorry for... um..." Cat looked up at the wrong moment. A sudden flock of butterflies unleashed in her stomach, stealing her words away. Men at court, including the knights and guards she used to train with, never went around ladies, especially a princess, half-clothed. As a result, Cat had only seen one bare-chested man before, and that was a very different situation.

For someone so lanky, Cat was not expecting Thomas to be so well built. The muscles across his chest and arms were well defined.

"Um..." Cat looked at the ground, the cliff face, the rag in her hand, anywhere but Sir Thomas' exposed chest. A hot pink blush rose to her cheeks. She struggled for the next word to say, but the swarm of butterflies had swept it away. She opened her mouth to speak again, not meeting his curious eye.

A shrill giggle bubbled out of her. Cat placed her face in her hands to stifle it.

A broad smile lit Thomas' face, followed by his own throaty laugh. His sullen mood melted away. "I thought your laugh would be beautiful."

The sound of the arrowhead burying itself in the target was immensely satisfying.

Emma smiled to herself. It was short lived.

Two days she had been confined to quarters. King Kristoff seemed to think the confinement would either put Emma in a more helpful mood or flush Cat out of her hiding place. But Emma was already in a helpful mood. She told the king everything she knew, except the part about the compass and the crone. Cat left the palace, going east, and Prince Thomas went after her. The sooner the king believed her, the sooner he would find Cat and bring her home. She hoped Ryder was having more luck convincing the king than she was.

At least her aim was improving.

Emma chose to use her confinement as an opportunity to practice her archery without interruption. She stood on the balcony, loosing arrows into the target she hung on the heavy door. Nine of her ten arrows peppered the center of the target. All tightly packed around the center. The tenth arrow waited, poised on her bow string.

She took aim and let the arrow loose.

It buried itself into the suddenly open door, almost marrying Ryder's handsome face.

"You spoiled my shot! That doesn't count as a miss."

"Spoiled your shot?" He gave her a questioning glance. "I think an arrow through the eye would have spoiled my whole day."

"It would have hit closer to your throat." Emma set aside her bow, smiling at her fiancé. An arrow certainly would have spoiled his beautiful stormy eyes. "Are you allowed to see me? I thought being confined to quarters meant I lost all of my toys."

"Officially, I am not here at all. Sir Guy returned from the mountains last night. He claims to have news." Ryder's lips, so often set in a serious frown, played at a smile. "*Officially*, I will not be there either." Emma looked over Ryder. He wore a dark cloak over his tunic and breeches, all dark as well.

"You mean to do some spying." Emma dropped onto the delicate couch beside the fireplace, finding the silk slippers she had left there to warm, and pulling them on. "Is he in the throne room?"

They crept down the hall to a secret panel that Emma pushed open, slipping inside. Moisture ran down the stone walls, making the passage slick and damp. The smell of mildew stuck in Emma's nose. Judging by his pinched expression, Ryder did not care for the smell either. Ryder had never liked the passages between the palace walls, connecting the older parts with the new. Too many secret halls dead-ended, forming an impossible maze of stone. He needed Emma to guide him down to the throne room where another entrance was hidden behind a heavy tapestry.

It took several minutes for them to reach the small alcove. Emma's feet grew colder with every step against the stone floor. She slid a small panel open, just an inch. Light filtered through the thick tapestry that hid them. Sir Guy's high nasal voice filtered through as well.

Emma placed a finger over her red lips, leaning close to listen.

"My men and I caught up with the princess on the mountain trail, Your Majesty."

"The mountains?" The king's voice boomed. Now he had to believe Emma. "Tell me, why did you not retrieve her and bring her back to the palace?"

"We lost her in the forest."

"You lost her? How did you lose a five foot tall girl traveling alone on foot when you commandeered my fastest horses?" It was nice to hear the boastful knight be put into his place.

"Had she been alone and on foot, I would have caught her, your grace. She was neither. A man had her on horseback; he was the one who dragged her into the woods where we lost the trail."

Emma glanced at Ryder. He was stony, unmoving, still reserving judgment on whether or not Prince Thomas had actually gone after Cat until he had proof. It was not Emma's word he doubted, but the character of the man she sent after Cat. Ryder claimed the prince was nothing more than a self-absorbed rake, unwilling to sacrifice his sport and comfort for anyone. Emma knew differently. She knew the first moment she saw Thomas with Cat that he loved her, and that they belonged together, though she did not know who he was at the time.

"A man was with Cat," Emma whispered. "It was the prince; he caught up with her. He'll protect her."

King Kristoff's booming voice blanketed the throne room. "Do you believe you could describe the man she was with?"

"I did not get a clear view, sire, but he treated her roughly. I believe the princess has been kidnapped; they were traveling toward Salene. I sent three of my best trackers to find their trail."

A lie! Emma swallowed her gasp, pressing her fingers to her mouth. She turned away, not stopping until she was in the daylight again. "He's lying!" She fixed Ryder with a stare. "Why would he lie?"

"Perhaps he misinterpreted what he saw or..."

"No! He's lying. He wants your father to believe Cat was kidnapped. I'm going to find out why. Does he know about the assassination attempt?"

Ryder nodded. "He was the guard on duty."

The scent of lemons and fresh baked pastries swirled around the kitchen. Evander tapped a finger against the tabletop, waiting for Simon and Marcus to get off duty and come looking for him. They would undoubtedly have questions when they heard about his sudden resignation. They would come pounding on the bakery door any minute. That's what friends did, they looked out for one another. They depended on each other. That thought filled Evander with the bitter taste of guilt. Cat had been his friend once, a long time ago, but he had not looked out for her. Maybe if he had, he would have been able to protect her from Guy and Carswell's plotting.

"That's it!" Lydia slammed the pan of miniature lemon cakes onto the table in front of him. "If you are going to mope around in my kitchen, then you are going to work. I need these cakes iced for the morning."

Evander pulled the bowl of sticky sweet icing toward him, spinning the knife between his fingers. This was what his life would look like, now that he was no longer a guard. Slow hours ticking by, filled with mundane tasks and his sister's scolding voice. He swiped a thick layer of icing over the cake.

"While you're working, you can tell me why you suddenly decided you did not want to be a royal guard anymore. Not that I don't *love* having you here." Lydia's tone was sweeter than the icing and Evander knew it would make him just as sick.

"Princess Catiya ran away." Evander swiped a second sloppy layer over the cake. Icing spilled over the edge of the bowl like the closely kept secret he just shared. No one outside of the royal palace knew Cat had run away. They all believed she was confined to her rooms.

The pan Lydia was pulling from the oven clattered to the floor. She spun around, watching him with wide, uncertain eyes. A thick stunned silence filled the room. The cloying heat of the open oven melted the icing dripping from Evander's knife. "You're certain? I thought she was just in hiding somewhere."

"Yes." Evander continued, ignoring the pile of cakes around Lydia's feet. "And Lord Carswell and Sir Guy are involved in a plot to kidnap Cat and take her to King Bastian."

"You're still on that?" Marcus' low growling voice in the doorway made Evander flinch. He turned in his seat. Marcus leaned against the door frame. Somehow, he seemed larger than ever. His arms were the size of barrels, folded over his chest. His shoulder length brown hair was tied into a low ponytail, much like his hero Captain Roderick always wore. As if emulating the captain would make him as great a man. Behind Marcus stood Simon, looking almost like a child next to the larger man. "We watched Sir Guy for over a year. There's no proof he's a Salenian spy; he's just obnoxious. Careful Lydia," He stepped in, resting a hand at Lydia's back, pulling her away from the open oven door. "You'll burn yourself."

"This time I have proof." Evander grit his teeth, waiting for his friends to sit. At least he had enough proof for them. He would need their help proving it to the king.

Simon stepped around Marcus and Lydia, kneeling in front of the oven, gathering up the cakes strewn across the floor. He moved to the table, shoving one of the cleaner looking cakes into his mouth. "What? You cannot sell these, right? I'd hate to see them go to waste."

"I overheard Carswell giving Sir Guy instructions to obtain Cat and take her to king Bastian. I swear it is the truth."

"Why didn't you go to the king?"

"Because Carswell knows that I am the one who let Cat escape. If I take what I know to the king, he will only twist it around. That's why I need your help."

Thomas let out a bored sigh, watching the forest stretch out in front of them. The forest had softened over the course of the day from a stretch of dense woods to a thin cluster of trees growing between tall rocks. They had descended from the mountain. In another day or so they would probably reach populated areas again, unless Cat's magical compass turned them back eastward.

Their ever eastward journey made Thomas nervous. A tight knot had formed in his throat, tightening with every mile that passed. They were heading toward the Salenian border.

A Volentian princess and the Crown Prince of Reinsaffira were sure to stand out in any Salenian village.

Thomas glanced across the clearing at Cat as she gathered an armload of sticks. Her long copper hair was tied into a tight braid that hung almost down to her waist. She had changed that morning into a simple square collared dress with a set of riding breeches beneath. The dress was green; the only adornment was a line of golden vines stitched around the collar. The color complimented her skin and drew out the fire in her hair. Looking at her only made Thomas more certain that she would stand out anywhere they went. She would certainly stand out at the Reinsaffiran court, filled with elegant blondes and brunettes, all with coy smiles. There was nothing coy about the satisfied smile on

Cat's lips or the way she moved with decisive stomping strides. In so many ways, she was just like the girl he had dreamed her to be; smart, stubborn, and passionate. Everything she did was filled with the same fire that made her hair seem to glow. There were also so many ways in which she was different than the timid princess he had imagined her to be when they first met. Cat did not belong in the stifling ball gowns he always pictured her in. She needed to be able to move freely, in soft airy fabrics, surrounded by trees and the lilt of bird songs. She belonged outdoors with a sword in her hand. But Cat was naive too. She had lived the sheltered life of a princess, trapped behind palace walls. Everything about the forest ignited a look of wonder in her eyes. As often as Thomas saw it, he always wanted to see it just once more. He wanted to show her every wondrous thing there was in the world and watch her fall in love with it over and over.

Thomas' breath caught when Cat looked up, her dark eyes catching his. He looked away, snatching a piece of firewood out from the roots of a nearby tree. She had moved on again when he risked a second glance at her. The only thing Thomas was certain of was that he was just as much in love with the princess in front of him as he had ever been.

A thought crossed Thomas' mind as he examined the tall trees and large stones around him. There were stories about ancient magical places that survived on the borders of Salene, including caverns made of glowing crystals. Thomas' geography was not as good as his history, especially when it came to Volentia; he never had any need of it. He set his bundle of firewood between the two tents Aiden was setting up in the clearing, feeling a surge of annoyance at the man's presence. Not that he was ungrateful to Aiden for his tents and guidance through the unfamiliar woods, but Thomas would have preferred to spend the time *alone* with Cat. How was he supposed to convince her he loved her if they were constantly watched? He knelt at the pile of saddle bags, digging into his pack. Under his spare shirt he found a folded map of Volentia, unfurling it to study the intricate drawings.

There, nestled against the mountains, labeled in careful curving script, was what he was looking for. The Crystal Forest. The story was that the mountain side was formed out of the same magical crystals magix used to channel their power and the caverns could soak up any light they found so they glowed, like warm starlight, the moment the light was extinguished.

He had seen a cave entrance while gathering firewood, just a few minutes ago. If they really were in The Crystal Forest, it would be a sight worth seeing.

His gaze flashed to Cat. It would be a sight worth showing.

Without pausing to think, Thomas dug deeper into the bag, fingers closing around one of the candles he had brought along. Something clattered to the ground with the candle. A small silk pouch. He knew what was in it; that did not stop him from lifting it off the ground, opening the pouch, and emptying the contents into his upturned palm. The sapphire ring glinted in the evening light. Such a simple trinket. It weighed next to nothing. The silver band was unadorned except for the star sapphire framed by two sparkling diamonds. It was the ring he had intended on giving Cat when their betrothal was officially announced. It had only been a few days, but it felt like a lifetime ago. They were different people now, or they would be by the end of their journey.

His gaze snapped back to Cat, his fingers closing around the ring. Somehow, the cave seemed like a far better place to tell her than the pavilion he had originally planned to use. He would tell her all the things he originally planned to; he would ask if there was any hope for him.

The ring slid back into the small pouch. He tucked the pouch into the pocket of his leather riding jacket. Now was the time.

"Princess."

Cat startled at the breathy whisper at her ear, dropping her pitiful bundle of sticks. Thomas' fingers brushed her elbow. She knew it was him.

She pressed a hand to her heart. "You frightened me."

"That's because you need to be more aware of your surroundings."

Cat smacked Thomas' shoulder. His ever present smile faltered.

"Come with me for a moment." His grip on her elbow tightened, just enough to pull Cat toward him. She could pull away from him if she wanted; he would let her go. "There's something I want to show you."

She followed.

He led her into the trees, away from their small camp. As the shadows darkened overhead, a dizzying buzz started to thrum in her chest. Not quite a sickening anxious feeling. Something else. It thrummed like anticipation in her blood. Her heartbeat quickened. Cat's feet skidded against the mossy ground. Quite suddenly, she was unsure if she wanted to follow Thomas into the shadows. The quiet thrum tugged her forward, making her ache to lean into him and listen for the race of his own heartbeat.

Was that what falling for someone was like?

Cat chewed her lip in thought. Falling for Thomas was not an option for her, not with a prince waiting for her.

"Where are we going?"

The mouth of a cave appeared between a break in the trees. "Have you heard the stories of the crystal caves?" Thomas released Cat's elbow, pausing at the entrance. Using both hands to strike a match and light the candle he carried with him. "The crystals in the caves absorb light and will reflect it back for hours. I believe this may be one of them."

Extinguishing the match, Thomas took Cat by the hand, tugging her into the dark space. She let herself be tugged along by the gentle pull of his fingers.

The stony ground was rough, sloping downward at a steep angle. Cat could hear water dripping somewhere in the distance. In the dim light, she could see a series of crystals glittering in the low ceiling. They did not glow though. Cat stepped out, distracted watching the shimmering stones above her, and found only air. She stumbled forward, heart dropping to her toes.

Thomas' arm wrapped around her waist, catching her against his chest.

Cat's heart thumped hard. She glanced up at Thomas. She could see him smiling in the flickering candlelight, laughing at her. Her face and neck grew hot.

His arm did not move from around her waist and Cat did not step back. She knew she ought to. She felt frozen, unwilling to lean closer or to step away.

"Ready?"

"For what?" Cat blinked back her confusion.

Thomas lifted the candle to his lips, blowing away the small flame.

Darkness enveloped them.

Then it happened.

Glittering blue lights sparkled to life around them, surrounding them in starlight. Cat's breath caught. It was amazing! Like standing at the center of the night sky. The crystals glittered, blue, green, white, and a thousand other colors.

Cat's skin prickled with awareness, feeling eyes on her in the dark. She looked back up at Thomas, watching her watch the twinkling lights. His always charming smile faded into a serious, thoughtful expression. His hand moved slowly from her waist to her cheek, fingers tangling in the loose tendrils of hair. The pad of his thumb brushed over her lip. Cat's heartbeat stuttered. The tingle across her skin sparked at his touch.

The wonder etched across Cat's face was enchanting. Thomas watched her, mesmerized as she watched the twinkling lights surrounding them. She seemed to glow and glitter as brightly as the crystals did.

Then she looked up at him.

This was it. The perfect moment. The ring in his pocket pulled at his attention.

Another thought struck him. How would Cat react when he told her who he was? Would she hate him for the mere fact that he was the prince she was told to marry? Would she agree to marry him for that same reason? If only there was a way to know if she wanted him for just being *him*.

Thomas could feel her heart pounding under his touch when their eyes met, and every thought was driven out of his head by the over-whelming desire to pull her closer to him. To lean down and kiss her, here in this secluded, magical place. To kiss her not as the prince she was being forced to marry. Not as the princess he had dreamed about for years either. Just as a man and a woman who wanted to be together. He wanted to touch her and feel her and know her just as she was.

His hand slid to the back of her neck, tangling in her hair. He was going to kiss her. Cat startled. She could feel him pulling her close, the warmth of his skin pressing through her dress.

Then she remembered.

Thomas was a knight.

Cat was engaged to a prince.

Eventually, she would have to return to the palace. To her life and responsibilities as a princess. To the prince who would be waiting for her. She could not fall in love with the man standing before her. Cat pulled back. Cool air coming between her and the knight. Her hands twisted together in front of her. "We... We should be getting back. I didn't finish gathering firewood."

"Right." Thomas' hand dropped to his side.

"Thank you for showing me this place."

Thomas smiled, but it was lopsided, almost defeated in the fading light. "You left the palace to see the world. I did not think it would be right for you to miss something so beautiful."

They walked back to the camp in silence. An ache forming in Cat's chest. Guilt pulled her downward. Cat twisted her braid between her fingers. How could she do that? How could she forget, even for a moment, that she was a princess, that she had responsibilities? She had so desperately wanted Thomas to kiss her in the cave and was so certain he would. She could not allow herself to forget again. Leaving the palace was not about falling in love, just like it was not about running away from the prince.

She took in a deep breath as they neared the camp, hoping her blush had faded enough that Aiden would not notice.

Cat twirled her braid again, twisting it around her knuckles, focusing on the forest around them. Birds flit across the tree branches, knocking red and orange leaves to the ground. The leaves crunched under Cat's boots. She elongated her steps to crush a leaf just off the path. It crinkled in a satisfying way, and it pulled her a little farther away from Thomas.

A voice boomed ahead of them, startling the birds to silence. Aiden's voice followed, though Cat could not hear what he was saying.

In a flash of movement, Thomas gripped Cat by the elbow, pulling her down behind a rock on the edge of the clearing, shielding her from prying eyes.

"There they are! Thomas! Cat! Come out here."

Cat grit her teeth. It had been her idea to let Aiden travel with them. He knew more about healing and forestry than Cat or Thomas did. She had thought he would be helpful. Now the idea felt unbearably naive.

"Forgive my companions, Thomas is a bit protective of his new wife," Aiden lied smoothly. Was this a trick to betray them?

"It's okay," Thomas hissed into her ear. "It's just a Ruzeme wanderer troop." He rose to his feet and, taking Cat's hands in his, helping her to her feet. She was careful to turn away the moment her feet were stable.

Cat balked. Her eyes widened the moment she saw the wagon.

The man standing next to Aiden had shaggy black hair and dark skin. Cat recognized him. He once pulled Emma onto a makeshift stage to play a princess in need of rescuing. She had seen the troop of actors several times. Whenever their travels brought them close to the city, they performed a special show in the park in front of the palace. The man was sure to recognize Cat. If he recognized her... Cat was unsure of what would happen. Ruzeme wanderers were not technically loyal to any king. They should not care about one wayward princess. Except her father was a great supporter of their troop. That had to buy some loyalty.

She glanced back at the boulder, worry gnawing at her. She could not crouch behind it all night and it would be even more suspicious if she ran straight to her tent. What choice did she have but to keep walking toward the wagons circled in the clearing? She dipped her fingers into her long braid as she walked, following Thomas' long strides, unwinding the braid so her copper hair fell around her face, hoping to hide her telltale freckles and green eyes.

Aiden gestured to Thomas as he spoke to the man. "These are the companions I was telling you about. We've been traveling northeast, away from the Volentian palace"

"Away from the palace you say?" The leader tilted his head studying them.

Cat turned her face away from the man's appraising eyes and watched the other wanderers as they set their camp and cook fire. There was an older woman with crinkled gray hair sitting at a small table who caught Cat's eye. The old woman ignored everything around her, mending a shirt with careful stitches. Cat had never seen the woman before; she did not perform when the troop came to the palace.

"Well," Thomas threw an arm around Cat's shoulder, playing the part of the doting new husband, the part which Aiden had cast him in. "Near the palace, but it is an easy landmark."

"Then it is lucky we met you," the man laughed. "My troop was invited to the palace to perform at a special festival for the princess' wedding."

Cat tensed. She clenched her jaw, fighting the urge to bury her face against Thomas' chest, to run and hide. Thomas' grip on her shoulder tightened, as he angled his body so he stood between Cat and the man.

"You must join us for the evening and tell us all about your travels."

Thomas opened his mouth to speak.

"We would be honored to join you, my friend," Aiden shouted.

As the afternoon turned to night, Cat's worries about being recognized lessened. Her nerves were untwisting. No one *seemed* to recognize her. She took a bite of the meat pie she had been served by their host; he said his name was Malaki. No one would ever expect to see a princess out in the woods, especially not a princess they believed was safely tucked away in a palace, preparing for her wedding.

The fire danced in front of her, warming Cat's face and hands. She rubbed her palms together. The evening air had turned cold and Cat imagined she could see pale frost forming on the grass. Her breath slowly turned to wisps fog. The summer turning to autumn around her.

A lively set of plunking notes sounded around Cat, pulling her thoughts away from the cold. A dark-haired man sat across the fire plucking at something that resembled a lute but was not quite right. The notes swirled through the twisting smoke, dancing around Cat in a fast cadence.

"Would you care to dance princess?" A rough hand pushed toward Cat, palm up in invitation. "We always dance after our meal."

A jolt of nerves passed through Cat's body like lightning. She turned her gaze upward, looking at Malaki. He leaned over her, extending his hand.

"I'm not... I mean... I don't." Her throat felt suddenly too dry to form words.

"Are you trying to tell me you are not a princess or that you do not dance?"

"No... I mean... Why would you think I'm a princess?" She forced her eyes to remain on the man in front of her instead of darting to Aiden and Thomas across the fire.

"In Ruzeme, every man is a lord because he is the master of his own fate, but there are some who are blessed with exceptional destinies." Malaki gestured to Cat's long red hair. "There is a legend that claims those with fire in their hair also have fire in their blood because they are descended from the guardian of fire himself, making them princes and princesses."

Cool relief swept through Cat. The man was just trying to charm her.

"Well, my dear princess, will you join us in a dance?"

Cat slipped her hand into the man's, letting him help her to her feet. The rest of the wanderers had risen as well, forming a circle around the fire as the music swept around them. She linked hands with a woman on her other side following the wanderers in the intricate pattern of steps.

Thomas forced himself to remain seated when the music started and their host approached Cat, asking her for a dance. He spooned another bite of meat pie into his mouth. The savory taste of onion and spices made his mouth water. It was a cool evening and the hot dish kept him warm.

"It seems everyone who meets our *princess* is drawn to her. They all want to make her happy, protect her..." Aiden's words grated against Thomas. He watched the people around him for a reaction. No one moved. The music covered their words.

"Trust me, she does not need anyone to protect her."

"Really?" Aiden shook his head in a light fatherly way. "Then tell me, if she does not need you to protect her, why are you following her around scowling like that?"

Thomas clenched his jaw, choosing not to answer. Aiden had given him no reason to share any secrets, his or Cat's, but Thomas had found himself wondering more and more who Aiden had been before becoming a bandit. The man spoke like he knew about headstrong girls. Had he been a father once? And how did he know so much about magic when most people in Reinsaffira and Volentia believed it was nothing more than a myth? What was it he believed Cat could save his wife from?

"If you're not here to protect her, then you should be dancing with her."

"I don't believe this is the right moment." There was still a stinging pain in his chest from the moment Cat pulled away from him in the crystal cave. If he danced with her and felt the warmth of her skin against his again, he knew he would want to kiss her again. The afternoon showed him that he had to earn Cat's trust. That she deserved to be charmed. It would take time. Falling in love would not be a sprint of passion.

"Trust me, life is shorter than you think. You have to make the moments you have right."

What did Aiden know about it? About anything? The moment was not right.

Thomas glanced at the old woman on the edge of the firelight. She had discarded her mending, replacing it with a thick stack of cards that she shuffled on a low table. She waved him over, gesturing to the seat across from her.

If it meant getting away from Aiden...

Thomas stood. His muscles still felt stiff from days of riding and sleeping on the cold ground but it was starting to abate, giving way to simple exhaustion. He shuffled his feet as he walked over, dropping into the chair across from the woman.

Her gnarled hands set to laying out the cards on the worn table cloth.

He laid a hand on hers. "I'm sorry, I don't need my fortune told."

Thomas already knew everything about his future, everything that mattered. He was the crown prince. One day he would inherit the throne, and he did not want to know when. He glanced over his shoulder at Cat. The only other mystery that mattered was already settled.

The old woman continued dealing out the cards.

"Malaki said you were to perform at the Volentian palace." Thomas pulled two pieces of parchment from his pocket. Each sealed with a dollop of deep blue wax and pressed with his signet ring. The indentation of a sea dragon protected the contents of each letter. Thomas laid them out on the table, covering the cards. One for his brother Phillip, explaining where he had disappeared to, and one for Prince Ryder. The one to Ryder had been more difficult to write. How to explain to the prince that he intended to protect Cat at the same time he would not return her to the palace? "Will you deliver these to Prince Ryder for me? I'll pay you."

The woman turned over the card at the center, revealing a picture Thomas did not recognize. "You are destined to fall in love with a powerful woman."

"Yes, I know." He sighed. "I'm destined to save her, and she is destined to save the world." Amora had read his fortune before. Thomas did not need to hear it again. "Please, will you deliver my letters? They must go to the Crown Prince of Volentia. No one else. It is a matter of life and death." He glanced back at Cat. Aiden had joined her in the whirling dance, whispering something to her as he turned her in a wild spin. He was telling her something that made lines form on Cat's forehead. Probably trying to convince her to give up the jewel he tried to steal on their first meeting. Aiden had not explained why, but he believed the necklace would save his wife.

At least Cat was safe and not drawing attention to herself.

"It is not a matter of life and death," the old woman glared over the table. "There is no danger that can be averted by getting word back to Volentia." She unveiled the remaining cards. "The danger is much closer."

The hair on the back of Thomas' neck rose. An itch. A need to glance back at Aiden. He fought against the pull.

"Something is lurking in the shadows that will pull you apart. You must not let it." The old woman rose, moving with unexpected grace and fluidity. The scent of nutmeg followed her as she circled the table. "I will take your letters to the prince but know that he will not be able to help you."

"What are you doing?" Cat's lilting voice made Thomas jump, startling out of the chair. The letters were gone from the table, whisked away by the old fortune teller. Only a series of colorful cards remained on the table.

Cat was smiling, her face flushed from exertion.

Thomas forced himself to look past her, searching the small crowd for Aiden. The older man ducked into his tent on the edge of the clearing.

"Are you having your fortune read?"

"Oh... yes. It seems I am to watch the shadows for danger." Thomas tapped his finger against his leg. Searching for the next thing to say. He could not find it.

"Sit down, my dear." The old woman returned to her seat, holding a blue porcelain box in her gnarled hands. "I will give you a reading."

Cat hesitated, chewing her lip in thought. Thomas slid out of his seat, creating a space for her. She took the seat, smoothing the wrinkles in her dress with her fingers.

The box was filled with colorful rocks that almost looked like glass. The woman pushed the box at Cat. "Choose."

Her fingers brushed over the colorful stones. The colors seemed to shift under her delicate touch, landing on a smooth pink stone that shimmered in the evening light. She traced a crack in the glassy surface with her thumb. The woman instructed her to hold the stone to her heart and tell it her dearest wish.

A line formed between Cat's scrunched eyebrows; she pulled the round stone close to her heart, closing her eyes in concentration. Thomas smiled to himself, noting once again how much Cat wanted to believe in all of it, the magic of the world. The compass. The fortune teller. She just could not see it in herself. Cat had to be a magix; it was the only thing Aiden told them that Thomas knew he could believe.

Cat handed the delicate stone back to the old fortune teller.

The woman took it. The stone's rosy hue seemed to dim as the woman ran her fingers over it. "Legend says that just like our history is set in stone, so are some people's destinies. Our choices can wear them away, like the movement of water in a river, but they can be read by those with the knowledge." The woman paused. Her pupils widened as her finger skimmed over the long crack in the stone a second time. "And yours goes back hundreds of years."

He watched Cat roll her eyes. Of course, her destiny had been written for generations. She was a princess. She had been destined to be a princess, with all of the responsibilities that came along with that, from the moment her ancestor first took the Volentian throne.

"You don't believe?"

"It's not that," Cat laughed. Her nose crinkled, her hair cascading over her shaking shoulders. "What else does it say?"

The woman ran her fingers over the stone's surface a second time. Her gaze darted to Thomas then back to Cat. "Your destiny is entwined with another's. The road ahead will be difficult and painful, but at the end of it... your choices... the power you hold, will change the world. Trust your heart, my dear." She pushed the stone back into Cat's palm. "You know what you want and what is right. You are free to make that choice."

Emma drummed her fingers against the brick wall, waiting for Sir Guy to appear. He was sure to be off duty soon. Whatever he was up to, Emma planned to find out.

The problem with Emma's spy spot was that she could not see. The small passage wound between the kitchens and the small chambers reserved for the knights and guards who stayed in the palace. The brick walls were thin and cracked, perfect for eavesdropping. This passage was originally meant for knights to reach the royal apartments in an emergency, but the doors had been sealed decades ago. Now it was just another hall leading nowhere.

It had taken Emma more than an hour to pace out the corridor until she was certain the wall she leaned against was Sir Guy's.

"The arrangement was that you deliver the girl to us. Where is she?" A woman's voice echoed on the cold stone. Something about the voice scratched in Emma's ears. Familiar.

"I was not expecting the prince to follow her, but that problem will be dealt with soon. I have been given permission to go after her. You will have her before the next full moon. As we agreed."

Emma's eyes widened. He had been telling the truth when he told the king someone was trying to kidnap Cat. *He* was.

She did not need to hear anymore. Emma needed to do something. She could not go to the king. Perhaps she could stop Sir Guy herself.

She jumped to her feet, sprinting through the palace.

Sir Guy's room was empty by the time she reached it. The bed was neat and made and a gilded mirror stood in the corner. There was nothing else. No evidence anyone had been there. Not even a warm ember in the hearth. Where was he? Emma turned and rushed toward the stables, hoping to cut him off.

To reach the stables from the knight's quarters, Emma had to go past the guest wing, where the Reinsaffiran Royal Family was lodged. She was more concerned with saving her friend than with the impression the next queen of Volentia rushing through the corridors would make, until she slammed into someone coming out of King James' apartment.

Both toppled to the ground.

"Oh, your majesty! I'm terribly sor... Lord Carswell?" Emma looked up at the duke as he stood, brushing dust from his jacket. A blond man who was richly dressed, like royalty. A man she was familiar with, though she never would have expected to see him on the palace grounds again. "What are you doing here? You were banished from court!"

"Lady Emma, charming as ever." Carswell smiled, rising to his full height, making no effort to help Emma stand. She would not have accepted his hand even if it were offered. Carswell was the worst kind of lord; spoiled and entitled. He once tried to bully Cat into marrying him and there were rumors that he spoke openly of Ryder being unfit to rule. "As it happens, I am here visiting the Reinsaffiran royal family. King James is an old friend of my father. Or have you forgotten that my uncle is the duke of Cordawnia? My cousin was once engaged to the crown prince, though he broke off the engagement to waste his life as a rake and scoundrel." Carswell lifted an eyebrow at her. "I believe the rumor was that he was found in bed with three other women on the night their engagement was to be announced."

The sound of Emma's racing heart pounded in her ears. Her fingers twitched, wanting to form fists and that would smash against Carswell's smug face. "Whatever you are trying to do, you won't get away with it. I'll tell the king you are here and he'll..."

"Oh, my dear Lady Emma, I'm afraid the king has much bigger things to deal with than me, at the moment. Is it true that my lovely Princess Catiya ran away with the very same rakish Crown Prince of Reinsaffira? The one who is famous for seducing half the women of his own court? I'm sure he will have a great deal of fun with her. But... I wonder what the king will do when Prince Thomas grows bored with her?"

The back of Emma's hand crashed into Carswell's jaw. Crimson blood immediately trickled from Carswell's lip where her betrothal ring caught him. "How dare you?"

He swiped the blood away. A sickening smile curled his lips. "I had worried it would be difficult to watch you lose everything, but I must say, you are making it much easier." There was no feigned politeness in his manner.

He turned away from her.

"Whatever you are trying to do, it won't work! I will stop you!"

But Carswell was already gone. Emma was alone. Left wondering what it was he said to King James. She stalked away, toward the stables. Sir Guy's horse was already gone. The minutes lost to Carswell had stolen her chance to stop him. A light breeze pulled at her skirts. It was fully fall now. The arbor would be turning orange and red. If panic had not been twisting inside her heart she may have been able to enjoy the light weather. She could not.

"Lady Emma?"

She spun around. A guard stood at the end of the stalls, holding a freshly polished saddle. It gleamed a deep brown.

"What are you doing out here?"

Ryder sat, brooding, in the solarium attached to his room. Dark hair falling into his storm colored eyes. He looked up as Emma let the door clang shut. Simon trailed behind her.

"Emma? What is going on?" He was by her side, arms wrapping around her, in the span of a breath. Ryder could read the panic and anger in her golden brown eyes. "What's wrong?"

"It was a trap! Sir Guy and Lord Carswell! They were plotting with the crone to kidnap Cat! I heard him! It was a trap and I let her go. Whatever happens to her, it will be my fault!"

Emma crumpled, weeping against his chest.

"It's not your fault. You know Cat. Once she gets an idea in her head... well... you could not have stopped her. This is not your fault." Ryder turned to Simon poised to question what was happening. He did not have the chance.

"It's worse. Lord Carswell is here, and he plans to take Princess Catiya to Bastian."

Thomas did not stay at the table for more than a few minutes after

Cat sat down. He stood so abruptly it made Cat wonder if she had driven him away. The thought gave her a quiet, sinking feeling. She quickly shrugged it off, tucking the stone the old woman had given her into her pocket. It was a nice fortune. Cat liked the idea of her choices changing the world.

Across the small camp, Thomas caught her eye. He was standing by the fire with his arms crossed, but that was not what caught her notice. Cat did not care what Thomas was doing. It was the woman with dark brown hair who approached him that Cat noticed. It was hard not to notice her. She wore a long red dress with a fur stole draped over one shoulder. She was tall and very pretty. Cat remembered seeing her perform when the wanderers came to the palace, she was a fire dancer. The girl glanced at Cat then turned to Thomas, speaking to him for a moment before taking him by the hand and guiding him toward the ring of dancers.

Cat crossed her arms and turned away, suddenly feeling very tired. Not that she cared who Thomas danced with or how pretty the girl he chose to dance with was. It was not as if she had come over to the fortune teller to see if he wanted to dance with her.

She stood, her chair bumping against her knees and crashing to the ground. The sound made Cat jump, kneeling down to pick it up. "I'm so sorry. I didn't mean..."

"It's quite alright, my dear *princess*."

The title sent a chill up Cat's spine before she remembered the story Malaki told her, the legend regarding her red hair. She forced herself to take a deep breath.

"Only an accident."

"Right." Cat brushed a stray lock of hair away from her face before picking up the chair. Her gaze flitted, just for a moment, back to Thomas and the girl. She turned back to the old woman, offering her a quiet smile. "I must be more tired than I thought. I... I should go to bed."

Aiden stretched out on the cold ground to sleep, bundling his cloak under his head. The music still danced through the night air, soothing his tired body. This was the sort of place where he was most happy, with the sky and the trees and the grass. Although, after everything Aiden had lost, no one could truly call him *happy* at any time.

Sleep never came easy. There were too many images that swept through his mind in the quiet of night. Always the same; the awful day years ago. It came to his mind again, just like every night. The image of his small woodland destroyed, a burned-out husk. His wife and daughter gone. Aiden had not slept in a home since that day; always sleeping in stables or under the open sky in the woods. It was easier that way. Always easier to keep moving.

Not tonight. Aiden pushed the images from his mind. *Please, not tonight.*

When he closed his eyes, the memories swirled around him again. He pressed his face into the grass, the smell drowned out the memory of the scent of baking bread… only for a moment.

Olivia always smelled like fresh baked bread, even though she only baked on the first day of every week. She had been baking on the awful day. There had been a smudge of flour on her cheek when he kissed her goodbye.

Aiden balled his fists against his sleepless eyes, willing the memory to fade away. It was no use. No amount of drink could drown his mind enough that the memory would not resurface in the quiet of night. He was cursed. Cursed to relive the same day over and over in his mind. It was his fault that Bastian had found them. If he had not been so careless, Lyse would never have gotten sick and Olivia would not have turned to shadow magic to save her. That was how Bastian found them.

The rustle of fabric drew Aiden out of his memories. A dark haired woman with gleaming lavender eyes leaned over him, watching him.

He saw the magic working, a glowing blue light that emanated from the vial in her hand. He could feel the magic too. It felt hot against his forehead, where she touched him. He clutched the crone's wrist.

"You cannot hide from me, Olivia."

The woman shifted, uncomfortable, eyes darting away, but Aiden knew those eyes. He knew the rounded half smile that curved her lips. He knew every inch of the woman before him. The pitiful creature was what his wife became after Bastian twisted her will and the magic inside of her. Her hand slid out of his. She laid down beside him, resting her head against Aiden's chest. As if the years had only been seconds.

"You have to keep the girl out of Bastian's reach." Her voice was dry and cracked; it scraped against Aiden's ears in a painful way. "He cannot be allowed to take her magic."

It was the same thing Olivia told him the last time she appeared. The same warning.

"I'm trying." Aiden brushed a finger down his wife's arm, remembering the feel and warmth of her skin. "I'm going to take her heart stone. I should have it soon. Then you'll be free,"

Olivia shook her head. "It won't be enough. She's the daughter of the prophecy."

The daughter of the prophecy? The magix destined to free The Darkness?

"The only way to protect the world is to kill her. You have to end her bloodline."

Aiden's heart dropped. Cold swept through him. "If she's the daughter of the prophecy, she cannot be killed. I would need…"

"An enchanted. She carries a blade that can only be wielded by the descendant of a guardian. It will work." She pulled his hand to her heart. Pressing his fingers into her skin. "You have to pierce her through the heart with it. It is the only way to protect the world."

"No!" He pulled his hand back. Sitting up to look at the woman who had once been his wife. Olivia had appeared to him several times in the years since she had been taken. Each time she warned him of the danger, the coming *darkness*. Each time she showed him more of the beast she had become. The last time she had been Olivia just long enough to tell him the only way to stop The Darkness was to find the Volentian princess and destroy her magic. "No! I won't kill an innocent girl. Even if I could, I can't wield an enchanted dagger."

"You must find a way."

"But... Olivia, she has the light. She can save you. She can undo Bastian's hold on you. She can..."

The crone pushed away from him. Every scrap of his wife was draining away, buried beneath layers of twisted magic. "You are wasting your time. You cannot save that girl any more than you can save your foolish wife."

Black smoke filled the tent, extinguishing the lantern.

Aiden reached out, but it was no use. She was gone.

Cat pulled her boots from her tired feet, wiggling and stretching her now free toes. A groan falling from her lips. She had not realized how long the evening had been, but she enjoyed most of it. She had danced and eaten and had her fortune told. It was so different from the celebrations and dinner parties she was used to attending. Now that her useless jealousy had faded, Cat found herself smiling.

She undid the lacing at the front of her dress, slowly pulling it off her shoulder.

The flap of her tent opened and Thomas ducked inside.

"What are you doing in here?" Cat pulled her dress closed, hastily retying the laces.

"Please, don't stop on my account."

"What are you doing in here?" She glared at him. Clenching her teeth. "You can't just come in here and... and..."

"You know, you don't stutter as much when you're angry." He cocked his head to one side, studying her.

"Thomas!"

"Relax. Aiden told our new *friends* that you and I were married." Something passed over his face, a cloudy thought that Cat could not read. "It would be suspicious if we did not stay together." Thomas turned his back on her, securing the tent flap. "Besides, I don't trust these people. So far everyone we have met has tried to hurt you. I don't plan on giving these people the chance."

Cat knew the Ruzeme wanderers would not harm her. They were patroned by her father. Besides, no Ruzeme wanderer would harm a fellow traveler. It would go against their beliefs. Cat glanced back to the entry. Just beyond the crisp fabric, the campfire still crackled and danced, warding off the night. The sounds of music and laughter had died away as people made their way back into their wagons and tents to sleep. The only real danger was if one of them had recognized her.

Thomas secured the last two toggles that held the fabric in place. He turned back to fix Cat with those penetrating blue eyes that she could not look into. They saw too much of her. She crossed her hands over her body, hiding herself, remembering he had just been flirting with the beautiful girl outside.

Her fingers brushed against a lump in the pocket at her waist. She dug the lump from her pocket, the stone the fortune teller had given her. The pink stone was smooth and warm in her palm. The surface gleamed like glass in the lamplight. The old woman had told Cat that her choice would change the world.

"Do... Do you really believe I'm a magix?" She finally met Thomas' gaze. "You, Aiden, the fortune teller, you all say I have this power and that my choices will matter but I..." She had to take in a deep breath to steady her words. A laugh formed inside of her instead. The whole idea was absurd. "I've never been allowed to choose anything, not even my clothing. How am I supposed to make a choice that will change the world? As for power... I wouldn't even know where to start. I don't know anything about magic. I don't know how to save Aiden's wife. I don't know how I summoned the light you saw."

She set her lips in a grimace, looking away from Thomas. Was that embarrassment he saw on her face? He watched her unconsciously toy with the stone hanging from her neck.

Thomas' arm inched toward her. He did not understand magic, but he wanted to help. His fingers found her, brushing Cat's occupied hand, clasping her fingers and pulling them away from her collarbone. His fingers slid over the callouses on her palm, stilling the princess' fidgeting.

Her hand was so small, and icy cold. He wrapped both hands around it, hoping to warm her skin. Cat did not pull away, but she would not meet his gaze either.

Rough callouses were worn on her palm from years of training with a sword, giving him an idea.

"Maybe you need a teacher."

"A teacher?"

He shrugged. "Someone taught you how to wield a sword. It took time for you to learn how to climb rocks as well, didn't it?"

Cat's eyes finally met his. There was a line of freckles under her left eye that reminded him of a cluster of stars. The look she gave him was not her usual harsh glare. It was soft, unguarded. "This isn't like that. I... I don't need a teacher because I can't do magic."

"Have you ever tried?"

All at once, Cat realized Thomas was holding her hand. She pulled back, fingers tightening around the pink stone in her palm. It thrummed, warm and comforting against her fingers. Not quite so comforting as his fingers had been.

"Wh-what?"

"Have you ever tried to do magic? Or do you remember doing magic by accident?"

"I would not even know where to start."

The lantern at the center of the room flickered, drawing Cat's attention. Aiden had called her a light magix. Her memory strayed to the fire in the old tower. How had the fire started so suddenly?

Cat set the stone aside, lifting the lantern. "Maybe."

She closed her eyes, trying to remember what it felt like when she summoned the light. The fear when the shadows attacked her. The anger when Aiden tried to steal her mother's necklace. The sweeping emotions that overtook her, always followed by the unexplainable. Her eyes opened again, meeting Thomas' encouraging gaze. It was hard to replicate those feelings. Light and warmth rushed to her cheeks, and she ducked her head. Cat focused on the fire. The light dimmed between her fingers. She focused on the light and warmth buzzing in her core.

Cat had an idea, a thought about magic, but it was crazy. Then again, it was possible. Fire never bothered her. She could not ever remember being burned.

With a deep, steadying breath, Cat dipped her fingers into the flames. It was flickering and warm. Thrumming. The flame crept up her fingers, coming to rest in her palm. Flickering. Dancing.

A smile lit her face. "I did it!"

"Cat! Thomas! I need to speak with you!" Aiden's voice rang out on the other side of the fabric. He forced his way through the entrance, his eyes widening, taking in the sight of Cat and Thomas sitting on the ground. The sight of Cat holding the dancing flame in her hand. "You can wield fire magic? That's impossible."

Cat's eyes felt heavy and grainy. Morning dew clung to her hair, making Cat shiver. She pushed her tangled hair away from her face, wishing she could fall back asleep. It was too early to be awake.

Something woke her.

A sound she was not expecting.

There it was again. A hammering. Wood knocking against wood. Metal jangling in the still morning air. Cat recognized the sound. It took a moment, but she knew it. The wanderers were hitching their horses to their wagons.

Moving slowly, so as not to wake Thomas, who slept curled on the ground in front the tent door, Cat got up. She had to lift her long dress to keep from stumbling over Thomas' sleeping form.

She emerged into the morning mist. It clung to the grass like clouds against a mountain top. It was a gray day. The clouds were heavy with the promise of rain. A breeze swept through the clearing, ruffling Cat's hair. On the far side of the road, the wanderers loaded the last few items into a set of drawers on the side of one of the wagons. It was still dark, but Cat could not be certain that it was not the storm growing above them.

"You're leaving? So early?"

The men paused their work, Malaki turning toward her. He wore a bright golden shirt that contrasted with the dark weather. It seemed to warm the space. "Ah, Princess."

Cat balked before remembering he had called her 'princess' the night before, referring to her fiery hair. He said she had fire in her blood. Cat's fingers twitched against her thigh. If only he knew how right he was.

"Yes, we have a long way to travel, if we are going to reach the city by nightfall."

"Oh..." Cat found herself chewing her lip, her fingers twisting against the heavy cotton of her dress. "You said you were going to perform at the palace. Would... Would you take a message to Lady Emma for me?"

Malaki's eyebrows drew tight. He was watching Cat in a way that made her feel like a book, every inch of who she was written across her skin.

"Would you tell her that I'm... That I'm fine and that... that I'll come back as soon as I can. Tell her to tell..." Her throat felt dry, voice straining against the words. "Tell her to tell... my fiancé that I will come back. I just... I have to do this first."

"We can take a message for you, but would you prefer to take it to her yourself, your highness?" A smile twitched on Malaki's lips at the same time that Cat's blood pressure dropped, making her head spin. "There is some space for you."

"You knew who I was?"

He tugged lightly at a lock of red hair clinging to Cat's shoulder. "You tend to stand out." Malaki frowned. Maybe it was the weight of his gaze, or the weight of the rain filled sky, but Cat felt her spirit crushing. "Don't worry, your secret is safe, but are you certain you do not wish to return home?"

She dipped her hand into her cloak, fingers closing around the brass compass. "I can't. I have to do this. There's... there's something I need, and I won't find it at the palace."

The old woman, Cat still did not know her name, she found herself wondering if she had one at all, appeared in the mists. Ethereal and otherworldly, like a creature from an old fairy story. Cat suppressed a shudder. There was a familiarity of the movement, the similarity to the crone who gave her the compass. Though, she was not sure why the thought of that crone sent a shiver down her spine.

"My dear girl, there is no need to go chasing after something you believe you need, when it is right in front of you." Her dark eyes flickered, like a gleaming coal in the center of a dying fire.

Cat glanced over her shoulder. She did not need to; somewhere in the last few days Cat had become attuned to Thomas' presence. A sense of something important happening, like she was standing on a precipice. He stood at the entry to the tent, watching her with his arms crossed.

She returned her attention to the woman. "You told me that I needed to trust my heart. That my choices will affect the world. This is my choice. But please, will you take my message to Emma and... the prince?"

Ryder folded his hands in front of him, contemplating the letter he just read, as well as the unusual messenger who delivered it. ... And the meeting between two kings earlier that day. Everything that day had been unusual.

Prince Phillip sat across from the solarium from him.

Silence clung to the air.

The younger prince opened his mouth to speak. His voice felt out of place in the broken quiet. "Lord Carswell claimed your sister fled because she was afraid of what would happen if it was discovered that she, like her mother, was a magix. He also accused her of..." Phillip looked down, not quite embarrassed, just hesitant. "He claimed that she called their engagement off because she was having an affair with a Reinsaffiran knight."

"That is untrue!" The same anger Ryder felt when he found Carswell with his sister at the center of the labyrinth surged forward. "Carswell is a brute who was banished from court after he tried to force himself on my sister. Ask anyone. Ask Lord Arik; he saw the whole thing."

"Trust me, when it comes to women, my father won't trust anything Arik has to say. But he does trust Carswell. That's not the problem though. The problem is the accusation of magic."

"Cat has no magic." Ryder took a long drink of his wine. He would have known if Cat was magix. There were no secrets between them. Even if there were, there were no secrets between Cat and Emma and Emma would never keep that kind of a secret from him. "She would have told me."

"Carswell claims she confided in him, and your mother *was* from an ancient Salenian bloodline. It's enough for my father."

Ryder's chest ached. He rubbed his sternum, hoping to alleviate it. "So, the alliance is finished then?"

"I have never seen my father like this. He believes Carswell and he is furious. It is like he has gone mad, hungry for war." Phillip shook his head.

Ryder tapped the letter resting on the table in front of him. Another pack of secrets. Keeping secrets created this mess. "What about this letter from your brother? Doesn't that prove Carswell's story is false?"

The letters had arrived moments before, delivered by a troop of traveling performers who had been summoned for Cat's wedding. A wedding Ryder doubted would happen now. The traveler claimed he met Cat in the woods, traveling with two men. She did not act like a captive, but she refused their offer to travel back to the palace with them. The man told him that Cat had promised to return. Then he handed him the letter from Prince Thomas. The letter proved she had not been kidnapped.

Phillip lifted his own letter, turning it over in his hands. "It is my brother's handwriting, and the seal is from his signet ring, but it does nothing for the accusation of magic." The golden prince leaned over the table, as close to Ryder as he could get. "I'm afraid that bringing this letter to light would only send enemies to your sister and my brother."

Ryder reread the carefully scrawled words.

Phillip was right. Emma was right. Cat was with Prince Thomas and Sir Guy and Carswell were lying to them. There was nothing Ryder could do now.

"Secrets," he grunted. "They hardly seem worth the cost."

Phillip stood to leave. "No, they do not." Ryder wondered what the younger prince's letter had said, but he had chosen not to share. There was still a moment to ask. Phillip's hand hovered over the door handle. He turned back to face Ryder. "I believe you are aware that when the alliance was first negotiated my brother came to Volentia in secret."

"I am."

"What I doubt you know is that after my father returned, my brother begged him to let him return to Volentia to court a beautiful girl with red hair he claimed to have fallen in love with." The door groaned as Phillip pulled it open. "My brother is a great many things, but he is in love with your sister and will do anything to protect her and bring her home safely." Then he was gone. Leaving Ryder alone with his thoughts and those words echoing in his head.

Ryder stared down at the muddied parchment.

Prince Ryder

Cat is safe.
I will keep her safe and bring her back.
I promise.

Prince Thomas of Reinsaffira.

He had no choice except to trust Thomas, as much as the thought roiled his stomach. In any case, he had to warn him about Sir Guy and Lord Carswell's treachery. Whatever Thomas had planned, he had to get Cat back to the safety of the palace. No one could be removed from the palace against their will, or so the legends claimed. Ryder set his own pen to paper, scrawling a short note of his own.

A tall man with dark hair stood at Arik's door. He was stiff and imposing. Arik paused on the threshold. "Excuse me, sir, where is Evander? He is my usual escort."

The man crossed his barrel sized arms. Speaking in a low growl that was soft as velvet. "Evander had resigned his post."

Resigned? Arik had known Evander for five years. He had been Arik's escort since he first became the ambassador to Volentia. And they had been friends since the day they rescued Princess Catiya from Lord Carswell. Friends may not be the exact right word to describe it. They were, at least, friendly. Arik was certain Evander would have told him before resigning his post. He was even more certain that Evander would not resign at all; he loved being a guard. He loved protecting the royal family.

"I'm going to have to ask you to come with me."

"Come with you?"

"I would highly recommend it," the new guard grunted. He adjusted his stance, muscles flexing as he moved. A little voice in the back of Arik's mind told him this man could crush him without thinking. He did not want to go anywhere with him, not with tensions in the palace being so high.

Arik's thoughts went back to the moment the day before when Lord Carswell appeared in the king's suite with a bottle of fine wine. He claimed the princess ran away because she was a magix. That she was a danger to Reinsaffira. The room boiled over with anger so quickly. Arik had to retreat to his own room, as if he could hide from the crumbling alliance.

Before Arik could think of an excuse, the guard grabbed Arik by the arm, dragging him from the room. Another guard stood on the other side of the door; Arik vaguely recognized him. He vaguely recognized most guards in the palace. This one had brown hair that hung around his shoulders. He came to stand on the other side of Arik, guiding him down the hall.

"What are you doing? I'm..."

"The Reinsaffiran ambassador. We know." The smaller of the two men spoke, keeping his voice low. Not quite a whisper. "Don't worry, we're not going to hurt you. We need your help saving Princess Catiya and Prince Thomas."

Arik's feet sputtered to a skidding stop. The larger man kept a hand hooked on Arik's upper arm, pulling him down the hall. "What? What do you know about Princess Catiya? And Thomas?"

"Not here. It's not safe." The larger man's grip slackened.

Arik continued to follow.

The three left the palace, walking down the main thoroughfare to a small bakery a few blocks away from the palace.

The bakery smelled like cinnamon and fresh baked bread. It was a small, warm space with a long counter and an organized display case. A swinging door behind the counter revealed a large kitchen that was golden with afternoon sunlight. A plump young woman wearing a lavender apron leaned on the counter, arranging a tray of muffins. Her curves looked so soft. Arik assumed she was not the reason these two men had dragged him here.

"Simon? Marcus? What are you doing here?" The girl looked up with disinterest.

"We're here to talk to Evander," the larger man grunted. His voice was much softer when he spoke to the woman.

"Well," Arik leaned on the counter in front of her, tracing the wood grain with his finger. "I'm here in search of something delicious."

A meaty hand snagged the back of Arik's shirt, hauling him back away from the counter. "I would highly recommend not flirting with Evander's sister."

"Marcus," the girl laughed.

So, the larger man was Marcus, making the smaller man Simon. Arik recognized him now, he was one of Prince Ryder's bodyguards, Arik had seen him several times with Evander.

Arik sat in the airy kitchen, listening to Lydia hum a cheery tune as she dusted flour over a pan. Evander and the two other guards sat around the large square kitchen table. He wanted to be shocked by what they were telling him. The knight searching for Cat and Thomas was a Salenian spy. He and Lord Carswell were working together to deliver her to King Bastian. Arik tapped a finger against the table. His best friend was in danger. There had to be something he could do.

"Can't you go to the king? Warn him about Sir Guy's plans?"

"Unfortunately, no." Evander kept his tone even. His voice and jaw held tight. "We would need proof and we cannot get it."

"And the king would not believe us," Marcus chimed in.

Arik's eyebrows drew together. "Why?"

Silence followed, except for the uncomfortable drum of fingers against the wooden table and Lydia's stirrings throughout the kitchen.

Evander rubbed the back of his neck as he searched for an answer. "When it comes to matters involving the princess... we..."

"They're not the king's favorites." Lydia set a bread pan at the center of the table, immediately slapping one of the men's hands away. "He believes they cannot be objective about her safety. It probably has something to do with the fact that Simon was in love with her for two years and Evander used to help her sneak out of the palace to gamble."

"Hey! I wasn't *in love* with Cat!"

"And Cat was perfectly capable of sneaking out on her own." There was a series of eye rolls around the room. "Fine. We were friends with Cat... Princess Catiya, but when the queen was killed... it was decided that we were not appropriate influences for a princess. It's easiest to say that the king does not trust us, but he might trust you. You could speak with him, convince him to let us go after Cat or..."

Arik shook his head. "I don't believe I can do that, but..." He did have one thought. There was a place Thomas almost always turned up, though he doubted he would, with the princess in tow. "I may be able to find him and convince him to bring her back before Sir Guy does."

Magic, it turned out, was almost boring in its simplicity. Aiden had droned on about the history of magic and the way it worked for days. According to legend, what people called magic was a byproduct of the creation of the world. The farther from the center of creation one traveled the less magic permeated the world. Somewhere on the other end of the world, beyond the borders of Brotid there was probably a land that had never even heard of magic.

The people of Salene and Ruzeme lived at the base of an impassable mountain range. This is what the Salenians considered the center of creation. The place where magic started. No one knew what was beyond the mountains, but even the people of Volentia and Reinsaffira agreed the impassable range was dangerous. There could be anything beyond the border lands; dragons, monsters, anything. The magic of creation seeped into the earth and the blood of the people. That was where magix came from. At least, according to legend

Cat sighed, lifting her compass out of her pocket, checking that they were still heading the right way. The arrow pointed, unwavering, north east over the plains.

Maybe Thomas was right, maybe the compass was broken. Almost two weeks had passed, and Cat felt no closer to finding whatever it was she needed than she was the night she left the palace. Though she could not be certain. Cat had never seen a magic compass before being handed this one. Other than the small tricks she had managed since Aiden had started teaching her and the nightmares that Cat could not help but wonder if they were really memories, Cat had never seen magic of any kind. There was nothing in Aiden's lessons and explanations that could help her understand the compass. Still, it was in and out of her hands every few minutes, distracting her from Aiden's droning lecture.

Cat looked up from the compass. Catching Thomas watching her movements out of the corner of his eye. She looked away the second their eyes met. What was he watching for? The way his eyes searched her face made her fidget. She reached down to smooth her nonexistent skirts.

Thomas smiled at her when she looked back up. He did have a lovely smile, when he was not being smug and irritating. Cat watched him ride along. His brunette curls had grown shaggy, curling at the back of his neck. It was not until Cat's horse splashed through a creek that Cat realized she had been staring at him, paying no attention to where she was, or the information Aiden continued to give her on the *complexities* of magic. She had to make a more concentrated effort at indifference. Cat was not on this journey to fall in love. There was a prince waiting to marry her, one she intended on going back to. Cat could not afford to fall in love... ever. That was the sort of thing better left to the lucky, like Ryder and Emma.

"There's a river up ahead," Aiden circled back to her and Thomas. "It seems as a good a place as any to make camp."

Cat nodded. The sun was sinking low and she doubted they would find anywhere better before dark.

She watched Aiden climb down from his horse. He had been different since the night they met the wanderers. She could not name it. It was something in his manner that changed. He was willing to explain how magic worked during the day, but when evening came, he avoided Cat. Always setting to work on the fire or tents as fast as he could without going near Cat. The only time he chose to speak with her over the crackling fire was when Cat removed Emma's jeweled dagger from her belt, asking questions she could not answer.

It did not matter.

Once the horses were brushed and picketed, Cat sat at the base of a tree. Every muscle in her body ached. Her arms ached from use and her heart ached with worry that the journey was nothing more than the errand of a fool. How would she recognize what she needed when she found it? Cat rubbed her forearm, working away the dirt and tension. She was filthy with travel. Cat never worried much about a little dirt. At court she was constantly being lectured on her appearance, dirt smudged across her face. Her last governess, before it was decided that Cat was old enough to be the lady of the royal family, had taken it upon herself to teach Cat a lesson on cleanliness by scrubbing her face with a hard brush until her jaw was raw. That woman disappeared after Cat's mother saw the line of blood.

The grime clinging to Cat now felt absurd, even for her. She did her best to keep clean, but it was difficult making camp in the woods every night. Her hair was growing knotted as well. It needed a good cleaning before she could brush the snarls free.

"I think it is safe to have a fire," Thomas announced, standing suddenly. He stretched to his full height. "I'll gather some firewood."

Aiden nodded, rummaging through his saddlebag. Then he stepped into the woods without a word.

Cat was alone. Invisible. Listening to the river dance over the rocks.

She glanced around. Alone. Cat was alone. The river was secluded by brush and a large weeping willow with branches hanging down into the water. She grabbed her bag and headed toward the inviting babble of the river.

Thomas stepped into the clearing, singing softly to himself. It was an old ballad, something sweet he half remembered from childhood. A bundle of sticks pressed into his chest and arms.

"Where is Cat?"

Aiden entered the clearing, carrying his own bundle of sticks. "I had assumed she was with you."

The sticks clattered to the ground. Thomas shook his head with irritation. She could not have been gone for more than a few minutes. He stooped, searching for any clue of what happened to Cat. There was no sign of struggle in the clearing. Knowing Cat, she had stood up and walked straight into some kind of danger. That girl could find danger in a meadow populated only with butterflies. Thomas suspected that, if he had not insisted on traveling with her, she would have died within a day of leaving the palace. He was not quite certain she was worth this much trouble.

Two long strides and Thomas was out of the clearing again.

"Where are you going?" Aiden jogged after the taller man.

"To find her before she gets herself hurt."

Aiden fixed Thomas with a hard stare. After a minute he shook his head in a noncommittal way that Thomas took for agreement. They went in different directions, searching for signs of struggle or danger.

"Where is she?" Thomas muttered under his breath, feeling more annoyed than worried. Then his booted foot sunk into the warm water, soaking him up to his knee. He had been too distracted in his search to notice that the path had fallen away. The water was warm, steam rose up from it. The river must have been connected to a hot spring somewhere beneath the ground.

A movement on the other side of the swaying willow branches caught his attention.

Careful not to fall all the way into the clear running water, Thomas pulled himself back onto the bank. His eyes fixed on the mysterious movement.

The creature was too slender to be a deer. It bent over the water. The dribble of water splattering against the stones stopped and the beast rose. Thomas' eyes widened; the silhouette belonged to his troublesome princess. She pulled a comb through the waist length hair that hung wet and loose around her. Her white tunic was soaked, clinging to her arms and hips. She let her hair tumble over one shoulder, twisting it methodically into a long braid.

He turned to shout to Aiden that he found her.

The shout caught in Thomas' throat. He did not want to interrupt this private moment, did not want Cat to know he had seen her. Thomas would find Aiden quietly and inform him of Cat's safety. He took a step back.

"You love that girl." Aiden's gravely voice resonated behind Thomas.

A crimson blush warmed his cheeks, spreading to the back of his neck. What Aiden must think of him, spying on Cat during such an intimate moment. Under normal circumstances... he would never... it was not what a gentleman would do. The blush grew darker, hotter.

"Whether you know it or not, I can see more than just a sworn knight. Be careful there." Aiden kept his voice low. Less than a whisper. "That story does not always have a happy ending."

Thomas glanced at the older man. The bandit's eyes were downcast, purposefully turned away from Cat.

"What story?"

"Women with magic in their blood. Their stories rarely have happy endings. Hers especially... I would guess. And it won't end happily for anyone who loves her either."

"I swore an oath to her brother to protect her. That is all." The half-truth fell easily from Thomas' lips. He could not admit to Aiden who he was or what he felt for Cat. His princess, the girl he had dreamed about for so long. He could not say that he loved her, that he was the person she was meant to marry. Not until he knew she loved him too. But he knew he loved her. He had known the first instant he saw Cat that she was rare, that she was all he ever wanted, that she was smart and caring and brave.

Thomas turned away from Aiden too fast, his foot catching on a root. He tumbled headfirst into the water.

All secrecy and quiet was driven from Thomas' mind. He pushed out of the water, gasping for breath, letting out a stream of curses. Aiden pressed a fist to his chest, laughing.

"Not one word, Aiden. Not one word."

"My God!" There was a flash of red hair between the swaying branches of the weeping willow. Her shadow snatching up a cloak and rushing behind the tree. "What are you doing here? I'm not..."

The water felt colder than ice against Thomas' skin. Heat rising to his cheeks. Everything he did when it came to Cat seemed to be wrong.

What were Thomas and Aiden doing there? Cat pulled her cloak over her wet limbs, searching for her clothes. How long had they been there? Had they seen her? Cat had been so careful when choosing this spot, the branches of the willow hung around a little cove on the riverbank. Steam from a hot spring bubbled up through the stone riverbed, warming the water. It had been perfect and private. Now she felt exposed in the open air.

Where were her clothes?

"Cat?" Thomas' voice shook. Was that concern? Embarrassment? "Are you all right?"

Cat was not alright. She wanted to scream. She was mortified, not to mention indecent. No *proper* way to phrase that came to mind. A hand pushed back some of the branches. Cat found her voice. "Stop! I don't... I'm not... Just stop!"

The branches stilled.

Through the leaves, Cat could see the tall knight take a step back. Water dripped from his shaggy hair. Soaked from the top of his head to the tips of his boots and beginning to shiver. "Cat, I..." he was searching for the right words. "I'm so sorry for intruding. If I had known... well... You were missing and I thought..." His voice dropped low when she did not respond. "Princess?"

"I was bathing! Am I a child that I need to ask your permission?" The breeches, tunic, boots, and necklace sat under a small pile of leaves. Cat grabbed them, clasping the necklace around her neck. It was still a diamond when she looked down at it, not the deep blue stone she remembered her mother wearing. Cat hesitated before finishing dressing, glancing back through the branches. Her soaked tunic would have to be removed. How well could Thomas and Aiden see her? A chill crept into her muscles; the warmth of her skin lost to the autumn breeze. She pulled the cloak tighter around her.

"Why would you need to bathe?" Aiden laughed. It was as if he never met a woman before.

"Just because I've been dressing like a man, does not mean I want to smell like one," Cat snapped back. Unease was growing in the pit of her stomach. At this point it was obvious she was safe. Why were they still harassing her? If Thomas could see Cat as clearly as she could see him, then the tree made a poor dressing screen. "Now, would you please turn around so I can dress?"

"I'm insulted," Aiden continued to laugh. "It is not men who smell. You women are the ones always covering up your natural scent with soaps and perfumes."

"Soap is not for covering any smell, it is for washing it away. Something I strongly recommend you do as well."

Something deep in Cat's core pulled tight. A wave of dizziness settled on her skin, prickling as the breeze kicked up into a harsh torrent. The leaves and branches of the tree rattled. The wind caught the water's surface, soaking both men in the spray. As if by magic. No. Cat had to remind herself that it was not something like magic, it was magic. Magic she had done, but how? Where had it come from?

The air was growing cold. Cat's numb feet fought for grip on the tree roots. Her arms were losing feeling as pins and needles washed over her. She started to shiver.

"Now, would you please go so I can dress?"

"Cat," Thomas stepped forward again. "Are you sure you're alright?"

"Just go!" The magic pulled again. A hook that wrenched Cat forward.

Cat was suddenly burning hot, then icy cold. Numbness and exhaustion washed over her. Her feet slipped. Cat was falling. She hit the water hard but did not feel it.

Her eyes fluttered. She saw a blaze of orange above her. A fire? The next thing she knew, Thomas was dragging her out of the water. Cat gasped for breath as he lifted her, consumed by her need for air. She was only vaguely aware of his arms around her and her pounding heart.

"It's the magic." Cat heard Aiden speaking. His voice was so far away. "The heart stone is meant to channel the energy. It should not allow her to do anything beyond what her body can handle."

Heart stone? Cat tried to ask what Aiden was talking about. She wanted to put her feet on the ground. She was fine. Why wasn't her body listening?

"Either of those tricks alone would have killed most magix."

Thomas' arms tightened around Cat. "We have to get her warm."

Then there was only darkness.

Cat's heart pounded in her head when she woke. She was in a small tent with both Thomas and Aiden's cloaks piled on top of her. She felt a thrill of adrenaline when she realized she was wearing a dry shirt. Cat peered around the opening of the tent. Thomas and Aiden sat with their backs to her, staring into a small crackling fire. They spoke in hushed tones.

"They'll have seen the fire for certain."

"We should leave as soon as possible. Before first light."

Anxious to put the fainting spell behind her, Cat pushed back the cloaks and dressed, still feeling a chill in her veins. Her clean braid was already falling free of its bindings. Cat stepped out into the firelight, walking to Aiden.

"What is a heart stone?"

Aiden startled at her question, looking up at her.

"Cat," Thomas was on his feet. "How are you feeling? You should be resting!"

She held up a hand, eyes still fixed on Aiden. "You said something about a heart stone at the river. What is that?" Cat doubted how much Aiden actually knew about magic. She had no one else to ask, Cat had never met a magix... as far as she knew. At least, she had never met anyone who was willing to speak openly about magic without dismissing it as mere legend.

"It's that gem around your neck." He patted the ground beside him for her to sit. "A heart stone is a special kind of gem that was gifted from the sea. They look like diamonds, until they encounter a magix. They used to wash up on an island just off the coast. Before the Reinsaffirans came from the west, Salenian girls would journey there when they turned sixteen. If the stone they found changed color, they would begin learning to control their powers."

Cat lifted the gem in her palm. Still a diamond. Always a diamond. How could that be possible?

"A water magix will turn to a sapphire. Earth, an emerald or sometimes amber. Stone will turn purple. A wind turns milky white, like an opal."

"And fire?"

"No one knows. Fires were wiped out centuries ago. Betrayed by one of their own. The heart stone harnesses your magic. It is what allows magic to flow out of you. Even the most powerful magix can do nothing without it."

That was not right. It could not be. A diamond still hung from the chain around Cat's neck and yet, she had done powerful magic. The memory of the fire in the old tower tickled the base of her skull. Had she been responsible for that fire? She had no heart stone at the time.

"But mine... it's a diamond and..." The flickering orange light. Had she set the willow by the river on fire? Cat glanced around and realized they had moved far from the river's edge. "Are you certain?"

"I am. Yours is a diamond because you are not an ordinary magix. You are a light magix." He had called her that before but what was the difference between a light magix and a fire magix? Why could she wield both? "The first in history. I am certain about that as well."

Thomas stood with a huff. Moving to the tent, taking it down piece by piece, his form casting strange shadows in the firelight. "If you are rested, we ought to get moving. We cannot stay here too long, unless you want to be caught by the Volentian knights who are tracking you. We need to get someplace safe where we can hide for a day or two until they move on. I know a good place that is not too far from here. You may not like it, but they will never think to look for you there."

An "L" shaped crack in the tabletop took up Emma's whole focus. Annoyance crossed her face as she pressed her fingers against it.

"How could King James say such horrible things?" Her voice was rough from hours of disuse. Emma had barely spoken since the Reinsaffiran royal family left, brooding

Ryder looked up, blinking across the table at her.

"Cat is not a witch! We would have known if she had magic. *I* would have known." The memory of a blinding light dissolving a shadow that was trying to drown Cat formed in Emma's mind. She pushed it aside. Magix were horrible selfish creatures, like Bastian. Cat may be stubborn but she was also kind; she always did what was right no matter what it cost her.

"You and I both know that is not the reason Cat ran away. What does it matter what the Reinsaffirans think?"

"And you just stood there, letting them say those awful things, about her... about me... about Volentia. You didn't say anything when they tore up the alliance like it was nothing." Emma was not angry at Ryder. It had been more than a week since Cat left. Almost as long since they found out about Sir Guy's treachery. She was frustrated, not knowing what was happening out in the wilderness. The reports from Sir Guy were no help. It was impossible to tell what half-truths made up the whole. Panic rose inside of her, burning her throat whenever Emma thought of it. "What if Prince Thomas didn't find her? Or if he did find her and tried to take her back to Reinsaffira where they want to kill her? Or..."

"Enough Emma." Ryder let out a huffing breath. "You are going to worry yourself to death. Then I will have no beloved as well as no sister."

Emma rolled her eyes. She had little intention of relinquishing her worry, no matter how warm Ryder's half smile made her feel.

Ryder was not so boisterous as Emma; she knew the same concerns nagged at him. Lord Arik had left a few days before the Reinsaffiran royal family in search of Prince Thomas, although she was not sure if that was a good thing or bad. For the first time, Emma found herself wishing Cat was less impulsive, that the two of them had taken the time to come up with a real plan before Cat went tearing off into the darkness. Sending Prince Thomas after her was not enough, not with so many forces working against them.

Ryder reached out across the table, placing a hand on Emma's. She could feel his strength seeping into her, helping her hold the weight of her anxiety. Ryder knew as well as she did that her fury was directed at herself for letting her best friend fall for such an obvious trap. Now there was nothing she could do to help or even warn Cat. The feeling of helplessness was bitter and cold in her stomach.

A deep sigh escaped Emma as she leaned into Ryder's grasp. She tried to think of what Cat might do, where she might go. Would she tire of her quest and trust Sir Guy to bring her home? Had she already?

The sign above the door swayed in the breeze. *The Peach Tree Inn.* The bright letters gleamed against the polished wood.

An uneasy feeling crept up the back of Cat's neck. An inn did not seem like the best place to hide. The town stretching out behind it was too small. Not a single person roamed the streets, though it was barely dusk.

Cat's muscles ached and her head was starting to pound with exhaustion. She swayed so much in the saddle she was certain Thomas' arm around her was the only thing that kept her in it. They had ridden hard all day to get there before nightfall, hoping to outrun Sir Guy and anyone else who might be tracking them.

"Are you sure we can hide here?" Her eyes slid toward Thomas. He looked perfectly calm.

"Amora is very discreet; she'll understand our predicament." His shrug was graceful and easy. Someone so tall and lanky should not move with so much ease. "I doubt anyone will even think to look for you here." Thomas hopped off the horse, handing the reins to Aiden.

Cat found herself following Thomas, down the stone steps that lead into the inn. The smell of stew cooking somewhere in the kitchens made

Cat's stomach growl. In their rush to put distance between them and Sir Guy, she had not eaten since the night before. Cat took in a deep breath, relishing the smell. Something sweet and fruity was baking as well. Where had the inn managed to find fresh peaches?

The door was red with a peach tree and a fairy scene painted across it. The story was not one Cat was familiar with. A beautiful young woman was stealing fruit from an orchard. There was something strange on the next panel. Before Cat could study it, Thomas threw the door open, and a blast of warm air and sound hit her. Dozens of people were packed into the common room. The whole population of the little village had to be inside.

A clear-skinned woman with short cropped hair bustled behind an enormous podium that blocked the entrance to the common room. She was young, no older than Cat, but her movements had an ancient quality to them. Graceful and tired. She was quite possibly the most beautiful person Cat had ever seen. It was like she was made of moonlight, her skin shimmering.

The woman eyed Cat. "I am not taking anyone new just now. Sorry miss."

Cat opened her mouth to respond then realized she did not understand what the woman meant.

"It is just as well, Amora," Thomas spoke behind her. "This one would be rubbish at any job you found for her."

"Thomas!" The woman brightened, charging at Thomas, flinging her swanlike arms around his neck.

"Look at you! You've grown so tall!"

"I am exactly as tall as I have been since the day we met." Thomas suffered through the woman's cooing appraisal, like a dutiful son. "It is good to see you too, Amora."

Envy stabbed at Cat's stomach. She rolled her eyes at the display and the sour jealousy that burned her throat. What did she care if he had a flirtation with yet another beautiful girl?

"Perhaps it is something else then." The woman's gaze flitted, ever so briefly, to Cat. She smiled a bright starlight smile, full of mischief and moonlight. "What are you doing here? I heard a rumor," she glanced at Cat again, "that you were getting married."

There was a second pang of jealousy, this one sharp in Cat's chest. Thomas blushed, rubbing a hand against his neck. Cat rolled her eyes at her own reaction. She did not care. In fact, Cat felt bad for any girl Thomas might marry, he was such a nuisance.

"Rumors of my engagement may have been *exaggerated*. As for my purpose here..." He gripped Cat's hand, pulling her into his chest. He wrapped an arm protectively around her shoulders. "This is Cat, and we need a favor."

Amora had ancient eyes. Wise beyond the years her body carried, tired and sad as well. A heavy weight of knowledge hung behind them. They studied Cat, taking her in in full. "Exaggerated indeed." The way her eyes drank them in made Cat feel embarrassed, too exposed to this stranger. There was nothing to be embarrassed about. She was betrothed. Thomas was only there to protect her. The only feeling Cat felt for him was irritation.

"What is the favor?"

"There are some Volentian knights searching for Cat. She needs a place to hide until they pass."

"I see. Lyse!" Amora turned sharply to a blonde girl coming out of the kitchen. This one was young, maybe nineteen at the most. A flour-streaked apron covered her gossamer silk dress.

"Madame?" She fluttered her painted eyelids.

"I'm giving up my room for the night. I'll be sharing yours. I will see that you are compensated of course."

"Of course. I had no plans to take any customers tonight."

Customers? Cat struggled to work out what the girl meant. It did not sound like Amora was asking a guest to give up her room.

The girl picked up a tray, circling the room to gather empty tankards.

Amora turned back to Thomas. "There. The two of you may make use of my rooms. Thomas knows where they are. Are there more of you?"

This time Cat answered. "Aiden, our companion, is still with the horses. He and Thomas can share a room."

"Hmm." Amora nodded. "First, we'll get you cleaned up, then we can worry about your friend's accommodations. If you are going hide among the girls, you will have to look like them. Not like..." Amora waved a hand vaguely at Cat' stained tunic and messy hair. "This."

The girls? Customers? The realization widened Cat's suddenly innocent feeling eyes. The common room was filled with beautiful girls who fluttered in thin silks. "This is a brothel!" She pushed away from Thomas. Why was he so familiar with a woman who ran a brothel?

"I did say you probably would not like it."

"I can't stay here!" If Cat was found in such a place, she would be worse than ruined.

"Do you have a better place to hide?"

A dozen better places came to mind. Half of her wanted to storm out and find Sir Guy. Parading around, pretending to be a whore was the worst plan Cat could think of. Her reputation still mattered to her, even if she had run away from her responsibilities. As thick as he was, Thomas should know at least that much by now. Even Sir Guy would have known that.

That... that was why he had brought her here, she suddenly realized. The thought tasted bitter and metallic. No one who knew Cat would search for her in a brothel. He was right about that.

Cat let Lyse guide her up the stairs. She would figure out what to do later.

Amora spun on her heel to face Thomas the instant the small woman was gone. Eyes flashing, she tapped her foot, folding her arms over her chest. She was not his mother but, in that moment, he shrank away from her as though she were. In many ways, Amora felt like a mother, one he had disappointed.

Though she looked young, Thomas knew the truth, knew Amora was ancient. He knew her story, and was one of the few people alive who did. She had once been one of the first people to sail from Brotid to Reinsaffira after the broken lands were cursed. After stealing a peach from a magical grove of trees, Amora was cursed with eternal youth and beauty, becoming one of the guardians, the eternal beings responsible for protecting the last remnants of magic in the world, watching everyone she loved grow old and wither even from memory. A steep price to pay for a peach. But that was why Thomas brought Cat here. If anyone could protect the last fire magix, it had to be a guardian.

"If I did not know better, I would say you just brought the missing Volentian princess into my establishment."

Thomas lowered his gaze.

"The very princess who was said to have run away upon the announcement of her engagement to *you*, your highness."

"Don't say that so loud! Cat doesn't know who I am. She believes I'm a knight."

"Why would she believe that?" Amora's eyes narrowed to slits.

"She made an assumption and I have not told her otherwise."

Amora's graceful hand whacked across the back of Thomas' head. Just hard enough to sting. "Whatever you are planning, it's stupid! What do you think will happen when she finds out who you are?" If there was one thing Thomas could say about Amora, she was never afraid to tell anyone the truth. She had seen and raised so many kings in her long life that a crown prince was little more than a child to her.

Then, she wrapped him in another hug. Just like his own mother might do.

"Amora." Thomas pulled back, holding her at arm's length. "I think she's in danger. She's a magix." There was so much more to this than Thomas originally guessed. The magic compass and the crone weighed so heavily on his mind. Then there was the toll magic took on Cat... it could not be an accident that her powers had been kept from her. Amora knew so much about magic, perhaps she would know something.

"A magix? Are you certain?"

"Beyond a doubt. Amora... what do you know about fire magix?"

"Other than the fact that they are extinct?"

"They *were* extinct."

Bewilderment flashed across Amora's face. She shook her head. Her skirts swished as she moved toward the kitchen door. "We should continue this conversation somewhere more private."

Lyse pushed Cat into a bath of steaming water that smelled like peaches. The whole brothel smelled like peaches. Cat dipped her head beneath the surface as she scrubbed the leaves and dirt out of her tangled hair. The hot water soothed her sore muscles as it washed over her, her copper hair floating around her. The steam and warm water drew the exhaustion up from her skin, into her eyes. Cat chewed her lip, glancing at the blonde girl hanging a series of silk dresses on a nearby dressing screen. She felt awkward sitting there in the silence.

"How... How long have you been... here," Cat finally asked after an excruciating minute. She never liked it when servants waited on her during these kinds of moments.

"Amora found me in the Border Lands almost ten years ago. She brought me here."

"What about your family?"

"I don't have one. Something happened to them. I don't remember."

"Oh." How terribly sad. A little girl alone in the Border Lands, not knowing what happened to her family. A question ticked into Cat's brain. Did Amora save her or was she responsible? There was definitely something about the woman that felt mysterious, dangerous.

"In answer to your next question; no, I'm not a whore. The young women who are brought here are taught many things. Most become seamstresses or cooks. A lucky few, the ones with the aptitude, even learn medicine. Only the ones who choose to take on *customers*. It's a pretense that keeps the rest of us safe and allows them to pay for their board."

"If you're not a..." Cat's voice trailed off. Somehow, she did not like the words whore and prostitute, they felt wrong to say. "What do you do?"

"I'm a pastry chef. I'm quite famous for my peach tarts, actually." Lyse swept up one last dress, hanging it over the dressing screen with the rest of Cat's options. All in different sizes that looked like they might be close enough to fit Cat. "I was once offered a job in the palace kitchens but I wanted to stay here."

Cat could not understand why a girl would choose to stay in a brothel if she could have another sort of income and home.

"This isn't the kind of place you think it is."

The door to the room opened an inch, silencing Lyse.

The beautiful young Madam slid into the room. Cat's eyebrows scrunched. The woman in front of her could not be old enough to warrant the way Lyse spoke of her. She would have had to be practically a child herself when she rescued Lyse in the Border Lands.

"You may return to the common room, Lyse. I would like to speak to our guest."

"Of course." Lyse smoothed the creases in her silk skirts. "May I go to the kitchens and use some of the peaches and fresh cream?"

Amora looked sad. She placed a tender hand on Lyse's cheek. She sighed. "As much as you need. Now, go on." The door closed. "Poor thing. She has been in love with your companion for as long as I have known him, and I am afraid he will always be blind to it, especially now that his affections are elsewhere."

Cat slid deeper into the foaming bubbles, hiding herself from the mystic feeling woman. Light footsteps padded around the large tub to a wardrobe painted with fanciful scenes, the same that was painted on the main doors. Amora removed a thick cotton towel from the shelves.

"Thomas tells me you are a princess. I am not certain I believe him. Shall we see if we can make you look like one?"

"He told you I was..."

"You will find that it is hard to keep secrets from me." The woman held up the towel for Cat. "You may tell me your story if you like. I have heard many stories, but I never tire of them."

The towel was warm, as if it had been hanging beside a fire, and was as a large blanket. Cat wrapped it around her shoulders. It hung down to her knees. She dried herself and put on a thick robe. Amora pushed Cat into the velvet cushioned chair, plucking up a comb.

A different room, a different lady, but this part was always the same and Cat dreaded it. People were always trying to twist Cat's fine hair into elegant styles, ripping and pulling at the snarls it collected. This would be excruciating.

With one long smooth swipe, Amora slid the comb through Cat's hair, gently removing a line of snarls. Amora had quick, clever hands. The snarls vanished in a matter of minutes. She cooed over the softness and the bright color of Cat's hair, and other frivolous things.

Cat set her jaw, unwilling to say anything about her quest. She wanted to. Something about the eternal-feeling woman made Cat want to tell her all of her secrets. It almost made her less angry with Thomas for bringing her here. She supposed Thomas had to tell Amora something about Cat, to explain why she had to hide.

When Amora was done combing her hair, Cat reached up to tie it into a loose braid.

Amora smiled before pulling Cat's hands away from her hair. "Oh, no my dear. The way you wear your hair suits you, but it will make you far too recognizable. The idea is to hide in plain sight." Amora's fingers worked to untangle Cat's braid, pulling her long hair down to drape over one shoulder, and pinning it back to expose her neck.

Cat clenched her jaw, keeping her mouth shut. She hated having her hair and makeup done; it always felt like people were trying to cover up who she was. Though she supposed that was the nature of hiding. Just as she suspected, Amora then turned Cat's face toward her, swiping a series of brushes over Cat's eyelids and lip. She painted a mask of makeup over her features, making her up like a doll. But, when Cat caught a glimpse of herself in the mirror, before Amora shoved her behind the dressing screen, she found herself staring back... or a version of herself. Her freckles were not covered up like they usually were and the golden eye makeup made her green eyes snap. It was a sultry effect that she never would have been allowed to wear at court, with her hair mostly unbound and yet still exposing her neck and shoulders in a provocative way.

Dressing was difficult. The gowns were made of such thin material that Cat thought they might crumble in her rough hands and her muscles were so sore she could hardly maneuver herself into the wispy silk.

Finally, Cat stepped out from behind the screen, letting Amora turn her to face the mirror in the corner.

"There," she cooed, "now you look like you belong."

Cat gasped. It was hard to believe that this woman was really her. Her hair was a shade brighter, bleached by the sun, and the dress clung provocatively to her curves, plunging deeper than anything her father would have allowed her to wear. She did not feel quite like herself. She did not feel like a princess either.

"I dare say, not even Thomas will recognize you."

Hopefully no one else would either.

So, this was the famous Peach Tree Inn? Aiden lifted his tankard to his lips, weaving his way through the crowd. The room was hot and smelled of peaches. A lute player plucked out a quiet tune in the corner. Across the room several girls were dancing.

Aiden turned back toward the entrance, away from the crowd of beautiful young women, back toward the barn. He would rather spend his evening alone with his nightmares of Olivia than in this place filled with empty pleasures. He bumped into a girl carrying an overbalanced serving tray. A pink ale sloshed over the sides.

"Woah!" He reached out to steady the tray. "Careful there."

"Oh... thank you."

That voice! It was painfully familiar. So familiar it ached. Throbbed like a distant echo in Aiden's ears. He looked up at the girl with the tray. She had round lavender eyes and golden hair framing her round features. A perfect ghost. A distant memory that stood before him. She was the exact picture of Olivia on the day they met.

Impossible.

This had to be a nightmare.

An illusion like every other one that came to him when the nights grew dark.

Aiden blinked. Clearing the image of his wife away.

The girl remained the same. Long blonde hair and lavender eyes. He realized, as she brushed past him, that she was not quite like Olivia. The girl was too tall, her willowy frame was a little too delicate. Olivia had never been delicate. She had hard muscles from years of tending their farm. Perhaps, Aiden thought as he watched the girl walk away, if Olivia had lived a different life... it did not matter, she was an illusion. A fading memory.

"Lyse!" A voice rang out like a bell across the common room and the girl turned, smiling.

Aiden felt his jaw drop as he watched her call back to the other girl, chatting about some gossip that Aiden could not hear. He was both right and wrong. The girl was not Olivia, but he had known her once, when they were both different people with different lives.

It could not be possible. His daughter, Lyse, died when Bastian came to steal his wife's magic and burned their farm to the ground.

Hadn't she?

The room was suddenly too warm. Aiden's throat was dry, shattering his voice until he could not speak. Aiden spun toward the door again, finding a young woman with ash colored hair leaning against the podium, scraping the tip of a feather quill against the ledge, her cheek resting on her palm.

"Excuse me, madam..."

"Sorcha," the girl droned back. She did not bother to look up at him, swirling the ink over the blank corner of the page. "My name is Sorcha."

"Sorcha. What can you tell me about that girl?" He gestured back toward the young blonde as she passed out tankards of sweet ale.

Slowly, Sorcha rolled her gaze away from the page, following his outstretched hand. "Lyse? She's not available. She's only here to work in the kitchens." Sorcha returned her focus to the spirals she was drawing on the ledger.

"No," Aiden shook his head, a wave of relief sweeping through him, cooling the heat in his skin. "Where did she come from? How long has she been here?"

A heavy sigh dropped from the woman's lips. She set her quill on the podium with a loud thunk. "I don't know. Amora found her in the Border Lands. She's been here for year. Since she was a little girl."

"In the Border Lands? Are you certain?"

"I think so. She was orphaned in some sort of fire."

Cold swept through Aiden. He gripped the edge of the podium, swaying on the spot.

"Is there something you actually wanted? I'm very busy."

"No, thank you." Aiden turned back to the door stumbling into the night air. He needed to get out. He needed to think.

The common room was very much the way Cat imagined any inn's to be, only louder. She had never actually been in one before. She pulled herself deeper into the shadowy corner she had half-hidden herself in, folding her arms over her airy gown. No, gown was too formal a word. The dress was more a series of sheer silk petticoats. The material felt flimsy. Cat felt too exposed, every movement revealing more skin. How did the other women manage to move with so much comfort and ease? They looked like leaves dancing on the wind.

Cat chewed her lip, silencing her complaining thoughts. Amora was taking a huge risk hiding her. The least Cat could do was act grateful.

The room was filling up with strangers, men jockeying for the attention of the prettiest girls. For once, Cat was relieved that she was not generally considered beautiful. There was a chance she might not be noticed. A chance that she would not need to use the words Amora made her repeat over and over before coming down to the common room; *I have been previously engaged.* She tested the weight of the verbal shield.

The stink of wine slapped Cat across the face. A man's arm slid around Cat's waist. A second plucked up a lock of her loose hair, painting it across her cheek. The owner of the arm was a medium-sized man with black hair and the sort of smile that told Cat he usually got what he wanted.

She started to slide away.

The man's grip on her waist tightened. "You're a new peach. Where did Amora pick you from?"

"I'm... I'm not..." Cat's voice was soft, getting caught hallway through her throat. "I mean... I'm sorry, I'm pre... I'm previously engaged."

"Poor fool does not seem to be here." He pulled her closer into him.

A hand, one that Cat had come to recognize as easily as her own, clapped the man on the shoulder, wrenching him away from her. "Be careful who you call a fool," Thomas growled. "This one is spoken for."

The dark haired man looked from Cat to Thomas, eyes wide. "Of course, begging your pardons, *sir*."

Cat masked her relief the same way she had tried to mask her fear. A wisp of loose hair fell across her forehead.

Thomas rested a hand against Cat's waist, dragging her to the far side of the room, where the musicians were plucking out a tune. Tingles followed his hand at the small of her back. He pressed into it as he guided her into the shadow of the staircase.

"Thank you," she found herself whispering.

"You look pretty." Thomas leaned close to Cat's ear. Her thanks going unanswered. Had he not heard her? Or was Thomas being false to his nature and choosing not to gloat?

Well, if he missed her saying thank you, that was his problem.

"Right," Cat scoffed. "Now that my face is washed, and I'm drenched in silk and perfume."

"No... well, yes, but..." He released his grip, turning to face her, folding his arms over his chest. He would be menacing if it were not for the broad smile that lit his face. "You are the most infuriating woman I have ever met. I am trying to compliment you. You look pretty now, with your face washed and covered in silk. You are always beautiful. "

Cat could not look at him. Her gaze dropped to her shuffling feet. He was not the first man to call her beautiful, for one reason or another. He was the first one she believed. Thomas brushed aside the stray lock of hair, fingers lingering on her cheek, tilting her face up to meet his gaze. Thomas took in a deep breath, as if preparing to speak. Preparing for something. Cat reminded herself of all the things he obviously was; a scoundrel who frequented brothels, a rogue knight, a charmer who was *not* her betrothed. She could not reconcile the man before her with those thoughts. She could not pull herself away.

Thomas' fingers slid from her cheek to the back of her neck, tangling in her hair. "Cat, I..."

A heavily scented blonde pushed between them, dragging a man by the hand. "Clear a path!"

Whatever spell they were under broke. Thomas gripped Cat's hand, pulling her into his lap in a large plush chair. Her protesting was silenced with a quick word. "This is the best way to keep the other men away from you. Remember, you're playing a part."

It is just a game. Cat wrapped her arms around the knight's long neck, forcing a smile.

Thomas smiled as well, his eyes focused on the world around them, scanning every face that appeared in the entryway.

A shiver made Cat pull closer to the warmth of Thomas' chest. He was freshly bathed as well; his brown curls were clean and brushed back, and his usual leather riding jacket had been traded for a clean, soft, cotton shirt. He started singing under his breath, thumb tracking across Cat's bare arm. It was the same tune he sang so many times before as they traveled together. Cat had grown used to his off-key voice.

"What is that song?" She could never hear all the words. It was not one of the bawdy tunes full of jokes and twisted phrases designed to make Cat laugh.

"Just an old lullaby. It's a fairy story from Brotid. The sun loved the moon, but he had no place among the stars. Instead, he traced a path through the sky for her to follow, so he could always lend her his light."

The story was familiar, Cat could not say why. It was comforting, hearing him sing. Cat listened to the verse while watching the crowd flit through the room.

Unconscious of her movements, Cat lifted a hand to the back of Thomas' neck, brushing her fingers through his curls. She wrapped one curl around her finger then let go only to gather it up again a moment later. His hair was silky soft. His low singing paused for a moment. Realizing what she had been doing, Cat dropped her hand to her side. "Sorry."

"I didn't mind." Thomas slipped his fingers against hers. Lifting her hand lightly in his, he pulled her close to him, but not so forcefully that she could not stop him. She let him lift her hand, brushing the pad of his thumb over her rough palm, draping it over his shoulder. Cat could feel the warmth of his skin through his shirt. The feeling sent a fresh wave of shivers across her skin.

Only a game, Cat reminded herself. This was a game. A way to avoid suspicion. The thought left a sick feeling in her stomach. Cat wished she was somewhere else; sitting like this, with her legs draped over Thomas, her body pressed into his chest, was confusing her.

This time Lyse rescued her, approaching on silent, slippered feet.

"Your... I mean, Sir Thomas. I brought you this." She placed a cream tart on the table beside them, turning a magnificent shade of pink. Cat felt a surge of pity, remembering Amora telling her the younger girl had been in love with Thomas for years, and here Cat was sprawled across his lap, her own confused feelings twisting in her stomach.

The tart was a little round thing with puffy pastry and five peach slices placed in a perfect circle on top. The luscious scent would put Lydia and her bakery in Royal City to shame. Cat's mouth watered.

"I remembered how much you enjoyed my peach tarts. I thought perhaps you would like to try my latest recipe."

Thomas' smile made Lyse turn an even brighter red. The shy girl in front of Cat did not seem at all like the confident and outspoken woman Cat met earlier. This seemed more likely to be the real Lyse, dressed in a simple dress with flour on her apron.

"Lovely little Lyse, you should be the finest pastry chef in the three kingdoms."

"It's really no talent of mine. Without the peaches Amora grows to trick you, I would seem like a very poor baker."

The music changed to a reel Cat was familiar with. Lyse glanced over her shoulder at the dance floor, replacing her blush with a tired smile. She took Cat's hand, pulling her to her feet. "Come dance with me, Cat." Several women were already twirling across the open dance floor.

"What? No, I can't. I don't know the steps."

"It will be fine. Take off your shoes and dance with me. It will be such fun!"

With every tug at her arm, Cat moved farther from the safety of Thomas' arms.

"Don't worry." He let her go, hands sliding away from Cat's waist. "I'll be right here."

There had been no shoes in the whole brothel that would fit Cat's large feet. She still wore her riding boots but slid them off at Lyse's urging. Bare-footed, Cat followed Lyse into the thick of dancers, reeling with the other girls in a wild chain. They all twirled; smiling, clasping hands, and leaping about. Cat had never felt like a great dancer, except when she was holding a sword. This dance was different somehow. Meant for the pure joy of it. Everyone moved so quickly and there was no pattern to the steps.

When the music slowed, Cat and the other girls were breathless and laughing. Several flopped to the floor, fanning themselves.

Cat turned, searching for Thomas or Aiden.

The room was starting to empty. It still felt crowded.

Thomas' bright blue eyes struck Cat. She hated the way it made her melt, her skin flushing. It was as if he saw every inch of her in one appraising glance. A broad smile lit his face. Thomas was still sitting in the chair, leaning forward to watch her, his index finger resting against his lip. Had he watched her the whole time she danced with Lyse? Cat looked away. No one ever looked at her the way he did. His gaze felt heavy. Safe.

"He is in love with you." Lyse fiddled with her wavy hair. "I have never seen him smile the way he does when he is looking at you."

Cat shook her head. Lyse was still very young. When Cat was her age, she believed she saw love in many places that it never was, including in Thomas' eyes. "I assure you; he is nothing more than a friend."

Lyse squeezed Cat's hand, hard. "I have known Thomas nearly as long as I can remember. And I have never seen him look at anyone the way he looks at you. That is reserved only for you."

Whether or not that was true and what Lyse believed did not matter. Eventually, Cat would have to return home. A prince was waiting for her. That was her reality. Thomas, this journey, it was all a fantasy. One she could not live in. What Thomas might feel for her and what she might feel for him did not matter.

"Well, I do not love him."

"If you say so." Lyse left Cat standing alone at the center of the room.

Thomas met Cat in four strides, placing his hands on her hips. The notes of a new dance plunked out on the lute. Cat's heart pounded. Was Lyse right?

The red door swung open, and Cat's breath caught. Fingers tightening into fists around the soft fabric of Thomas' shirt. She pulled him into the shadows under the stairs. Every other thought crowded out of her mind by cold fear. "Oh no! No! No! No!"

"What is it?" Thomas ducked his head, searching the common room. "The Volentian knights? Sir Guy?"

"No," she hissed back. "The man who just walked in. I... I *know* him." Worse, he knew her. "He'll recognize me. He'll..."

"Arik? I doubt he'll be looking for you, he's a Reinsaffiran."

Lord Arik was not just a Reinsaffiran. He was the ambassador to

Volentia. He knew Cat. And he was cousin to the prince she had left behind. It would be his duty to both kingdoms to drag her back to the palace. Away from Thomas. Away from this one chance at freedom. Or worse, he could tell the world where he found her.

"You're shaking."

Cat looked up at Thomas. He wrapped his long fingers around her shoulders. She could not still the tremble vibrating from her core. "He cannot find me here. I'll be ruined."

"He won't. Trust me." In one quick movement Thomas swept Cat over his shoulder, laughing loudly.

"What are you doing?"

"Just trust me." He bolted up the steps.

Two small lamps hung above the lily-white bed, lighting the meticulously kept room. Orange light cast long shadows against the gossamer bed curtains. It had been years since Thomas first woke up in that bed, unaware of where he was. Amora had found him, an injured, foolish young man. She brought him here and possibly saved his life. From that day on, Amora had been his safety net. His advisor. She taught and protected him, and now she would protect Cat too.

He set Cat on her feet, turning to bolt the door.

"You can't manhandle me like that!" Cat spun around, her fists clenched and eyes blazing. She was still flushed from dancing. Still beautiful. He wanted to make her smile again the way she had in the common room. He wanted to be certain nothing bad ever happened to her. "I'm not some whore for you to…"

"My mistake." The joke rolled easily off his tongue. He leaned against the door, keeping a safe distance between himself and the princess. Better to avoid temptation. "You can see how I might get confused; all things considered." He gestured to the loose bundle of silk she wore. It felt like too much of a stretch to call the thin layers of silk a dress. Her long, exposed arms and shoulders and loose hair left dizzying thoughts in his head. He knew they should not be alone like this. Though that was only a distant vague thought.

Cat's lips twitched, the barest hint of a smile. Then her fingers tightened into fists again, stubborn anger winning out over the amusement.

"Don't worry, *Princess*, it's hard to forget who you are, no matter how you are dressed. Though, if Arik saw you at all, he would think I was just a patron, and you were one of the girls."

Cat's shoulders softened. The hard set to her jaw relaxed until her lips formed a gentle pout. They were painted a pale red that reminded him of fresh strawberries. He wondered if they would taste like strawberries as well. She stood just within reach. One step forward and he could wrap his arms around her and find out.

He straightened his spine, keeping himself out of reach.

"Well, I'm not."

"I know that!" The ache in his arms to hold her grew unbearable, listening to the rustle of her silks as she looked around the dark room. They wrapped, unbidden around her waist. Before Cat could move or force out a response, he swung her around, pinning her against the locked door. His hands slid up her back to the laces holding her inside the dress. "I know you are a princess. Just like I know you are beautiful and clever and so much more than a man like me could ever deserve. Things like that are hard to forget." His gaze zeroed in on her face. Her shocked green eyes. They were so close he could see little flecks of gold within them that seemed to mirror her freckles. "And I would never want to."

He watched her eyes search his face. He could read surprise in them, but not fear. Their lips were a breath apart. He could feel her pulse racing in her skin. Did she want him? Cat did not move or push him away. Just looked up at him, waiting. Holding her felt right. She curved perfectly into him. He wanted to kiss her barely parted lips. A single perfect moment to hold onto as long as he lived.

Not yet.

Not now.

Thomas wanted her to trust him with her heart. Thomas wanted more than this moment. He wanted a lifetime of moments. No matter what it took, Thomas planned to win them.

He forced his arms to his sides, trembling with the effort. "You should probably stay in here for the rest of the evening, just to be safe. I'll... um... I'll go down to the kitchen and find some food." His blood burned. "Don't open the door for anyone. I'll be right back."

The door shut behind Thomas with a dull crushing thud. The air in the corridor was stale and cold. The colors felt muted. At least, he could breathe and think with a wall between him and Cat. Thomas ran a hand through his hair. It was not just that he wanted her more with each passing day. The closer she was to Thomas, the more of his world she took up. Her laugh was sweeter than any music and her smile was brighter than any star. Without her the world was dark and colorless. With her the rest of the world vanished.

"Please tell me that was the Volentian Princess you whisked up here a few minutes ago."

"Arik!" Thomas spun to face his friend. "What are you doing here?"

Arik leaned against the wall. His tight muscles and stiff movements betrayed the casual posture. Sir Trenton stood behind him, an imposing figure with blond hair hanging against his brawny shoulders.

"Looking for you. Please tell me that was the princess with you. You weren't in there long enough for it to be someone else."

Thomas glanced back at the door, keeping his voice low. "Yes, I have been traveling with her."

Sir Trenton held his hand out to Arik, waiting until Arik dropped a shining gold coin into his upturned palm.

"Good. Get her. We need to leave for Volentia. Now!"

The words hung in the air, ringing in Thomas' ears like a bell that could not be un-rung. He focused on the door again. Cat was just on the other side, possibly eavesdropping. Or relaxing, pleasantly unaware of anything happening outside of the low lamplight of their room. "Why?"

"She's in danger. Sir Guy is searching the village for her."

That did not make sense. Sir Guy was a Volentian knight. One of Princess Catiya's guards.

"He's a traitor. When he catches up to her, he plans to take her to King Bastian of Salene."

Bastian! The man who had killed Cat's mother. Thomas choked on the thought.

"There's more," Trenton grunted.

"Not here. Somewhere more private." Thomas interrupted, spinning on his heel, stalking down the stairs toward the kitchen.

Thomas arranged a tray of fruits and cheeses for him and Cat. He even found a loaf of warm bread, while Arik and Trenton explained what had happened. How Arik learned that Sir Guy was a spy, but the men who discovered it could not go to the king. How the palace was the only safe place for the princess. How it was up to Thomas to convince her to return... to force her back to Volentia if he had to.

"If you think I have the power to convince Cat to give up on anything she has decided she wants, then you know nothing about her." A thought struck him. Just a small idea. "I may be able to get her to the Reinsaffiran palace though." It was much closer and better guarded. "If a group of Reinsaffiran knights caught us before Sir Guy..."

"That will not work." A heavy sigh filled the room. Arik glanced at Trenton, as if the other man could explain better than he could. He twisted the ring around his finger. Trenton did not move, his jaw and muscles were tight, as if he were made of stone. "Princess Catiya cannot go to Reinsaffira, because..." Arik gave the ring another twist. "Because there is no longer an alliance between Volentia and Reinsaffira. Which mean she is no longer your fiancé."

The words soaked up all of the air in the room, leaving nothing for Thomas to breathe. His lungs burned from the lack of oxygen. "Why?"

"A rumor reached your father that Princess Catiya is a magix, and that her mother was one as well. She would not be safe anywhere in Reinsaffira."

Thomas' jaw clenched in anger. It was impossible for anyone at the Volentian court to know about Cat's magic. She did not even know until her fight with Aiden.

Aiden! Was he a traitor? Was he how Sir Guy kept finding them? He *had* vanished moments after they arrived at the Peach Tree.

"Where did this rumor come from?"

"A man named Carswell," Trenton grunted.

"An irritating man."

"He claimed she told him herself and that was why she ran away."

Fire and anger swelled in Thomas. His fists tightened, keeping him from lashing out. That was an impossibility.

"You need to send her back to Volentia." So sensible, especially coming from Arik. It was jarring to see the man who spent his whole life chasing after every shiny thing that caught his eye with so much responsibility weighing down his shoulders. "Or send a message to Volentia and have Prince Ryder pick her up. The sooner the better. If Sir Guy finds you with her, he'll kill you. And if our knights find her with you..."

"No." Thomas took as firm a tone as he could. "I swore I would protect her, and I intend to.

Arik stammered a moment. "Thomas... you'll be risking your life for..."

"A woman who will never be mine? That does not matter. I am staying with her."

"I know how you feel about her, but even you have to accept that this is not possible. Sending her home is protecting her. No one would see it as a dishonor if you..."

"I would." Trenton muttered, taking a bite from a peach. Juice dribbling through his beard. "A true king keeps his word."

Defeated, Arik pushed himself away from the large kitchen table. Of all the people in the world, Thomas thought Arik would understand why he could not leave Cat. He already left her once. "I think this is foolish but I can give you a chance. I'll keep Guy away from here as long as I can."

Thomas took in a deep breath. He stood before the colorful door at the end of the long hall, unable to reach for the handle and step inside.

Everything had changed. Ten minutes ago, Thomas was engaged to the princess on the other side of the door, and his greatest concern was how to tell her who he was and how to keep her out of the Volentian guards' reach until he was certain she loved him. Now... Now she was in danger, real danger with real evils, and worst of all, she was no longer his.

No! He was not going to let anyone hurt her and he was not going to abandon her. Thomas gripped the door handle hard enough that the carved decorations left indents on his fingers and palm. He was going to marry Cat, no matter what it took.

The door pushed open.

He stepped inside.

A fire iron swung, rattling against the door. Thomas ducked when it swung again. He reached out as quickly as he could, fingers wrapping around the metal. Cat pulled at it then looked up, her eyes rounding. The iron slipped from her hands.

"Thomas? You... You were gone for so long. I was afraid..."

"I can see that. Did you plan on starting a war by cracking open a Reinsaffiran ambassador's skull?" He turned the fire iron in his fingers. He had dropped the tray, fruit and cheese littering the floor. The loaf of bread somehow still rested on the tray. Thomas set the iron aside, kneeling to gather up the spilled dinner. "You might have succeeded too. You certainly did a number on our meal."

"It was better than nothing."

Time caught up with him. "Did you say you were afraid? As in, you were worried about me?" An amused smile quirked his mouth.

"I was afraid you weren't coming back."

"So, you missed me? How interesting."

She took the same stubborn posture Thomas had grown used to seeing, clicking her tongue. "I was afraid you had been caught and that Lord Arik had found me. That's all."

Thomas laid the gathered food out on the tray. A less than pretty arrangement. Smiling to himself. She had been worried about him. The light thrill of joy was short-lived. "Cat, I have to tell you something."

At the exact same moment, Cat started to speak. Her words tumbled out in a rush. "I think I owe you an apology." She dropped onto the chest at the foot of the bed, tucking her hands into the folds of her dress.

"What?"

"I think I may have been misjudging you and... well... I'm sorry. H-how did you," she shook her head, steeling herself against the stutter her words tripped over whenever she became nervous. "How did you become so familiar with this place and Madam Amora?"

Thomas rose, setting the plate on the tidy desk and taking the wooden stool Cat had left for him. "Amora has a habit of collecting lost things and people. She found me when I was lost. We've been friends ever since."

"You were lost?" Lines formed on her forehead as her brows drew together in a question.

"Once, when I ran away from my own betrothal." He watched Cat out of the corner of his eye for her reaction. The change was subtle. Her eyes widened for a second then narrowed too much. She smoothed a wrinkle on her skirt before leaning forward to take a hunk of cheese and bread from the plate. Cat's movements were too stiff, too deliberate.

"You were betrothed?"

"An arranged marriage, to a girl who deserved much better than me. I couldn't force her to marry me, so I left. Unfortunately, my horse threw me and, somehow, I ended up here."

"So, you are a gentleman," she whispered. "And is that why you did not drag me back to the palace, that first morning? You couldn't force me to marry a prince I did not love?"

Even knowing that she believed she was speaking about someone else, it stung to hear her say she did not love him. This would all be so much simpler if he had just dragged her back to Volentia that first day. "That is part of it. It is also easier to rescue you without having to commute. You seem to attract danger."

A rare, genuine smile lit her face. One just for him. It was a small gift that he treasured. "Ah yes, danger and I always find each other. Rumor has it we planned to wed at the end of the year."

"At last, the truth."

Her smile brightened. An easy silence stretched out between them. Thomas selected a grape from the plate, rolling it between his fingers before popping it in his mouth.

"I know very little about you. Are you from a great family, in Reinsaffira?"

"In a way." Now would be the perfect moment to tell her. It would be so easy. The words would not form. The veiled lie came out instead. "Most would consider me fortunate in my birth."

"You wouldn't?"

Thomas let out a sigh. Cat knew him better than she thought. "For many of the same reasons you would not always consider yourself fortunate. Some expectations are hard to live up to."

Her smile faded. That heavy sadness she carried filled Cat's eyes. The explanation of who he was faded from his thoughts. He would give anything to trade her sadness for another smile. What made her so sad? Did she love him and still believe she would have to return to marry someone else? Hope flickered like a candle in his chest. Warm and comforting. Telling her who he was could bring her smile back... but only for a moment. Telling her who he was would lead to warning her about the danger. Then she would go home and leave him forever.

"I'm tired," Cat stood, brushing her hands down her long skirt. There was only one bed in the room. She chewed her lip, glancing at the large, invitingly soft, feather mattress covered with a thick down comforter.

There was easily enough room for two in the bed, but Thomas knew she would never suggest it.

"The bed belongs to you, Princess." Thomas picked up his bag, removing his bed roll and laying it out in front of the locked door. "I will sleep on the floor."

"A true gentleman."

"Not this time. Consider it a debt I intend on collecting later." Thomas settled on the floor.

The sound of silk curtains pulling shut drew his eyes upward. The princess' form was softened, not quite hidden, by the flowing curtains. It was a simple trick caused by the lamps hanging above the bed. Her back was to him, her long limbs pulling at the laces of her dress. He lowered his eyes, heat rising in his neck and cheeks. There was a splintered floor board that needed to be repaired at the edge of the door jam. He glanced back to her, pulling on a simple shift and reaching up to dim the lamps. The ache for her grew in the pit of his stomach.

Emma could not sleep. Nightmares that faded away the instant her eyes fluttered open plagued her. She was miserable, helpless, and useless. The world was spiraling into chaos away from her tenuous grasp. She could not just lay there with anxiety clamping down on her ribs. Emma had to get up. She had to move.

The blankets fell to the ground. Emma dug her hands into the mattress, forcing herself to sit up. The room was cold. The marble floor was like ice, freezing her toes. A deep, velvet darkness blanketed the room, obscuring everything. It did not matter, she knew the space, and she had to move.

Emma shrugged on a robe, following her feet to the door.

The corridor was empty and silent. At least the air felt freer. Her lungs prickled with every breath of cool air. Each breath came a little easier as she moved farther from the nightmares that woke her.

"Has there been any word on Lord Carswell?"

Emma spun toward the harsh whisper. Two guards stood on the far side of the door to the royal wing.

The vice tightened around her ribs.

"Nothing. Perhaps if you wrote to Fara. She may know something of his plans."

"She has not seen him in five years, and even then, she knew very little of his plans."

Emma backed away from the door, ducking into a shadowy alcove. Her breath came in short spurts. The figures were moving. Emma's shoulders bumped into the wall as she pressed into the darkness, away from the voices of the strangers.

Click.

There was a quiet whisper of wind that rustled her long hair. A musty stale scent followed it. Emma spun around, her fingers running along the seam of the panel. A round stamp marked the entrance of a secret passage. Emma thought she knew every passage in the palace. There should not be one here. Footsteps echoed down the corridor. A lump formed in her throat. Emma did not think; she pushed the panel open and ducked inside, letting the door slide back into place.

Darkness enveloped her.

The tunnel was musty and damp. A chill swept over her skin. No one had been in this space in years. Emma could feel it deep in her core.

She stepped forward, her toe nudging something solid. A box containing a half-burnt candle and a series of matches. She struck one, filling the passage with the smell of sulfur. Emma was standing at the top of a spiraling staircase. The tug of adventure pulled her forward, down into the depths of the castle.

The staircase ended in a stone room lined with shelves. Emma's fingers danced across the spines of the books. She chose one at random, sliding it off the shelf, flipping it open. Ancient Salenian scrawled across the page.

"What is this place?"

Hay smelled. It was always described as sweet. All Aiden could smell was the musk of moisture and wood rot.

He lifted the bottle in his hands to his lips, drinking down the last of the bitter ale. Drowning his failures. For years he had left his daughter here, alone. He should have searched for her. Should have somehow known she was alive. Aiden tilted the bottle to his mouth one last time. A few drops dribbled over the edge. Empty. He still felt the well of shame inside of him.

"Olivia!" He threw the bottle. It flew through the air, shattering against the barn wall. "Where are you? Why didn't you ever tell me?"

Silence echoed back.

Olivia did not appear. Nor did the horrible image of the crone she had become.

Aiden rested his head against the bale of hay. Waiting, the cold creeping over the barn floor as the night air froze. His hand dipped into his pocket, finding the small lump of wood he carried with him. A trinket that barely filled his palm. A toy he once carved for his daughter, a long time ago. The toy swan's long neck was worn smooth. Its large feet, perfect for floating, balanced on his palm. For all the years that he carried the trinket, he had never considered the person it belonged to might be missing it.

"Why are you here?"

Aiden looked up expecting to see his wife. Wrong again. Just like he was wrong about everything.

The woman with mousy brown hair and blue eyes, as ancient as the sea, stood in the doorway. A rough spun shawl was draped over her shoulders, thin protection against the chill in the air.

"Isn't it obvious? I'm getting drunk. Or I was." He waved a hand at the shattered glass. "That's what you do when you realize you have failed everyone in your life."

The woman hardened her stance. "Why are you traveling with the princess? If I am not mistaken, you are from the Border Lands, which means you are not one of her guards. Why would a Salenian choose to follow a lost princess through the countryside?"

"Until a few hours ago, I planned to use her powers to save my wife. She's a light magix, you know. *The* light magix." His words slurred together. Aiden shook his head, had he just said all of that out loud? Was it a secret? He could not quite remember.

The woman's eyes narrowed. "The daughter of the prophecy? Are you certain?"

"He is." The grate of Olivia's voice was unmistakable. No, not Olivia, the monster Olivia had become. Or, something in between the two creatures. He could not see her. "Just as certain as he is that our daughter is alive. Which is why he is going to kill the princess and destroy the key to freeing The Darkness. Before my men find her, and it's too late."

Something startled Cat awake. Her eyes flew open, only to find Thomas, leaning over her, his fingers pressed to her mouth to stifle her shout. She glared at him with hard, questioning eyes. Thomas lifted a finger to his lips in a shushing motion. He pulled the curtains closed, lighting the lamps before kneeling on the mattress beside her.

Thomas motioned to the door and Cat's ears perked at the sound of raised voices on the far side of it.

"As I told you before, *Sir*," Amora's stern voice was solid as oak. "This is a legitimate and *legal* establishment. You have no right to search it and I will not allow you to disturb my customers."

"And I will not let you interfere with my search for the Volentian princess," Sir Guy spat back at her. "I will tear this business down in search of her, if I have to. Now, unlock this door!"

"You think I would not know if a princess was hiding in my establishment?"

"I think you would know. And I think you are hiding her. Now, unlock this door before I break it down."

Her eyes widened with fear. "We have to get out of here. Where do we go? What do we do?"

"We hide."

How could Thomas be so calm? He was almost smiling, tucking a lock of Cat's hair behind her ear. Her gaze cast around the room. It was small and tidy and lacking in any place to hide. A wardrobe stood in one corner with an ancient looking mirror beside it, but Guy would search there. There was no way they could both fit under the bed. Where else was there?

"Where?"

"Right here."

Thomas rested a hand on Cat's cheek, the other firm on her lower back. He was so close to her that Cat could feel the heat of his skin. Slowly, Cat understood what he meant. There was no place to hide which meant... Cat recoiled, pulling away. "I can't. We can't. I'll be ruined!"

"I'm not going to let that happen. I promise." He guided her back against the pillows so she lay beneath him. Cat could feel the heat of his skin through his shirt. "Do you trust me, Cat?"

Her eyes flew to his mouth. To his lips hovering just inches from hers, and then back to his eyes. There was hesitation in them and something else Cat could not recognize. Even a blind woman could read the depths of those clear blue pools, but Cat could not. She bit her lip, heart pounding. She thought she trusted him. She wanted to trust him.

A heavy pounding on the door and the sound of a lock turning made the decision for her.

"Yes."

Thomas' lips crashed into hers, swallowing the word. Kissing her. It was a nice kiss, soft at first but filled with passion, different than any other kiss she had received. Cat had been kissed before. There were men who courted her; gentlemen who traveled miles to kiss her hand and whisper sweet lies, every one of them leaving her with nothing but chapped knuckles. This kiss was burning. Thomas' hands slid over her body, wrapping around her waist, pulling her into him. She found herself arching her back, trying to draw closer to him. Lifting her chin to let his lips travel to her throat. His tongue darted over her skin, tracing the patterns within her freckles.

"This was a mistake," he murmured against her skin. "You have no idea how much I want you. How long I have been thinking about you." His hand slid to her thigh. Rough fingertips making her shiver as he ghosted them across her skin, finding the hem of her nightgown. His kisses trailed up cheek again, drawing her earlobe between his teeth.

Cat gasped.

Was this what it felt like to be desired? Cat did not know. The men who courted her only ever wanted Cat's title, not her. No one had ever wanted her.

Her heart pounded, hands sliding down the firm muscles of his chest. She knew she wanted him. Wanted to feel his weight press down on her. Wanted to be closer, to feel his skin against hers.

As if reading her mind, Thomas slid his hand beneath her nightgown, the only barrier between them slowly vanishing. Pressing his palm to her stomach. Feeling her. His skin was warm against hers. Could he feel her racing heart? Dragging the fabric up as he kissed her, hands inching closer and closer to her breast. Wanting to feel her as much as she wanted to feel him. His desire tangling up with her own.

Something snapped tight like an elastic band inside of Cat. He wanted her, but Cat was engaged to a prince. What she was feeling was impossible. A lie. Someday she had to return to Volentia and marry a prince, secure the alliance with Reinsaffira.

The truth of the situation brought her back to the moment, enough that she could force her eyes to the door.

Thomas let his kiss wander to her collarbone. "You are perfect. I wish I deserved you. I have something I need to tell you."

Through a gap in the bed curtains, Cat could see the door hanging open and the flickering light from the hall. The doorway and the room were empty, except for her and Thomas.

"I... I th-think they're gone."

"For several minutes now." He caressed her cheek, tugging Cat's attention back to him so he could recapture her lips. He was not stopping or pulling away.

Cat fell into the kiss, wanting to lose herself in the moment again, but... "Stop! Thomas, please stop." Cat pushed her hands into Thomas' chest, pushing him away.

He pulled back, looking at her with a mix of lust and confusion. Cat could read those thoughts in his eyes.

"I can't do this! I'm engaged. I'm meant to marry the prince of Reinsffira." Cat forced herself out of the bed, as far from Thomas as she could get. Stalking over to the door and pushing it closes. The lock clicked into place. She did not turn back to face him. Her blood was too hot. She could not look at him. "We cannot do this.'"

She could hear his footsteps approaching her. She shivered the second his fingers brushed over her arm. "Cat," he sighed, "there is something I have to tell you..."

"Please don't. I don't think I can say no a second time. I don't... I don't want to be just some girl you seduced."

"You could never be."

"Don't lie to me." Cat rolled her eyes. "I know your type. And I know my obligations. I'm a princess and someday I am going to go back to Volentia and..." her voice felt like it was cracking under the strain of what she was about to say. "And I am going to marry the prince, if he is still waiting for me."

"He will be."

She felt suddenly cold. Cat crossed her arms over herself to stave off the chill in the room. How had it become so suddenly cold? She finally forced her eyes to meet his again.

Thomas was frowning. That thing she could not read had returned to his eyes. "I know the prince and he would wait for you until the end of time." He let out a heavy sigh. "If that is what you want, I will take you back to Volentia tomorrow. Or anywhere else you want to go."

Thomas couldn't breathe. He needed air. He needed to be away from Cat and the temptation to kiss her again.

He waited until Cat returned to the bed, curling up with her back to him, though he was certain she was not asleep, before stepping out the door. It thudded closed behind him. He let his head rest against the painted wood.

The Peach Tree was quiet and ice cold. Somewhere down in the common room, he could hear Sir Guy continuing his search. But Cat was safe. Guy would not search a room he already believed was a dead end. He knew that much.

The only other thing Thomas knew was that he was an idiot. He should have told Cat who he was the moment he met her. There were thousands of times he could have told her. Should have told her. Now, his own carelessness would cost him the girl of his dreams.

He took in a deep breath.

Thomas was not sure how long he leaned against the bedroom door, but the lamps were dim when he stepped back in, locking the door behind him. The curtains were parted, just enough to show Cat's red hair. She was asleep. Thomas swept the curtain aside, kneeling in front of the bed. Cat stirred but did not wake.

"Cat." He sighed, raking his fingers through his hair. "I am the Crown Prince of Reinsaffira." He touched a lock of her hair and leaned in to kiss her cheek. "And you will never be just some girl to me."

The ghostly blue light the handheld mirror cast, blinded Sir Guy. Anyone could sneak up on him in the darkness and heavy rain; he would never see them coming. Still, he stared into the light, waiting for something... someone to appear in the glass.

Suddenly, she was there. A woman with dark hair and paper-thin skin appeared on the glass' surface. The crone; a shriveled, aged sorceress with a single lock of golden hair tucked behind one ear.

"Your constant failures are growing increasingly difficult to abide." Her voice was low and sharp like gravel. More like a bullfrog than a woman.

"Perhaps you should provide me with better information. The girl was not in the brothel. I searched every inch of it."

"You stared the girl in the face and were too blind to see her. The failure is yours. She hides most cleverly, even now, in the arms of a prince. You have failed to separate them as well."

Sir Guy stood. Rage coursing through his veins. It burned his skin. "I'll get her. I will drag her out and kill the prince before her eyes."

"No. I will collect the princess myself. Go to the Border Lands and await my instructions."

The light faded, leaving Guy blinking away the dark spots hovering in his eyes. Return to the Border Lands? The girl was there for the taking and he was to concede the hunt? Guy was growing tired of the crone's commands.

A persistent knocking woke Thomas from his light slumber. Pale light seeped in through the window, barely dawn. He leaned against the locked door; a thin blanket draped over his shoulders. It was no surprise he felt stiff and uncomfortable. His neck ached from sleeping in the uncomfortable position.

The knocking grew louder and more urgent. Worried the sound might wake Cat, Thomas stood, pulling the door open an inch.

"Finally! Thomas," Amora shoved the door open, dropping a pile of clean folded clothing into his arms. A simple green dress was at the top of the pile. "Get dressed. We need to speak."

"Right now?"

"I would have preferred to speak last night, but you seemed occupied. Get dressed." She pushed the door closed.

Thomas set the dress and a pair of wool breaches that were much too small for him on the night stand by the bed. Cat still slept soundly, curled in a tight ball. Tangled red locks of hair clung to the girl's cheeks. He brushed them back, exposing her freckled skin. Thomas smiled, watching her stir, tightening her grip on the pillow beneath her. "It doesn't matter what my father says. I am going to marry you."

Thomas sighed. He had to tell her today.

He pulled on a fresh tunic and stepped out the door, where Amora waited. Before he could speak, she grabbed him by the arm, dragging him down the hall. "That girl is in danger." She balked at the top of the stairs, shoving Thomas back into the shadows.

A graying knight wearing a deep blue cloak lined with gray fur was speaking with one of the women. It was Sir Robert, one of his father's most loyal knights. Thomas should have known his father would send men of his own.

Amora rounded on him, glaring. "Is there anyone who is not looking for you?"

"I guess not."

She smacked the back of his head, "This isn't a game! That girl is in *real* danger."

"Ow! I know. The guard who was searching for us last night is a Salenian spy; he plans to take Cat to King Bastian."

"Bastian?" The name rolled in Amora's mouth, taking on a questioning tone. She kept voice low. Thomas realized he had never seen the ancient woman look confused or frightened before. Both emotions hung in her crystal eyes.

"I don't know what he wants her for, but he wants the alliance between Reinsaffira and Volentia to fail." Thomas glanced toward the common room. The girl being questioned, gestured toward the door, he could not hear the words that passed between them. Sir Robert nodded once before turning away.

Thomas was out of time with Cat.

"Amora, will you do something for me? If I am unable to, will you protect Cat? Make sure she returns to the Volentian palace?"

"You know that girl will never forgive you, if you make her love you and then abandon her."

"I have no intention of abandoning her."

Everything was bleary in the morning light. Cat rolled onto her back, trying to bring the room into focus. Even before Thomas had woken her, Cat had not slept well. After... It took so long for her heart to stop pounding and her mind to stop swirling with thoughts. Thoughts that still had no conclusion. She pushed herself up, the room coming into focus. It felt dim and gray in the morning light, though still tidy. It felt empty. No, it was empty. She was immediately on her feet, spinning around in search of Thomas, or evidence of Thomas. Panic constricting in her chest. There was no trace of him in the room. Even his saddle pack was missing. The swell of panic tightened. Her eyes widening. Had he left her? Alone? Cat did not really know where she was or how to get anywhere.

She shook the thought from her head, her tangled hair flying. She was being stupid. Why would he leave her after the things he said the night before? Even if he did not care about her, she knew he cared about *her* prince. But she thought he cared about her.

There was a pile of fresh clothing on the bedside table, waiting for her. It was the only other change she recognized in the small room.

A shiver passed through Cat, prickling the skin on her arms. The room was cold. She picked up the folded clothes, a simple green dress that had been cropped at the knees and gray woolen breeches. All were clearly borrowed and somehow still made to her exact measurements.

As she lifted them to dress, a piece of parchment fluttered to the floor. It was a note written in beautiful handwriting. Cat had to read it twice because the words made her heart flutter. She had to tamp down the feeling, reminding herself of who she was and who Thomas was.

No matter what you believe, you will never be just another girl, not to me. But there are things you don't know, things I have not told you. Things that can no longer wait. I'll be waiting in the stables when you are ready. Though I am afraid what I must tell you will make you hate me.

-Thomas.

Cat slipped the note into the pocket of her dress.

The swirling thoughts from the night before suddenly fell into place, ordered and clear. Everything felt clear in daylight. She had to find Thomas.

She found him exactly where he said he would be, in the stables behind the brothel, brushing a dappled gray horse. Thomas kept his back to Cat, the long brush strokes turning deliberate. Cat watched him for a moment before clearing her throat.

"Good morning, Princess." The brush moved to the horse's long neck. Thomas turned toward her, moving with the same slow deliberation he used to brush the horse. He set the brush on a small shelf on the edge of the stall. Cat's heart did a small skitter step. The pale blue tunic he wore brought out the summer sunshine in his eyes. Cat would have thought that after what happened the night before she would have stopped being surprised by how handsome he was. Now she did not think that would ever happen.

"Before you say anything, there is something I want to tell you."

"I'm yours to command, Princess. Ask me anything." An errant curl fell across his forehead. Cat stepped forward, her fingers flexing to brush it. She pulled back, reminding herself she was engaged. There was no future between her and Thomas. "I... Last night... You asked me to trust you."

His smile faltered. "I remember."

"I... I didn't. I wanted to but I didn't. But I do now. I trust you." Cat chewed her lip. Somehow it was hard to think of anything when he looked at her. Heat rose to the tips of her ears. She wanted so desperately to kiss him again. Wanted to tell him how she felt about him, even if they could never be together. Telling him would only hurt him, which was why she needed to go home. Why she had to tell him to take her home. "Which is why..."

Something clattered on the stone street outside. Thomas' eyes darted toward the sound. He stepped between her and the sound, fingers wrapping around hers, tugging Cat away from the swinging stable door. Cat followed, pulled into him by some magnetic force. "Wait. Before you say anything, I have to tell you something. I should have told you weeks ago, but I was selfish. I wanted to be with you."

Cat blinked back her surprise. Thomas wanted to be with her? *Her?*

"You wanted to be with me. W-why?"

"Because I love you, Cat." His voice was a low, husky whisper that sent a wash of shivers and tingles through her arms and fingers. Butterflies were batting their wings against her ribs. "No matter what else happens today, I want to be sure you know that. I love you and I am going to fight every day to protect you and prove I deserve you."

His grasp on her hand tightened, pulling her into his chest. Cat did not decide to do it; her body moved on instinct. She raised herself on her toes to meet his kiss and gripped his shoulders. This kiss was not like the ones he had given her the night before, fevered and frantic with need. It was gentler, kinder, deeper. Warmth followed his arms as they wrapped around her waist. Holding her tight.

A perfect kiss.

A perfect moment.

Then Cat's mind caught up with her body. She and Thomas could not be together. It did not matter if he loved her or that she loved him. She knew for certain in that moment that she loved Thomas.

"Wait." For such a small word, it was difficult to manage. "I can't... We can't... It's not that I don't want you. I'm..."

"I know. That is the other thing. Cat, I have to tell you who I am. I am not who you think I am... I wish that I was but..."

"Who does she think you are?" A man's voice broke them apart. Thomas stepped between Cat and the door again. Three men stood on the threshold, blocking the midmorning light and casting long shadows. Each wore the deep blue of the Reinsaffiran flag. Knights. They had found her. This was not how Cat had imagined her adventure would end. Her eyes darted between the men, locking on a familiar man with light brown hair. Arik. So, he did see her in the common room. It did not feel like a coincidence.

"I'm sorry Thomas," Arik muttered. "I delayed as long as I could."

"I know you did." Thomas turned back to Cat. "Do not worry. I can handle this." He flashed them a smile. "Good morning gentlemen."

"Good morning, your highness," the graying knight at the center placed a hand against his heart, bowing at the waist.

Highness? Cat felt a surge of fire and anger burn through her chest. Anger she had no place to put. She pulled away from him. The idea of his touch suddenly made her skin hot.

"*You* are the prince?" Her hands balled into tight fists. Pain was sparking in her palms. The urge to hit something was building to a tempest.

"Cat... Please..."

She push him away from her. "You lied! Have you just been laughing at me this whole time? The stupid princess who didn't... who couldn't... who was too dumb..." She could not think of anything else to say. All this time she had been telling him her secrets; about her mother, about wanting to choose for herself. He had acted like he sympathized, like he wanted to help her. It was all a trick. A lie. A game he played with her aching heart.

Thomas' gripped her wrists, keeping her fists from slamming into him. The idea of his touch made the anger inside of her burn and spark. "I was trying to tell you. I wanted to tell you."

"You lied about everything!"

"No, Cat I ..."

Cat felt the magic rage to life, flickering orange and red inside of her. Her hair fell into her face.

A look of shock and sorrow crossed Thomas' face, morphing to fear. He backed away from her. A swell of fear was filling Cat as well. Power burned inside of her, threatening to consume her. She had to release it. Even in her anger, she did not want to hurt anyone. Did not want to hurt Thomas.

A hand came to rest on Cat's shoulder. Arik spoke and she was certain he meant to calm her, but the pounding of her heart drowned out his words. She knocked Arik back, and a blue and orange flame sprouted on her fingers, unbidden and unintentional. Fire surrounded her, pushing the men back. Only Thomas stayed near. Fear hanging on his face.

Cat backed away, leaving scorch marks on the straw covered floor with every step.

Through the fire Cat could see the men's faces. They all seemed to say that it was time for her to disappear. She did not want to hurt anyone. She could not control the flames swirling across her skin.

Cat turned away, running for the far door as fast as her legs would take her.

"Cat!" Thomas called with an edge of panic.

"Let her go, sire. She's not our concern."

The wind blew cold, pulling at Thomas' cloak when he and the knights mounted their horses. Arik looked pale; his burned arm was tightly bandaged in scraps of blue and white linen. Still smiling, telling one of the younger men that maidens love brave knights, especially those who could prove it with scars. Thomas understood Arik's meaning, though he disliked the idea that Cat would be turned into the villain of whatever story Arik attached to the burn.

Thomas saw the look in Cat's eyes when the fire started. He could not imagine being unable to control such a large piece of himself.

Exhaustion from using magic would overtake Cat soon. If they were going to search for her, he and the knights needed to start. He just hoped she was still safe. Knowing Cat, she would run immediately into someone with plans to hurt her. They had to find her and take her home.

Cat would go home, and Thomas would keep Aiden with him for questioning about Sir Guy's scheme.

Thomas pulled his hood tight around her face. We must start our search, if we are to find Princess Catiya."

"There is no need to worry about that, your highness," Sir Robert answered. "Your father wants you returned without delay."

Sir Robert's response did not make sense. Thomas scrunched his forehead. "Then we must start our search immediately. Volentia is our neighbor, if not still our ally, and she is in danger. We have a responsibility to…"

"She *is* a danger, and we have no responsibility to Volentia. Our orders are to return you to your father, not go chasing after a witch."

Witch? Thomas recoiled at the word. Sir Robert's meaning was clear. Cat and her safety did not matter. Anger rose in his throat, leaving a bitter taste in his mouth. "She is not a witch!" His hands tightened into fists. "And I am not going anywhere without her."

"He's been enchanted," one of the young knights whispered. Only Arik and Trenton knew the truth.

Robert looked at Thomas for a long moment. The gray that peppered his brown hair quivered as he shook his head. "My prince, we have been ordered to give you no choice." The hilt of a sword slammed into the back of Thomas' head.

Stars exploded in Thomas' vision.

He swayed on his feet, forcing himself to stay upright.

Darkness fell on him all at once.

"This was not the plan!" Arik's voice echoed in the distance.

"Plans change, sir. Get him back on the horse. I would like to reach the palace before dawn."

The trees all looked the same. All unfamiliar. Cat's lungs burned. Still, she ran, not stopping for bearings or breath. She refused to stop for anything. Fog surrounded her, thick and cold. She pushed through low hanging branches hidden by mists. Scratches now covered her face and arms and her legs ached. The pain did not matter. Nothing really mattered in that moment. Although, the burning in Cat's legs was starting to matter. Her arms were growing numb as the magic drained and her energy vanished. Only the desire to get away from Thomas propelled Cat forward.

No, she reminded herself. *Prince Thomas.* He had lied to her, lied about everything. He should have told her who he was from the beginning instead of playing around at being a knight.

A tree root wrapped around Cat's boot, pulling her, face first, to the ground.

The moss was soft and cool. It soothed the aches filling her body.

After a long moment, Cat forced herself into a sitting position, leaning against the tree that had tripped her, folding her legs against her chest so she could rest her forehead on her knees. She did not know how long she had been running or how far she had gone or even where she was. The heavy fog obscured everything around her. All she knew was that she was in Reinsaffira alone and lost.

Without thinking, Cat pulled the brass compass from her pocket. Watching the arrow spin without stopping.

Cat tossed the broken, useless thing to the ground. Folding her arms to guard against the cold that crept in. The dagger strapped to her hip, the clothes she wore, and the compass was all she had and the compass was no longer working. Volentia was to the south. In the morning Cat would point herself south and go home. If she was lucky Sir Guy would find her on the way. Suddenly she was quite tired of this adventure and everything to do with it.

She probably would not even have to wait until morning, the Reinsaffiran knights were probably searching for her. They would find her and take her home... or directly Reinsaffira to marry Thomas. It was their duty to her *betrothed*.

Cat pushed the thought of Thomas away before tears could slip from her eyes. She focused on home. It would still be warm in Volentia, it was always warm in Volentia, but soon Ryder would insist that she and Emma needed to wear their warmest cloaks when they went outside and have fires lit in their rooms. A dull ache filled Cat's chest, thinking about Ryder hurt almost as much as thinking about Thomas. She had betrayed him and Emma and everyone else she cared about.

A twig snapped, breaking Cat from her thoughts. Had they found her already? Her fingers wrapped around the hilt of her dagger. No sound followed. It was nothing. Just a passing animal. Her grip on the leather hilt tightened.

"I have been tailing you for quite some time."

Cat spun, staggering to her feet. Her blade ready as she faced the voice. Six men had circled her. Each looking rougher than the last. The voice belonged to the dark-haired man at the center. Bandits. Slavers. The same slavers she had fought the night she met Aiden. Cat chuckled, trying to appear unconcerned, though her head was starting to pound, and her eyes were growing heavy. "And you have chosen now to attack me because you think I am vulnerable? An easy target?"

"No. Just a valuable one. After that recent display, I have no doubt that you are the girl I have been looking for."

Exhaustion made Cat's head heavy. Using magic had drained every scrap of her energy. Even the dagger was too heavy in her numb, shaking hands. Still, she would not be taken without a fight.

One of the men grabbed at her. Cat danced away, swinging the dagger at him. It whooshed through the air.

"Careful. We don't want to mar that pretty face."

They did not want to hurt her. It was Cat's only advantage. If she could just get away. Her whole body felt heavy, as if her soul was drifting off into darkness. Cat was not sure if she could run any farther or if she could fight the men off. She had to try. She swung the dagger blindly at another man who grabbed hold of her shoulder, dragging her back by her cloak. Something snapped in her ear. Cat's cloak broke free of her shoulders. She stumbled as the fabric fluttered to the ground.

The world around her was falling out of focus. Her only chance was using the last of her strength to summon the fire again. "You will find that underestimating me is a dangerous mistake," she growled, gritting her teeth.

The flames did not come. Her core was cold as ice. Cat's fingers flew to her neck, in search of her heart stone. The gem was missing. Cat had lost it somewhere. Her eyes darted around in search of it. She would never find it in this fog with the men grabbing at her. Cat was so dizzy. Another swing of her dagger and darkness closed in around her. Her knees dropping to the mossy forest floor.

No.

Cat tried to push away the rough arms that wrapped around her.

Then there was nothing, just hard ground.

"Make sure she is alive. She's no good to us dead."

The last thing Cat was aware of was a pair of calloused hands groping at her neck and wrists for a pulse before the warmth of nothingness welcomed her.

PART

THREE

Part Three

The creak of damp wood, groaning as it rocked against the river's current, was the first thing Cat was aware of when she woke. She knew with certainty that she was on a boat before even opening her eyes. Her nausea and the smell of water confirmed it. A boat to where?

The next thing she was aware of was the pounding, relentless pain in her head.

Bile rose in Cat's throat. She rolled onto her side, letting the contents of her stomach spill into a bucket left beside the pallet she slept on. The sound only made her feel sicker, shakier. Cat spit the last of the foul taste from her mouth and moved to wipe the drivel from her lips, but she could not move. Her wrists were bound tight, holding her hands behind her back.

It was easy to miss the dull pain from her arms being forced behind her when every muscle in her body ached from the use of magic. Now she could not ignore it. Every movement chaffed her wrists, bringing more pain to her stiff and aching arms.

She tried squirming her way out of the bonds, unwilling to be helpless when one of her captors came to fetch her. Kidnapping was almost certainly not the limit of the men's treachery.

"Struggling will do you no good."

Cat flinched. She had not heard the door click open or the man enter.

He stood in the shadowy doorway, leaning casually against the door frame. "My best man tied your wrists. I doubt even I would be able to undo those knots with both hands available. He has a talent with ropes." The man pushed the heavy door closed, bolting it behind him. Dressed in dark colors, the man became a shadow moving through the candlelight.

Cat cringed, backing into the wall. Her chest constricting around her pounding heart. The naval officers who came to the palace enjoyed telling gruesome stories about pirates, black hearted men with no regard for laws or life. The reality was worse.

A long silver blade flashed in the candlelight. The pirate twirled it between his fingers. "I did not want you trying to escape and getting hurt after all the trouble I went through to find you." He wrapped a hand around Cat's arm, pulling her up until she was sitting. He twisted her around so he could see the ropes. The blade slid through the bindings, freeing Cat's hands. "But now that we are in the deepest part of the river, I don't think we need to worry about you trying to escape. You look smart enough to know that you won't be able to. Right, darling?" He tugged gently at a lock of Cat's fiery hair.

Cat pulled away. Gritting her teeth against the pain in her bruised wrists. "I... I know what you are trying to do," Cat stammered. Her voice only sounded a little braver than she felt. "You... You are trying to make me trust you. Don't you dare touch me!" She flinched away, banging her hip against the corner of a small writing desk. The cramped cabin was beautifully furnished, not the sort of place most prisoners would be kept.

"You listen to too many stories." He slipped the knife back into his belt. "You know, I almost gave up on you, but when I saw your little display, I knew you were exactly the girl I was looking for."

"Looking for?" She glanced around as she spoke, searching for a clue as to why he had taken her and where they were going. The man was wrong about one thing, Cat was not smart enough to *know* she could not escape. If he was dumb enough to untie her, then she would be dumb enough to use every resource available to escape. A large cabinet and a bookshelf, filled with leather bound volumes, covered an entire wall of the modest cabin. The other wall was taken up by a large bed and a writing desk. She realized the pallet she slept on was a bench in front of a line of small windows. This had to be the captain's quarters.

The pirate smiled. "There's a very powerful man who is willing to pay handsomely for any red-haired magix found wandering the wilderness between Reinsaffira and Volentia. After seeing your abilities... I have never been more certain that you are the one he is looking for. Terrible shame for you, but you are going to make my crew and I into wealthy men."

A lump formed in Cat's throat, almost choking her. He was going to sell her to someone who had been searching for her. Someone who did not want the alliance with Reinsaffira. Was it the same person who sent the shadows after her so long ago?

"I'm Princess Catiya of Volentia! My father is King Kristoff. I... I don't know what this other man promised you, but if you take me home, my father will pay you double! He'll give you whatever you ask. I promise!"

The pirate's eyebrows rose with surprise. He surveyed Cat's face, taking in her features. "Princess Catiya? Queen Anya's heir?" His voice was full of reverence and surprise. He gripped her arm tighter. "You are Queen Anya's daughter?"

"Yes!" The lump in her throat made it hard to speak. "Please... If... If you take me home... I promise my father..."

"Will reward me with a noose." The pirate stalked to the far end of the cabin. A nervous energy emanating off his twitching arms. "Piracy and slave running are punishable by death in Volentia. And what do you think they will assume if I am caught in Volentian waters with their lost princess in my cabin?" He ran his hands down his face, tugging at his beard. "No. I cannot take you back to Volentia." He was pacing now. Back and forth across the narrow room. Muttering to himself. "The princess. Bastian ordered... Anya's daughter... and she's a fire magix..." He spun away from Cat, stalking to the door, unbolting it. He turned back, jabbing a finger at her. "Stay there!"

The pirate disappeared, pounding up the steps.

Cat pushed herself to her feet, hurrying to the open door. She could see the dark-haired man but no one else. He stood at the top of the steps, pointing and shouting orders. Cat held her breath, trying to hear over her racing heart.

"You! Turn the ship around!"

"Captain?"

"Turn us around NOW! We're going to The Block."

"Captain Tristan, are you certain? If she is the girl Bastian is after and he finds out we didn't deliver her..."

"She's Queen Anya's only daughter. What do you think will happen if we take her to Bastian?"

The ship listed to one side.

Cat stumbled, gripping the door to remain standing. Captain Tristan continued to shout orders. Something about sending a message. Cat had stopped listening, steeling herself to run. This might be her only chance to escape. She had just taken a step onto the stairs when the ship listed a second time, making her stumble.

A rough hand gripped her by the arm, dragging her back into the cabin. He held her so tight Cat was certain her arm would be peppered with bruises. "I told you to stay put!" The pirate shook her. "Why are you here?"

"You kidnapped me." Cat struggled to pull out of his grip.

"No! Why aren't you at the Volentian palace?"

"I..." Cat could not think of an excuse. Telling him she was following a magic compass sounded stupid. Admitting she had been running away was even worse. Her thoughts went to Thomas. "I... I was tricked."

Too many thoughts were swirling around Cat's mind to say much more. Captain Tristan had said something about Bastian. Why would Bastian be searching for her? Even going so far as to hire a group of thugs to hunt for her. Was the compass a trick? What about Thomas? Was he in danger? Thinking about him only hurt now that she knew he saw her the same way everyone else did; a piece to be moved across a board.

Thomas was groggy when he woke. His head pounded. The light felt sharp in his eyes and there was a sore spot on the back of his head that he was afraid to touch.

It took a moment to recognize his surroundings; the soft feather bed and deep blue curtains. His own bed in the Reinsaffiran palace.

It was the single most unwelcome sight he had ever seen.

Then he saw Arik, stretched out on the chair by the fire, and that became the most unwelcome sight he thought he ever saw. Betrayed by his best friend. A man he had trusted for years. A man who knew how important Cat was to him.

Cat! Thomas had to find Cat! She was alone and in danger.

Thomas pushed himself up to face Arik. "Where is Cat?"

A wave of dizziness forced him back against the pillows.

"Trenton is searching for her. He left as soon as we got you here. If she is going to be found, Trenton will find her."

"And believe me, he had better find her. I would hate to see what Prince Ryder would do to you if you turned up without his sister." Phillip let the bedroom door close behind him, leaning on the wall in a casual manner.

"Listen, Thomas, no one believed Sir Robert would actually leave her out there I would have stopped him if I did."

Thomas sat up, slowly this time, struggling to pull himself out of the bed. "I need to be there when he finds her. I need to talk to her."

"You need to rest," Phillip said with a scolding tone. "Father wants to see you when you are ready and I think you will want your strength back before you face him."

"I am ready now. What hour is it?"

"Almost evening."

Evening? Cat had been alone for hours, almost a full day. He did not want to think about the sort of trouble she could have gotten into in that time. Had she already been captured by King Bastian?

Thomas brushed the tangles from his hair with his fingers. Static energy built in his core, it needed to be released. "Arik, you said Sir Guy was planning to take Cat to Salene. Do you know why?"

Phillip sputtered. "Sir Guy? The princess' guard? He intends to sell her to Salene? How did you learn this?"

Arik stiffened, shooting an annoyed look at Phillip. "I am not completely without friends in the Volentian court. Most people think I'm delightful and charming."

"Did you tell the king or Prince Ryder? They have to know…"

"They already know King Bastian wants to harm the princess," Arik sighed. "It's why Kristoff added the marriage clause to the alliance."

Ice rushed through Thomas' veins, pooling in his heart.

Arik continued, answering Thomas' question before it could fully form in his mind. "The Salenian throne passes through the female line. Princess Catiya is the rightful queen of Salene and a threat to his reign."

"What?" Both Thomas and Phillip spoke at once. Eyes wide with surprise.

"Why didn't you tell me that?"

"We haven't exactly had a lot of time to talk recently."

The pieces snapped into place, sharp and in focus. Bastian, a man who murdered his twin sister for the throne, would not hesitate to hurt Cat. "I have to speak to my father." He stumbled to the wardrobe, his head throwing him so off balance that he had to steady himself against the doors.

"I don't know how hard they hit your head, but you do not want to go see Father right now. Trust me. You want to put it off as long as possible."

"I can't wait." Thomas pulled a fresh tunic over his head. "Cat is in danger." He tugged on a clean pair of boots. The hard leather refused to mold to his feet. "Gather your things, I will need you both to be ready to leave as soon as I return."

"Are you even concerned about the trouble you are in? Or what it means that the Volentian alliance is finished?"

"It doesn't matter. I have to find Cat before Bastian does. He wants Reinsaffira and Volentia at each other's throats while he uses her to gain power. Are you with me or not?"

"Well, I'm all for it," Arik laughed, jumping to his feet. "Let's go annoy the king and prevent two wars. Should I find Jason as well?"

"Hopefully she can go twenty-four hours without needing a physician." Thomas pushed through the door. A solid scolding from his father could not be worse than most of the dangers he had already put up with on his journey Cat.

The shutters and curtains of the king's study were closed. The stifling darkness was only worsened by a large fire that let off more heat than the cramped room ever needed. Smoke lingered in the air, clinging to the furniture, stinging Thomas' eyes.

King James hunched over a large map. His shoulders rounded with exhaustion. Eyes gray with clouds. The king... Thomas knew in that moment his father was thinking only as a king... glanced up at Thomas, giving him a brief appraising look when the door thudded closed.

Thomas straightened his spine, trying to look more princely than he felt. The dizziness was gone, replaced by a dull headache. The king returned his attention to the map, ignoring Thomas with practiced deliberation. This was part of Thomas' punishment. He would wait until he believed Thomas looked contrite enough to be acknowledged.

Finally, after Thomas began to sway from the weariness inching up his legs, King James grunted to the lords surrounding him. "I will speak with the prince in private. Leave!" A wave of the king's hand and the lords scurried away.

Muffled silence filled the room.

The king rose to his full height. His arms folding over his chest. An imposing figure full of disappointment. "If you are going to be king of this land someday, you must learn to behave like one."

Thomas stiffened. He knew better than to respond with any of the thousand quips that clung to his tongue.

"A king puts the needs of his country above his own selfish desires."

"I believe I have done that."

A raised hand told Thomas he was not yet permitted to speak. "He does not disappear on the night his betrothal is announced only to be found weeks later in the company of a known criminal and a witch!"

The urge to defend Cat crept up his spine. "I believe you mean my fiancé. I was found with my fiancé and I would very much like to get back to her."

"She is a witch and you are no longer engaged to her." King James let out a groan, running a hand down his face, exhausted. "You are restricted to the grounds until further notice, *and* you will accept, without complaint, the next suitable marriage I can arrange for you."

"Do you really expect me to behave like one of your courtiers? A wave of your hand and I will scurry back into the shadows? That has never been my nature."

"No. You have always been predisposed to mischief. It's terribly inconvenient."

"And love. Or have you forgotten?" Forgotten that he had sworn Thomas could marry the girl of his choosing, and that girl had always been Cat.

The two stared at each other, waiting for the other to blink.

"Restrict me to the grounds if you must but know that I will not stay. I swore I would protect Princess Catiya, and I intend to. And of course, we cannot forget that you gave me the right to choose my own bride. I have chosen Princess Catiya. I am going to find her, I am going to marry her, and I am going to stabilize the alliance with Volentia, as you asked me to do."

"Oh? How do you intend to do that when there is no alliance with Volentia? Don't worry about your honor, my son," he laughed, shaking his head. "No one knows you were with the princess all this time. She is someone else's problem now."

"Actually, it is well known that Thomas was with the princess." Arik strolled into the study, a confident and casual swagger to his hips. "There were witnesses at the Peach Tree Inn as well as three *trustworthy* Volentian guards who all know."

"And I have been in contact with Prince Ryder."

"If Thomas were to resurface without her. Well...." Arik let his voice trail off with a knowing tone.

"You would threaten your own people with war? Over a stupid girl?"

"No. War threatens us either way and it hinges on Cat's... Princess Catiya's safety. Or were you not aware that she is the heir to the throne of Salene? Surely the historians who confirmed her bloodline also discovered that." The popping of the fire echoed off the stone walls. "My feelings for her do not matter. Princess Catiya was lured from the palace by King Bastian, and he means to use her to gain full control of Salene and to weaken Reinsaffira and Volentia. We are being manipulated." Thomas felt his jaw tensing as the next words formed in his throat. "Let find her and return her to her home. She will regard me with hatred for the rest of her life, but she will be safe, and we will have time to counter whatever else Bastian plans."

King James tried to dismiss the information with a wave of his hand. "You have been enchanted by the witch's magic. When your head is clear, you will realize how unlikely such events are."

A laugh bubbled in Thomas' chest. One he could not hold inside. "Father, Princess Catiya would have to be able to control her magic in order to enchant someone. The fact remains that I love her and that will not wear off with time. And it will not change the truth. Restrict me to the grounds or let me go after her with an entire army at my back; it does not matter. I am going after her. Once she is safe. I will do whatever you believe a future king should do."

Most of the books on the line of shelves were useless to Cat. Some contained sea charts and maps, the borders marked with dotted lines, but there was nothing that helped her know where she was or what to do. She moved to the desk, hoping Captain Tristan was a foolish man, the sort who would leave keys or weapons lying about. Even a letter opener would be enough. Cat opened the roll top, tisking with irritation when it held only papers. The captain was not a foolish man, even if he was a disorganized one.

Cat picked through the papers. The parchments were water stained. She picked up one, studying it. A royal Salenian edict offering a reward for the capture of a fire magix. She discarded it. The letter told her nothing the captain had not already.

Captain Tristan had been reasonably forthcoming with Cat. He told her King Bastian had offered a reward for any magix with red hair they found, and that the consequences for not delivering her would be severe.

Of course, then he locked her in the cabin.

Cat slammed the roll top desk shut. There was nothing that would help.

She dug her hands her hair, groaning. "If only I still had my compass. It could show me what I needed to get out of here."

The compass did not work that way, Cat knew that, even if it was not broken and lost in the woods. Like everything else that mattered to her; her mother's necklace, Emma's dagger, it was all gone. She was trapped. Captured by pirates. No one knew to rescue her and there was nothing she could do to rescue herself.

And it was all her fault!

Cat dropped onto the window seat. She never should have left Volentia. She never should have accepted the compass. Emma had known better. She had insisted there was a rational way to get out of the trouble Cat created. Emma was never so brash and impulsive as Cat.

Emma.

The thought of her friend hurt. Cat missed her. If Emma had been there with Cat, she would know what to do. Strategy and patience always fit better in Emma's head than it did in Cat's.

Cat pushed the thought from her mind. No one was going to save her; not Emma, not Ryder, and especially not *Prince* Thomas. Cat needed to focus. There was a way out of this nightmare. She swiveled around on the bench, pressing her hand to the window. Running her finger along the edges in search of a lock or hinge. Only worn, varnished wood that was smooth beneath her fingers.

"You're wasting your time there. Even if those windows opened, you'd never be able to swim to shore. The currents would sweep you out to sea."

Cat spun around, masking the sudden pounding of her heart. She had not heard the door open. "I wouldn't be so sure about that. I am an excellent swimmer. And why should I listen to you? You're just a pirate. You don't know anything about me."

Captain Tristan's dark eyes flit over Cat, appraising her. He held a bowl and a loaf of bread in his hands. Steam swirled over the bowl. The hearty scent made Cat's mouth water. "There is no need to get snippy, your highness. I brought you dinner." Her captor set the tray on the desk before walking to the cabinet. He unlocked it, revealing a collection of colorful bottles, selecting a broad square bottle filled with amber liquid and two glasses. "Make no mistake," he continued, splashing the liquid into the glasses. "I don't doubt your capabilities, but I've seen men much stronger than you dashed against the rocks on this stretch of ocean. But if you insist on trying to swim to freedom, I'd recommend eating first. You must be hungry." Captain Tristan slid one of the full glasses toward her.

"I'm not." Cat lifted the glass, sniffing it with care. Some sort of spiced alcohol. For a moment, Cat wondered if it was drugged, until the captain took a long swig from his own glass.

"You are not a convincing liar. Don't worry, none of it is drugged and no one on this ship will harm you. You have my word. Now, go on and eat all that. It won't do to have a princess starve on my ship. It would damage my reputation as a gracious host."

She examined the bowl, a thick, hearty stew full of potatoes, carrots, and chunks of beef. Cat snatched up the loaf of bread, tearing off a hunk and dipping it in the broth. "Where are you taking me?"

Captain Tristan drained his glass. Reaching across the table, taking Cat's untouched glass. "The Block. You may not be familiar with it; it is not a nice place."

"It is an island off the coast of Reinsaffira where pirates sell the things they steal." Cat quirked an eyebrow at the pirate, crossing her arms and keeping her eyes hard and sharp. "Is that what I am? Something to sell?"

"It is more of a smuggler's haven. The market for slaves, and other such atrocities, is not so lucrative as the stories may have led you to believe. I mostly deal in valuable magical items, things required for potions, that sort of thing. So, really, you have nothing to worry about. Consider yourself a guest on my ship."

"A guest?" She surveyed the lavish prison.

The captain smiled over his glass. Propping his feet up on the table. "I do not usually store cargo in my cabin, Princess."

"Then what do you plan on doing with me at The Block?" She did her best to hide the quiver in her voice.

"I have a customer who is a Volentian Lord. I'm arranging to meet him there. He will return you to your home."

"Which lord?" Who would risk consorting with pirates and smugglers? What Volentian lord would be so foolish?

"His name is Carswell. I believe he is a duke of some sort."

"The duke of Rook." Cat suppressed a shudder. Not foolish. Arrogant. Cat would have preferred to stay the pirate's captive. Everything Carswell did was about power. He would return Cat to the palace and her father, the king, would be indebted to him. Carswell could request anything. The shudder actually broke through this time, refusing to be suppressed. "You said King Bastian would make you and your crew rich men. Why would you give that up to help me?"

The pirate's smile faltered. "You know, I met your mother once, a long time ago. She was still a princess then; I doubt she had even met your father yet. She was helping a little boy gather firewood. She would have been a good queen. The people of Salene remember that." He stood with one abrupt motion. "Get some rest, your highness, and clean your face. We should arrive at The Block in the morning."

The scorched footprints ended in the mist covered woods on the banks of a wide river.

Darkness was settling on the forest. Soon, even the best trackers would be useless, and Thomas had never been counted among even the adequate trackers. Still, he was not prepared to give up and make camp. Every minute wasted took Cat farther away. It had already been two days.

"We should make camp." Phillip edged his horse closer to where Thomas stood. "We won't find her in the dark."

"No!" Thomas turned around the small clearing, surveying it, striding across the thick moss. Something about the clearing gave him a sick feeling in the pit of his stomach. A tingle ran up his spine, making its way over his arm until it seemed to settle around his left wrist. A feeling Thomas had not felt in a long time. Cat had been here. He could feel it in the air, sense her in the swirling mists. She had been here, and something had happened. Thomas did not want the knights escorting them to trample any clues to where she had gone.

His long legs took him across the clearing in three strides. The fog made everything difficult to see. Even his feet were obscured. His toe snagged an unseen tree root, sending him sprawling in the damp moss. Thomas groaned, more out of annoyance than pain. If he could not even see a tree root, how could he... The gleam of metal caught his eye, cutting off his line of thoughts. A small, round hunk of brass. Thomas picked it up, his fingers brushing across the cover, wet with dew and intricately carved. Placing it in his palm, he sat up to examine the object. A compass. He found the clasp, opening it. The arrow spun.

Cat's magic compass.

In Thomas' hands the arrow only spun, occasionally wavering in a nonsensical direction, pointing to the west. It was supposed to point to the thing Cat needed. The thing that led her out of the palace in the first place. It was not something Cat would abandon in the woods.

"Phillip," Thomas called out to his brother, the only one of his companions he trusted. Arik had not been able to join the search for fear that his wound might get infected.

Suddenly, Thomas could see everything. The moss around him was scuffed and torn. A pile of dark green fabric lay in a rumpled pile at the base of the tree. Thomas gathered it up in his hands. Heavy velvet with golden fastenings. The scent of peaches clung to the cloak. A sparkling diamond necklace lay hidden among the roots beneath the cloak. A few feet away a golden dagger glinted in the waning light. These were Cat's things. Things she would not willingly leave behind.

Images of Cat being attacked and kidnapped by bandits or Sir Guy flooded Thomas' mind. His hands balled into fists.

Phillip knelt next to Thomas.

"The princess has been kidnapped."

"How do you know?"

Thomas held out the diamond. It filled his palm. The broken chain dangling. "This necklace belonged to Princess Catiya's mother." He forced himself to use her proper title. "She would never leave it behind. Someone took her."

Phillip found a scrap of torn material in the dirt. Turning it over in his hands. "You may be right." He pointed to the black stitching on the yellow fabric. "I know this emblem."

Cat stumbled on the last step, still unaccustomed to the sway of the ship. A rough hand wrapped around her elbow, pulling her up onto the deck. She glared at Captain Tristan. A small crowd had gathered on the deck of the ship, pausing in their work long enough to see the spectacle of a princess.

The ship was small with only one mast and sail, designed for short trips down the coast, not the open sea. Cat thought it might be able to manage the great river, if the draft was shallow enough. It was a pretty ship. The sails were purple, and the deck had been scrubbed until the boards gleamed. The salty breeze stirred the sail and lines.

A man in a black silk shirt ran up the gangplank. "He's late, Captain."

"He'll be here." Cat folded her arms. Carswell would never miss the opportunity to be Cat's rescuer. She looked out over the docks, wondering which ship Carswell might be on. What would he want from her in exchange for taking her home? Cat would never be free of the debt to him. Freedom. It was all Cat wanted, no, needed. There was nothing else her lost compass could take her to. And it was the one thing she would never truly have. Cat leaned on the rail of the ship, letting the defeat wash over her. "What will you do with me, if he doesn't come to collect me?"

"We can worry about that in a few minutes. Don't you think?"

"I'd rather worry about it now," a familiar voice shouted.

Cat leapt out of the way when a hooded figure dropped down on the deck, between her and the captain. His hood slipped back enough to reveal Thomas' face. Cat's heart thudded to a dull stop. The sight of Thomas beside her elicited a dozen emotions. The most prevalent was anger. He winked at her, wrapping an arm around Cat's waist. "My apologies, for taking so long, Princess. Also, for this." He scooped her up, lifting Cat off her feet. He grabbed a rope hanging from the mast.

"Thomas! What are you doing?"

"Trust me."

"I am never trusting you again! You are a liar, and I don't need you to rescue me!"

He ignored her, gripping the rope tight, swinging them over the rail. A sick butterfly feeling filled Cat's stomach as wind rushed around them.

They landed hard.

Thomas stumbled, dropping them both against the boards, rattling Cat's teeth. An involuntary grunt of pain burst from her throat. Cat teetered when he set her on her feet, regaining her balance. She folded her arms over her chest, watching Thomas draw his sword.

Chaos erupted around them.

Men burst from the ships around them. Cat did not know which were the prince's knights, which were smugglers and pirates, and which were Carswell's men.

The meddlesome prince pulled Cat behind him. "Stay behind me. I will keep you safe."

Cat shoved him, forcing his hand away from her. "I do not need you to keep me safe. I had a plan. There's a Volentian lord here. He was going to take me home!"

"You're untied!"

"Well spotted, halfwit! I wasn't a prisoner!" She still could not get her heartbeat to slow or the swarm of butterflies to stop stealing her breath. He came to rescue her. Thomas came to rescue her! She did not have to do it all alone. She did not have to face Carswell. Thomas was there for her. *Prince Thomas*, Cat reminded herself. The same man looking down at her with wounded eyes was a prince. He had lied and tricked her. Anger colored Cat's cheeks again.

Thomas pushed her behind him, pulling her out of her thoughts. A group of ruffians descended on them, including a man with a flash of blond hair hidden under his hood. Cat thought that might be Carswell. She had lost track of Captain Tristan.

"Which lord?"

"Carswell." The name left a bitter taste in Cat's mouth. "He's the duke of Rook."

Thomas spun around. "You can't trust him."

"I can't trust you! And I don't need you to protect me." Cat punched a man who had grabbed at her.

"You know in my experience, when a gentleman saves a lady, she thanks him. Sometimes with a kiss."

"If you think I am ever going to kiss you again, then you are mad!"

"Fine." Thomas' arm slid around her waist again. He leaned over her, spine curving as he dipped her. Her hair cascaded over her shoulder. Cat was forced to wrap one arm around his neck to keep her balance. "I'll kiss you then."

His lips pressed into her hers, cutting off the protest on the tip of her tongue. His mouth curled into a smile.

Cat's own mouth formed a thin line. She pressed a hand into the prince's chest, pushing him away from her. "In case it has escaped your notice, this is a life and death situation." Cat spun from his grip, straightening her dress. Her anger flaring inside her.

"How right you are," a cold voice hissed into Cat's ear. An arm pressed into Cat' stomach, knocking the air from her. A stranger held her tight. A blade teased the soft skin of her throat. Sharp and cold. "Now then, your highness, lay down your weapon and I won't have to slit her pretty throat." There was something familiar in the man's voice.

"I would not do that," Thomas grit his teeth. "You will only make her mad."

For a moment, Cat was relieved. She was out of Thomas' reach and the pirate should be easy enough to deal with. Just like Captain Roderick once taught her, Cat thrust her elbow back, ramming it into the man's stomach. The grip on her waist loosened enough for her to squirm and kick her way free. Her fingers twined around the hand holding the blade, twisting it free.

She spun around to aim the blade at her attacker. Eyes widening. It was not a pirate but Sir Guy.

The knife slipped from her fingers.

How had he found her?

"Cat!" A sudden grip on her wrist forced Cat off balance. She landed against Thomas' chest. The prince's long fingers wrapped around hers. Holding her tight, afraid of losing her again. Blood trickled down his chin, his lip split open. A bruise was forming under his trimmed beard. "You're hurt!"

Cat brushed her free hand over her collarbone. It was slick and warm with blood. The cut stung but would do little more than that. "I'm fine. I need a sword."

Thomas ignored her request. He dragged her down the dock, rushing into a shadowed corner. He produced a silk handkerchief from the pocket of his cloak. Cat let him press the cool fabric to the cut, ruining the familiar handkerchief further.

"Look out!" Cat pulled him away from the swing of a blade.

He spun, fighting the man away. Then he turned back to smile at her, as widely as his cut lip allowed. "You just saved me."

"Please don't make me wish I hadn't."

"I don't have much experience with being rescued, but I believe the protocol would be to..."

Cat slapped him, just hard enough to keep him from leaning close to her again. She could not let him kiss her again. Could not let him confuse her heart anymore than he already had. "If you kiss me again, without my permission, I swear I will kill you myself."

Thomas swiped at the bloody hand print she left on his cheek. "Fair enough. I'll settle for repaying you instead." He swept Cat off her feet again, swinging her over his shoulder with ease. Being suddenly upside down made the world spin. Cat was not fully aware of her surroundings as they rushed through a narrow alley. Then she landed on a pile of netting, a large knot sticking in her spine. Quiet splashing told her she was on yet another boat. This was a small fishing boat with a heavy rudder and small sail.

"Apologies for the rough landing." Thomas extended a hand to Cat. She had no intention of accepting it. She pushed his hand away, forcing herself to sit up. Thomas and a familiar blond man stood above her. The boat was already moving.

Cat searched her memory for the younger prince's name. "Prince Phillip?" A swell of embarrassment hit her. The last time Cat saw him, she had nearly knocked him over and thrown a considerable fit.

Phillip smiled; the same broad smile Thomas so often wore. "Welcome aboard Princess."

Phillip fidgeted with the controls, guiding the fishing boat down the coastline. The princess huddled at the front of the boat. She looked smaller than he remembered. Her shoulders were slumped. Her striking red hair was dull from the dirt clinging to her braid. Blood stained the square collar of her dress. Her flashing emerald eyes were harsh, and Phillip felt a swell of relief that they were not directed at him. The force of her eyes was crushing. It was hard to see whatever it was that his brother saw when he looked at her.

"Forgive my saying, but she does not seem to be worth all this effort."

"She is," Thomas growled back.

"Calm down. I just meant that I expected a girl you were willing to risk your life for to actually like you."

"She does or," he let out a sigh, raking his hand through his hair. "She did. It's a little complicated, but I'm sure she will forgive me, eventually."

Phillip raised a questioning eyebrow. He examined his older brother. His brother who was always laughing, who shirked every responsibility, had never looked so sad... so serious. Thomas sat with his legs stretched out and arms crossed, his eyes never leaving the girl.

"You may not have that kind of time. Does she know about the alliance?"

Thomas did not answer.

"The only girl you've ever cared about, and you keep lying to her."

Phillip thrust the rudder at his brother. Striding toward the sour princess. "May I sit with you?"

"Not if you intend on trying to soften my mood toward your brother."

Phillip took that as a yes.

The princess frowned, glaring at the coastline.

"You shouldn't do that."

The princess' hand clenched into a tight fist. Her wrists were scratched and raw from being tied up. A lump formed in Phillip's throat. He thought she said she had not been a prisoner. "What shouldn't I be doing?"

"Being so angry." He shrugged. "Of course, the choice is yours. You get to feel whatever you like."

The princess softened a little. She still held herself firmly with clenched fists. Her teeth sank into her lower lip. "Well, I *feel* angry. Wouldn't you? If someone lied to you? Tricked you?"

"He also risked his life to rescue you, when he thought you were in danger."

"We both know he did not do that for me. Just to salvage the precious alliance. Another lie."

Dark blue water glided beneath them. Tall cliffs along the coast steadily gave way to white sand beaches. The sun glinted off the water. The princess hunched her shoulders, watching it all pass. Her anger giving way to sadness. She believed that. Phillip had to tell her.

"There is no alliance between Reinsaffira and Volentia. After my brother returns you to Volentia, he is going to return to Reinsaffira, and probably never see you again, unless there is a war, and we happen to reconquer Volentia... I doubt it." Phillip's gaze slid back to Princess Catiya, watching for any reaction. "Thomas would have told you, if you would let him speak to you at all."

The princess lowered her eyes. Her dirt-stained fingers smoothing the wrinkles of her short-cropped dress. "I would not expect *Prince* Thomas to tell me anything of significance," she muttered under her breath. She turned her face away again, watching the beaches slip past.

Maybe she did feel something for Thomas, something deeper than. Her deep green eyes shimmered with tears. Maybe she felt something deeper than anger for Thomas.

Phillip rose to return to the rudder. At least now she knew.

"Phillip," Princess Catiya reached out, catching him by the sleeve of his shirt. He paused. Hovering for just a moment. "Thank you, for coming to help. I know you did not have to."

"Oh, but I did have to, because my brother asked me to." He stepped back to the rudder.

Thomas was on his feet at once. "What did you say to her?"

"I told her the truth."

It felt like sleepwalking; the rock of the boat, the way it drifted along the shoreline. Cat was not entirely sure how long they spent on the small fishing boat or how long it took to reach the beach, where Phillip and Thomas moored the boat. She did not remember climbing out of the boat and stumbling through the sand to a campfire surrounded by logs. Cat leaned against one of the logs, her legs curled against her chest.

She felt... numb.

There was nothing left inside of her to feel. The anger that had burned so hot finally sizzled to coals, leaving scorch marks across her heart. The pain dulled until even the betrayal was a distant ache. There was sadness there too, deep and rumbling, running under the turbulent surface.

A shiver traced across Cat's skin. She pulled her legs closer to her chest, huddling against the late autumn chill.

"You're shivering. Here," Thomas laid a cloak over Cat's shoulders, dropping onto the log at her back.

"I don't want your cloak."

"Good, because it's yours. The one you lost near the Peach Tree."

Cat's gaze darted to Thomas for less than a breath. He did have his own cloak still draped over his shoulders, a beautiful royal looking velvet cloak with a fur collar. She still considered throwing the cloak off, not wanting anything from him. A gust of wind silenced the thought.

Thomas laughed. "He always said you were stubborn."

"Who?" Cat's eyes snapped onto the prince. He was smiling to himself, his gaze fixed on the fire.

"Arik. The ambassador from Reinsaffira. He always said you were stubborn. I just never realized it was to this extent." Thomas continued to smile. Cat could not fathom what he found so amusing. "It is beautiful to see you hold on so tightly to what you want and who you are."

"You would be the first to think that. Or is that another lie?"

He raked back his hair. "I never actually lied. You were the one who said I was a knight. I just... never corrected you."

Cat's fingers tightened into fists. Her nails dug into her palm. The embers of anger igniting. "A lie of omission is still a lie! You deliberately deceived me. Why?" He was silent for a long moment. Exasperating the annoyance surged in Cat's chest. "Surely you can tell me now that I'm not going to be your wife. Was it a trick? Were you testing me?"

"No! Nothing like that."

"Then why? Why not just tell me who you were?" Cat could not stay so close to him; it confused her. She was on her feet in a second. Her feet pounding against the sand as she stalked to the edge of the firelight. She kept her back to Thomas... the prince. It was easier to stay mad if she did not have to look at him.

"I have a reputation in Reinsaffira. You can ask your brother about it, once you are home, as a great seducer of women. I... It is deserved, but unearned."

Cat's brows drew together, forming lines across her forehead. What did that even mean? Another part of Cat's mind turned, spinning like a top. He was a scoundrel; she should have known when she saw him with the girl in the woods, when he kissed her. Her heart sank in her chest.

"Every girl I ever kissed, ever seduced... every girl who ever wanted me knew I was the prince of Reinsaffira, and I knew that. It did not really matter... until..." his voice faltered. Until what? Until meeting her? If it was not a lie, it was the sort of thing hundreds of men had said to thousands of women. The sort of thing Cat could not believe. She could almost feel him moving, raking his hands through his hair. He moved like an electric current through her skin. "There was this girl. I did not know her name or where she came from... I did not know anything about her except that she was smart." Thomas let out a laugh. "She was always reading. And she was kind and brave. I saw her once; a village was under attack, and she offered to trade her life in exchange for the lives of villagers she had never met."

Cat flinched. Turning to look at Thomas. Seeing him with new eyes, remembering a dream about a man with blue eyes who comforted her when she was frightened. A man who promised to find her. She shook the thought from her head, dismissing the memory as what it was, a dream. Forcing herself to the man she knew.

"How did you know about that?" No one knew what Cat did in Rook.

Thomas took her question as an invitation to step forward. Just one small step closer. "I saw it. See, the thing about this girl was I did not even know if she was real. She only lived in my dreams, but I wanted to believe she was real. I searched everywhere for her, even though I did not know her name or where she was. Until I found her... in Volentia." A sigh fell from him, pushing him forward another step.

The vague memory scratched at Cat's mind again. She stared at Thomas, trying to remember the man's face, but all she saw was him, the man who had traveled with her for the last few weeks. It could not be real. Those were only dreams.

"I knew then that it didn't matter why anyone else wanted me, so long as when she wanted me, when *you* wanted me, it was me and not my title." He hesitated for a breath. Then, lifted his hand to a stray lock of hair that clung to her cheek. His hand rested there, warm and rough with callouses. Cat stilled. Even her breathing slowed. She was unsure if she wanted to lean into his touch or pull away, but was paralyzed in the in between. "Cat, I love you. I have loved you since the first moment I saw you and I am afraid I will love you for the rest of my life."

Thomas' thumb tracked across her lips, drawing Cat's eyes up to him. Somewhere in his speech he had moved close to her, holding himself at arm's length. An easy distance to cross. His eyes were close enough to read every thought behind her own. They were a deep warm blue, the color of the sky on summer nights, studying her as if he would never see enough of her, memorizing her. Thomas believed what he was saying. Every word. A thrill of electricity pulsed through her.

He was going to kiss her.

"Please don't." Cat turned her face away. Back to the cold night. "I don't know how to trust you."

Thomas' hand slipped away. "Then I will go with you and prove you can trust me."

"Go with me where? Back to Volentia?"

"Wherever you choose to go." Thomas turned away. He produced a box from his pack by the fire, holding it out to Cat. She lifted the lid. Nestled in the bottom of the box was her compass, her mother's necklace, and Emma's dagger, wrapped in a scrap of cloth.

Emma sat on the edge of the bed, waiting for Ryder to return from his meeting with his father. He was not normally out so late, but things had been strange since Cat ran away and the Reinsaffirans called off the alliance. Ryder was busy trying to hold the kingdom together. To fix things, the way he always did.

Besides, it was not as if he knew he was keeping her waiting. Emma was not even meant to be in his room. She was meant to be asleep in her own room, but how could she be when everything that happened was her fault and she needed to fix it? There was only one thing she could do to fix it. Emma had to find Cat and bring her back. She had decided much earlier that day, Emma had to find Cat. She was in danger and

Emma would never let her face that danger alone. Unfortunately, that meant leaving Ryder.

The door opened.

Emma startled, jumping to her feet and running a hand down her hair to smooth the curls. She was wearing her favorite dress, a deep purple and silver one that shimmered in the moonlight. Just like the lovely clip in her hair and the betrothal ring she wore. Perfect. This was the image she wanted Ryder to remember.

He paused in the doorway, eyes meeting hers. Emma knew he was questioning why she was there. Working it out in his mind.

Ryder flashed a mischievous smile that made her feel effervescent. He closed the door, holding down the handle so it did not even click as the lock engaged. Leaving them completely alone in the low light. "You're not supposed to be here." His smile widened.

"Oh?" Emma feigned the most casual look she could. "Is this not my room? How embarrassing." She walked to the door, looking up at him. She could feel the warmth of his skin through his shirt. Could almost imagine that she could hear his heartbeat quicken. "I guess I had better go."

Ryder's hand caught hers, pulling it away from the door handle. "Why would you do that?"

"Because I'm not where I am supposed to be."

"I agree." He brought an arm around her waist, drawing her into the warmth of his chest. "You are supposed to be right here."

Emma smiled, her arms twining around his waist. "You're right, this is much better." Emma kissed him.

It felt like every other kiss. Tender and warm, full of unspoken words. The worst of them was goodbye. The one word she refused to say to him. Not because she did not think she would come back, but she knew he would not understand when he woke the next morning and she was gone. The weight of that secret exhausted her.

"Your heart is beating so fast." Ryder rested his cheek on top of Emma's head. "Is something wrong?"

"No," she clung to him, soaking in his warmth. "I'm just... I love you."

She stood on her toes to give him another kiss, just enough to show her sincere affection. Affection she wished she could remain in forever. "How was the meeting with your father and his advisors?"

"I see." Ryder threw his head back to laugh. "You are here to seduce me for information."

"Oh no. I am here to seduce you but I don't particularly care about the information."

His fingers tangled in her long curls. "Losing the alliance has complicated things with the dukes. My father will have to go to them to smooth things over."

"When will he return?"

"Not for at least a month. He needs to ensure we have their support if... if Reinsaffira chooses to attack."

Emma lifted an eyebrow. That was very interesting news. It would make getting away less complicated. Otherwise, Ryder would try to stop her. "And you will need to stand in for him as regent until his return?"

"Emma." Ryder's deep baritone vibrated off the marble floor. "You are up to something."

"Up to something? Ryder, I am insulted"

"I know you, Emma. You have a half-formed scheme brewing in that head of yours. What is it?"

There were times when how smart Ryder could be and how well knew her was very annoying. "Just because I am in a good mood does not mean I am up to something."

He raised an eyebrow. "That is exactly what it means, and whatever it is, you want to be sure I am too busy to stop you."

"That's nonsense."

He pulled her back into him, tilting her chin up to kiss her again. Emma let him, relishing the warmth of his skin. "You can tell me what you are planning now or you can tell me in an hour when you start to feel guilty. It's your choice. I don't mind either way."

"Fine," she pulled away from his kiss. "I was planning to leave the palace."

Ryder froze. "What?"

The words started tumbling out of her before she could think. "I'll come back! And I'll bring Cat with me. I'm going to find her. She's my best friend. I can't just sit here and wait for news that Sir Guy has betrayed her or..." Emma's voice broke off. Some feelings turned to glass when she tried to put them to words. Fears she could not speak of without admitting they could be true. "I should have kept her from leaving. I should have known better..."

"Emma! This is not your fault, and you can't fix it by tearing off into the wilderness too." Ryder's black curls fell across his forehead. He pushed them back. Emma's lips parted, ready to protest. "Please. I cannot lose you."

She raised her caramel eyes to meet his. Ryder's eyes were clenched shut, as if the thought of her leaving caused him physical pain. A grimace etched across his features.

"You won't lose me." Emma took a step back. She suddenly found herself unable to look at Ryder. Her attention was pulled down to the marble floor, tracing the swirling green with her toe. "She doesn't know about Sir Guy. I have to find her before something happens to her."

Ryder opened his mouth to speak. To reassure her. To tell her again that none of this was her fault. He did not get the chance. The door clanged open.

A dark haired guard rushed into the room. Simon, one of Ryder's personal guards. His hair had fallen from its ties, covering half his face. Panting and resting his hands on his knees. "Sire... I... I apologize for the interruption. There..." Simon took in a series of panting breaths. He must have sprinted the halls searching for them. "There is a messenger outside with word of Princess Catiya. He said he would only speak to you."

"A messenger?" Something burst inside of Emma. "From who? About what?"

Simon's eyes darted to Ryder, hanging with a question.

"It is okay," Ryder nodded.

"I did not recognize him, but he claims he was sent by Prince Phillip."

This was Evander's life now.

It had been weeks since he resigned his commission and he still could not ice a cake to Lydia's satisfaction. Every time, she grimaced at the mess of sugar he spilled across every cake. Finally, she pulled the bowl of icing away from him, tossing a broom into his hands, telling him she hoped he would be more proficient at sweeping, since it was closer to a sword.

When he was not doing his best to battle back the dust of the bakery, Evander spent his time skulking in the park in front of the palace, listening to every whisper that reached him, listening for any word of Cat or Sir Guy. Always nothing. You would think someone so consistently and noticeably out of place as Cat would turn up somewhere. Someone should have noticed her. Simon and Marcus had not turned up anything in their own investigations either. There was nothing he could do to stop Sir Guy and Lord Carswell. There was nothing he could do to find Cat. He was stuck, sweeping floors and icing cakes forever.

Evander swept the broom over the pale wooden floors, kicking up more dust than he gathered. Getting used to the idea that he was no longer a guard, destined for heroic gestures, was proving impossible.

"Evander!" The door crashed open, knocking a series of empty platters to the floor. Simon panted in the doorway, a wide smile on his face. "You won't believe it!" He panted. "I ran all the way here! It's incredible!"

"You ran here? Simon, it's midnight! What's going on?"

"Cat! She's coming back. The Reinsaffiran prince is bringing her back."

"What?" A surge of adrenaline burst through Evander's veins. He rushed to his friend, gripping his shoulders. "How..." Evander pulled Simon into the bakery, slamming the door shut, sliding the bolt into place. The dark street could hide any number of listening ears, including Carswell and his spies. "How do you know this?"

"A messenger arrived at the palace earlier this evening, a Reinsaffiran. He would only speak to Prince Ryder." They retreated into the kitchen as they spoke. "I was there. You should have seen the look on Lady Emma's face. I knew it had to be good news. I don't know all the details. It seems that something happened recently and the Reinsaffiran prince is bringing her home. It will be more than a week's journey, but she's coming home."

Evander was speechless, dropping into a chair by the work table.

"Well… this is good news. Aren't you happy?"

Happy? Evander was thrilled. Electricity buzzed across his skin, raising the hairs on his arms. Cat being home would make her easier to protect, except that he still was not a guard, and he still had no proof that Guy and Carswell were traitors. The danger was still real.

"Who else knows about this?"

"Who else knows? Evander this…"

"Doesn't change that Carswell is a traitor and Guy is a Salenian spy. Both of whom planned to take her to King Bastian. That's not going to change no matter where Cat is. We have to do something about that." Evander wanted to hit something. His fist slammed down on the work table. Knocking a bowl to the floor. It shattered. A satisfying sound until he looked over at the mess he created. Sugar mixed with shards of pottery strewn across the clean floor.

"Would you two stop shouting? I have to be up in a few hours." Lydia appeared in the stairway, Marcus lumbering behind her. "Did you break my best mixing bowl?"

Simon pointed an accusatory finger at Evander.

"I'll replace it. First, we need to get proof of Carswell's treachery, before Cat returns. Hopefully the prince can protect her until then."

Ryder brushed a curl away from Emma's face, letting his fingers linger on her cheek. She stirred in her sleep, clutching her book to her chest. He realized it had been weeks since he saw her sleep soundly. Even the night they found out Cat was returning, Emma had not truly slept. Worry had robbed her of rest to the point of finally crashing, falling asleep on a chaise at the center of the library. He should take her back to her room, where she could have a proper rest.

He lifted the worn volume out of her grip.

"I need that," she muttered sleepily. Emma did not open her eyes. Instead, she rolled onto her side, gripping the book tighter.

"I'm sure it will still be here in the morning... when you're rested." He smiled, helping her to sit up. "Unless you're not really all that tired. In which case, I can think of several other things we could do until morning." He watched Emma's delicate movements, the blush that rose in her cheeks. Her fingers smoothing her skirts and messy hair. Her lips parting in a half smile.

Now that the constant worry about his sister was coming to an end, Ryder found himself relaxing, just like Emma had, which meant he had to work much harder to hold himself back from Emma. Their wedding could not come soon enough. Perhaps it could be moved forward, when they had Cat back. The people of Volentia needed something happy to focus on.

Then Emma frowned, the moment coming to an abrupt end. "Why do you think Cat is coming back? Do you think something happened to her?"

"Emma, you're torturing yourself with what could have happened. She's safe. She's coming home. She will tell us everything else when she returns."

She glanced down at the book, fingers tracing the soft leather cover. "What if she does not make it back?"

"She will."

Emma shook her head, her hair cascading over one shoulder. "She was lured out of the palace for a reason. Someone wants to hurt her.

What if they succeed before she comes back? What if Carswell was right and she is a magix?"

Ryder took her hand. Squeezing lightly. Reassuringly. "First of all, Cat would never trust anyone, Carswell least of all, with a secret she had not trusted you with first. It's actually very annoying. And second, the prince is bringing her home along the coast. It's the safest possible route. She'll be home in a few days."

"I still should have stopped her or gone with her. All of this is my fault. Volentia is in danger because of me."

Before Ryder could reassure her, tell her once again that there was nothing she could have done to stop Cat from tearing off into the wilderness, a voice purred in the shadows. A sinister voice that made the hair on Ryder's neck stand on end.

"So, good things really do come to those who wait." Carswell stepped out from behind the shelves. "I never expected my exploration of the royal library to be so informative. Did I hear correctly that our lovely future queen is the spider responsible for losing the princess that sparked a war?" He leaned against the shelf. Casually crossing his arms.

"You!" Ryder bolted to his feet, heat rising in his cheeks. "You have no right to be here. You were banished from court."

"You forget, I am still the ambassador to Salene. Perhaps, I came to make a report. Though, I think what I've just learned will be considered far more interesting to King Bastian."

"You son of a..."

"Swearing in front of a lady?" Carswell clicked his tongue. "Hardly a princely thing to do, even if she is a treacherous snake. What will people say when they learn the two of you conspired to end the alliance with Reinsaffira? I daresay they will not be pleased. I wonder what they will do to you. I suppose all that is left for me to do now is rescue Princess Catiya, unimpeded by the two of you, of course." He rubbed his chin in thought. "She won't make a good wife, but I will not have to worry about that for long."

Ryder's hand flew to his hip, searching for his sword. Only air. There had never been a need to carry a weapon within the palace walls, until that moment. Ryder understood Carswell's intent. It was the same intent he had when he set his sights on Cat years ago. Power. It was always about power.

Ryder lunged at him. He would not be threatened in his own home. Not by this man.

He tackled him, knocking him to the floor. Grappling with him until his arms ached.

Suddenly, the duke went limp, falling to the ground. Blood seeping into the carpet. Emma over them, a bloodstained knife in her shaking hands.

"Emma, what did you do?"

"He was going to kill you!"

Ryder followed her gaze. Carswell held a small knife of his own.

Emma clutched the ancient book tight to her chest as she ran through the corridor. She had taken it from a hidden room she found beneath the royal wing, a place she definitely was not meant to snoop around, and she did not want it to be found and taken away. Emma needed it. If she was going to learn anything about the crone or the magic compass or why the crone needed Cat in the first place, she had to keep every ounce of information she could find on magic.

So far, all Emma had learned was that magic was far less interesting than fairy stories made it sound. In fact, it was almost boring.

Captain Roderick sat at his desk in the small office outside the royal armory. He looked so serious, poring over documents and maps. His spine was straight. His long dark hair tied into a neat ponytail. "Sir! Come quickly. Prince Ryder and I need you in the library."

"My lady," Roderick blinked, looking up at her. "What is the problem?"

Emma paused, balking under the captain's gaze. How was she going to explain the situation in the library to him? "I... We were attacked by Lord Carswell." Emma took in a deep breath. She could get through this, even if her blood-stained hands were shaking. "Gather some guards and bring them to the library. At once!"

Captain Roderick nodded, rising from his seat. "I'll gather the men."

Ryder was waiting in the corridor outside the library. Afternoon light hung in his dark hair, making it look almost blue. He jumped when she brushed her slender fingers against his sleeve. His beautiful storm-colored eyes falling on her. "What did you tell Roderick?"

Emma sighed. "Only that Carswell threatened us in the library."

Ryder nodded. "Good."

He turned back to the library doors, pulling them open. He paused in the doorway so suddenly that Emma did not notice his hulking form rooted in front of her. She walked into him. The large volume tumbling out of her arms.

"Ow! My love, what are you doing?" Emma reached for him.

He flinched away.

"He's gone. Carswell is gone." Ryder turned back to the corridor. His eyes darted into every dark shadow.

"What do you mean gone?" Emma forced her way past Ryder, into the library. She paced the carpet where the treacherous duke had fallen. Nothing. The plush carpet felt cool and dry under her slippered feet. But she was certain blood had stained the ornate pattern only a few moments before. Emma was certain of it. It was like he had never been there at all.

Goosebumps traced up Emma's arms, a shiver striking her. She had seen someone else disappear as if they had never existed, the woman responsible for all of this, and she knew how the crone had done it. Emma turned back to the doorway in search of her book. Her quarry sat directly in front of Emma, balanced in Ryder's hand. He studied the page intently.

"Emma, where did you get this?"

There was no time to explain. She pulled the book from his hand. The picture drawn across the page was of a beautiful woman transforming into a hideous old crone. She was close to the right place. She just had to find it, turning the pages with quick fingers. "We think all magic is the same, but it's not. There are three kinds of magic; Magix are born with magic and can control natural elements. It's natural. A person can be born with it, but without some kind of stone to direct the magic it remains dormant. Then there is magic that can be harnessed in potions and powders that can be used without being born with it." Emma's deep caramel eyes rounded, flipping back to the drawing. "Then there is shadow magic. It's the most dangerous." She tried to keep her tone even. "The book is written in ancient Salenian, but I think I understand it. They derive their power from Shadow and it... it does something to them. It's like being a conduit. Whatever it is, they become more power-ful. Some can even travel hundreds of miles in a single step." Emma flipped over the pages again, fingers glossing over the places where the ink was faded and washed away. "It all makes sense. A shadow magix, they're not a real magix they can take someone's power and..." She was speaking so quickly she doubted she was making any real sense.

"Emma!" Ryder gripped her wrist. "Where did you get that book?"

"Where I got it doesn't matter! Listen to what it is telling us. Carswell and the crone, they are both Shadow magix. He's alive and he knows where to find Cat now. And he can travel hundreds of miles through shadows!"

Ryder ignored everything Emma was saying. He grabbed the bool out of her hand, snapping it closed. "You cannot be found with this book. Anything to do with magic is... you have to hide this book."

"Why do you think I wouldn't let you take it from me earlier? Listen to what I am saying."

His lips unexpectedly brushed against hers. The kiss startled Emma just enough that she fell silent. "I believe you," he whispered, "but this is dangerous."

Footsteps announced Sir Roderick and the other guards' arrival.

Ryder rose to his full height. "Carswell has escaped." His voice was sure. Unwavering. "Search the palace for him; he could not have gotten far." His hand clasped around Emma's. "I will escort Lady Emma back to her chambers. Two of you, come with me and guard her door." He swept up the book and pushed it into her hands. "She may be attacked again."

"Ryder, he won't attack me. He is gone."

"He may be gone, but his accomplices may not be." He half dragged Emma from the room. "Tomorrow you can explain everything to me." He handed the book back to her.

Blood stained the damp stone floor beneath Carswell's feet. Not crimson; nearly black. Everything looked black in the dank ruined castle, even the burning liquid the crone poured onto his back. Fire shot through Carswell's wound, burning his veins. The pain almost made him wish the sorceress had left him to die in Volentia.

"You were told to wait in Volentia." The crone's grating voice scolded, echoing off the stone walls. "Not to announce our plans to the crown prince."

"Do not forget, I do not answer to you or your master," Carswell growled back, gritting his teeth against a second jolt of burning pain. "I was doing what was necessary to ensure the right future."

"And for it, you received a knife in your back and proved yourself a traitor." Her gnarled, steady hand pressed a rag into the wound.

Carswell tried to breathe through the searing pain.

"I cannot undo the damage you have done."

"I can." Carswell's eyes turned toward the dark-haired knight in the corner. "The damage would not have occurred if your spy had acquired the princess as we agreed. Perhaps we should find a new knight. One who knows how to keep a bargain."

"I did as agreed!" Guy spat, hands shaking with anger. The two men glared at each other. Carswell broke first. Not out of fear, but out of simple need. The knight was an oaf, but a useful oaf. They may still need him.

"You *agreed* to bring Princess Catiya here, the day after her betrothal was announced. You could not even manage to capture her when she was gift wrapped and delivered to you." The crone pressed a second rag into Carswell's wound as she spoke. Her voice rough with her anger. "All you claimed to need was her outside the palace walls. And you!" She glared at Carswell. "Your task was even simpler. All you needed to do was wait for the opportune moment." The crone walked to a small table between Carswell and Guy, picking up and studying a series of vials. "Do neither of you understand the precariousness of the situation we are in? We must perform the ritual at the next turn of the moon, or everything will be lost."

A trick of the light fooled Carswell's eyes into believing her black hair was silver, almost perfectly white. Then the illusion faded. She glided to a tall mirror in the corner.

"Tell me where she is! I will not fail again."

Carswell crossed his arms, pushing himself into a sitting position. "You had the opportunity to grab her at The Block. You failed. You failed at every attempt."

"Quiet! I will fetch her myself." The woman spoke into the mirror. Carswell wondered what she saw there. No image reflected in the clean glass. Was she seeing Bastian or was something darker hiding behind the reflection?

The heavy book lay open on Emma's lap, weighing down the blankets until she felt trapped beneath them. Her eyes were growing heavy. She glanced at the candle beside her, burned down to the stand, wax dripping onto the polished nightstand, ready to burn out. The sun would rise soon. In an hour, maybe two. Emma knew she ought to sleep, but she pressed on. Her eyelids drooping, she read the small print. Trying to find the meaning in the ancient letters. The book had stopped speaking to her. Emma was lost in the unfamiliar words. She knew what the crone was. What she did not know, and could not find, was how to fight her or what she wanted with Cat.

Her eyes fell shut for a third time. Emma shifted her weight so the book was laid open on her pillow, resting her head against the pages, inhaling the thick scent of old parchment. She would count to 100 then continue her work. There was no time to waste if she was going to find a way to keep Cat safe, once she returned. No one was going to be safe until she found a way to defeat the crone, the creature that lured Cat out of the palace and sent spies and raiders and those horrible shadows all those years ago. Until she found out why the crone wanted Cat in the first place.

1, she counted silently, 2, 3, 4...

Emma found herself standing in a ruined courtyard. She held a light bow in her hand. The pull against her shoulder told Emma she had her quiver filled with arrows as well. She pulled one from the quiver. Ominous, thick mists swirled around her. Emma spun around, searching for the source of the sick nervous feeling growing in the pit of her stomach.

The mists rolled across the cobblestones, clearing a path to the edge of the courtyard. Another girl with a sword in her hand stood under the gate. At first glance, Emma thought the girl was Cat, but when she looked again... she was all wrong. Everything was just slightly off. The girl's hair was too dark and her skin too pale. The woman's eyes that sent shivers across Emma's skin. The woman had crimson eyes.

The arrow Emma had prepared loosed before she could even think to aim, flying through the air.

Emma's aim had always been exquisite. The arrow struck the woman's heart. There was something about the heart. Emma's instincts told her that was the source of magic and that was how to defeat this woman; the crone she had come to despise.

Time slowed.

Emma stared at the woman, the arrow sunk into her chest, as she collapsed. She wore a wispy dress, the white gossamer fabric flowed around her, joining with the mist. A golden crown was nestled into her blood red hair. Blood, dark as her hair, soaked through the gown. The arrow protruded from her chest. Emma's aim had been true. She turned away, not wanting to see the horrible scene she had caused.

"Emma?" A quiet, familiar voice whispered across the fog.

"Cat?" Emma swiveled on the spot, unwilling to believe the trick her ears were playing. Eyes widening when they landed on the woman who lay dying on the ground.

The blood red hair lightening to a fiery copper. The red eyes that had left a chill in Emma's soul had turned to a soft emerald green.

"No!" The bow slipped from Emma's grip clattering to the ground. She ran to Cat, her dress tearing when she dropped to her knees at Cat's side. "No. No. No. Cat! I'm so sorry. What do I do? Tell me what to do."

The mist around them thickened. Emma did not know what to do. How had Cat transformed so much that Emma did not recognize he? Was this what magic did?

"Please. Cat. You have magic. You can save yourself. Please!" Blood covered her hands. Cat's white dress was stained a deep red. "Please Cat! Ryder! Help!" Emma called through her tears.

The jumble of blankets tangled around Emma, holding her down as she startled out of her dream.

Only a dream.

Ryder leaned over her, a cool hand pressed to her cheek. "Emma! Emma what's wrong? The guards said you were screaming in your sleep."

Her tears were hot, burning her eyes. It had not been real. The tears ran down her cheeks anyway; she tried to blink them back. The sight of her oldest friend covered in blood hovered behind her eyelids. The image would not leave her mind. Something about the dream was too real. An icy cold crept through her, starting at the pit of her stomach. "They're going to take Cat's magic and she'll become a shadow! We have to find her."

"That's not going to happen."

Wind swept over the beach, bringing a chill with it that made Cat shiver. She pulled her cloak tight around her, dipping her hand into her pocket, retrieving the compass that weighed her down. Thomas was taking her home. Curiosity still drew her to it. There was something, somewhere that she needed. It was not Thomas. It could never be Thomas. Even if he had not lied to her, his duty was to Reinsaffira and hers was to Volentia and no matter what he said, that would not change when they made it back to Volentia. By all rights, they were enemies now, and he was probably going to be imprisoned the second he stepped onto Volentian soil. But there was *something* out there that she needed and knew she would never find now.

The needle of the compass spun slower than ever before.

Cat dropped the compass into her lap. It landed with a clink against the jeweled dagger Emma had loaned her. The dagger was heavy. She ran a finger across the hilt, savoring the memory of her friend and her home.

The two items pulled her heart in two different directions.

"You're not considering running away again, are you?" Thomas adjusted his horse's saddle. Smiling at her. Always smiling. That same bright smile and teasing manner she had grown so accustomed to in such a short period of time.

"It's a big world." Cat shrugged. "And I've seen very little of it. There's always some part of me that is thinking of running away."

"Well, stop thinking about it." Prince Phillip appeared over the crest of the hill, throwing a small bag at his brother. Thomas caught it, tucking it into the saddle bags. "Because I am going to Reinsaffira, and he is going to Volentia and neither of us are going to go tearing off into the wilderness after you."

"I could go alone. I'm not afraid of the wilderness."

Prince Phillip laughed. "You, alone in the wild. I doubt you would last a day."

"I might."

"You were captured by pirates in less than a day. You were captured by *pirates* miles from the ocean. You really think you would survive alone in the wilderness? Without anyone to help you?"

Cat's eyes narrowed. Her cheeks grew hot. "I do not recall asking for your help with the pirates, or now for that matter."

"Of course. You don't need help from anyone." Phillip threw up his hands in obvious exasperation. "I only hope that when you die, which you will, your father and brother don't blame us for it and start a war. All because you are a stubborn princess who doesn't accept help from anyone. Whether you need it or not. Princesses," he grunted under his breath. "Even the intelligent ones tend to be rather useless. The sooner we get you back to Volentia the sooner everything can get back to normal."

"I'm not useless!"

Unsure of whether or not Phillip was including Cat among the *intelligent* princesses, she stood and stormed away. Her hands clenched into involuntary fists. She felt childish as she stomped her feet through the sand. Recent events told Cat she was not one of the intelligent princesses. An intelligent princess would have figured out who Thomas was at the very beginning. An intelligent princess would not be conflicted over running toward danger or returning home.

Cat rounded a bend, moving until she was out of sight of the two princes. She dropped onto a large stone, examining the dagger again, running her sleeve down the blade to clean it. She was not useless. Cat had been able to read as long as she could remember, and she knew every legend and fairy story from Brotid as well as Salene. She could speak the common language as well as ancient Reinsaffiran, and Salenian. There were other things. Roderick used to tell Cat that her skill with a sword rivaled that of any man. No one else in Volentia could climb the Dragon's Tooth. Even this dagger. Emma had once told Cat that this dagger had come from her birth mother's country and that only the descendants of a guardian could wield it. Surely, she could not be useless.

"I'm not useless."

"What's that, Princess?" Thomas' focus on her felt heavy.

"I'm not useless. I'm not a useless decoration in constant need of protecting and saving."

"You do get captured an awful lot." His smile flickered.

Cat grit her teeth, rising to her feet, the dagger gripped in her hand. "Well, I won't be captured again!"

"You shouldn't listen to Phillip; he's just cranky."

"And he's wrong!" The dagger shook under her tight grip. "I'm not useless. My mother was a warrior. She taught me how to protect myself and..."

"So, it is a family trait." Thomas laughed at his own private joke. "Cat, I don't believe that you are useless."

"No, you just think I am some stupid girl who could not figure out you were a prince. A convenient wife to bear your sons and a hostage to ensure my father honors your alliance." She glared up at him, waiting for Thomas to respond, but when her eyes met his, they were full of sadness. Watching her.

"I have never said any of those things, Cat." He took a step toward her, lifting his hand to caress her cheek. A new shiver traced through Cat's skin. The same silver shiver she felt whenever Thomas was close to her. It circled her wrist, tracking up her arm. Warming her despite the breeze. Her heart did a little skitter step. "I don't believe any of those things. Cat... I... I think you're amazing and I..."

The sound of footsteps brought the world back into focus. Cat pulled away from Thomas, tucking her chin against her shoulder and turning away. Phillip stood at the turn of the bend, glaring at them, arms crossed. "Are you two ready? We need to get moving if we are to reach the rendezvous." He spun back toward the horses, leaving Cat and Thomas alone again, but the moment between them was shattered.

Thomas raked his fingers through his hair. "I had better go help him with the horses. His mood will only worsen the longer we make him wait." He turned away, leaving Cat alone on the beach. A whole new wave of feelings overwhelmed her.

"What am I doing?" Cat ran a hand down her face. What was wrong with her? She wanted to kiss him and believe the things he told her. She just could not trade a single moment for a lifetime of heartache. "He will have to leave," Cat reminded herself. Thomas could not stay in Volentia. It was better to let him believe she did not want him. It was better to keep reminding herself that she could not trust him. Cat found the compass in her hand again. Absently tapping her thumb against the edge of the glass. The arrow made a long lazy circle, pausing on the bend in the coastline where Thomas had disappeared before suddenly swinging off to the east.

"Father, I need to know exactly why you arranged this marriage for Cat." Ryder stormed into his father's private study, trying to catch him before he left to meet with the dukes. The king looked pale. He claimed the stress strained his aging heart. Ryder suspected it was really the fear that kings were not meant to show.

"It was the best thing for the alliance."

"The truth! I want the truth about Cat's engagement. Does it have something to do with Mother's death? Cat's alleged magic?"

"Your sister's name is Catiya. Try to muddle your way all the way through it at least once in your life." Ryder's father glanced up from his stack of papers. He could be hard and unforgiving if he chose to be. He was not the only one.

Ryder glared back.

"My sister has been missing for weeks because you tried to force her into a marriage after giving her your word that was the one thing she would always have a choice in. We have knights lying to us. Lord Carswell has been here and the Reinsaffiran court sowing seeds of war, and he threatened me, and Emma. It all started because of Cat's betrothal. You owe me the truth."

The king sighed, sinking deeper into the cushioned chair. Lines etched around his eyes. A weight of exhaustion rounded his shoulders. "I had hoped she would just accept the betrothal. She would have been safe and out of Bastian's reach in the Reinsaffiran palace, unable to take the Salenian throne." He gestured for Ryder to take a second plush chair beside him, filling two silver chalices with wine. "Make yourself comfortable, son. The explanation is long."

The king took a long drink. Ryder leaned on his knees, restless with anticipation.

"Your mother and I were young when we met during the war. She was promised to a prominent lord in Salene. She could not take the throne until they were married. It is a very ancient law, something about complimenting magic. Instead, she married me and was banished for it." The king shook his head. "Anya always did whatever she pleased. Your sister most unfortunately shares that trait. Her decision broke centuries of tradition and left no descendant to take her place. It was decided Bastian would take the throne until such time as Cat could prove herself worthy of the throne."

"I know all of this."

"What you do not know," he pressed on with a hint of irritation, "is that Bastian believes in an evil lurking in Salene. Your mother called it The Darkness. An old Salenian legend about a great evil and a girl destined to defeat it or unleash it. She never believed it could be true but Bastian did. And Bastian believes Catiya is that girl."

Ryder thought back to the day Cat ran away. His father had asked him about magic. What had Emma dreamed the night before? Something about Cat being twisted into something unrecognizable and evil. "He believes Cat has magic."

"Anya and I hoped it would remain dormant; it should have been without a heart stone. If there was no reason to believe Catiya had magic, Bastian should have stopped chasing her. But he didn't. He never will. Reinsaffira has powerful protections against magic. Wards woven into the walls of their ancient castle. I knew if I got her there, she would be safe."

"But she's not safe. You said it yourself, she is too much like Mother to ever allow anyone to make her choices for her."

"Most unfortunately." The king placed a sad, tired, hand over his eyes. "At least we know Bastian does not have her yet. We would know if he did."

Ryder leaned back in his chair. "What do we do?"

"We hope she comes back before Bastian finds her. Then we find a way to salvage the alliance. With a bit of luck, I will still be capable of arranging a marriage for her that will make it impossible for her to ascend the throne. I only hope it is enough."

That was it? The king's only plan was to wait and hope Cat wandered back to the waning safety of the palace then force her back into the same situation that drove her away. Ryder fumed. Rising to his feet, knocking the heavy cushioned chair back. "That is madness."

He did not know what he was doing or planning to do; Ryder stormed out all the same. The heavy door slammed shut behind him. He would not sit around waiting for Bastian or some darkness to capture Cat and use her for its own purposes.

The morning felt unusually warm to Emma. She lifted her curls off her neck. Beads of sweat dotted her hairline. The fire cracked and popped in the low hearth. Emma wished the servants did not insist on heating the palace indiscriminately once Autumn hit. There was no need for this burning heat on such a lovely day. It was too hot. She could not focus. Tossing the book aside, Emma headed toward the balcony doors. Wind ruffled her hair when she opened them. The cool breeze swirled through the room, soothing her.

It was almost midday but Emma still wore her dressing gown. The night had been long and difficult. After the dream she could not sleep or even close her eyes without seeing visions of blood and Cat sprawled out on the courtyard bricks. She buried herself in the book from the catacombs. The hours leaching away her hope little by little. Sun, moon, stars, magic, it was all so confusing and complex. Trying to read ancient Salenian did not help. There were stories about shadows being controlled by magix, and stories about a great evil trapped in a mirror. None of it made sense.

Emma pulled her dressing gown tighter around her, suddenly cold despite the heat. Still deep in thought when the door to her chambers pushed open of its own accord.

"Have you slept at all?"

Emma turned to face Ryder, forcing a smile. "No more than I am sure you slept. How is the king?"

Ryder threw his hulking form onto the couch beside the fireplace. "My father is an old, mad, fool! Once Cat returns... if Cat returns, he plans to simply arrange a new marriage for her and go through all of this again. As if he has washed his hands of her. I have to admit; I am not far behind." The prince's eyes were dark and heavy.

"You won't."

"I might. Did she even consider that there would be consequences when she ran away?"

"I think she was more concerned with what would happen if she stayed." Emma knelt beside him, resting her hands on his arm. She could almost laugh at Ryder and his brooding, He was as stubborn as his sister, Emma loved him for it. "Besides, I know you won't give up on her when she comes back and immediately tries to run away again because you are afraid to find out which one of you I love more."

"Do not worry, I won't make you choose, but when my father announces that he is pursuing another marriage for her, you cannot let her run away again." Ryder's eyes locked on Emma for the first time since entering the room. Widening. "Why aren't you dressed? It's not... I shouldn't..."

Emma's smile broadened. "I believe I was in my chambers and that you barged in uninvited."

The two stared at each other, waiting for the other to make a move. It was Emma who finally lowered her gaze. The light breeze made the fire dance, and the change in the light made Ryder's hair gleam.

"I've been reading since dawn. I had not stopped until just before you came in *uninvited*. I suppose I forgot to dress. Did you learn anything else from your father?"

"Get dressed and I will tell you."

"Honestly? You cannot control yourself long enough to just tell me?"

Ryder rubbed the pain and tiredness from his eyes, finding a spot on the wall to focus on as he spoke. "I won't be able to concentrate properly."

Emma rolled her eyes, stepping behind the privacy screen. "Fine. Tell me while I change."

His exhausted voice rumbled, relating what the king had told him. "I knew it did not make sense that Bastian was just after the throne. Cat came of age years ago. Why come after her again now? My father said it had something do with The Darkness."

Emma pulled a simple lavender dress over her head. The static material made her hair crackle. She chewed her lip in thought, stepping out, fully dressed. "Better?" Ryder's sigh of relief told her it was. "I have been reading and there is something about *The Darkness* and using a girl's magic and blood to unleash it." She picked up the book The cover crumbling in her fingers, the spine held together by only a few threads. "What if that is what Bastian has always wanted Cat for? Could she be this *daughter of the prophecy* with magic to free this Darkness?"

"I thought you did not believe Cat had magic. 'She would have told you.'"

"She would have... if she had known."

The compass arrow wavered, pointing eastward again. The waves lapping at the sand beach at Cat's back soothed her, stilling the nerves that danced up her spine. Whatever was on the distant end of the compass needle was to the east. Not the south. Not in Volentia.

"We're close. I can feel it."

Cat snapped the compass closed, dropping it into her pocket. She was supposed to be gathering firewood. She needed to focus on the tasks at hand.

"If we get up at dawn tomorrow, we should be able to reach the palace by tomorrow night." Thomas spoke behind her. A pile of sticks clattering to the ground. "Is something wrong?"

Cat's shoulders slumped. She spun around, dropping onto a smooth driftwood log in front of the crackling fire Thomas had coaxed to life. Her fingers knotted in her lap. Thomas sat beside her. His fingers brushed hers and her skin heated at his touch. She jolted, stiffening. One more thing Cat did not need to confuse her. One more decision she did not know how to make. She pushed her long hair away from her face.

"You know, you can tell me if something is bothering you. Are you concerned about the gossip when you return to Volentia?" He smiled. "I would have thought you'd be used to all that by now. You *have* been a princess your entire life, after all."

"You do make it easy to continue to be annoyed with you." Cat swept back her long hair, starting to twist it into a braid. Thomas nudged her with his shoulder. The loose braid slipped from her fingers and fell in front of her face again. "Fine. I'm just... I'm afraid I'll regret it."

"Staying annoyed with me? I'm certain you will."

Cat slugged his arm, without deciding to do it. "Going home. Not finding out what's on the other end of this." She pulled the compass from her pocket again. Heavy and cool against her palm. "What if this is my only chance to have an adventure and I'm squandering it? What if... What if I'm not ready to go back to Volentia?"

It was a stupid question. Pointless to even consider. The *prince* was taking her home and that was the end of it. Thomas had responsibilities and so did she. This adventure had always been nothing more than a dream. One it was time to wake up from.

Thomas' fingers brushed over hers, plucking the compass from her grip and opening it. "I already told you, it does not matter to me where we go. Volentia, Reinsaffira, out there. I will go with you. I will fight for you. If you want to keep following that compass then I will go with you, because I love you."

"Thomas!" Cat rose. They had been through all of this before.

His hand was on her wrist in a flash of movement, pulling her to a stop. "Please wait."

"Is it really that simple to you? Abandoning your family, your responsibilities, your kingdom without thought, just for me? How can you do that?"

"I don't believe there is anything *just* about you." He brushed his long fingers through his curls. They had grown shaggy and unkempt. Messy in an endearing way. "It's easy, really. You decide what is most important to you and you do what it takes to get it. Can I ask..." he tugged lightly on her wrist a second time, pulling her back toward their driftwood bench. He held out the compass in his other hand. "Why is this so important to you? You had other options the night you ran away, but you chose to follow this compass. Why?"

The reason was so heavy on her shoulders. It pulled Cat down onto the seat. "My mother. She..." Cat twisted her fingers together. "I suppose you did not know that my parents did not meet in a palace. She actually robbed him in the forest in Salene."

"I thought your mother was a princess before she married your father."

"Technically, she was a queen. It's complicated. She had left the castle in order to protect her people when Reinsaffira cut off trade with Salene. No matter what it cost her, she always made the right choice for her people. She was always brave. She was all the things that I am not. I had hoped that... because the person who gave me this compass also had this," Cat's fingers found the glittering stone resting on her collarbone. "I hoped the compass might lead to something that would make me more like the person she wanted me to be. That that was why she wanted me to have it." The words tasted sour. Cat's throat tightened as she spoke. She dropped the stone, letting it land against her collarbone with a thump. "And I can't even make the decision to keep going after it because I'm selfish and scared. It doesn't matter what's at the end of that stupid compass. I've already made every wrong choice and ruined everything. There's nothing that can fix that."

She curled in on herself, pulling her knees to her chest, suddenly shivering. A light breeze off the sea swirled around her. The fire flickered and sputtered. The orange glow fading into darkness. Cat stretched her fingers toward the dying coals. A blaze of light danced off her fingertips, setting the pile of branches burning anew. The lightest trace of a smile formed on her lips.

"What choice should you have made?" The prince curled his arm around Cat's waist. A different kind of warmth emanated off him. Cat leaned into his touch.

"Staying in Volentia... marrying you." Her chest tightened. That was the decision her mother would have made. Ryder would have done the same thing. It was the best thing for Volentia's people, and that was her only duty as a princess. If she had stayed, Reinsaffira and Volentia would still be allies.

"I would have liked that but..." She could feel him shaking his head as he spoke. "Would you have fallen in love with me, if you had?"

"Who said I love you?"

Thomas shot an annoyed look her way. "Fine. Would you ever fall in love with any man who was chosen for you? A man who dragged you away from your home and family?"

"No." Cat shook her head. Cat would have never given herself the chance to love him. She would never have forgiven him for simply being the person someone else had chosen.

"I did not believe so. You seem stubborn that way."

"I'm a princess; the preferred term is headstrong. But that is not what matters. What matters is securing the alliance with Reinsaffira. Princes and Princesses are not given the luxury of love."

"You need to worry less about what others will give you. For better or worse, you did make a choice and now you can make another. Cat..."

Thomas' voice caught. He pressed the compass into her palm. Cat watched his Adam's-apple bob as he swallowed, preparing to speak. Whatever he wanted to ask was weighing heavy inside of him. "Cat… would you choose me now? If you believed you had that choice?"

"Yes," she whispered. "I would."

Thomas lifted her hand, pressing a kiss into her cold fingers. Silver shivers washed over her skin. "Then we can save the alliance together, and afterward, if you want, we can go find what is on the other end of that compass."

Cat leaned her head on the prince's shoulder. She shivered again. Exhaustion washed over her, hitting like an unnatural weight. "Okay."

Thomas startled awake. A shiver tracing over his skin. Stars twinkled in the velvet sky above him. The fire had died down to ash. There was not even smoke swirling above the charred sticks. It must have just been the cold that woke him. It was October now, after all, and the nights were cold.

Just the cold.

Thomas pulled his cloak tight around his shoulders, letting his eyes drift closed again.

The shiver ran over his skin again.

Thomas jolted. Not cold. Something else had woken him. A sound? A feeling? A sense at the back of his mind that was familiar. Almost a memory. Like the magic of the dreams, he once had about Cat and the shadow that ripped her away from him.

He sat up, peering through the darkness to the place where Cat slept. The darkness was thick. Writhing. Alive. A shadowy hand was clamped over Cat's throat. She gasped for breath, stretching an arm out toward Thomas. Her green eyes were wide, fluttering as her skin paled.

"Cat!" Thomas forced himself to his feet, staggering toward her.

Trying to push the thing, the shadow away from her. It dissolved in his hands only to reform. Cat was fading away with it.

He did the first thing that came to his frantic mind. He grabbed Cat's hand. Her fingers curled around his wrist, trying to hold onto him as he held onto her.

Light flashed.

Darkness pressed in around them both. Ice cold and binding. Burning his skin.

Then, suddenly, Thomas found himself standing in a dark but familiar forest. Trees leaned in around him. He knew this place. The memory was burned into him. It lived in his skin. Everything was just as he remembered it from his dreams. The first moment he saw Cat. The dream where he held onto Cat and a shadow pulled her away from him. Just as it was doing now. "Cat! I'm not letting you go this time. I found you and I will not let you go." The shadow pulled at her. Thomas' grip tightened as her fingers slipped from his grasp. She was fading away. They would be separated and he knew he would never find her again.

The shadow pulled her away, dragging Thomas with her deeper into the night.

A jolt went through him. Thomas stumbled forward, landing in the mossy clearing. It was very much the same as the forest he just stood in, only more real. Tangible. He realized he was sprawled on the ground, Cat's ice-cold hand still in his grip. Thomas pushed himself up, leaning over Cat. She was so still. Too still. Her skin was almost gray. Her eyes closed. Thomas' fingers brushed across her skin and throat, searching for a pulse.

"Cat! Cat, please! Please wake up!" Her skin was still warm.

"Relax, she will live." A scratching, gravel voice sounded. Thomas spun toward it. A woman sat hunched on the far side of the clearing. Her skin was a similar shade of gray as Cat's. Exhausted. Panting. Dying. "If I was able to kill her, she would have been dead long before you ever met her."

"You!" He knew her. The crone who lured Cat into the wild with the compass. Why was she here? Cat's dagger still hung from her belt.

Thomas snatched it up, ready to attack the woman. The hilt grew hot. Burning hot against his palm. His fingers clenched, trying to hold onto the blade, but he could not. The dagger slipped from his fingers, falling to the ground, the pale opal gem on the pommel gleaming a deep red. Thomas risked a glance away from the crone at his burned palm. An angry burn blistered where he gripped the dagger.

The crone approached. Shuffling toward him with stiff aching movements. Her gnarled hand was balled into a fist.

"What do you want? Why did you bring us here?"

"Us? No. You were never supposed to be here. Your insistence on getting in my way has been so very frustrating, but that is over now." The crone was so close now he could smell the heat of her breath as she spoke. "Her." The crone sneered, looking down at Cat's still form. "Her I want to see dead, and her power buried beneath the indifference of time. Unluckily for her, that choice is not mine to make, and what Bastian wants her for will be so much worse. But you don't have to worry about that." She lifted her hand, palm up to reveal a pile of glittering white dust and blew it into Thomas' face and eyes. "You won't live long enough to see it."

The sun was shining, gray and green, when Cat's eyes fluttered open just past dawn. Her throat ached. Her neck and shoulders were stiff. Cat tightened her cloak around her shoulders, curling up on the bed of moss, soft and safe. She was not ready to wake up.

Moss?

The question formed quickly in Cat's mind. They had made camp on a secluded sand covered beach. There certainly had not been moss there.

Cat pushed herself up, scanning the clearing. Her shoulders and neck were too stiff to move. Her skin was sensitive to the touch, tender with bruises. Nothing was familiar. The only thing she recognized was Thomas' sleeping form beside her.

But where were they?

"Thomas?" Cat reached out, shaking Thomas' shoulder, still scanning the clearing. He remained still. "Wake up! I... I need your help!"

"Oh, he won't wake. Only he can break free of the spell." Cat knew that voice. It scraped her ears and mind, sending shivers through her.

Cat dug her dagger out of the grass, leaping to her feet. Spinning. Searching. "Where are you?"

"Right here, little dove." The crone stepped out of the trees. Cat recognized her in an instant. The woman who had given her the compass. She did not understand. Was this a vision? An illusion? How could she be there?

In an instant the woman's dry hair softened, lightening to a silver blonde. Her wrinkles faded away. Transforming the woman. It startled Cat; she knew this woman as well. A memory from years ago, when this woman approached Cat in an alleyway and tried to bury a knife in her heart. That was why the voice was so familiar. It was the voice inside every shadow that haunted her nightmares. Cat's blood turned to ice.

"You have proved to be challenging prey, but the hunt is over, my dear."

"Who are you?"

The crone returned. Stringy dark hair falling in her face. She grimaced, as if the transformation hurt. "It does not matter. I am not the person you need to worry about. Say goodbye to your prince. He will not be joining us."

Cat glanced back at Thomas. "What did you do to him?" The filigree wrapping the hilt of the dagger dug into Cat's palm. Anger filled her chest.

The crone lifted her hand, palm up, revealing a glittering handful of diamond dust. "You'll see." She smiled, blowing the dust into Cat's eyes with the gentleness of blowing a kiss. It sparkled at the edge of Cat's vision.

The world slowed around her.

Everything felt heavy.

The dagger clattered to the ground and the gray light faded away.

Cat was falling.

PART

FOUR

Part Four

Ice cold drops of water splattered against the stone floor, hitting Cat's cheek. The sensation pulled her out of a dreamless sleep. Rough stone dug into Cat's hip and shoulder, draining the heat from her body. Her head throbbed with a blinding pain. It was the second time in a week that she had awoken unsure of where she was. Cat tried to study her surroundings through bleary eyes.

A sick sensation rose in her stomach. Shame and guilt welled up inside of her, making her head hurt.

Cat clenched her eyes shut against the sudden pain and nausea.

That witch tricked her, and Cat had stupidly fallen for it! She was so stupid! Selfish need had blinded her and put everyone she cared about in danger. She had fallen into a trap.

She opened her eyes again.

Cat was in a narrow stone cell. Gray brick walls loomed over her, less than four feet apart. Black iron bars blocked the narrow doorway. The bars were old, dripping with rust. Somewhere above her a slit of an open window let in the dwindling light and freezing rain.

Cat clenched her eyes shut again. Her head still throbbed. Her wrists and throat ached. Every part of her felt heavy.

The witch was the last thing Cat remembered. The powder she flung at Cat must have been a sleeping drug. But why bring her here?

A scuffling and scraping sound in the distance drew Cat's attention back to the doorway. The world slowly becoming sharper, more focused.

The sharp sound continued. Like dragging feet approaching her dim little prison. Panic rose to the back of Cat's tongue. She had to get out before the shuffling feet brought their owner to her.

Pressing her shaking palms into the stone floor, Cat tried to stand, ignoring the rush of dizziness. Cat took a tentative step toward the cell door. A weight tore at Cat's wrists. For the first time since waking, she looked at her hands. Heavy manacles and chains hung from her wrists. She pushed away the false hope. There would be no escaping. No one was strong enough to pull free of the tight chains she was at the end of. The steel manacles bit into her wrists. The door was still a foot away.

Cat's travel-stained clothes were gone as well, replaced by a loose white gown. Her arms were exposed and her feet were bare. Goosebumps prickled her skin.

"Poor little butterfly, caught in a web," a thin voice growled at her. A hulking figure with crimson eyes stood on the far side of the bars. King Bastian. Cat backed away, bumping into the wall, wishing to be away from him and his unnatural eyes.

There was nowhere to go.

Bastian unlocked the cell door. Metal screeched as he pushed it open. The man was massive, nearly seven feet tall. He wore a heavy purple cloak over blood red robes. A jeweled crescent moon broach held the cloak in place. The Salenian royal crest. Cat had seen it in her mother's jewelry.

"King Bastian." Cat tried to sound brave. She failed. Her voice was trembling as much as her legs. "You have to release me! If you return me to my home, you will receive anything you want in ransom. I promise."

The wall was ice cold against Cat's back.

Bastian stepped into the cell. His claw-like fingers ran along Cat's collarbone. Cat winced, feeling blood draw to the surface of her skin. His eyes appraised her and the blood he had drawn. "Ransom? My precious little princess, there is nothing your father can offer that is more valuable than you."

"Me?" Cat pushed Bastian away from her, struggling against the weight of her chains. "Whatever you want with me, you won't get away with it. Thomas will…"

"Thomas? You mean your weakling prince? You should know better than to count on his rescue. Isn't he a *liar*?" Bastian flung her own words back in her face. "Even if he manages to wake from his sleep, he will never find you. And your family? Why would they come looking for you? You abandoned them. You destroyed everything they worked so hard for. Didn't you wonder why your brother or Lady Emma never went searching for you? Deep down you knew they always believed you were nothing more than a self-centered, spoiled princess." Bastian's mouth curled into a cruel smile. "Besides, even if someone was coming to rescue you, once the connection is formed, it cannot be severed. I am afraid your story does not have a happy ending."

Bastian turned away from Cat. He paused in the doorway, holding out a silver key to an unknown accomplice in the shadows. "Sir Guy. Escort my niece to the great hall. It's time."

A familiar knight stepped into view.

Cat shook her head in disbelief. Thomas had told her about Guy betraying her family after he pressed a knife to her throat at The Block. Still, she could not fully believe it. Guy had sworn an oath to protect Volentia. To protect her. Her father gave him a home, trained him to be a knight.

Cat scrambled back, finding only the brick wall against her back. Guy grabbed her wrist, pulling them forward. Cat struggled to pull free of his grip.

"Stop fighting me!" He unlocked the manacles, twisting her arms behind her back and dragging her forward. "My king assures me that, so long as you cooperate, draining your magic will be relatively painless."

"Why are you doing this?" Cat kicked feet forward, bracing them against the stone steps in front of her, slowing their way. Guy's grip on her only tightened, wrenching her arms harder behind her back until pain shot through her shoulders.

Guy slipped on the steps. Dropping Cat on the hard stones. Before

Cat could scramble away, he grabbed her by the hair, dragging her to her feet.

"Why would you betray Volentia like this?"

"Betray Volentia," he hissed into her ear. His breath burned her neck. "I am not Volentian. I'm Salenian and unlike your coward of a mother, I have no intention of abandoning my people. Once my king is finished with you, he will be unstoppable. We will burn Volentia and Reinsaffira to the ground and take back what belongs to us." His grip on her hair tightened. "Now move. Or I will break that pretty face of yours."

The sun-bathed field surrounding Thomas smelled like lavender and honeysuckles. Tall grass swayed around him, dancing on the wind. Thomas smiled to himself, resting his head on his arm, enjoying the beautiful summer day. Summer on the Northern Isles was always Thomas' favorite. It was comfortable and mild. He picked one of the delicate white and yellow flowers that dotted the field, plucking the petals and letting them fall into the tall grass.

There was something he was meant to be doing. Something important. It nagged at his mind as he let the last petal fall to the ground. It had to do with Cat and Volentia.

"Cat!" Thomas startled. Where was Cat? He had been with her and then something happened. Thomas had to find her.

He pushed himself to his feet. Urgency filled his veins as he scanned the field for Cat. For any trace of her red hair. She had to be there. Cat had been with him and then there was that shadow and the crone and... She was in danger. She was...

Thomas stumbled to a stop.

Cat was standing in front of him.

The sick feeling of worry vanished.

Her long red hair was swept up, elegantly styled to frame the glittering diamond tiara she wore. Not the rose gold tiara he remembered from his dreams. Not the crown of a Volentian princess but a Reinsaf-firan princess. *His* princess. Thomas paused to take in the sapphire blue dress that clung to her, eyes settling on the ring on her left hand. A silver ring with a glittering sapphire. The same ring that had weighed down his pocket for weeks. Which could only mean... she really was his.

"Princess!" Thomas ran to her, wrapping his arms around her waist. His princess. Perfectly and beautifully his. She laughed as he spun her around; arms tight around his neck. When her feet finally touched the ground, Cat gripped Thomas by the collar, lifting herself on her toes to kiss him.

Thomas hesitated, pulling back. He looked around the field. A place he knew well, but he did not know how he had gotten here. Or how Cat had gotten here. The last thing he remembered... It was hard to focus on anything outside of that moment, but Thomas was certain Cat had been in danger. There had been a forest and before that they had made camp on a beach on their way to Volentia.

"This isn't real." He stumbled back, pushing Cat away because it was not Cat. The crone had taken her away from him. "Where is Cat?"

The figment's eyes burned. "What are you talking about, Thomas?" The timbre of her voice was wrong. It felt flinty and dull.

Thomas took another step back before the thing could draw him in again. He knew Cat. This was not her. Cat was unpredictable, like a flash of lightning. This creature looked like her but lacked Cat's move-ments. She smiled too easily. Too seductively. As if she were a fantasy meant to trap and distract him.

"You're not her. This isn't real."

"Why does that matter?"

"Because it isn't real! Cat needs me. The real Cat. I have to find her." He tried to push past the figment, scanning the familiar field. How had he gotten here and how did he get out? His eyes lit on a pond on the edge of the tree line. One he knew did not belong. It had never been there before.

The figment gripped his arm, pulling Thomas back. "You'll never find her. Even if you do..." She smiled, a cruel smile unlike the one he had become so familiar with. "You cannot ever have this." She swept a hand, gesturing to the world around them. To the crown and dress, her engagement ring glinting in the golden light. "You can never have her. You know your father will never let you marry a magix. He will never let her tainted blood near the throne. But if you stay here with me and you will have everything you want."

"No!" Thomas stumbled back, creating much needed distance between him and this thing. The real Cat was somewhere and she needed him. Even if what the spirit said was true. Even if he felt a pull toward her. If he succumbed to this fantasy, Cat would die.

He sprinted to the pond. Staring into it. The reflection was wrong. It was all trees and a gleaming moon. A different world than the one he stood in. This had to be the path back.

"You want to find your princess?" The figment's voice hissed into his ear. Her fingers curled around his arm. "Then let me take you to her." She dragged Thomas beneath the surface so quickly, he did not have the chance to take a breath. She pulled him down to the stony bottom. Disappointment burned like the suffocating feeling in his lungs when there was no way out, only a lake bed at the bottom. His body called out for air but he could not wrestle out of the figment's grip. She forced his body against the rocks, smiling all the while. "You are already too late. She is going to die and there is nothing you can do to save her."

Thomas tried to shove her away.

Sand and air bubbles swirled around him, stirring up the lake bed to reveal a long knife buried there. He reached for it, grasping the hilt.

Thomas lifted the sword to kill the creature, but, when he looked up, it was Cat's face he saw.

Cat.

No. It wasn't Cat.

This was a creature of magic who was trying to keep him from Cat. And Cat was in danger. He clenched his eyes shut, shoving the knife into the creature's gut. The crimson tang of blood swirled around Thomas. The creature's grip loosened, hands falling away. She drifted to the lake bed, no longer Cat, but the image of the crone who had taken her. Thomas pushed himself up, swimming toward the pond's surface.

He startled awake, gasping for breath.

Thomas was stretched out on the moss in a wooded clearing. It was the same clearing the crone had brought him to. Gnarled branches blocked the setting sun. He had lost a full day, maybe more. Thomas could not be certain. There was only one certainty in Thomas' mind; Cat was in danger. He had to find her.

On the far side of a clearing stood a glittering lake. Gleaming in the moonlight. It was the same lake Thomas saw in his dream, he was sure of it. Thomas stumbled to it. Scrubbing the cold water over his face, waking himself just enough to think clearly.

The lake surface smoothed, revealing a woman with dark brown hair standing over him.

Thomas lurched back. There was nothing, just air and emptiness behind him. No woman. No one. He leaned over the water again. The woman still stood there, her image wavering in rippling water. There was something about her that reminded him of Cat, not in the way the figment had been like Cat. It was just a sense. No, not Cat. The woman's forehead was the same shape as Prince Ryder's with the same worried creases etched across it.

"Prince Thomas!" The woman's voice was strange. A dim echo. As if she were speaking from a great distance. "Prince Thomas! Catiya needs your help. You have to hurry. Before it's too late."

Thomas' eyebrows knit together in confusion. He was going mad. "Where is she?"

The woman stretched out a hand, pointing out over the lake. Thomas followed the woman's gaze out into the forest. In the distance, through a gap in the thick trees, he could see smoke rising up from a distant valley. "Sybilla's ruined castle. You must hurry, before the moon is at its peak." Her image wavered, fading into the murky water.

"Wait! How do I find her?"

The woman was gone.

Bruises were forming on Cat's arms as she struggled to get away from Guy's relentless grip. He had dragged her into a great hall, though, calling it a great hall felt like a stretch. It was a menacing place. Torches bathed the crumbling limestone in red light. The full moon shone through a circular window at the zenith of the curved roof, open to the night. There was a rough stone altar covered in vines on the far side of the room.

Guy dragged her toward it.

Bastian stood beside the altar, sharpening a knife in the pale moonlight, silently watching the moon track across the sky.

A shaft of moonlight hit the altar and the torches dimmed. The light being pulled from the room.

"The hour has come." Bastian lifted Emma's jeweled dagger in his hands. "Begin."

Guy's grip on Cat tightened, forcing her left arm into the shaft of cold light.

The crone stepped out of the shadows. Her eyes were heavy with sadness when she looked at Cat. She rested her palm on Cat's cheek. The woman's hands were ice cold, freezing Cat's blood in her veins. Then the crone closed her eyes, singing in a clear ringing voice. The unfamiliar words drifted over Cat, a strange language she did not recognize.

The song sent fear bubbling through her; building in the pit of her stomach, stretching over her skin. She twisted in Guy's grip as Bastian approached. "Please, don't do this."

Bastian ran a hand over the blade. He drew close to Cat. The dagger was definitely Emma's; Cat recognized the glittering opal. But that should be impossible. The dagger was meant to be magic. Only Emma and Cat had ever been able to hold it for more than a few seconds.

He pressed the blade to her skin, cutting deep into Cat's arm. Heat and pain burned through her skin. She bit her lip, holding back a shout of pain.

Bastian lifted the dagger a second time, cutting his own forearm.

Blood poured from both wounds.

The crone worked quickly, producing Cat's heart stone and an empty vial. Capturing the dripping blood in the vial, she twirled her wrist, mixing the blood within the glass, continuing her chant. It started to glow, turning to a sickening, inky black that soaked up every ounce of moonlight. Next, she lifted the heart stone into the moonlight, letting the blood pour onto it, binding Cat's magic to Bastian. Cat could feel it, a link forming between her and her uncle. She could sense his thoughts and the pain burning through him, the same pain that burned through her, but unlike Cat, the binding seemed to strengthen Bastian. Cat felt her body sagging in Guy's arms, all of her strength slipping away. The diamond turned pitch black the instant the blood touched it.

The crone turned away, still singing her horrid tune. Her voice grew sad as she placed the necklace, Cat's mother's necklace, around Bastian's neck.

He straightened his shoulders, setting the dagger aside.

There was a pull at Cat's magic.

Orange flames burst from Bastian's hand. His lips curled in a cruel smile. "Very good. Make sure we have enough of her blood."

The crone produced a second vial, gathering the blood that dripped from Cat's arm, before pouring a black goopy liquid over the cut. Fire burned through Cat's veins, tracing all the way to her heart. There was no biting back the scream that ripped through her body as the cut sealed, sapping the strength from Cat's body.

She collapsed in Guy's arms.

When Cat woke a moment later her wound was sealed, stained an inky black, like she had been burned. Every inch of her skin ached.

The moon had passed out of the hall.

Bastian stood tall; Cat's heart stone glowing a deep red, nearly black against his chest. She could feel her strength and magic pull toward him, draining.

"Sir Guy," Bastian rumbled, "please escort Princess Catiya back to her *chambers*."

"You might as well kill me," Cat heard her own voice, distant like a half-remembered dream. "Just like you killed my mother."

"Your mother's death was a tragedy that could have been avoided, if she didn't foolishly believe a lie she had told herself."

"And what lie was that?"

"That you would be a worthy queen. You should thank me. If she had lived, she would have seen how foolish you grew up to be." Bastian lifted Cat's chin, forcing her to stare into his crimson eyes. "You murdered your mother, and now you have made her sacrifice a waste." He shoved her face away with a look of disgust. "Take her away."

Guy lifted Cat in his arms. His touch was almost gentle as he carried her out of the hall.

Phillip thought the council room was darker than usual. Perhaps it was just the way his father fumed in the large throne at the head of the table. A quiet rage pulsed off his skin, fuming at Phillip's news.

"How the devil did she get away from you?" The storm broke loose. "You had one job, make sure your brother and the Volentian princess return here, and somehow they just slipped away from you?" His hands slammed on the table. "You let them get away! And you're lying to me about it. It's the only explanation."

"Why would I lie? Why would I help Thomas break his word?"

"You are brothers." His father waved a dismissive hand. "I know you have always idolized him. I doubt there is anything you would not do if he asked."

Phillip exhaled, gathering his words. He was not sure what to tell his father. Thomas and the princess should be back in Volentia by now. His father was not likely to send men there. There was no reason to keep the truth from him any longer. "You are right. He asked for my help. I gave it to him. When I left, he was taking the princess back to Volentia, where he planned to stay until the problems with the alliance could be resolved."

His father rolled his eyes, drumming jeweled fingers on the table. "There was a time when I had a great deal of hope for this kingdom's future. I believed that when Thomas strayed from his path, you would guide him back to it. Instead, you aid him in his foolishness. As if Arik was not bad enough. Now... It seems my only option is to live forever. Neither of you are capable of bearing the weight of ruling."

"If that is your plan, then I see no reason to deny my brother the right to choose the princess as his bride."

The king snorted, annoyed by the very notion. He rose, moving to the door. He muttered a command to the guard, something Phillip did not hear. "And you think that is a good idea? Even though she is a magix?"

"What she is is the girl your son has been in love with for years."

"No! She is a Salenian magix! A danger to our way of life. What happens when her powers get the better of her and she kills your brother? Have you thought through the consequences if something happens to her or your brother?"

Captain Roderick slid the ribbon from his hair, letting the loose ponytail fall free. A dull ache was forming behind his eyes.

The window in his quarters looked out over the city. Overlooking the main thoroughfare that cut through the rows of shops and houses, stretched out before him. He leaned against the stone window sill, watching the ebb and flow of people through the street. As if he could pick out two people among the hundreds. Still, he kept watch, knowing that even now, as the city quieted, and the streets emptied, he would not be able to see Cat's approach.

The messenger said she would be returning with Prince Thomas by the coast. Even if she was coming from as far north as the sapphire beach, Cat should arrive any day now.

But the seconds and days ticked by, and Cat did not arrive.

His chest tightened with anxiety.

Roderick tapped out a nervous rhythm on the window sill. The inkling of danger was nothing more than his anxious mind. He shoved the worries away, searching the street for a wisp of red hair.

"My lord?" One of the younger guards stepped into the room. "There is a man at the gate asking to see you."

Hope bubbled up in his chest. Roderick spun around to face him. "A man? Who is he?"

"Evander. The guard who tendered his resignation a few weeks ago."

The bubble burst.

Not the prince returning Cat.

It felt strange to worry over Princess Catiya. She was capable of handling herself; Roderick had done everything in his power to be sure of that. In fact, he had not truly worried about her until Lord Carswell vanished. There had been a shift that night. A turning point he barely recognized, but felt in his heart. A distant, looming danger, drawing close enough to finally see.

"Bring him up." Roderick dropped into a chair by the window. Defeated.

It took several minutes for the guard to return to the palace gate and escort Evander up to Roderick's chambers. By the time he stepped through the door, Roderick had recaptured his hair in the low ponytail, regaining a small semblance of decorum.

Evander had always been an excellent guard. He was loyal, honorable, and a good fighter. Roderick hated losing him from the royal guard. Evander still carried himself like a soldier, with stiff shoulders and a straight back, standing tall in the center of the room. Waiting for an order. Something told Roderick this was not a social call.

Roderick gave Evander a second appraising glance before rising from his chair and pouring two chalices of wine. The life of a civilian did not seem to be agreeing with the young man. The definition of his muscles was already fading with disuse. His blond hair was shaggy and dusted with a white powder. Flour, perhaps, from his family's bakery. A waste of his talents. That man needed a sword in his hand.

"Good evening, Captain. Permission to speak?"

"I am no longer your captain, Evander." Roderick handed one of the crystal chalices to him. "There is no need for so much formality."

Evander did not move, glancing at the wine and setting the chalice aside.

Roderick shrugged, taking a long drink from his own glass. "To what do I owe the pleasure of this visit? Has Marcus finally proposed to your sister?"

"Not exactly."

"I did not think so. Shame. I could have used some happy news today. Go on then, what is this about?"

"Has Princess Catiya returned yet?" The words rushed out of Evander all at once. Half yelled. Half whispered.

The words grew heavy the instant they hit Roderick, thudding into his chest and turning to lead.

"No." Roderick took another long drink of his wine, letting the sweet liquid warm his throat. "Princess Catiya has not been found yet." His gaze flickered back to the window. Hoping that would change soon.

"What about Lord Carswell? Has he been found? Since his disappearance after threatening Lady Emma?"

"How did you... Of course, Simon and Marcus. Those two need to be reminded of what is a secret."

"Sir," Evander pleaded, dropping into the chair across from Roderick and clasping his hands together in front of him. "Please, I need to know. Has there been any sign of Lord Carswell since the night he disappeared?"

"You know I cannot tell you that." As much as he would have liked to. "You resigned your commission."

"But you don't understand. I only resigned my commission because..."

"Because you let Cat run away."

"How does everyone know that?" Evander's eyes rounded with shock. His jaw tensed.

"I assumed as much. I think, had I been in your position and the choice was between my future as a guard and the lifelong guilt of betraying my friend, I would have let her run away as well." He had once. Before Kristoff married Anya, he helped the future king leave the palace and travel to Salene. When the choice had been between Roderick's commission and helping his best friend find the bandit who had stolen his heart, Roderick had not hesitated. Of course, that story was for another time. "The question is, why you didn't come to me the moment you let her go?"

"I couldn't, for the sake of my family. Carswell is working with Sir Guy, he is a Salenian spy, and he is going to find Cat and take her to King Bastian. I have to know where he is. That's where Cat will be. He's going to use her to take the Volentian throne."

**

Cat's arm burned. The heat tracing through her veins scorched her heart. Every movement sent a pulse of pain through her body. She did not remember being placed back in her cell; she must have fainted again. She wished she knew how long she had been out. The light was gray and watery. Was it morning or evening? Cat rolled onto her side, forcing herself to sit up. A wave of dizziness swept over her, knocking her back to the ground. Her head pounded, but she forced herself to remain conscious.

When she tried to sit up again, Cat moved slower, keeping her weight off her bandaged arm.

Moving at all was awkward and slow without the use of her left arm and a heavy chain hanging off her right. Every movement forced the too tight manacle to bite into her wrist. The metallic smell of blood filled the stone cell.

She finally managed to sit up, leaning against the back wall, panting for breath.

"Bastian is right, you are stronger than anyone gives you credit for. I heard your mother could barely stay conscious while her magic was being drained, let alone move."

Cat opened her eyes, straining to see through the waves of dizziness and the dull throbbing in her head. A hazy figure stood in the door of her cell. Something was wrong. The rust covered bars were missing. The door was open and the man stood within her cell. A man who was blond and thin, his thick hair hung almost to his shoulders. A man she knew.

"Carswell?"

He was older, five years had passed since Cat last saw him.

Age agreed with him. He was still handsome, with a neatly trimmed beard and a loose tunic that hung off him in an effortless way. This simply could not be possible. Carswell was in Volentia, governing Rook. This was a figment, an illusion brought on by pain and hunger. "What... Why are you... here?"

"You always did have a way of getting to the heart of a matter quickly." Carswell leaned over, appraising her, brushing a wisp of hair away from Cat's face, proving he was real. "One of the more annoying things about you."

"I... wha..." Cat swallowed hard. Words were too hard to form.

"Don't struggle too hard, *Princess*. I prefer you silent."

Cat pulled away from Carswell, pushing herself to the back of the cell. Her hands were slick and clammy. Her heart was suddenly hammering, forcing the pain through her body. "You're helping Bastian? Stay away from me!"

Carswell glared, his sinister smile flickering. He was exactly the same man she had refused so long ago. "You must be confused after your recent ordeal." He gripped her burning arm. "You no longer give the orders, Princess."

The fog in Cat's mind started to clear. Thoughts and words were coming faster with every second. Carswell never did anything for free.

Everything was motivated by power. The man who had wanted to marry her only wanted the power she would give him. There had to be something she could offer him. "Wha- Whatever Bastian has promised you, if you help me, I promise you will get it. My father..."

"You have already tried this trick; it did not work then and it will not work now." He leaned close to her. "There is nothing I want more than you. Your blood holds the key. Once Bastian is done with you, you are going to give me everything I want."

"No! I won't do anything for you! Thomas is going to find me and he'll..."

"Thomas? That fool of a prince. You think he is going to save you?"

"He will. He will find me and..."

"He might. He might wake from his dream state, and he might find you. I admit, there is some link between you. I imagine he will follow it right here to you and that he will try to save you from Bastian. Heroes like that are so predictable." Carswell pulled Cat to her feet, pinning her against the wall. Roughhewn stones dug into her bare shoulders. "But he won't save you. He can't break the connection between you and Bastian. The moment he tries... do you know what Bastian is going to do to your handsome prince?" His voice was hard and flinty, hot against Cat's skin. "Bastian is going to use your magic, that dragon fire that burns inside of you, he is going to rip it out of you and use it to burn him alive. You will feel every second of it, you will see it, and there will be no escaping the knowledge that YOU murdered the only person who ever loved you."

"No. I won't let him."

"You won't be able to stop him. And then, no one will stand between me and everything I want."

The way Carswell ran his fingers over her skin reminded Cat of the last time he had been so close to her. A memory that had not disturbed her waking thoughts in years. A memory of him pinning her to a pillar at the center of the rose labyrinth. Evander and Arik had found them then, saved her. But no one would find her this time. No one was coming to help.

There was a sound in the distance. Footsteps on stone steps whispering down the corridor.

"Help!" Cat did not know who she was calling out to. She did not care. Anyone was better than Carswell.

"Help? Who do you think will help you here?"

"What are you doing?" Sir Guy appeared in the doorway, holding a small tray of food. Not the hero Cat would have hoped for. "No one is to be down here, king's orders."

"I do not take orders from King Bastian."

"Then take them from me." Guy set the tray aside. "The girl is not to be harmed. I will not allow you to touch her."

Carswell sneered, running a thumb across Cat's trembling lips. "Always interruptions when I want a private moment with you. This will only take a moment." He released Cat, turning to face Guy. Cat slumped to the ground, lacking the strength to even stand on her own. Shaking, she watched Carswell step toward Guy. "This girl is mine to do with as I please. If you really do wish to see your pitiful family and village again, I suggest you walk away."

"I won't let you harm her. She belongs to Bastian until he releases her to you to return to Volentia."

"Very well." Carswell wrapped a hand around Guy's throat. He slammed Guy into the wall, shaking the stone cell. Crumbling mortar rained down on Cat. "You think you can stop me? You are playing against forces you cannot imagine, and you have long since outlived your usefulness." A crushing darkness burned between Carswell's hand and the flesh of Guy's throat. It burst through the room, blinding Cat. Then nothing moved. Guy slumped to the floor.

Carswell turned his cruel eyes back on her.

"I'm not yours." Cat's voice was a breathless whisper. "And I never will be. Even if my father believed you rescued me, he would never force me to marry you if I refused." That was what he wanted. He wanted Cat's hand and her father's throne. He would not get either.

"Perhaps not, if I were only your rescuer." He dragged her to her feet again as if she weighed nothing. The heavy manacle pulled at her wrist, the chain tangled around her. "But he would never deny the father of your child."

Carswell's meaning required no emphasis. Every muscle in Cat's body tightened.

"No!" She used the few ounces of strength remaining to struggle against his grip. "I... I will tell my father that you were here, what you did to me. He will revoke your title and burn your land and Ryder will... Ahh!"

Carswell wound the chain around her wrists, forcing her arms painfully above her head. The little blood in her fingers drained, leaving tingles and sharp pain running down her arms. Metal clanked in her ears. He produced a bottle of sour green liquid from his pocket. "I doubt you will be telling them much of anything." The bottle cast sick green shadows across Cat's face. "Do you know what this is? It took me years to find the ingredients. Most came from the southern deserts beyond Ruzeme. I doubt I will be able to produce a second dose, since the pirates who supplied it are all dead now, thanks to you. Not that it matters, I was saving it for just this moment." He worked one handed to unstopper the bottle, never moving his body away from hers. Holding her in place. Cat's legs shook from the strain of standing. Her wrists ached as the weight of her body pulled against the chain. "It is a special kind of magic that forces the drinker to keep any secret. A few drops of this, sealed with a kiss, and you will never be able to betray any secret I ask you to keep."

Faster than lightning arcing across the sky, Carswell forced the liquid over Cat's lips, emptying the bottle. The bitter liquid burned her mouth and throat. Carswell threw the vial to the ground. The glass shattered. He covered her nose and mouth until she was forced to swallow the burning potion.

His lips were on hers, forcing a harsh, fervent kiss on Cat.

"You will never tell anyone anything that happened within this castle. It is our secret, and it is sealed behind your lips."

He dropped Cat. She fell, hitting the cold stones. "Please, Sir Guy."

One last desperate hope. She reached for the knight's lifeless form. "Help me."

Guy did not move. Only Carswell's shadow looming over her. "No help is coming for you. You are mine."

"Bastian won't keep his word," Cat spat the words at him. It was all she had left to fight him with. "He is going to kill me, and you will be left with nothing. Whatever you do to me, I will never be yours and you will never rule Volentia." Cat clenched her eyes closed, refusing to show the fear in her eyes or the way her core trembled.

Thomas ran a hand down his face, trying to push away the fog of exhaustion. His legs ached after hours of trudging through the woods toward the rising smoke. It was the only lead he had, and he could not lose it.

It was almost dawn.

Every time he paused, Thomas heard the voice of the mysterious woman again, urging him to hurry, drawing him toward the smoke when he lost the twisting path.

The ground fell away in front of Thomas, opening into a deep ravine. Thomas stumbled to a stop, teetering on the edge.

A mound of gray stones that could have been a castle at one time, though now it seemed to be little more than a ruin, stood at the end of the ravine, where the two cliffs met.

The old queen's palace.

He was not certain if the voice on the edge of his mind came from his imagination or from the woman he saw in the water's surface.

His fingers flexed into fists. Thomas had been wrong to follow the smoke. Cat was not there. No one could live in that ruin.

Movement along the cliff face caught his attention. Thomas watched a dark-haired woman as she crept down a stony path almost hidden among the rocks. Thomas' eyes followed the woman, his heart in his throat. Was this an illusion? A trick of his exhausted mind? Could he really be seeing the same woman he saw in the lake's surface? Then he saw what she was walking toward; a well-used stone road cut through the forest.

He looked closer at the ruin. Smoke. Smoke rose into the sky around what must have been the kitchens or great hall. His attention returned to the woman. She was harder to see now, wavering like a reflection. She walked purposefully toward the hidden side of the old castle. Perhaps she was leading him to a way in.

It took Thomas more than an hour to pick his way down the cliff to the trail, careful never to glance over the edge, fighting his way through a tangle of brambles and bushes to a rusted gate on the far side of the ruin.

Up close the castle looked even more like a ruin. Vines and brambles tangled around the crumbling stone; thorn bushes grew out of the slitted windows. A rotted oak panel, once a solid door, lay on the ground beside the rusted gate. Inside was a long, dark corridor, stinking of mildew.

Thomas hesitated; uncertain he was ready to learn what was hidden in those depths.

Thomas! Help! Please!

The words whispered in the distance like a voice at the back of his mind.

Thomas took a deep breath, shoving away the fear.

He stepped into the cold dark. The floor was slick with water and filth. The cells he crept past were filled with thorn bushes. Surely this was a waste of time, no one would choose to stay in such a place, let alone hold a princess captive. Still, the whispered call tugged at his chest pulling him past moss-covered walls and rusted bars. Thorn bushes snagged his arms, leaving long scratches.

The corridor ended in a winding staircase that led further into the darkness. Thomas pulled his heavy hood up, hiding his face. If someone was lurking in the darkness, he did not wish to be seen or recognized. At the bottom of the stairs was another long corridor of empty cells.

These ones were swept clean, except for a heap of white and red rags in the farthest cell. Silently cursing, Thomas turned back to the spiraling staircase. There was nothing here.

A soft sound turned him back. His eyes fixed on the farthest cell.

What he had first disregarded as the remains of a former tenant quivered in the pale light. His eyes raked over the long red braid; he knew that braid and the pale freckled skin shivering on the stone floor.

"Cat!" Thomas rushed toward her. "Cat! Princess!" He reached the cell, yanking at the metal bars. They did not move. Neither did the trembling woman. "Cat." He called out again, kneeling and stretching his arm through the bars to reach her. To touch her and know she was real.

Cat stirred, moving slowly, as if even the slightest movement pained her. She lifted her head and turned to look at him with blotchy, red-rimmed eyes. Cat had been crying. Dried blood and bruises covered her cheek, neck, and arms. A torn, loose-fitting gown hung off of her, exposing her legs. The wisp of fabric could not protect her from the cold and bare stone floor. A heavy manacle circled her wrist, so tight Thomas could see long red lines where it bit into her skin.

"Thomas? You cannot be here." She reached her free hand toward him, straining against the heavy chain, as if she believed he would evaporate. As if she thought he was an illusion brought on by pain.

Tears welled in Thomas' eyes. He reached for her, closing the gap between them. His fingers brushed lightly against hers, then twined around hers.

"You're real," she sighed. Her features shifted. The momentary serenity of relief faded away, her eyes widening. "Why are you here? It's not safe. You have to go! If Bastian finds you here, he will kill you."

His grip on her fingers tightened as she tried to pull away. "No. Cat, I'm here to rescue you. You're hurt. Did Bastian do this to you?"

Cat looked away. Her face was pale. Her jaw was trembling. "I... I cannot explain."

But she did not have to explain. Her face was streaked with blood and grime. The blood and bruises nearly glowed against her skin. It told him enough of what she had experienced in the days they were apart. Thomas thought of her smile. He would trade his life for the chance to see it again, to know she was safe.

"I have to get you out of here."

"Please... Please listen to me," Cat managed between sobs and gasping breaths. "You must go. You are in danger. I... I can-not watch you die."

"Don't say that. I won't abandon you! Is there a key?"

Cat shook her head, hair falling in her face. "Bastian keeps it around his neck. You... must... not... fight him. He has... too much... power." Each word was a struggle. Releasing his hand, Cat retreated to the back of the cell, resting against the back wall, panting with exertion. Far from his reach. He swept his arm through the air, trying to reach her. It was useless. "I can fight him. I-I am strong... strong enough to fight him." She folded her arms against the cold.

"You don't have to be. I am going to rescue you."

"You cannot save me this time. I will be safe until the next full moon. Please. You cannot fight him alone."

"Neither can you."

Cat let out a wail of pain, her hand flew to her temple. She pressed her fingers into her skin, trying to push away the sharp pain. Her teeth gnashed, stopping the shout in her throat.

"What is it?" Thomas reached for her. Even stretched to the limit, he could not touch her, not unless Cat reached out as well. He wanted to help her. To comfort her.

"He's here."

This time it was Cat who reached out. Her trembling fingers brushing against his knuckles. Thomas wasted no time, wrapping his hand around hers. Her fingers shook with strain. Her touch was so light. Her skin felt like ice. Cat gazed up at him, fear etched in her eyes. How or why she knew Bastian was near did not matter. She mattered. The presence of the witch king only strengthened his sense of urgency.

All of her strength spent, Cat's delicate hand started to release, fingers spreading away from him. Thomas' grip tightened. He had no intention of letting her go. She was his princess, and no one would take her from him.

"I am going to save you and when I do... when this over, I am going to marry you." He removed the small sapphire ring from his pocket. He had carried it from Reinsaffira. It was hardly a fine or special ring. Something he had purchased for her after his father arranged the marriage contract. Something he had hoped to give her weeks ago in the safety of a garden labyrinth. A star sapphire on a silver band. The only token he had to give her. He was going to ask now, like he should have done the moment he met her. "If you will have me?"

Cat nodded.

Thomas slipped the ring onto her finger, it fit as if it were made for her. "Take this as well." He undid his cloak, pushing it through the bars.

"No. He'll know you were here."

"Good. I want Bastian to know that I won't abandon you. Take it. I cannot watch you shiver."

She pulled it around her shoulders, slumping to the floor, no longer strong enough to sit up. Her shivers slowed. "Please. You have to go before he finds you."

"I'll come back."

Walking away from the woman he loved, knowing she watched him go, hurt worse than anything Thomas had ever experienced. Her eyes cut into him. Thomas turned back when he reached the stairs. His princess lay beneath the cloak, a mess on the floor. Her eyes were clenched shut; hands pressed to her head. He could not leave her, not like this. No matter what Cat said about Bastian, he could not leave her to this torment.

Hot tears slipped from Cat's eyes, splattering against the ice-cold stone. She listened to Thomas' footsteps, taking him farther and farther away from her. Too sore, too exhausted, too broken to move. Cat lay in the growing silence of her prison. She wished desperately to explain what had been done to her, what facing Bastian would do to them both, and why Thomas could not save her. The burning liquid Carswell forced down her throat did its work. The secret was sealed inside of her.

Searing pain ripped through the cut on Cat's forearm. A hook pulled at her heart. Bastian was using magic, *her* magic. So long as the two were connected, Cat would feel everything Bastian did. When he used her magic, it pulled from Cat's core, draining every ounce of who and what she was.

Cat clenched her eyes shut, willing the pain to stop. Thomas' image floated in her mind. He stood before her in the great hall, a sword in his hands. It was time for the lovesick fool to burn. He had been enough of a nuisance.

"NO!" Those were not Cat's thoughts. It was Bastian's evil and anger. His thoughts. It had happened before, over the few hours Cat had wasted in the dank dungeon. Glimpses of Bastian's mind. None had been this vivid. Cat could almost reach out across the void connecting her to Bastian and touch Thomas. The magic pulled through her again. Fire stretched from her fingertips, hot enough to burn any man alive. "NO!"

Gripping her bandaged arm, Cat willed the fire to cool. Her body. Her mind. Her magic. She would not let him do this. It was hers. Her magic. Cat had to have some control over how it was used. The harder she fought against Bastian, the hotter her skin burned; the more the pain of hatred burned through her soul. Bastian was stronger than her, he knew how to control what was only instinct for her. But she had to save Thomas. She had to send him away.

Smoke, or was it shadow, surrounded Thomas, enveloping him and filling the great hall, until she could see nothing.

A scream ripped through her.

The pain receded.

Cat's connection to Bastian faded away.

She gripped her bandaged arm, blood soaking through her fingers. It would be easy enough to let the blood flow out of her. To die in the cell, taking her magic with her. The thought was not so frightening. Dying was just a matter of closing her eyes and letting the darkness take her away.

Her thumb found the silver ring Thomas had placed on her finger. Spinning it round and round. Cat was stronger than that. Strong enough to fight. Strong enough to suffer until she found an opportunity to escape. She could not count on rescue or escape unless she fought for it.

The gossamer fabric of the dress ripped easily. Cat wrapped the rag around her wound, stopping the bleeding, waiting for it to seal up again. She could feel her heart beating under the bandage, pounding. Dizziness and the cold grip of death fell away. Cat would live. She pulled Thomas' cloak tight around her shoulders, brushing her tears away. She would live and she would fight.

Muffled voices filled the hall.

Thomas paused at the top of the stairs. An ancient sword hung on the wall just beyond his reach.

Hanging back in the shadows, Thomas listened, hoping the voices would let something useful slip.

"Why keep her in the dungeon cell," an unfamiliar voice whined. "Would she not be more secure in one of the tower rooms?"

"Do not play at concern. I know you are not worried about her security, only your own comfort when you *visit* her. Which I only allow because of your connection to... *her*. You know as well as I do that the princess cannot escape while the link is in place." Bastian paused, as if listening to the stirrings within the castle. He turned with a flourish, entering a room at the far end of the hall. The prince followed, snatching the sword off the wall.

The sound of Bastian just speaking of Cat, roiled Thomas' stomach. Sickened by the fact that the vile man did not care about the condition of his prisoner. Thomas snatched up the sword, gripping it until the leather dug into his palm. Bastian was a monster, not a king. Thomas had read enough stories to know it was his duty, as a prince, to slay monsters.

Thomas waited for Bastian to reach the heavy marble throne in front of a large round fireplace.

"Leave me," Bastian waved a hand at the blond man he had been speaking with. "I have other business to attend to." Thomas did not see where the man went, only heard the far door slamming shut. "Well, your highness, do you have something to say to me? Or would you prefer to skulk in the shadows?"

Emerging from the shadows, Thomas leveled the sword at Bastian. "Release Princess Catiya at once or I will release your head from your shoulders."

Bastian did not deign to look up. "Making demands of a king in his own court? Hardly princely behavior. We may be in the Border Lands, but my court is not without its graces."

"Perhaps not," Thomas growled. He was in no mood for games or banter. "It will be without a king if you do not release Cat and..."

"Go home, prince. There is no need to involve Reinsaffira in these matters." Bastian waved a dismissive hand, as if Thomas would turn around and leave. The foolishness of kings, used to giving commands. The man was unarmed. It would be so easy to lop off his head. First, he needed to undo whatever magic held Cat in this terrible place.

Thomas grit his teeth. "Release her and I will. Or would you prefer me to kill you?"

"I will not give you another opportunity to leave."

Any decorum in Thomas that might have questioned whether or not it was appropriate to kill a king in his own throne room, armed or not, was gone. All that mattered was the girl chained in the dungeons below his feet. All that mattered was the key that glinted in the firelight, hanging from Bastian's neck.

Steel flashed in the firelight.

Thomas charged forward. He never reached Bastian. The monster stretched out his fingers and deep blue flames swirled around Thomas. The air grew stifling hot, singeing his skin and hair. Just as the flames licked at his flesh, they turned to a billowing black smoke. Bastian evaporated before Thomas' eyes. *No!* Thomas spun around, the smoke clearing away.

He stood alone on the edge of a small village. A sign creaked, swaying in the breeze.

"Thomas?"

He ignored the sound of his name echoing down the road.

"Thomas! What are you doing here? Are you hurt?" Amora gripped his shoulder, turning Thomas to face her. "What happened? Where is the princess?"

Thomas looked up long enough to see Aiden emerge from the Peach Tree Inn. Anger flashed and burned inside of him at the sight of the man. "It was you, wasn't it? Why did you do it?" He pushed Amora away, chasing after the graying old bandit. When he reached Aiden he gripped him by the collar, pushing him against the wall.

"Thomas! What are you doing?" Amora grabbed his shoulder, trying to wrench him away.

"Were you working for Bastian? Keeping him informed of Cat's movements? Did you tell the pirates where to find her? Why did you do it?" Thomas' thoughts were a jumbled mess. The question why was the only clear thought in his mind. Why had Aiden attached himself to Cat if not to trade her to Bastian? "What did he promise you?"

"Stop this at once!" The small woman forced herself between the two men. "Aiden has been here! He could not have betrayed you. Stop it! He's Lyse's father! Would you make her an orphan a second time? Now calm down and explain what is happening."

Aiden did not give Thomas the chance to speak. "No. He is right. I lead Bastian's servants to Cat, but not for the reasons you think." Aiden fixed his gaze on Thomas. "The crone who serves Bastian, she is... she was my wife before he twisted the power inside of her. You and Cat know her as the crone who gave Cat her magic compass. She warned me of the king's plans for the princess. I stayed with you in order to stop his plans."

"How?"

"By putting a knife in her heart before Bastian could take her and use her power to unleash an even greater evil than any of us dare to imagine."

"The Darkness," Amora gasped.

Thomas ignored her. "What will happen to Cat?"

"Bastian will drain her of her magic. The ritual lasts from full moon to full moon. When the next full moon rises, he will cut out her heart and consume it. Then he will drain her blood and pour it and her magic out on the mirror that imprisons The Darkness. And The Darkness will destroy everything."

The full moon was only a few weeks away. Thomas had to work quickly. He had to get help.

"Thomas," Amora cooed. She stepped in front of him, taking his face in her hands, forcing his full focus on the ancient woman. Her eyes filled with concern, not just for him or Aiden, but something deeper. Fear. Thomas had never seen Amora wear fear before. "Where is Cat? Where is the princess?"

"Bastian has her." He pulled away from Amora, walking toward the stables. His fists tight. "I need to borrow a horse. I need to go to Volentia."

"Your own castle is half the distance."

"My father will not risk any men to save Cat. I need Prince Ryder." Thomas paused, turning back to Amora. "But I need you to go to Reinsaffira and find Arik and Trenton. Have them bring Jason to Volentia as soon as they can. Cat will need a healer and Jason is the best there is. We have to hurry."

Cold had set in over the last several days. Orange and red leaves spun through the garden on the light autumn breeze.

Emma sat on a bench in the park, just within view of the large palace gate, sketching, waiting for Cat to come back. Her adventures had grown dull without Cat. Picking apples, climbing trees, even midnight swims in the garden lake were not the same with Ryder rolling his eyes and laughing at her. She had never realized how lonely the palace could be.

At least her sketches were improving.

A commotion rose near the gate.

A group of guards rushed past her, shouting. Emma looked up, brushing a wisp of hair away from her face, craning her neck to see what was happening. The small hope that it was Cat finally coming home bubbled in her chest.

The hope dashed as the shouts turned angry and harsh.

Then saw what was happening.

Her pen slipped, leaving a long black line on the page when Emma caught a glimpse of a tall man trying to push his way past three guards. Filthy and exhausted, the man's movements were awkward and slow as he tried to push his way into the gardens.

Emma gasped.

She recognized him. But it could not be Prince Thomas. Not without Cat. Prince Thomas promised to protect Cat. Why would he return to the palace without her?

Emma stood, walking purposefully toward the commotion. Her eyes widened when one of the guards knocked Thomas to the ground.

"Stop! I know this man!" She lifted her skirts, rushing between him and the guards. She could not let them hurt him, not when Emma had plans to do so herself. "He is from Highcliffs." Emma glared down at the man she was now certain was the Reinsaffiran prince. He shied away from meeting her eye, face downcast. Paying no attention to the three swords pointed at his chest. "I trust you have an explanation for your appearance."

He reached out, gripping her by the hand. Long fingers engulfing hers. "I need to speak with you and Prince Ryder at once." Prince Thomas' voice was cracked and dry. Aching with a tone of desperate need. Emma saw he wore the large signet ring on his finger, perhaps he had hoped it would have gained him entrance to the palace. It might have if the alliance wasn't in tatters. "It is a matter of life and death."

"Of course, we'll get you cleaned up and then…"

His grip tightened, shaking with urgency. "Now."

His tone sent shivers of fear through Emma. She pulled him to his feet, leading him away from the guards, into the palace. Past wandering eyes that would surely lead to wandering rumors. There was a small solarium attached to Ryder's chambers, it would be safe and private enough for whatever Thomas had to tell them.

The windows were all open, letting in the sun and freshening the air.

Thomas studied the open room with a wary eye. "Is this place private?"

Emma smiled, brushing the filth from the hand he clasped. "Private enough." Every second she spent with Prince Thomas worried her more. He radiated urgency. It rolled off him in waves. Why was he so frantic? Where was Cat? The prince fidgeted with his shabby curls. Dark circles hung under his eyes. "You're exhausted. Sit down while I find Ryder."

Thomas did not sit. Not once while Emma was gone. The seats around the room were undisturbed when she returned. The only evidence of his presence was a path of dirt tracked across the marble floor in front of the windows. Prince Thomas hunched as he paced, covered in dirt and grim. He was not a prince anymore, just dirt and skin hanging off of tired bones. His eyes were no longer blue, but a distant, dark steely gray.

Emma realized with a start that he was not in the room at all. He was somewhere far away. Somewhere horrible. Maybe wherever Cat was.

"I suppose I should not be surprised. We have had so many unexpected visitors over the last few weeks." Ryder smiled, misunderstanding the situation. He glanced around the solarium. "Where is my sister?"

Prince Thomas collapsed into a chair, breaking under the weight of whatever he came to say. Burying his face in his hands. "In the Border Lands."

Emma's throat tightened.

She did not understand.

Could not understand.

Refused to understand.

How could Cat be in the Border Lands when the man who swore to protect her was here? A swell of pity for the broken and exhausted man fought against the anger and panic she tasted on the back of her tongue.

"Why aren't you with her?"

"I was, until Bastian took her. Please. I need your help."

"Bastian?" Ryder's mood turned to a dark cloud. "I do not understand. Your messenger said you were bringing Cat home."

"He took her from me. He has her in a dungeon in the Border Lands. I couldn't free her."

"You left her?" Rage burned away any pity Emma felt for the man. Her fists flew at him, beating against his chest. Thomas made no effort to defend himself. Ryder's hands wrapped around her wrists, pulling her back. "You left her," she shrieked. "You swore you would protect her!" Ryder's grip loosened, allowing Emma to collapse against the floor, her skirts pooling around her. "You left her."

Thomas leaned close, placing a hand on her shoulder. "I am going back for her." He looked up to Ryder. "I need your help."

"Drink this." The crone pressed a mug to Cat's lips. The hot liquid bubbling inside of it smelled bitter.

Cat turned her face away, stomach souring at the smell.

"Drink. It will give you strength."

Cat did not want strength. She wanted the pain to be over. Her body ached. Sharp pain stabbed at her core. Carswell had left her alone in her cell again only a few minutes earlier, after throwing Thomas' cloak aside and pawing at her body, reminding Cat in a cruel voice that her body belonged to him, just like her magic belonged to Bastian, and her future belonged to this unknown darkness.

The woman laid the cloak over Cat's bruised legs. It smelled of pine trees, just like Thomas did. The thought of him and Ryder and Emma forced Cat to drink, gulping down the horrible bitterness. He was coming back for her. She had to survive.

"You offered me a drink once before," Cat muttered between gulps. "Right before you tried to put a dagger in my heart." But that had been a long time ago. So long that Cat had not recognized the crone when she first appeared in her room.

"I did." There was no hint of sympathy, or was that remorse, in the woman's voice.

"Were they all you? The shadows?"

"Yes. Drink it all." She tilted the cup toward Cat's lips again. "It will help with the pain."

"Why?" Every word hurt to form. Her throat was bruised, though the crone's potion had begun to numb the pain and warm her.

"You are the daughter of the prophecy, the key to freeing The Darkness. I kill you; I save the world. Your life seemed a small price to pay."

Cat did not understand. She scrunched her face, trying to push away the mug. The crone chased her, pressing it to her lips again.

"Then why not kill me now?"

The crone shook her head. "I no longer have enough of my own will to defy my master." She took Cat's hand in her own. A strange and comforting gesture from the twisted woman. "But you do. You must drink all of this. The potion in it is strong, it will stifle The Darkness' plans and lend you strength. When we meet again, I will not be able to help you."

Roses blooming even in the early days of winter. The magic of the Volentian palace astounded Thomas. It was no wonder Cat loved this place.

Thomas stood at the center of the rose labyrinth, looking at the marble pavilion surrounded by blossoming rose bushes. The place he first loved his princess so long ago. What felt like a lifetime ago he had planned to bring Cat here to ask for her hand. In the hope that she might love someone who was chosen for her.

He lifted his knife to a white blossom, prepared to cut it away from the bush.

"Cat prefers the orange blossoms." Prince Ryder nodded to a bush on the far side of the pavilion. Thomas had not heard him approach.

"Fascination, enthusiasm, desire. It's fitting for her." Thomas tried to smile. The hurt of knowing where Cat was and that he had to wait for supplies before he could rescue her, weighed down his shoulders. His entire body sagged beneath the weight of his guilt and impatience.

"Cat used to love this maze when we were young, though I don't think she has set foot in it in years."

"It's a labyrinth, actually," Thomas' voice was flat. "A maze..."

"Has an entrance and an exit. Of course, you would know that." Ryder looked around, crossing his arms. Studying the pavilion and rose bushes. His voice was flat as well. "I thought Cat was the only person who could solve it without getting lost, until I saw you go through it."

"There is a string running through the bushes, marking the path. You never noticed it?"

"A string!" Ryder shook his head. "I should have known. She always liked that story." Ryder grew serious again. A stifling silence stretched out between them. "Why are you here? You should be resting while you can. The journey will be difficult."

Thomas turned back to the roses, his full attention on the blossom he selected. "I do not need rest and I will not find any so long as Cat is in that dungeon." Ryder was right. Now that he thought of it, the white blossom did not suit the girl he intended it for. He had wanted to bring Cat a piece of her home. Although, he doubted the flower would survive away from this place."

"I suppose that is for the best; you have no time for it. There are three men and a young woman here to see you. I had them escorted to your rooms." The crown prince's tone was as cool as it had ever been toward Thomas. He still held no trust for him, perhaps he never would. Like Lady Emma, he considered Thomas to blame for leaving Cat in that place. Even if he didn't, Ryder still did not believe Thomas deserved any love Cat had to give.

He was right.

"They are my friends. I hoped they would come in time." Thomas turned to a bush covered in red tipped yellow roses. He cut one, tucking it into the ruined silk handkerchief Cat had carried so far. He turned back to Ryder, ready to leave. The prince stepped into his path.

"Tell me what happened when you left her there."

"You would not believe what happened even if I told you, but believe me, if I had any choice, I would not have. Do you still believe I don't care about her? After everything"

"I believe you care about yourself more, but if you save her and she chooses you, I will not stand in your way. You may not get the same promise from Emma. She is not exactly forgiving." He rested a hand on Thomas shoulder, a threatening weight to his grip. "But know that if she does not survive this, if we are too late because you failed to protect her, or if you choose to save your own skin instead of her, I will kill you with my bare hands."

"If I fail to save her from that place, it will be because I died trying."

A slender hand wrapped around Emma's elbow, pulling her into the guest suite she had been walking past. She flung her arms out, one hand instinctively gripping the dagger at her waist. After Carswell's threats she was taking no chances.

A blond girl with wide round eyes stood before her. "You're Lady Emma, aren't you?"

"Yes." Emma's fingers flexed around the dagger.

"I thought so. You..." She hesitated, her eyes drawing toward her feet, blushing, "well, you look just like the princess described you."

The princess? Cat! Emma's mouth felt suddenly dry. She spun around, quickly closing the door behind her. "You've seen Cat? When? Where?" Had she escaped or...

"Several weeks ago, when Thomas... I mean, Prince Thomas, brought her to my home. I did not spend much time with her, but I liked her. Oh!" The girl suddenly gripped her skirts, sweeping them out in a wobbling curtsy. "I'm Lyse, my lady. I arrived today with Lord Arik and his companions and, well, I was hoping there was something I could do to help. I liked Princess Catiya. She was kind. And..."

The girl would have probably stumbled through her words for hours if Emma had not held up a hand, quieting her. "Maybe we should start at the beginning. Why are you here?"

"Amora sent me. She is a friend. She knows the ruin where the princess is being held, we think. She sent me with a map, but the men Thomas had me bring will not be enough to stop Bastian and the crone's magic. So, I was hoping there was something I could do to help."

Emma felt a smile curling on her lips. "I... I think there might be."

Afternoon sun streamed in through the shop windows. If it got too much warmer, the icing on the cakes would start to melt. Another mess Evander did not want to clean up. He set the broom behind the kitchen door. Out of sight. Years of training, wasted. All for nothing. Carswell was gone and he was nothing more than a coward who could not help anyone. Even Captain Roderick told him there was nothing he could do now.

The little bell above the door jangled.

Evander's shoulders drooped. Lydia was out making deliveries, meaning it was Evander's responsibility to deal with the customers. Knowing his luck, it would be one of the ladies throwing a party demanding to know why their tarts had not been delivered yet. Complaints he would have to remember and relay to his overly sensitive sister. There were so many more important things he should be focusing on, like finding Carswell.

"I'll be right with you."

"Oh, please, take your time. I'm in no hurry." The voice that answered was almost musical. It reminded Evander of a bird's flight.

Returning to the shop front, Evander saw a girl with long golden hair that had been tied up in an elegant half braid. She leaned over one of Lydia's displays, examining it. Her pink lips turned up in a smirk. Evander could not help the little gasp that escaped him, his breath catching in his chest. She was stunning. Perhaps the most beautiful girl he had ever seen. The sky-blue dress she wore drew out the reds and pinks in her golden complexion.

"Ahem." He cleared his throat, forcing himself back to the moment. "Those are rose apple tarts, the same that are served at the palace festivals."

The girl smiled, turning the plate to better examine the delicate flower crafted on the crust. "It's exquisite. You have a skilled hand."

"Actually," his face was growing warm, but it was a sunny day, "those are my sister's creations." He lifted a plate of lemon cakes that looked more like iced yellow blobs. "I'm responsible for these, and anything that looks like half the batter was spilled while being prepared." It had been. He had only just salvaged the lemon cakes by catching the batter with a baking tray.

"Ah... Well... You clearly have... potential."

"You wouldn't say that if you tasted them."

To Evander's surprise she picked a small lump from the tray, taking a delicate bite. Her mouth curved into a smile. "Mm. The icing on this is incredible. It pairs wonderfully with the lemon. Though your batter is not quite right. Next time you should try using a warm wooden spoon."

"And not spilling it?"

"That would also help."

Evander found himself smiling. The first genuine smile he felt in weeks, since resigning his commission. He leaned on the counter, drawing close to see the girl's round features. She smiled back at him. "That is what Lydia told me. Are you a baker?"

"An apprentice of sorts."

"Are you here to spy on us?"

"Oh!" The girl's eyes widened. Her hand immediately dropped into the bag she carried. Ducking her gaze away from his. "No, nothing like that. I was sent here by Lady Emma of Highcliffs."

"Lady Emma?" What could she possibly want? Not that she had never ordered pastries from them before, though, those orders usually came from the palace steward.

"Yes." The girl held out a rolled piece of parchment. "She asked me to order these things and have them delivered to the palace by sunset tomorrow. It's very important that we receive them by *sunset tomorrow*." Her tone turned hard and flinty. "This should cover the cost." She set a bag on the counter between them. It jangled, full of coins.

Evander unfurled the parchment with care, reading the list. Apples, hard cheese, dried meats... it was all travel food, simple and hearty. Nothing they sold in the bakery. Lady Emma would have known that. "I'm afraid this would make for a rather unconventional tea party. What does Lady Emma need these for?"

The girl's face paled. "That is a secret. Prince Ryder was most insistent that I not speak of it. Will you be able to gather it all and deliver it to Prince Ryder's private solarium in time?"

Evander quirked an eyebrow at her and the strange specificity of her words. There was only one reason the prince and Lady Emma would need so much food of this nature, if they were planning a journey.

A secret journey could only mean one thing; Ryder had found either Cat or Carswell.

Evander rolled the parchment up, twisting it against his palm. "I think we can handle it Lady...?"

"Just Lyse." She smiled again before hurrying out of the shop vanishing, like the last breath of summer on the autumn breeze.

Muffled voices sounded in the kitchen behind him, along with a sparkle of laughter.

Evander snatched up the bag Lyse had left. It was heavy, rattling with gold coins. More than twice what he would need to gather the supplies she asked for. He pushed through the kitchen door.

Lydia and Marcus stood on the far end of the kitchen. Marcus still dressed from his most recent shift at the palace. He hefted a basket onto a high shelf Lydia could not reach.

"Marcus, do you know where Simon is?"

"Already on his way to the palace." Marcus grunted back. "He has evening gate duty."

"Good. I need you to get me into the palace to speak to Prince Ryder. Tonight. Now."

"Again? Evander your obsession with Lord Carswell is going to get you killed."

"I think Prince Ryder knows where Cat is. He is planning to go after her. I'm going to offer my services and I want you and Simon to come with me."

Lydia dropped the heavy pan she had been moving. Leaving it at her feet. "How do you know that?"

The roll of parchment felt heavy between his fingers. Evander held it out to his sister. "Because he just sent a messenger with this order. Food for a secret journey. What else would he need it for?"

Marcus leaned over Lydia's shoulder, reading the list as well. "If you're going to wander through the royal wing, you're going to need to change. Do you still have your uniform?"

"I was expecting... more people. Is anyone else coming?" Arik glanced around the empty solarium. Thomas almost agreed. Trenton,

Arik, Jason, and Ryder. It did not seem like enough. Not to face Bastian and all his power. "Where did Lyse go?"

"I sent her to find what we need." Emma sat on a chair on the far end of the room, looking out on the sun filled afternoon. "She'll be back soon."

Volentia was too sunny, Thomas thought with a grimace. This place had no business being warm and sunny not when he knew Cat was in a cold dungeon. And everyone around him was too calm for that matter. Standing around discussing their plan, or lack thereof, in this comfortable space. A bitter taste rose to the back of his throat. No wonder Emma hated him.

"Seriously," Arik turned his whole body toward Ryder. "This is your entire force to rescue Princess Catiya? Where are your knights and royal guards?"

"I didn't ask any of them." Ryder's voice was the low rumble of thunder. He crossed his arms, dampening Arik's sunshine demeanor.

"There's the problem. I guarantee every single guard and knight in the city would volunteer if you only asked." Arik leaned conspiratorially toward Trenton, speaking loud enough for the whole room to hear. "It's every knight's dream to rescue a beautiful damsel from a monster. And *this* damsel is a princess."

"Whether that is true or not," Ryder rumbled over him, "it is inconsequential. Cat is being held in the Border Lands. I cannot lead Volentian knights across Reinsaffiran lands, not since your king tore up our alliance. It would be seen as an act of war. It is the five of us, or nothing."

The five of them or nothing.

Two princes, a physician, and two trained knights. It felt like nothing.

Thomas did not know how many men Bastian had under his command in the ruined fortress. There was the man Bastian had spoken to and the crone, he had not seen anyone else, but there must have been. For all he knew, there could be hundreds of soldiers hidden within the castle walls. Then there was Bastian's magic to contend with. The five of them may as well have been nothing compared to all of that.

Someone pounded on the door to the solarium. A silence fell over the small group. "Your highness, may I speak with you?"

Nothing in Ryder's demeanor betrayed even a second's panic or confusion. He rose from his chair, reaching the door in three long strides. He opened it, just a crack. Not even enough for Thomas to see the intruder. Whoever stood on the far side of the door could not see him either.

"Simon. This is not a good time." Ryder started to close the door.

A hand pushed through the opening, holding the door open. "We know you are planning to rescue Cat. We want to help."

Ryder's hand fell away, letting the door push open.

Emma sat up straighter, suddenly interested.

Three men in the green and gold uniforms of the royal guard stepped into the room. A formidable looking force, if also small. Each man wore a long sword on his belt. Arik smiled at them with a sense of familiarity. Of course, Arik knew these men, he had probably called them here, though Thomas did not know when he would have had the time.

"Is it true?" A blond man turned to Ryder. Of the three he was by far the smallest, though not small by any real reckoning. He had broad shoulders and held himself with a soldier's bearing. "Do you know where Cat is? Are you going to find her?"

"It is."

"Good. We're going with you."

"No, you're not!"

"Forgive me, your highness, it was not a request. Cat is in danger, and we are going to help save her."

"You are royal guards," Ryder tried to argue, the barest hint of a stammer lightening his tone. "I cannot lead you across the Reinsaffiran border."

"You're mistaken," the young man shrugged, "I'm just a baker. Not even a very good one."

The dark-haired guard behind him removed an envelope holding it out to the prince. "And Marcus and I resigned our posts ten minutes ago. We're going with you. Or we're going on our own. Either way, we plan to bring Cat home."

Ryder's shoulders sagged. He stepped aside, letting the door close behind the three men. "Gentlemen," he sighed, "meet Simon, Marcus, and Evander. They will be helping us."

"I told you," Arik smirked at Thomas. "There isn't a knight or guard in the world who doesn't dream of rescuing a beautiful damsel from a monster. We could raise an army if we had a few days."

"I would hardly call my sister a beautiful damsel. That's not why they are here."

The dark-haired guard, Simon, lifted his eyebrows in surprise. "Of course, Cat is beautiful. I always assumed that was why the king did not want us near here after she became The Rose Princess. Was I wrong?"

The strategy they worked out was simple. It had to be, going into a situation so blind. It still took hours to make the arrangements. The sun was set by the time Thomas rose from his chair, starting down the corridor toward the room he would share with Arik, Trenton, and Jason, feeling like he earned a bit of rest, though he could not be certain he would get any. Jason was already gone, gathering the supplies he would need to help Cat when they found her. Arik remained behind in the solarium, speaking with the three guards who joined them. He had not been lying when he said people outside of Reinsaffira liked him.

Thomas alerted to the sound of footsteps. He glanced over his shoulder to see who was following.

It seemed not all three guards had stayed behind. Evander had fol-lowed him out into the corridor. Thomas slowed his pace, half waiting for the man to reach him. They were close to the same age, Thomas thought, though it was hard to tell.

He fell into step beside Thomas.

"Thank you, for helping me rescue Cat. I cannot imagine it was easy..."

Evander stopped. Turning a glare on Thomas. His jaw was tight. "I'm not helping *you*. Do not make the mistake of thinking you are the only person here who cares about Cat. You're not."

Cat. Evander spoke her name with force and care, not bothering to stumble over her title. Thomas felt a sharp pang of jealousy deep in his stomach. Who was this man? Why did he care enough about Cat to resign his position and risk his life on the mere hope that he might help her? Thomas was not so foolish as to believe he was the only person Cat had ever cared about. Was this man a part of her history? Or a part of her present? The thought would not shake from his mind.

"I suppose this is the part where you warn me not to hurt her, or tell me how much you hate me for leaving her?"

Thomas started walking again. His feet beating rhythmically down the marble corridor.

Evander shook his head, long strands of his blond hair falling free of their binding. "I lost that right a long time ago. And she still saved my life. I only hope I have the chance to repay the favor."

"You're one of the guards, the ones she was friends with. Aren't you?" Cat had told Thomas about the men she trained with when she was young, when she told him how she learned to use a sword.

"A long time ago, yes. Listen, I don't know what Cat sees in you, but if she chose you, like you claim, it must be something special. Make sure you are worthy of her."

"I could never be worthy of her."

Emma's plan was nearly set. She spent every moment bustling around the palace. Making secret arrangements with Lyse and Evander. Avoiding Prince Thomas at every turn. Her rage had simmered into a quiet hate.

She made her way down the corridor, treading on light feet. To-morrow. They were leaving tomorrow at first light and there was so much to do.

The Reinsaffiran prince crossed her path, on his way to the small suite he had been hidden in. He wore a fresh cotton tunic without a trace of the dirt and grime he had worn the day he arrived. He carried a dried rose in his fidgeting hands. Thomas looked up just in time to see Emma try to avoid him.

He stepped into her path.

For a moment, Emma considered turning around, walking right back the way she had come. But this was the fastest way to the stables. She tried to brush past him instead. As if she did not even see him.

He sidestepped, blocking her way.

"Lady Emma, may I have a word?"

"No."

"Please, it will only take a moment."

Emma glared up at him, steeling herself against any pity that might swell in her chest when she met his eyes. They were always such deep oceans of sadness, almost like a night's sky when a storm rolled in.

"You promised to protect Cat," she hissed. "You promised she would be safe and you *left* her. Anything that happens to her in that dungeon is because of you."

Emma tried to push past him a second time.

Thomas gripped her by the hand, stalling her. His grip was gentle; had Emma chosen to keep walking she would have slipped away from him, though she could feel his strength in his quick movement.

"It was not my choice to leave her. I would do anything to save her. I would have willingly died trying to save her." The hurt on his face was plain. Tears hovered in his blue eyes. Emma swallowed the pity bubbling in her throat. It was easy to say such things when he was clean and safe and had a soft bed to sleep in.

"Then explain to me why you are here in the safety of the palace while she is there alone?" This conversation was overwhelming. Conflicting emotions crashed inside of Emma, buffeting her in their waves.

Thomas' fingers slid away, allowing Emma to continue down the corridor if she wished. "I wish I were there with her. I could not fight Bastian's magic. I wanted to. I tried but..." He let out a sigh, raking his free hand through his hair. "I was standing before him with a sword in hand one moment and then... suddenly... I was a hundred miles away."

It was not his words that rang true, though there was something about the way he constantly moved. Worry hung off of him like an ill-fitting shirt. Had Thomas rested at all since returning to Volentia? Something told her he would not have left Cat, if he had the choice. Emma paused, still refusing to look at the prince.

"She talks about you. You're the most important person in her life." He laughed quietly. "She was so worried about you. She tried to hide it but... well, she talks in her sleep." Emma looked at him. His form was blurry and quavering. "I am going to bring her back. I hope you can forgive me when I do."

Emma lifted her broad sword in her hands, inspecting the sharpened steel. Sunlight glinted off the blade. Come morning, Emma would have to say goodbye to Ryder, but after she would follow the men to the Border Lands. Her disguise was ready, thanks to Lyse. And the guards had agreed to claim her as a stable hand if asked. Emma would not be left waiting to hear the fates of the two people she cared about most.

Of course, a sword was not her preferred weapon; she was much more confident using the bow stashed in the stables with her other things.

A knock at the door made Emma jump. The sword slipped from her grip, clattering to the floor. She kicked it beneath the bed, rushing to the door. She was surprised to see Ryder standing in front of her. He wore a fine cotton tunic and dark breeches. His dark hair had been washed and swept to one side. Ryder's appearance gave the impression that he had just remembered a task he needed to do in the middle of something else. A rose, freshly plucked from the garden, hung from his hands.

It was easy to forget how handsome Ryder was. To disregard his strong jaw and smooth skin. It was even easy to grow used to his ever-changing sea green eyes. His presence and his features had become so much a part of her life she recognized them like a part of herself. This time they startled her, like waking up from a sleep to find his perfect beauty in front of her. The sudden reminder was too much. She could not look at him knowing what he was about to do, knowing that she might have to watch him die.

She turned away.

Ryder pressed a hand to her cheek, turning her back to face him. "What is it?"

"I can't ask you not to go." Tears shimmered, hot on her cheeks. "But I want to. I cannot bear knowing you might not come back."

"I will come back. If I am half so lucky in battle as I am in love, I will come back without even a hair out of place. I will bring Cat back too and everything will be the way it has always been, with one notable exception." Ryder brushed the tears away from her cheeks. Then, he knelt at her feet, wrapping his arms around her waist. "Emma, will you marry me?"

"I have already agreed to do that."

"No." He shook his head, hair flopping around his ears, refusing to settle where it was meant to. "I mean, marry me today. Now."

"Now? But Ryder..."

"Yes. Right now. Without worrying about court or kings or inher-itances, or anything else. Just you and me. Two people who love each other. I don't want to wait. I want to leave tomorrow knowing I will come back to my wife."

Emma lowered herself to the floor. She wanted to look Ryder in the eyes. Wrapping her arms around his neck, she pressed her lips to his. Leaving the deepest, gentlest kiss she could give there. "You are an idiot."

"That is not exactly an answer."

"But it is, because you never had to wait. If you had asked me the day we met, I would have married you then."

A broad smile lit Ryder's face. Placing his hands in Emma's, he lifted her off the floor, leading her out of the room. "Good, come with me. Everything is all arranged."

"Arranged? What would you have done if I had said no?"

He pulled her into him again, kissing her palm. "If I thought you might say no, I would not have asked."

A laugh pulled through Emma. The joy of simply laughing felt exquisite against her skin. "Am I really so predictable?"

"Only your heart."

Late into the evening, Emma laid her head against Ryder's chest, rising and falling with the steady rhythm of his breathing, deep in sleep. She willed herself to find the same contented sleep.

Sleep refused her.

Instead, Emma's worried mind ran over her plans for the fast-approaching morning. Saying goodbye to him, letting him believe they might not see each other again when she knew it was a lie. The thought left the bitter taste of bile in her throat. It was a lie she hated herself for. Telling him was too dangerous. If he knew she was there, his worry would put him in danger trying to protect her.

She had to live with the lie and hope it would do more good than harm.

Rain poured, splattering against Thomas' hood, soaking him. He glanced back at the small group who had journeyed with him to rescue the princess, taking particular interest in the stable boy Lyse had hired to help her with the supplies. He was constantly drawing Thomas' attention and curiosity. The boy wore ill-fitting clothes and a green cap that he pulled low over his eyes. Even in the evenings, when they made camp, the boy kept his distance from the rest of the group, sitting away from the fires checking and rechecking his bow. The only person the boy spoke to was Lyse. A suspicion was growing in Thomas' mind about who the boy really was. The boy was certainly trying to hide something. What? Thomas watched the boy push back his hood, trying to shake water from his cap. The movement felt familiar, almost feminine.

Thomas turned his attention back to Amora's small camp, the small row of tents and the cookfire. A less than impressive sight. Just to the east the forest loomed, dark and menacing. Trees pressed together into a wall, blocking any way of pressing into the forest.

He turned to Amora. The lithe woman leaned casually against a large oak tree with her arms crossed. "I thought you were going to meet us at the road to the ruined castle. You assured me you knew the way."

"I do and we have. The way is hidden with a powerful magic, but I can assure you, it's here."

Ryder scoffed. "Impossible. There can't be any magic strong enough to conceal a road through the forest."

"I suppose that, until a few weeks ago, you believed there was no magic left in the three kingdoms at all. Just remnants of old magix bloodlines. Like the roses protecting your castle in Volentia." She winked. "Do not believe every lie kings and history books tell you. Magic is not so easily driven from the land as you might think." Amora stepped around the large tree, disappearing. She emerged a moment later. "This is the road to Queen Sybilla's castle. I'm certain of it." Amora paused, her eyes locking on the same boy that prickled Thomas' skin with anxiety, perceiving something about him. The same secret that had been bothering Thomas. "Get some rest, all of you. We'll leave for the ruin at dawn."

The boy pulled his hood tighter around his face. For just a moment Thomas thought he recognized him. His tan hands were so close to

Lady Emma's coloring. There was a golden ring on the boy's left hand. A wedding band. Thomas let out a sigh. Not like Emma, it was Emma. He should have seen it days ago.

Thomas waited until night pressed in around them before approaching the boy who was not a boy at all. *He* sat near the forest inspecting the arrows in his quiver.

"I suppose I should not be surprised, seeing as you are Cat's friend." Caramel eyes turned on him, wide and round. Eyes he was certain belonged to *Princess* Emma. Thomas sat beside her. "I shudder to think of the kind of trouble you two get into together."

"You won't tell Ryder, will you?"

"Doesn't he deserve to know his wife has followed him into battle?"

"Knowing will only distract him and get him killed."

Thomas sighed, feeling more frustrated by the minute. At least it was Emma and not a spy. "He has the right to worry over the safety of the person he loves."

"So do I. That is why I am here. I am going to protect him."

"And who will protect you?" Thomas raked back his long curls. As if the familiar motion could steady his nerves. "I do not relish the idea of telling Cat her best friend was killed trying to save her."

Emma peered down the shaft of the arrow in her hand. "I do not need anyone to protect me. I have exquisite aim."

Blood stained Cat's hands. The sickening smell of iron filled the stone cell. Still, she pulled at the chain holding her. The manacle had loosened over the weeks she spent curled on the stone floor. If she moved just right, she might be able to slide her arm free.

She had to get free.

The rusted bars squealed in protest. Carswell pushed the cell door open.

Cold fear squeezed Cat's heart. She dropped the chain digging into her skin, flinching away from the leering man. He held a key and a length of rope in his rough hands.

"Get away from me!"

Carswell grabbed her with rough hands, binding her wrists together before unlocking the chain. The rope burned against Cat's raw skin.

Her sapphire ring glinted in the gray light. Carswell twirled it between his fingers as if he had not noticed it before, or simply had not cared to mention it. "It looks like your prince did not keep his promise. Are you still so certain he is going to save you?"

"I don't need him to save me." Cat kicked Carswell in the shin, turning to run.

Carswell's fingers dug into Cat's knotted hair, ripping her back. She was too weak to pull free. Cat forced her cry of pain to stay in her throat as Carswell's arms wrapped around her, holding her against his chest. "Did you really think I would let you escape? Let's go. His grace wants you cleaned up before the ritual." He dragged her through the castle to a heavy oak door. Steam poured out of the room when he wrenched it open, shoving Cat inside. Cat's teeth rattled, landing hard on wet floor boards. Her copper hair immediately grew frizzy in the damp air.

Cat pushed herself up, pain echoing up her bound arms, sitting so she could see what new torture she had been tossed into.

A large steaming bath was set into the floor at the center of the room. There was a large shelf filled with soaps and jars of salts beside a narrow stained-glass window. Several of the colorful panels were missing, making it hard to see the pattern in the fractured glass. The room was warm and looked at if it was used regularly, unlike Cat's stone cell.

This felt like a trick.

The idea of a bath, washing all the grime of the month, the feel of Carswell's touch, off her skin, pulled Cat to her feet. She wanted nothing more than to immerse herself in the steaming water. Shivers tracked up her ice-cold skin.

Cat leaned over the water, catching a glimpse of her reflection. A gasp escaped her. She had not realized the toll her misadventure had taken on her body. Where she once had firm muscles, all that remained were bones and blue veins under pale skin. The sight made her feel weaker than she already did.

"You're still dressed," the crone's voice grated, making Cat flinch. "Get moving. I won't wait all day."

Cat held up her tied wrists.

The crone clicked with her tongue, stalking over to Cat and pulling the ropes free. "Go on then. His Majesty wants you clean and dressed for the ritual."

Cat did not want to oblige the crone or her uncle's wishes but the steaming bath called to her, inviting her to wash away the aching bruises. She reached up, slowly removing the tattered remains of the dress she had worn for over a month, almost collapsing into the bath.

The water was warm and soothing. It soaked into her muscles. Cat curled her knees against her chest, crouching down so the water engulfed her up to her chin. Bubbles swirled around her. The crone hovered on the far edge of the room, glaring out the fractured window. This was the day, Cat realized. It was the only reason to finally take any interest in her well-being. It would end today.

Cat turned to look at the crone. She examined the ends of her long black hair. Cat remembered it being a golden blond, like Lyse's, with streaks of black when she first saw her. Now it was completely black. Had she lost herself piece by piece? Or was this who the woman was under her disguises.

"How did you become this way?"

"Bastian needed a shadow magix. If I did not take on the burden, he would have taken my daughter, Lyse." The name escaped her like a breath. Barely a whisper. "I gave up my freedom so she could grow up."

Lyse? Cat's ears perked. There were similarities between the woman standing before her and the confident orphan Cat met at the Peach Tree. Lyse claimed she did not remember anything about her life before the fire that destroyed her home. Could it be possible they were the same? Perhaps, if this was what her mother became, it was a blessing Lyse did not remember anything of her past. "I... I met a girl named Lyse, at The Peach Tree Inn in Reinsaffira. She did not remember what happened to her mother and father."

"If you are trying to bargain for your life, it is useless. Even if I had the will to defy my king, there is no way to break the connection between you. Either he must kill you and take your power or you must kill him and lose it." She sniffed. "And then, I will finally be free."

Cat studied her hands. "I hope you find her, when you are."

Painful minutes blurred together.

After getting cleaned up, Cat found herself laced into a gossamer white gown that exposed her shoulders and collar. The long wispy material tangled around her bare legs. Even with the laces pulled tight, the dress hung off of her. Her wrists were tied again the moment she was dressed. Carswell waited just outside the bathing chamber. He grabbed Cat by her bound wrists and pain shot through her. A wave of dizziness swept over Cat. She tried to pull away, but the world blurred around her, dizziness ringing through her.

Unsure if she had fainted, Cat found herself suddenly thrown onto the stone altar in the great hall. Carswell pinned her shoulders against the stone while Bastian worked to bind her to the stone with leather straps around her wrists and legs. The cool touch of metal drew her attention to Emma's dagger resting on the stone altar beside her.

Her hands were free, if only for a moment.

The crone was right. Killing Bastian was the only way to free herself from his hold. He was a monster and she had to stop him from hurting anyone else.

Moving slowly, sliding her arm across the rough surface, Cat reached for the hilt of the dagger. Dust ground into her open wounds. The dagger thrummed when her fingers wrapped around the opal pommel.

Her heart stone dangled over her, casting an unnatural black shadow, so close she wondered if she could access the magic. The two men must have believed she was still unconscious for all the attention they paid her and her small movements.

She gripped the blade, lifting it as quickly as her weak limbs allowed her to move. Cat swiped at Carswell first, cutting deep into his hand. Then she turned on Bastian, slashing the knife across his throat in one quick movement. Warm blood sprayed her face.

Bastian staggered away, blinking back a look of surprise.

Cat's arms fell to her sides.

A crooked smile formed on Bastian's face, revealing stained teeth. His fingers pressed to his throat, running the length of the wound. Pain stemmed from Cat's heart to her fingertips, watching her magic knit the flesh back together.

The dagger clattered to the floor. Cat gripped the blackened cut the crone had left on her upper arm, hissing from the pain.

How? How could he do that? It was the only coherent thought in her head. Where did Bastian find the strength to heal a mortal wound? It was impossible. Cat staggered, dizzy with new exhaustion. There was her answer. He took the energy from her, just like the magic. She forced herself to remain upright, in spite of the pain coursing through her.

"Poor little princess. Still fighting for your happy ending? If only your mother had taught you anything." Bastian stepped close to her. "The only way to kill a powerful magix is to pierce their heart. Magic comes from the heart. That is why I am going to cut yours out."

"What?" Carswell grabbed Bastian with his bloodied hand. "That was not the plan. The Darkness needs her. Alive!"

"The Darkness only requires the girl's power and her blood." The king wrapped his hand around Carswell's throat, his own bloodstained hands burning with a white-hot light, searing Carswell's skin. Cat could smell it burning, just like Carswell had done to Sir Guy.

"That is not all she needs! The girl has to live."

The energy Bastian pulled from Cat's body was too much. She collapsed on the stone alter, pressing her fists to her head. Flames licked at Bastian's hand, burning the life from Carswell, searing his flesh. Cat could feel his life slipping away and the joy Bastian derived from it. Killing him and destroying her in the process.

Something in Cat snapped. Her magic was light and fire. It was meant to show paths in the darkness and to warm campfires. It was never meant to destroy. *She* was never meant to destroy. She pulled into herself, willing every ounce of power back to her. It was her magic, and she would not let Bastian destroy her with it. She could feel his rage deep within her mind as the flames dimmed.

A final surge of power sent Carswell flying back, crashing into a wall.

Bastian rounded on her.

Had Cat been paying attention, she would have seen the shadows reaching over the altar, wrapping around her wrists and legs. But Cat could hear and feel nothing beyond Bastian's rage. The shadows' grip tightened, dragging her back into place on the alter.

"You are very strong. I have stolen power from many magix; not one of them had the will to draw their power back to them. You have done it twice. It is a pity your mother was never able to teach you how to control your power. With proper training you might have made a worthy queen." He picked up the dagger, carving an X over Cat's heart. "Instead, her love for your unworthy father made her weak. With your magic coursing through my veins, no one will ever dare challenge me again."

He raised the knife, ready to cut out her heart.

Cat closed her eyes. Trying to think. Trying to be brave. Trying to quiet the voices of pain and fear inside of her.

Waiting for the knife to fall.

PART

FIVE

 **Part Five**

The castle looked like nothing more than an unguarded ruin. The only evidence of life was the smoke rising from the crumbling tower. One Ryder thought, at first, would be easy to break into. Now, surrounded by hooded raiders in the courtyard, he was less certain of either. Sweat already pooled on his neck and back as the mercenaries raised their weapons. Ryder and his small band of heroes were outnumbered.

Ryder let out a sigh, lifting his own sword. There never was much hope this mission would be successful.

All he needed was to get inside. Evander and the others could handle the mercenaries while Thomas and Ryder handled Bastian. Urgency pulled Ryder closer and closer to the ruin. Something in his chest telling him to hurry.

An inky black smoke filled the courtyard, surrounding Ryder and Thomas in darkness and choking out all of the air. Ryder's eyes burned in the fumes.

The smoke cleared as suddenly as it appeared. King Bastian and a woman with dark hair and lavender eyes stood before him. The blond Reinsaffiran knight who Thomas called Trenton rushed at the pair, his sword swinging. Bastian flicked him away with a twist of his wrist. The giant man was a nuisance to him, nothing more. Power and dragon fire radiated off the king. This was why Thomas could not rescue Cat alone;

Ryder now understood the power the other prince had spoken of. The power that had killed his mother.

Amongst all of the chaos, Ryder felt a swell of relief. At least Emma was safe in Volentia.

The woman, who Ryder assumed was the crone Emma had spoken of, was terrifying in her own right. She did not move from place to place but appeared and disappeared in bursts of shadow, perfectly placing and avoiding blades. Had he not seen it for himself, Ryder would never have believed it. Everything he believed was a lie; magic was real and alive. The crone appeared beside him. Ryder dodged her blade.

An arrow whizzed into the place where the crone had just stood, striking the ground. She was gone.

Ryder's stormy eyes followed the arrow's path back to its owner. The boy Lyse hired to help with the horses stood atop a pile of rubble, but it wasn't a boy. "Emma!" Her long hair pulled back into a tight braid, the cap she wore as part of her disguise discarded at her feet, along with her heavy cloak. The disguise had been clever. Ryder had taken no notice of the boy who kept to the shadows. Even if he did not recognize her, Emma's aim was unmistakable. Emma never missed. Ryder pushed his way past the mercenaries to her side. "Emma! What are you doing here?" He tried to block her from the chaos around them.

"At the moment," she fired another arrow. It landed at the center of a mercenary's chest, downing him, "I am saving your life."

"You should not be here! It isn't safe."

"It's just as safe for me as it is for you." Emma knocked another arrow, following the crone's movements. "You don't have to worry about me."

"You know that is not going to stop me."

"Which is why I did not tell you I was coming."

The crone flashed into sight on the far side of the courtyard, sword raised at Prince Thomas' back.

Emma let her arrow fly, this time piercing the crone's heart. She prepared another arrow, watching the woman fall to the ground. Ryder and Emma hurried forward. The woman's hair changed, shifted to a pale blond. Aiden rushed to her side, brushing the woman's golden hair out of her face. Ryder and Emma rushed to Thomas.

For a moment, the fight seemed to slow. Stilling, and moving miles from where they stood over the crone's body.

"Are you hurt?" Ryder pulled Thomas to his feet.

"I'm fine." Dirt, sweat, and blood clung to the man's clothes. "It won't matter if we don't get to Cat in time."

Orange light bathed the courtyard as Bastian let out a blaze of magical fire that singed Ryder's skin, even from that distance.

"Right. You and Emma, get to the castle, find my sister." He fixed his eyes on Thomas, trying to press as much meaning into the look as possible. "Keep them safe." Ryder gripped his sword, testing the weight. "I will keep my uncle busy."

A heavy sadness came over Ryder when he turned back to the fighting. Sir Trenton lay motionless in the courtyard. Fighting Bastian meant sacrificing himself. If that was the price he had to pay for Emma and Cat's safety, he was glad to pay it.

"No." Aiden forced himself to his feet, drawing his too heavy broad sword. "I have unfinished business with His Majesty." He charged before Ryder could move. Ryder watched, stunned, for a long moment, unable to understand why the old rogue would risk his life for them. So many already had. "Go! Find the princess before it is too late."

Ryder turned, chasing after Emma and Thomas through the gate. Darkness engulfed him in time to hear Aiden cry out in pain.

"Where do we search?" Ryder's baritone vibrated off the cold stone walls.

"The dungeon is this way." Thomas hurried toward a narrow staircase.

Emma caught him by the sleeve. "Wait. I read about this. Bastian has to perform the ritual in the light of the moon. Is there a great hall?" Her eyes darted around the dark castle. "This way! It has to be this way."

Both Emma and Thomas ran in different directions. Thomas for the stairway and Emma down the corridor toward a set of heavy oak doors. Ryder's head swiveled between the two, paralyzed with indecision. Instinct told him Emma was right, but Thomas had found Cat in these ruins once before. He took a tentative step toward the stairs, glancing back to the heavy doors Emma had disappeared through.

A cry of anguish, like shattered glass, echoed through the castle.

"No!" Emma was screaming.

Ryder ran for the doors, hesitating when he reached them. He did not want to know what would cause Emma to make that sound. Prince Thomas was beside him in a second, panting for breath. He did not hesitate, pushing through the door, balking just inside, as if buckling under an unrealized weight. Ryder remained paralyzed in the corridor; teeth clenched. He did not want to see what was beyond that threshold.

A second shattering cry and a gulping sob rang out. Ryder had no choice. Steeling his courage, he stepped through the door. Whatever pain Emma was facing, he would not leave her to face it alone.

Thomas stood just on the other side of the door, a single tear sliding down his cheek when Ryder reached him. He was shaking, hands balled into fists until his veins bulged beneath his skin.

Emma lay in a crumpled heap at the base of a stone altar, her onyx hair splayed over her face. She was trembling, her body racked with sobs. Finally, Ryder forced his eyes to slide away from Emma, to the white stone altar bathed in silver moonlight. The source of so much pain.

 Long copper hair, brushed clean and straight, framed a motionless, pale woman draped in a white gown that was stained red with fresh blood. Cat. Cuts and bruises covered her arms. Blood dripped to the stone floor. She looked so small and fragile in the wispy silk gown that turned her pale skin to ice.

It was all for nothing.

He was too late.

Thomas stepped forward. Moving slowly, deliberately. It felt like an eternity before he reached the altar, stepping past Emma as if he did not see her. For Thomas there was only one thing in the room. Only Cat.

Ryder followed, afraid to step into the room and make it real.

So much emotion and pain filled the space and yet... Ryder felt nothing. Just a void in his heart and an ache in his muscles. Ryder stretched out a hand to Emma, pulling her up from the floor. Blood and battle stained Emma's hands and clothes. Her face was scrunched, trying to control the relentless sobs. He said nothing. There were no words of comfort to give. All Ryder could do was pull her his chest, wrapping his arms around her, holding her.

"She can't be dead," Emma whimpered into his chest.

The feel of Emma's sobs breaking against his ribs brought misty tears to Ryder's eyes. Why didn't he feel anything? He did not understand.

The healthy color in Prince Thomas' cheeks was gone. The silent tears that streaked his face splashed against Cat's skin. Cat did not move when he cupped his hands around hers or brushed hair away from her face, pulling Cat close to him. Ryder tightened his grip on Emma, afraid she might slip away as well.

It was a wonder Cat had survived as long as she had. The long weeks of imprisonment showed on her body. The Cat who left Volentia two months earlier was strong with sturdy legs and shoulders. She had always been like that. Not this thin, frail thing cradled in the Reinsaffiran prince's arms.

Thomas brushed the hair and glittering dust from Cat's face. "You couldn't wait just a little bit longer?" He whispered; forehead pressed to hers. "I was going to rescue you."

"What makes you think I need you to rescue me?"

The cracked voice was so small, Ryder could not make himself believe it was real. Emma lifted her head, turning back to the scene.

Cat's eyes were open. Her lips pressed against the grief-stricken prince's ear.

Thomas ran the heel of his hand along his cheeks, pushing the tears aside to look at the girl. "Cat?"

Cat sat up, arms trembling under her own weight.

"You're alive!" Thomas swept her up in his arms so fast Cat had to wrap her arms around his neck. He spun her through the air; joy and disbelief filled his voice. "How... How is this possible?"

"I... I don't know." Lines formed on Cat's forehead. Thomas set her back on her feet, but Cat did not move away from him. She was gazing up at Thomas. Her raw, damaged hands slid into his. He braced her against his body, helping Cat remain standing. For just one moment, it seemed Cat and Prince Thomas were completely alone in the world. She had not even noticed Emma and Ryder standing just a few feet away, the two people she once claimed to love more than anyone else in the world. Her eyes only found the prince who pulled her close to him. Ryder almost laughed at the scene. Cat had actually gone and fallen in love, and with the very person she had been told to fall in love with.

"Cat?" Emma unlaced her arms from Ryder's waist, throwing herself at Cat. "You're all right!"

Cat blinked at them. Startled. "Emma? Ryder?" Her arms flew around Emma's neck, stumbling to catch her in a hug. "You're here? I thought I would never see you again!"

Cat clung to her best friend; arms tight around her shoulders. Tears burned her eyes. For so long she had believed she would never see Emma or Ryder again, that she would die in Bastian's dungeon. She had come so terribly close when the alarm went up and the crone threw that glittering powder, that made her eyes and body heavy, over her. Then, just as suddenly, she woke to Thomas' blue eyes gazing down at her. It felt like a dream. Any second she would wake and find herself still tied to the altar, waiting for the knife to fall.

Everything hurt. Her whole body trembled. Still, she could not bring herself to let go. Cat looked up at Ryder, standing over them, then to Thomas, finally stepping back to see Emma, whose face was streaked with tears. A piece of her heart shattered as she looked at them. They had believed she was dead. She almost was. She would have been if not for them. They gave her so much, risked so much, and all Cat had given them was pain. She was selfish and did not deserve the love they held for her.

Not again. Never again.

The dagger still lay on the altar. Cat placed her palm on the hilt, clutching it in her shaking hands. She could feel Bastian in the distance, pulling her magic away from her. Between that and the injuries peppering her body, Cat did not have the strength to stand on her own. Her legs shook and she collapsed onto the floor. It did not matter. She would find the strength and she would kill Bastian. She would make sure he could never hurt anyone she cared about again.

"Where is Bastian?"

"Don't worry about that now." Thomas knelt beside her, an arm twining around her. Warmth spread beneath his touch. "We're going to get you out of here."

Cat shook her head. "I cannot leave. Bastian and I are connected. He..." Pain swept through Cat. She dropped the dagger, gripping her head. A flash of Bastian's mind, the hate and rage, ran through her. He was beneath the castle, running through a long corridor. He would escape and come back to finish her. "The only... way to... break... the connection is..." Cat grit her teeth. Even this little information was kept inside of her by Carswell's spell of silence. Cat clenched her eyes shut against the pain. "I cannot leave so long as Bastian is connected to my magic."

Ryder nodded. "Emma, stay here with Cat. Help her get cleaned up and bandaged. Both of you get out of here at sunrise, whether we have returned or not. Thomas and I will deal with Bastian."

"Do not make decisions for me as if I am not here!" Cat grit her teeth. "I know how to fight Bastian. It has to be me." Another scream of pain wrenched through Cat.

"You cannot even stand. Stay here. We'll come back for you."

"No... I..."

"Catiya!" The rumble of Ryder's voice set her back. It had been a long time since her brother had given her a command. She had almost forgotten how irritating he could be when he tried to protect her. His need to protect her would kill him. Ryder did not know how to fight Bastian. "If you ever, in your life, listen to reason, listen now. You are not strong enough. You need a physician. Stay here with Emma. Stay safe. We'll come back."

Cat leaned against the stone altar. Helpless, reluctant, watching Ryder and Thomas leave. They did not know how to kill Bastian and she could not tell them. The bitter taste of secrets burned in the back of her throat. Another secret Carswell's cruelty had forced on her. She could not stop them either, not when she was too weak to even stand.

Emma knelt beside her, drawing strips of linen out of the pack at her hip. An easy silence fell between them. As if weeks had not passed, as if nothing had changed. The silence sent more pain bubbling to the surface. If Bastian was allowed escape, he would use Cat to hurt Emma and Ryder. Cat could not allow that. These were the consequences of her choices. She would be the one to face him.

Emma started wrapping the bandages around the wounds on Cat's arms, stifling the slow trickle of blood. Her eyes scanning Cat for new injuries, quirking her eyebrow at the silver ring on Cat's finger. She steeled herself for Emma to mention it.

"This is a new dress." Emma said instead. "I like it, apart from the blood."

A laugh glittered inside of Cat's chest. She felt a sparkle of joy for the first time in weeks.

Then the joy shriveled in her chest. A shadow fell over them, drawing Cat's eyes up. "This really is a touching reunion. So lovely seeing the two of you together again." Carswell stood over them. His shirt was torn at the collar, revealing a hand shaped burn on his throat. His injured hand was no longer bleeding, but he had not bandaged it. "It's a shame I have to cut it short."

Cat cringed back, her shoulders knocking against the stone altar. There was no strength in her to fight Carswell, just like there was no strength to save Ryder and Thomas from Bastian. She could not breathe through the fear constricting her lungs.

Fortunately, Emma was there. She shoved her way between Cat and Carswell, drawing her sword to point it at Carswell. "You! What are you doing here? Get away from us."

Carswell's lips curled into a sneer. "Isn't it obvious? I'm here to rescue Princess Catiya." He moved with unnatural speed, shoving Emma out of his way, gripping Cat by the wrist, dragging her to her feet. He pulled her into his chest, pressing a knife to Cat's throat when Emma scrambled to her feet, fumbling with her bow. "Don't! I do not believe the princess can spare much more blood."

"How are you still alive?" Bastian killed him. Cat saw it.

"You saved my life. Don't you remember, Love? When you took your power back from Bastian."

"Not the smartest thing I have ever done."

"No," his voice was low and husky, growling in her ear. The heat of his breath sent shivers up her spine. "But it was terribly convenient. Now I will save you and you will free The Darkness. Then, with the crown prince and his lovely fiancé gone, we will rule Volentia together. Just like I planned."

"No! I am not going anywhere with you." Cat's eyes locked on Emma's. They were hard and calculating, her bow string pulled tight. "Emma, shoot him. He won't hurt me. Just shoot him." Cat's skin crawled at Carswell's touch. Fear and memory cloying at her throat. "Please."

The arrow flew. Hitting its mark, embedding in Carswell's right shoulder. Not a mortal wound. Cat's body covered too much of him and Emma had been trembling when she released it. It was the only time Cat ever saw her miss. It was still enough. Enough for Cat to stumble away. Emma caught Cat, dragging her out of the grand hall, away from Carswell.

An image flashed through Cat's mind as Emma dragged her through the castle. She could see Ryder on the ground, writhing in pain, electricity coursing through his body. She gripped Emma's hand. "Ryder is in danger!" Cat looked around. She felt a tug at toward the stone staircase. "This way!" Cat pulled Emma down a narrow staircase that ended in a long dark tunnel.

"How do you know?"

She shook her head. "I can feel it."

The girls rushed into the darkest depths below the ruin. Rushing water echoed off the rough walls. They found themselves in a cavern beneath the foundations. Cat heard once that some ancient Salenians built their castles above caves and near moving water; she could not remember the reason why. The long tunnel ended in an abyss. A shaft of impenetrable darkness dropping down into the earth. It could be miles until the river below reached the surface, if it ever did.

This was where Bastian was. Cat could taste his hatred and desperation in the air. The hairs on her arms prickled, standing higher the closer she moved to the edge. Unfamiliar emotions swirled through Cat. Images of Thomas and Ryder flashed in her mind, coupled with hatred, a desire to kill. The closer she drew to him, the less Cat could tell if her mind belonged to her or her villainous uncle. A blazing light appeared, burning into Cat's eyes and lighting the chasm. The princess immediately missed the dark.

The tunnel opened into a round chasm. It rose a hundred feet above them and plunged even farther down. Other tunnels opened into the rough walls. There was a tunnel just above them to one side with Thomas kneeling on a ledge trying to shield Ryder. Bastian floated on a cloud of shadow, eye level with Cat, burning white flame held in his outstretched hand.

Cat shivered, feeling her power drain.

Her fingers found the strips of linen strips covering her wrists, clawing them off. The bandages stifled her, making her fingers feel clumsy. She needed control. She turned to Emma, studying her with sad eyes. Emma looked older than Cat remembered. Her ebony hair frizzed, pulling free of its braid. Her cheekbones were sharper. Cat gripped her hand, drawing the dagger. She had been so focused on her own need for adventure and freedom that she had been blind to the needs of the people she cared most about. Selfish. And the last thing she ever did would be selfish too. Cat had to be sure the friends who risked so much to save her were safe.

Taking a shuddering breath, Cat slipped the sapphire ring from her finger, dropping it into Emma's hand. "Do something for me, Emma?"

"Anything."

"Return this to Thomas for me. Tell him... tell him I really did want to marry him."

Cat let go, sprinting with the little strength she had inside of her. The dagger clutched in her hand. Cat leapt into the air. Letting that invisible tug of magic draw her toward Bastian.

"No! Cat!"

Too late. The dagger landed, burying itself in Bastian's chest, pinning him to the wall. She scrambled to hold onto the ledge behind him with her free hand.

Cat ignored the voices echoing around her and the pain in every part of her. There was only Bastian. Hatred mingled with her fear.

The closeness made it impossible for Cat to know her own thoughts and feelings. Rage, fear, pain, it all filled her like the static crackle of thunder.

The only way to kill a powerful magix is to pierce their heart. Magic comes from the heart. That is why I am going to cut yours out.

Bastian rested a hand on the wound on his chest. Black smoke oozed from it, filling Cat's lungs. All she could see were Bastian's crimson eyes, draining to a pine forest green. "How very clever of you."

Cat was alone in the dark. Falling.

Her fingers tightened on the dagger. It started to slip from the stone. Pain shot through her shoulder as gravity pulled her toward the abyss.

"Cat!" Her name sounded in the dark.

"I'm here," she called back.

The flickering light of a torch appeared above her, followed by Thomas' voice. "Hold on Cat. I'm coming." She looked up to see him scramble onto a narrow ledge, climbing toward her. His hand stretched toward her. "Just reach for me Cat, that's all you have to do."

She twisted her free hand around to him, fingers brushing, and then he caught her, pulling her into his chest. Cat felt the narrow ledge beneath them and the pound of Thomas' heart.

"Cat! You're so stupid! Why did you do that? Why couldn't you let me save you?"

"You did save me." She reached up, pressing a kiss to his lips.

Wrapping her arms tight around his shoulders. She tried to put everything she could not say into the kiss. Relief washed over her. Her thoughts were hers. He was hers. They were together. Cat pulled back, looking up at him. She lowered her eyes. Unsure of what she could say. "Thank you."

Thomas' thumb tucked under her chin, drawing her eyes back up to him. "Why are you thanking me?"

"I... I have been told that when a gentleman saves a lady, she is supposed to thank him. Was I misinformed?"

Thomas pulled her close to him, his arms so tight around her she could not move. He studied her face in the flickering torchlight. Butterflies danced in Cat's stomach and chest. "In my experience, when a prince saves a princess, she slaps him for impertinence."

"I will try to remember that. If..."

He cut off her quip with another long kiss, telling her everything she ever needed to hear. She was safe. Cat would not pull away from him again, no matter who looked on.

Exhaustion took her. Cat collapsed into Thomas' arms.

Cat woke. She was laying on a table. Her body refused to move, as if she were bound. Something tight was wrapped around her burning wrists. For a moment she was afraid she had dreamed it all and only awoke to find herself still tied to the stone altar.

A man leaned over her, brushing a salve over the X cut over her heart with gentle hands.

"Thomas?"

No. Her eyes were coming into focus. The man was similar to Thomas, though not quite like the man she loved. His hair was too light and his movements were too steady and purposeful to be Thomas. Still similar pointed features, and startlingly similar blue eyes.

Cat was growing tired of waking up in strange places. She tried to move.

"You probably should not sit up. You've lost more blood than you can spare." The man spoke with a kind tone, his focus never wavering from his work.

"You must be Jason." Her cracked, aching voice sounded harsh and unfamiliar even to her own ears. "Thomas spoke of you. He said you were his best friend."

"Did he?" Jason pressed a gauzy bandage to the wound over her heart, shifting his attention to the black scar on her forearm. "I would have thought that distinction would belong to Arik."

Cat stared up at the ceiling. She was still exhausted, but a feeling of safety and warmth spread over her. Her eyes fluttered closed, mind drifting away. It was quiet. No hatred burning through her. No Bastian. She was her own again. "He said you taught him which berries were good to eat." Something startled her. The memory of the chasm. They had been together. Where was he? She tried to sit up.

Jason pushed her back to the table. "That is not a good idea, Princess."

"Where's Thomas?"

"He is waiting just outside. You can see him once you are dressed." The physician forced a smile. The salve he put on her arm was starting to burn in her raw skin. Cat realized her arms were bandaged again, all the way up to her elbows, more time had passed than she thought. After a moment, Jason helped her sit up so he could wrap bandages around her shoulders, covering the X Bastian had carved into her chest. "But Princess Emma is here, if you would like to see her."

"Princess Emma?"

"Am I mistaken? Isn't that the title given to the wives of princes in Volentia?"

Emma appeared beside the table, still dressed in her battle-stained tunic, hair now hanging loose. She had washed her face and her hands were clean of the blood and dirt. She took Cat's hand.

"I'm sorry I missed your wedding."

Emma shrugged, sweeping her hair over one shoulder. "You had other things on your mind at the time."

"There." Jason stood, turning to address Emma as Cat lay back down on the table, the effort of sitting up had exhausted her. "That is the best I can do without my equipment. What she really needs is rest and fresh clothes, the warmest you can find. I do not like the sound of her lungs."

"I'll see what I can do."

"Good." Jason turned back to Cat, smiling at her with those dazzling blue eyes. "Get some rest, Princess." The physician turned and made his way out of the room.

Cat had never been in this part of the castle before. It was warmer than the dungeon had been and she saw there was a plush carpet on the floor. Perhaps Bastian only kept the places he inhabited comfortable.

She let her eyes close again.

She had won. She never had to worry about Bastian again. "Will you still be here when I wake up?"

"I have no plans to leave."

"Good."

Thomas raked back his shaggy hair, waiting for Cat to reappear. He understood. Wounds needed to be dressed and Cat needed warm clothing, but waiting, being so far away from her, made him nervous. The longer they took, the more anxious he felt. He wanted to hold her in his arms and know she was real. He wanted to get Cat away from this awful place. He wanted to take her home.

The door he sat beside opened.

Cat stepped out of the room. She wore a simple green dress made of thick material with black fur trim. It was one of the crone's dresses. A black corset held the too large dress on her body. Her long copper hair had been braided, hanging over one shoulder. She kept her arms tucked behind her back. Thomas could see the bandages wrapped around her chest, over the neckline.

He did not believe she had ever looked more lovely.

Emma followed, dressed in a similar dark brown frock, keeping her arms stretched out to catch Cat if she fell. To say Emma had not left Cat's side since they found her was an understatement. It was impossible to pry her away. Neither prince minded. Thomas knew he had his whole life to spend with Cat.

He reached for Cat, knowing she was still too weak to stand on her own.

Cat pulled away.

Thomas watched her tug at her sleeves, trying to hide the bandages. Trying to hide the scars Bastian had left on her. He did not care if she was scarred. They were just as beautiful as she was. Proof of the strength no one believed she had.

Emma's caramel eyes darted between the pair. "I think I will go find Ryder." She slipped away from Cat.

Cat teetered for a moment before letting Thomas catch her, guiding her onto the bench beside the door.

He reached again for her bandaged hand; she pulled it close to her.

"You came back for me. Even when I told you Bastian would kill you."

"I told you, Cat, I won't let anyone take you from me." Kneeling in front of her, he placed a hand on her cheek, sweeping aside a stray lock of hair. "When I told you I loved you, I meant it. I meant forever. I will always come back for you."

Cat could not respond. She opened and closed her mouth, trying to form an answer.

Thomas looked away, studying the corridor, suddenly feeling almost shy. Watching how the mortar between the bricks and stones turned from gray to black. He hardly felt like the same man who caught a princess climbing in the arbor. Nor did she seem to be the same woman.

He let out a sigh. "Emma returned this to me, but I was hoping you would still wear it." Thomas reached for her hands again, hoping to place the sapphire ring on her finger, only smiling when she pulled them behind her back. "You don't have to hide from me."

"I don't want you to see."

Sliding his arm around her waist, Thomas found her bandaged hand. He ran a thumb over her palm. Gently, so very gently, pulling her hand from behind her back, he slid the ring onto her finger, brushing his fingers over the edge of the linen strips. The constant ache to have his arms around her subsided. He lifted her hand, pressing a kiss against her bandaged wrist. This was all he needed. She was all he needed.

Needed.

Thomas had nearly forgotten what he found when searching the crone's rooms for herbs Jason might use. The prince released her hand, producing a small brass object from his pocket.

Cat's eyes lit. "My compass!"

"So, what direction do we need to go next?"

She fiddled with the clasp, finally meeting his gaze. "You'll go with me?"

"My darling princess, I am never leaving you again."

Cat pushed herself up, taking a tentative step toward a nearby window. Looking out at the forest surrounding them. She fiddled with the cover before throwing it into the trees. Cat turned back to him, smiling. "So long as you are with me, there is nothing else I need."

Thomas laughed, lifting Cat in his arms, kissing her without hesitation. The sun was starting to rise when he pulled her close to his chest, resting his cheek against her hair. After fighting Bastian, what else could possibly keep them apart?

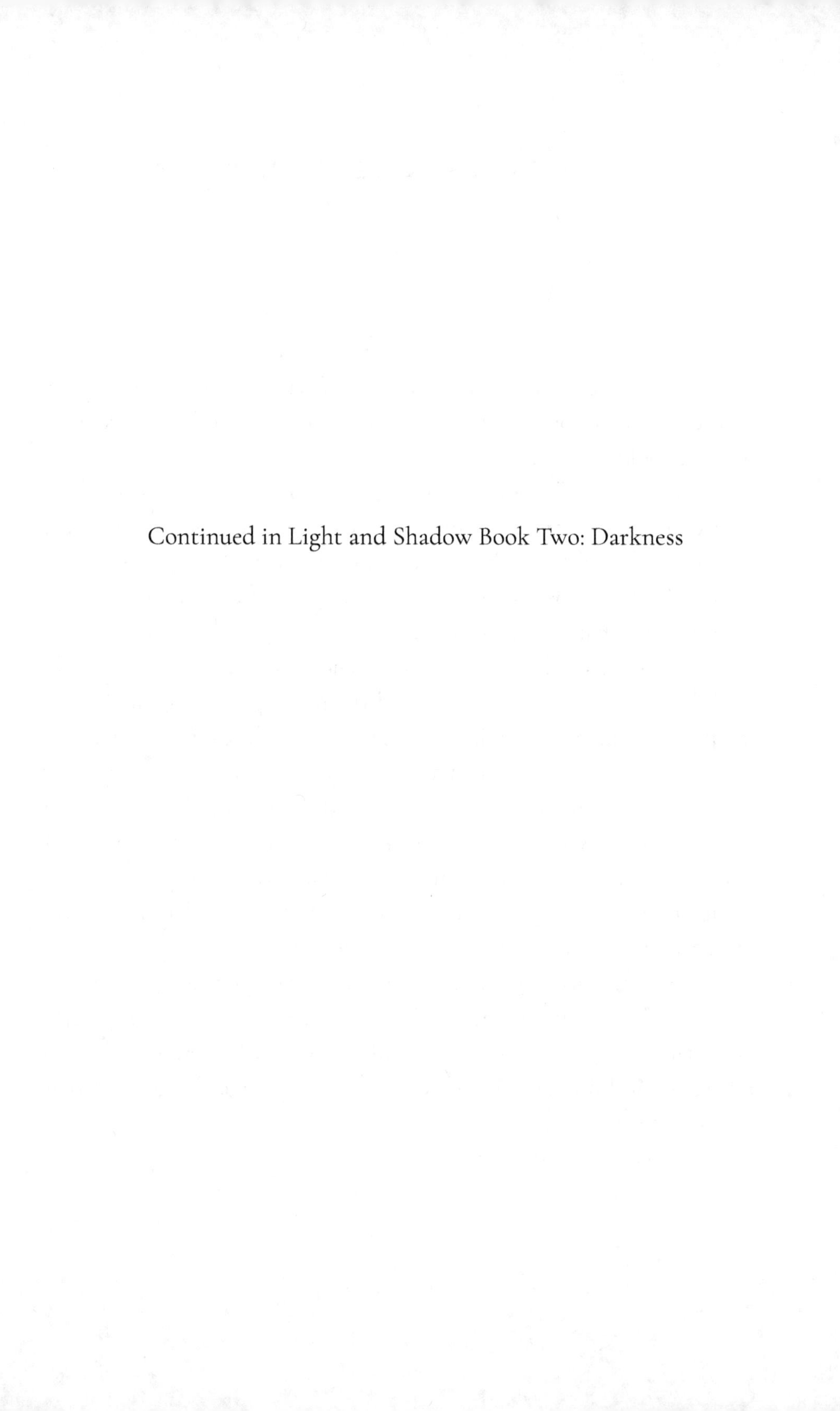

Continued in Light and Shadow Book Two: Darkness

Acknowledgements

As I said in the dedication, I wrote this book for my best friend, but I'm glad you read it too. Erin, I never would have gotten this far on this journey without you. You are the best writing partner and adventure buddy I could ever ask for.

A big thanks also goes to my line editor/beta reader, Bailey. You helped me make this book into the best possible book it could be. Thank you for all the work you have put into polishing my diamond in the rough and for loving my characters almost as much as I do.

The other thanks that really need to be said go to my brother, who made me sign his copy of my first novel and then refused to open it and read the inscription because he "couldn't ruin a signed first edition." To my parents who said I could be anything I wanted to be whether that was a pearl diver in the Bahamas or writer in Washington or anything else my ADHD mind came up with in the moment. To my writing mentor at Whitworth, Nicole Sheets, for making me into the writer I am today. And, most importantly, to my cats, who show every sign of being literate and who spent many days feeling displaced as my lap was taken up by my computer. You are the real MVPs.

My final thanks go to you, the readers. Thank you for choosing my book and for making it this far. I hope you loved it as much as I do and that you found some truth within its pages. I know there are so many wonderful books out there and I am so incredibly grateful that you have chose mine.

Thank you and I love you.

www.ingramcontent.com/pod-product-compliance
Lightning Source LLC
Chambersburg PA
CBHW071451140726
47997CB00005B/1686